Wife Support System

Wife Support System

Kathleen Whyman

hera

First published in the United Kingdom in 2020 by Hera

This edition published in the United Kingdom in 2021 by

Hera Books
28b Cricketfield Road
London, E5 8NS
United Kingdom

A CIP catalogue record for this book is available from the British Library.

Print ISBN 978 1 80032 395 7
Ebook ISBN 978 1 912973 48 4

Look for more great books at www.herabooks.com

Printed and bound in Great Britain by Clays Ltd, Elcograf S.p.A.

For my amazing mum, Susan, and in loving memory of my dad, John.

I love you both so much.

Chapter One

Erica

'Please don't leave.' Erica gripped the phone. 'Life won't be the same without you.'

'Sorry, but I have to.'

'If you won't stay for me, stay for Jasmine. She'll be devastated.' Erica tugged at the tips of her black, elfin crop, well aware she sounded desperate. But that's because she was.

A deep sigh came down the phone. 'Emotional blackmail won't work.'

'Will any other kind of blackmail?' Erica asked hopefully.

'No.'

'But, Jasmine—'

'You'll find someone else.'

'We don't want anyone else.'

The voice softened. 'That's nice to hear, but there are other nannies out there.'

Not that we can afford, Erica thought.

'Sorry,' Phoebe said again. 'But you're always telling Jasmine it's important to follow her dreams. That's what I'm doing. You should see it as a compliment.'

Phoebe's shock announcement that she was leaving and dropping Erica in the shit was about as complimentary as being kicked in the crotch. In pointy shoes.

'Moving to LA is your dream?' Erica's earrings rattled against the phone as she shook her head. 'You said in your interview that you love looking after children because they're genuine and natural. Not many people in LA fit that criteria. Especially not the children.'

'Being with the man I love's my dream. He's moving to LA, so I'm going with him.'

'You've never mentioned a boyfriend.'

'It's Grant.' Phoebe giggled. 'He asked me not to say anything.'

'Grant? From the studio?' Erica cringed at the thought of the cocky production director who hit on every female he encountered. Well, every female under twenty-five. As head stylist of *Sing to Win*, the talent show they worked on, Erica never revealed her age, but it was obvious she was older than the show's contestants and most of the crew. If they found out she was thirty-six, they'd stop listening to her styling advice quicker than they could type *#euthanasia*. Especially as she was actually forty-two.

'Yes,' Phoebe said proudly. 'I met him when you took me and Jasmine on that backstage tour. He's got a job on the US version of the show and said I can come if I want.'

'Are you sure about this?' Erica asked gently. 'You haven't known Grant long. Let's talk about it tomorrow when I'm back.'

'I won't be here. We're flying tonight.'

'Tonight?' Erica's legs went weak. 'You can't. You're on three months' notice.'

'*You can achieve anything you put your mind to. Don't let anyone say you can't.*' Phoebe recited another of Erica's quotes. Erica made a mental note to build Jasmine's confidence in isolation from now on. 'I'm leaving tonight,' Phoebe repeated.

Erica sank down onto her bed. This couldn't be happening. Without childcare she was screwed. 'Please don't do this, Phoebe. Can you at least hang on to say goodbye to Jasmine?'

'No.'

'But you've looked after her for eighteen months.'

'Yes. So you probably want to get me a leaving present.'

Erica was shocked into silence.

'I'd love some of the fake tan you use,' Phoebe continued. 'The stuff you get me from the studio is ok, but your colour's much nicer. Just tell me where you keep it.'

Being of Sri Lankan heritage, Erica had no need for fake tan, but Phoebe clearly hadn't figured out that her colouring was natural. And if she was that thick, then Erica didn't want her looking after Jasmine anyway.

'Goodbye Phoebe, and good luck.' Erica ended the call, placed the phone calmly in her lap and flopped back onto the bed. 'Fuck!' she shouted at the ceiling.

What had possessed her to come on this holiday? Things always went wrong when she was away. Louise and Polly weren't even real friends. They were *mum friends*. Their only common link was that they had children the same age. Great for play dates (ideally not at Erica's) and sharing lifts to parties and the odd sleepover (definitely not at Erica's), but not for going away with. But Louise had been so excited about winning a week in a five-bed Airbnb house and insistent she come, and it lessened Erica's guilt at Jasmine missing out on a half-term holiday. She'd convinced herself that if she kept on top of calls and emails nothing disastrous could happen, but this was proof that she needed to be there. If she'd been at home, Phoebe would have had to tell her face-to-face that she was leaving and Erica could have explained in a calm, rational manner that she had to work out her notice. Or hidden her passport.

Erica's phone pinged and she snatched it up, praying it was a text from Phoebe saying it was an April fool joke, even though it was the end of May. Instead, it was a request for an appointment with *Sing to Win*'s creative director at nine a.m. the following Thursday. Erica's stomach tightened. There was no way she could drop Jasmine off at school and travel forty miles in fifteen minutes. Especially not in heels. She took her iPad from her bedside table and opened her calendar. It was a mosaic of overlapping coloured boxes highlighting meetings she had, all of which coincided with Jasmine's ballet class or swimming lesson or dentist appointment or recorder recital. The iPad was heavy in her hands. She *had* to go to all her meetings. If she didn't, her career was over. Instead of being head stylist for *Sing to Win* and on most fashion editors' speed dial, she'd be picking out thongs for Z-listers to wear in the jungle. Everything she'd worked so hard for would be gone. Worse than that, she'd have to go to the recorder recital.

She dialled Dan's number. Why was *she* panicking about this? It was his fault they couldn't afford a nanny.

'Dan Ford please.'

'Of course,' a young man said, presumably the latest intern shadowing him. 'And you are…?'

'I'm his…' she hesitated, as she always did when having to describe her status. Common-law wife was too formal, partner sounded too business-like, and girlfriend seemed inadequate when they'd been together for ten years and had a child. Dan referred to her as his wife, but when she'd tried that approach, eyes invariably flicked to her bare wedding finger and her subsequent explanation sounded pathetic. As though she were desperate to be asked – which she wasn't; they didn't need a piece of a paper to validate their relationship – or had created an imaginary husband. 'Just put me through.'

'Dan Ford,' Dan said briskly.

'It's me.'

'Can't talk long. I'm on mute in a conference call.'

Erica could imagine him looking pointedly at his TAG Heuer watch.

'Phoebe's leaving,' she said.

'Shame. I'll miss her false nails blocking up the waste disposal unit.'

'Not as much as we'll miss her looking after Jasmine.'

'Just get a replacement.'

'By Monday?'

Dan choked. 'I saw her this morning and she didn't mention it.'

'No. She didn't say anything when Jasmine and I said goodbye to come here either. Very sneaky.'

'What are you going to do?'

'What are *we* going to do?' Erica corrected. 'You'll have to take Jasmine to school two days next week. I've got some early starts.'

'No can do. I'm in China. Comes with the territory when you're a partner.' The pride over his new position was evident in his voice. 'Wish I could have seen those shits' faces when they read my LinkedIn update.'

'I'm sure they're eaten up with jealousy,' Erica said. 'But it won't help me.'

'What about Louise and whatshername? Can't they help?'

'Louise works full time and Polly's looked after Jasmine all this week while I've been on calls. I can't ask her to do more.'

'You'll work something out. You always do. Shit, got to go, someone asked me a question.'

He hung up and Erica rolled her eyes. So much for Dan arranging childcare. The only arranging he did involved his bollocks.

She went to find Louise, Polly and some wine. All three were in the kitchen. Polly was at the table watching the children playing in the garden, red curls scraped back into a ponytail, the cuffs of her long-sleeved, white tee pulled down over her hands. Erica had never seen her in any other style top. She wore it with jeans in the winter and under a loose, chambray pinafore in the summer. Louise sat opposite, reading a magazine and working her way through a packet of custard creams. Crumbs coated her polo shirt. The table obscured her lower half, but Erica would bet her Louboutins that Louise was wearing combats. She smoothed down her green Stella McCartney dress. She was itching to give them a makeover, but Polly had no interest in clothes and Louise had no interest in clothes that didn't have elasticated waists and numerous compartments to store food items in.

5

Erica opened the fridge and took out a bottle of wine.

'Celebrating or commiserating that it's our last day?' Louise asked.

'Neither,' Erica said. 'I've had some crap news.'

Polly looked round from the window. 'What's wrong?'

'Phoebe's leaving.' Erica plucked three glasses from the draining board. 'She's going tonight and never coming back.' She opened the bottle. The twist of the screw top lid didn't soothe her as much as it usually did.

'Why?'

'She's following her heart. It'd be romantic if she wasn't dropping me in it.'

Louise tutted. 'I did warn you about Leos. Very impulsive star sign. Go for a Pisces next time.'

'There might not be a next time.' Erica had been lucky to get Phoebe due to a national shortage of nannies. Since having Jasmine, the power had shifted. Instead of having a selection of CVs and references to choose from, she had to partake in a bidding war, with families offering increasingly extravagant benefits to woo prospective nannies. Their own cottage, car and all-expenses paid holidays were commonplace. Erica's offer of an en suite, two tickets to *Sing to Win* and the odd tube of fake tan couldn't compete.

Louise bit into a biscuit. 'First world problems, eh? You'll be complaining that your cleaner doesn't get a good enough shine on your soap dish next.'

As it happened, Phoebe didn't clean the soap dishes as thoroughly as Erica would have liked, but, oh crap – Phoebe wouldn't be cleaning them or anything else from now on. How was she going to factor housework and laundry into her already over-stretched schedule? She didn't have time to even think about all the things that needed doing, let alone actually do them.

'Yes, it's a pain,' Louise continued. 'But it's hardly a crisis.'

'It is for me.' Erica threw her hands in the air and gold bangles chased each other up her slender, brown arms. 'It's alright for you – Nick does everything when you're away running your health and safety conferences. Couldn't do that if he wasn't around. How would you cope if he went to China every other week and the twins saw him more on Zoom than in the flesh?'

'Not much call for the editor of the local newspaper to go to China.' Louise wiped crumbs from the side of her mouth. 'Just as well. Nick'd hate being away from us.'

'What if it became part of his job and he had no choice?'

'I'd tell him to get another job.'

As Dan had just taken out a six-figure loan to buy into the firm as a partner, he'd be as receptive to that suggestion as an invitation to try waterboarding. Or taking Jasmine to a *Frozen* singalong.

'That's not an option for us.'

Louise nodded. 'I know. Don't mean to be flippant, it's just that it could be worse.'

Instinctively they both looked at Polly, who was still gazing out the window. Her fascination in watching the children play eluded Erica, but so did her willingness to wear chambray. Looking at Polly, Erica realised Louise was right. It could be a lot worse. But just because it could be worse, didn't mean it wasn't still crap.

'Shame we can't stay here,' Polly said, her eyes flitting from side to side as the children ran up and down the garden. 'Been lovely having everyone pitch in rather than doing it all by myself.' As far as Erica could tell, Polly *had* done everything by herself, unless she classed Erica providing green tea bags and Louise ordering last night's takeaway as pitching in.

'Been nice to have company too,' Polly continued. 'For me and the kids.'

Erica knew it must be hard for Polly going back to an empty house every day, especially one as big as hers. Polly had moved into the former B&B that she'd inherited two years ago, just before they'd met her, with the intention of transforming it

7

from a run-down hotel into a spacious family home for her and her two children. Like many good intentions – Erica was still wrestling with January's resolution to give up caffeine and *Keeping up with the Kardashians* – Polly hadn't actually renovated the B&B yet. Hard to find the motivation to do it on her own, Erica supposed. Dan might not be around much, but she knew he'd come home at some point. No one was coming home to Polly.

Erica's mobile pinged, reminding her that she hadn't confirmed Thursday's nine a.m. appointment. Without childcare, she couldn't go to that meeting. But one of her competitors could. Sighing, she picked up a biscuit – she'd go for an extra-long run in the morning to burn it off. Her stomach tightened as another reality hit home. Without Phoebe around to look after Jasmine, her six a.m. pre-work runs would have to stop. She ate the biscuit anyway. Maintaining the industry-expected size zero would be irrelevant if she didn't have a job. She may as well ask Louise now where she got her elasticated-waist trousers.

Polly must have noticed that Erica had finished her wine. She tipped the contents of her own glass into Erica's. 'Bit early for me,' she said.

Erica smiled her thanks. That was typical of Polly – always making sure everyone else was ok. Yes, she was a bit timid, but she'd entertained the children all week, playing endless games. Louise might not have been as hands-on, but she'd introduced Erica to the charms of the Harvester. Who knew eating out could be so cheap? The bill for the entire meal had come to less than a mojito in London. Erica took a sip of wine. Considering they weren't real friends, they weren't bad as housemates. Shame they couldn't really stay on at the holiday home, as Polly had suggested. If they lived together, she wouldn't have to worry about childcare.

She gripped the stem of her glass, as an idea formed in her mind. It started off small, but grew quickly, opening up like a row of cut-out dolls holding hands. If they lived together, she wouldn't have to worry about childcare. The children would love it and Polly wouldn't be stuck in that empty house. That empty, *enormous* house, with at least three living rooms and so many bedrooms that the doors had to be numbered so she could keep track. Admittedly, Louise didn't have much of an incentive to move in, but Erica never let a simple thing like logic dissuade her – she wouldn't have got so far in the fashion industry if she had. Dan wouldn't like it, but tough. If he wasn't prepared to help her, he couldn't complain. All she had to do was persuade Polly and Louise.

She opened her mouth, then closed it. Could *she* live with *them* though? Louise was a laugh, but Christ, did she moan. About everything and anything. Even the pattern in her cappuccino if it was off-centre. As for Polly, she was very sweet and well-meaning, but she was… Erica sipped her wine while searching for a word less unkind than 'boring'. She reached the bottom of the glass. There wasn't another word. Polly was dull. Especially in comparison to Erica's real friends from St Martins and London. But she was brilliant with the children, which was what Jasmine needed. And what could have happened if she hadn't been there when Jasmine ran out into the road that time didn't bear thinking about. No, she thought decisively, this was what had to be done. It didn't matter that they were boring and moaned and that their kids were, let's face it, fucking annoying. It would only be until she found a cut-price nanny.

She cleared her throat. 'Polly, you know what you said about us living together? There's a way we could.'

Polly looked round from the window. 'School's five hours away. We're late every day, as it is.'

'I only won this place for a week, remember?' Louise added.

'Not here – at home. It's the answer to all our problems.' Erica grabbed a fistful of air – it worked on *Sing to Win* when the judges were proving a point.

'What problems?' Louise asked.

Erica pulled her chair closer to the table. 'We've got the balance all wrong. Instead of living with our partners, or on our own, struggling to do everything by ourselves and only seeing each other now and then, we should do it the other way round.' She paused for effect. '*We* should live together and see *them* now and then.'

Louise crossed her arms and the buttons on her polo shirt gaped, revealing an inch of nude bra. 'Why on earth would we do that?'

'To help each other.'

Louise and Polly exchanged glances.

Erica tried again. 'What do we always complain about? Apart from the fact that Jon Hamm doesn't take his shirt off enough in *Mad Men*?'

'Who?' Polly asked.

'Never heard of him,' Louise said. 'Poldark's who you need. Though if you ask me, no one comes close to Mr Darcy.'

Erica shook her head. They clearly weren't appreciating – or even listening to – the benefits of the house-share idea. In fairness, it was hard to compete with Louise's detailed list of Colin Firth's benefits.

'Support,' Erica said loudly. 'Whenever we get together, we complain about not having enough support at home.'

Louise ran a hand over her mousey-brown bob. The aroma of Elnett hairspray wafted over the table. 'If you ask me, Dan should pull his weight more, then you wouldn't be struggling.'

'He's either away or working or moaning about how knackered he is.' Erica shook her head. 'Never occurs to him to help out at home. Typical man.'

Polly's hand went to a silver chain around her neck. 'Not all men are like that.'

Erica's cheeks burned with shame at her insensitivity. Polly had moved to the area after her husband had died so Erica hadn't met him, but he was bound to have been lovely and didn't deserve to be bundled into the same category as Dan.

'Of course not. Ignore me.' She gestured to Louise. 'Nick isn't.'

'Be nice if he just got on with things without me having to tell him what needs doing, though,' Louise tutted. 'I have to write lists. My conferences take less organising.'

Erica could picture Dan's reaction if she left him a list of jobs. She'd once asked him to hang a picture and he'd reacted as though she'd suggested he murder his entire family. It wasn't that he expected her to do it – he wasn't sexist – he felt such tasks were beneath both of them. Was elitist better than sexist? He was getting worse as he got older too. Those shitty bullies from school had a lot to answer for.

Polly's fingers closed around the pendant on her necklace. 'Wish we could live together. Safety in numbers.'

'What was that?' Louise's head jerked round at the word 'safety'. She took her role as a health and safety conference organiser very seriously.

Polly flushed. 'I mean, it'd be fun.'

Erica nodded. Now she was getting somewhere. 'Yes – fun. We'd be less stressed and the children would love it.'

'Where's this magical house coming from?' Louise said. 'You offering to put us all up?'

Erica winced at the thought of Louise and Polly's children on her muted white furnishings. 'Dan's there some of the time,' she said quickly. 'And it isn't big enough. But Polly's is.'

'My house?' Polly spluttered.

'It's ideal. You've got rooms you don't even use.'

'That's because they're unusable.'

Erica decided to ignore that point.

Louise frowned. 'It's not that I don't want to help, but you can't seriously expect me to leave Nick because your nanny's dropped you in it.'

'You're not leaving him. We'd stay at Polly's during the week to help with the children and go home at weekends. You could have date nights.' Erica winked at Louise. 'Escape the mundane crap of living together. Get the spark back.'

'Nick and I don't need to get our spark back,' Louise snapped. 'We're very active sexually.'

Erica winced even more.

Louise misjudged her expression. 'Don't beat yourself up, not everyone's relationship can be as fulfilling as ours.' She patted Erica's arm. 'I know you're in a fix, and this week's been great, but it's not real life. We haven't had to juggle school and work and all their clubs.'

'That's the beauty of it. We'd take it in turns to do the school runs and make dinner and the children would entertain themselves. You'd have more time for yourself.'

'You're like the snake in *Jungle Book*,' Louise tutted. 'Hypnotising us into your way of thinking.'

Erica's smile dropped. She didn't spend hundreds of pounds on Botox to be likened to a reptile.

'I don't think it'd work,' Polly said quietly. 'Sorry, but…' her voice trailed off.

Erica stared at her. 'You just said you wished we could live together.'

'Didn't realise you were thinking of my place. It's such a state. The bedrooms have got holes in the ceiling and I haven't had the walls painted since they were replastered and—'

'Superficial,' Erica said. 'I'll help you do it up.'

Louise snorted. 'How? You don't even paint your own nails.'

Polly shook her head. 'It's not just that. It'd be unsettling for the kids. After their dad, I…' She pulled her cuffs down over her hands. 'I need to keep things simple. Sorry.'

Erica's familiar feeling of guilt flicked two fingers up at the hope that had optimistically applied for tenancy. 'No, I'm sorry,' she said. 'Shouldn't have assumed you'd want us to move in. Or you, Louise. It's different for me, with Dan not around. Course you don't want to be away from Nick.'

'I do at times,' Louise said. 'His technophobia drives me mad. He hates mobile phones, thinks all gadgets should be banned, doesn't even drive. If he had his way, we'd be in horse-drawn carts and the kids would be playing cup and ball.'

'That's romantic,' Polly said.

'He's more romantic than my first husband; I'll give him that. His idea of romance was a packet of pork scratchings and half a lager and lime. And that was so he could chat up the barmaid.' Louise pressed her lips together. 'Had a completely different game of cup and ball going on there.'

'You're well rid,' Erica said. 'Nick's lovely.'

Louise picked up another biscuit. 'He might not be Colin Firth, but he'll do.'

Polly looked at Erica. 'Why not take a break from work for a while? Then you wouldn't need a nanny.'

Erica would have spat out her wine if she weren't so in need of the alcohol. Take a break? It had taken twenty years to build her business up; she wasn't going to throw it away now. Admittedly, Polly didn't know that she and Dan were living in their overdrafts and their credit cards were up to their limit, but she knew rehearsals for *Sing to Win* started the following week. If Erica took a break now her reputation as a reliable stylist would be as well respected as Donald Trump's hairdresser.

'Just seems like you're missing out on fun with Jasmine.' Polly ran her pendant back and forth along its chain. The scraping of silver grated in Erica's ear.

'We do have fun,' she protested. 'We're here, aren't we?'

'You've been on the phone most of the time. And you're always working weekends.'

'That's not true. I took Jasmine to see *Matilda* last month.'

'You could do things like that all the time if you weren't working.'

'Not at ninety-five quid a ticket,' Erica snapped, then felt guilty. Polly was only trying to help. 'I know you mean well,' she said. 'But you can't take a break in the fashion industry. I'd lose all my contracts and—'

'Not just the fashion industry,' Louise interrupted. 'I went back full-time after just three months.' She crossed her legs under the table. 'Stitches hadn't even healed.'

'Jasmine will always come first,' Erica said quickly, before Louise detailed the sorry state of her pelvic floor. 'But I won't give up my career. I've worked my arse off and I love it.'

'You won't need to,' Louise said. 'Nannies will be lining up to work for you.'

Erica shook her head. 'William and Kate got the last good one. I'm well and truly screwed.'

'Not necessarily.' Louise flicked to the back page of her magazine. 'Aries, aren't you?'

Erica walked to the fridge. If things had got so bad she was relying on her horoscope for guidance, then she needed another drink.

'A good opportunity is within your grasp,' Louise read. 'So long as you're willing to play second banana to a seasoned expert.'

Erica took a swig from the bottle. She didn't want to be a first banana, let alone a second one.

Louise eyed her. 'Steady on. It's only four o'clock.'

'Already?' Polly tucked the red curls that had freed themselves from her ponytail behind her ears. 'I'd best wake Summer or she won't sleep tonight.'

'Hang on, I'll read yours. Pisces – reconnect with family members you've lost touch with. It's never too late.' Louise smiled triumphantly. 'There you go. You never see Ian's family.'

'What?' Polly's face paled.

'Better than being a banana,' Erica muttered.

'Bet they'd love to see their grandkids.'

'No.' Polly's tone was abrupt. She glanced over her shoulder at the window. 'Where are the kids?'

'Family friends then?' Louise seemed determined to prove someone's horoscope was right. 'Or friends you met through the kids? Erica and I bonded over a breast pump.'

The words 'breast pump' made Erica shudder. All those hours she'd spent having her nipples suctioned so Jasmine had enough milk while she was at work. No matter how much she drained from her body, she'd still ended up with milk stains down her Chloé blouse.

'Louise, Erica.' Polly's voice was full of panic. 'The kids have gone.' She stood up so quickly her chair tipped over.

'They can't have,' Erica said. 'There's nowhere for them to go.' If there were an escape route out of the garden, one of them would have found it by now. They found everything, even Louise's secret snacks. Erica had never seen her so emotional as when she discovered they'd polished off her Curly Wurly stash.

'They're not up that tree again, are they?' Louise said. 'Tess is going to break something one day.'

The tree, probably, Erica thought, given that Tess had been the chief Curly Wurly consumer.

'No, they've gone.' Polly yanked the handle on the French windows back and forth. Her breath quickened, clouding the glass, as she struggled with the lock. 'I should have been watching them.' Her trembling words turned into a piercing scream as three pairs of hands slapped against the other side of the window. Louise's twins and Polly's son pressed their faces up against the glass. Jasmine hovered behind them, her large brown eyes unsure behind her dark fringe.

'When's tea?' Tess shouted. 'We're hungry.'

'Come in and watch TV.' Polly was visibly shaking. 'I'll wake Summer up, then bring you a snack.'

'You alright, Poll?' Louise asked.

Polly gave a nervous laugh. 'Need to stop watching the news. So many kids go missing, don't they? It's made me paranoid.'

Erica smiled, even though she agreed that Polly was para-noid. The children had been playing in a secure, fenced garden, not a remand centre on the guards' day off.

'Must get Summer.' Polly hurried out of the room.

'Why does she have to watch them all the time?' Erica whispered. 'She's been like it all week.'

Louise pursed her lips. 'If you ask me, you should be thankful she's so on the ball.'

Erica's stomach tightened with a mixture of fear and guilt. Louise was right. If Polly hadn't been watching the children so intently the night of the school Christmas show, she wouldn't have seen Jasmine run out to meet Erica, who was engrossed in a work call, and pull her away from an approaching car. Erica could still hear the screech of the brakes and Jasmine's shriek as she was hauled to safety. Erica had barely known Polly at the time, but she'd do anything for her now. Including putting up with her at-times-annoying best friend Louise, who she'd avoided since leaving the New Parents' Support Group they'd both belonged to.

Erica's phone beeped and the appointment request flashed up again.

'What am I going to do about work?' She tugged the tips of her cropped hair. 'Dan's in China all week and I've got to be in London by nine some mornings.'

'Tell you what,' Louise said. 'Drop Jasmine at mine on your way to the station. I'll take her to school with the twins.'

Relief flooded through Erica. Maybe Louise wasn't so annoying after all. 'Thank you.' Erica accepted the invitation on her phone. That was mornings sorted, but what about after school?

She looked at Louise. 'Is there any way you'd consider a house share? Just for a month, 'til I get childcare sorted?'

'No. Wouldn't be fair on Nick,' Louise said firmly. 'Polly doesn't want to anyway.'

'But if she changed her mind?'

Louise shook her head. 'I love her to bits, but I couldn't live in her house. It's not like this place, with en suites in every bedroom.'

'Polly's house has five toilets.'

'But I daren't use any of them since the time I had to flush a turd away with a bucket of water.'

Erica tried not to dwell on the image.

Louise looked around the luxury kitchen. 'Still can't believe I won this place in a raffle. If it was mine I wouldn't lend it out.'

Erica handed Louise her wine. 'If you hadn't won, I'd have had the brilliant idea of the house share.'

Louise drained the glass. 'Wish I'd won the lavende... now.'

Chapter Two

Polly

His piercing blue eyes gazed into hers. Polly stared at the photo, wishing he'd step out of it and back into her life.

Oliver had taken the picture. He'd only been five at the time and his photos were usually of the part of the person that was on his eye-level. Unfortunately this tended to be their genitals. Miraculously, on this occasion, not only had he got all four of them in, he'd also got their faces. Ian was saluting the camera with a beer. Their neighbour, Adam, tanned from making the most of the summer around his shifts as a fireman, stood next to him. His wife, Cheryl, and Polly sat on garden chairs, Cheryl looking at her phone rather than Oliver. Polly's curly red hair was twisted into a topknot, the sleeves of her tee pulled down over her hands. She hadn't known she was pregnant with Summer at the time. She hadn't known anything, least of all what was about to happen. Her throat tightened. It was still so painful. Just as nothing had prepared her for how blown away with love she'd be when her children were born, nothing had prepared her for how blown to smithereens she'd be when the man she loved died.

Her throat tightened. Her therapist assured her that over time the physical pain she woke up with every morning would subside to a dull ache, then to a numbness, until eventually she might not feel it at all. But it had been three years and the pain hadn't lessened. If anything, it had intensified. Once the initial shock of his death and the police statements and court cases had subsided, Polly was left with the cruel, hard fact that he was gone. Forever. Tears rolled down her cheeks. She still couldn't believe he was dead. It wasn't right, particularly not when other people seemed to go on forever. Just look at the cast of *Coronation Street*.

She closed the album. She never looked at photos of him, but the therapist said she had to if she wanted to move on. She'd done it, because she always did what she was told, but the trouble was, she didn't want to move on. She wanted the opposite – to move back in time and stop it happening.

She put the album in a cardboard box on the floor. Inside was a pile of letters from the family liaison officer and her solicitor, and some newspapers. *Local Man Killed* read one headline. Polly's throat contracted, as quickly as if someone had clamped a hand around her thin, pale neck. Struggling for breath, she desperately tried to recall the exercises the therapist had given her. Should she inhale or exhale? She tried to do both but couldn't do either. Oh God. She couldn't breathe. Helplessly, she watched her body shaking uncontrollably in the wardrobe mirror. Her green eyes were wide and full of fear. In the mirror, they merged together to form one eye. It glowered at her, triggering feelings of shame and self-loathing. It wasn't right that she was still here when he wasn't. Especially not when it was all her fault. She clawed at her throat. She couldn't breathe. Her reflection began to blur.

'Mum.' Oliver's voice was in her ear. She felt his small hand on the back of her head and a paper bag being held to her mouth. 'Breathe out.'

Her eyes flitted to his and she saw the panic on his face. 'Breathe,' he shouted.

Something inside her throat relaxed and air forced its way out into the bag and back in again, building momentum until she was breathing normally. She gazed at Oliver as she inhaled and exhaled. He watched the bag contract and expand, his eight-year-old brow furrowed. He hated it when she had a panic attack. Polly hated herself for being so pathetic. Oliver shouldn't be looking after her. His biggest responsibility should be remembering to clean his teeth, not dealing with her anxieties and trauma. It wasn't fair.

Polly put an arm around him. 'Thanks, poppet. I'm alright now.'

He tore at the edge of the paper bag. 'Are you still taking them tablets?'

'I won't stop unless the doctor says. I'm better though, aren't I? That was the first one in ages.'

'If you're better, why did it happen?'

'I looked at something I shouldn't have done. It shook me up.' She squeezed him tightly. 'We'll go to the park when Summer wakes up and you've done your homework.'

Oliver stiffened. 'Don't want to do it.'

'I know, but you have to.' Polly ruffled his hair, which was coarse and blond, like Ian's; so different to her red curls. 'What is it?'

Oliver's cheeks reddened. 'Have to write down stuff you do with your dad for a stupid Father's Day project.'

Polly's heart ached for him. 'Never mind the homework. I'll write a letter to the teacher explaining. Let's go to the park. We'll take the football.'

Oliver brightened. 'There's a football club there at weekends. Can I go?'

'Maybe,' she said carefully. She didn't like Oliver and Summer being with strangers. Or out of her sight, apart from school. Even then she checked Twitter constantly for updates on what Oliver's class was up to, although of course the school wasn't allowed to post photos of him. Her therapist said it was understandable that she had separation anxiety. It was one of the things they were working on.

Oliver prodded the cardboard box at their feet with his trainer. 'What's that?'

Before Polly could stop him, he'd lifted the lid and was peering into the box. He took the photo album out and Polly cursed herself for not hiding the box back in the wardrobe. His face grew redder with each turn of the pages, past photos of himself as a baby in his dad's arms, toddling after Ian in the garden, helping with that bloody barbecue. A newspaper cutting fell out and fluttered to the floor. *Tragic Death of Local Man.* Polly winced. She hadn't realised that was in there. The album slipped from Oliver's fingers and Polly snatched it up, shoved it into the cardboard box and screwed the newspaper article up.

'Why did he have to…' Oliver rubbed his nose with the back of his hand. 'No one else's dad is…'

'I know, poppet.' She went to hug him, but he stood up.

'I heard Erica talking when we were away last week.' He leant against the wardrobe. 'Something about moving here.'

Polly remembered the children hiding outside the French windows. She hadn't realised they could hear them.

'What was she on about?' Oliver asked.

'Erica suggested living together for a while, to help each other with childcare. But I don't want anyone else looking after you, and Louise—'

'Louise?' Oliver's eyes lit up. 'And George? George is moving in?' His face was full of hope. 'When?'

Polly pulled her sleeves down over her hands. When Erica suggested they all live together, she'd felt as though she'd been thrown a lifesaver. The old B&B she'd inherited was too big for the three of them, but she'd needed somewhere to go and had fond, if hazy, memories of the house. Her mum had grown up there, when it was a functioning B&B, run by Polly's grandparents. Polly had loved to hear the stories about the quirky guests who stayed, and remembered visiting when she was little, before her mum fell ill. The B&B had always smelled of cigarettes and some unidentifiable food item. She still caught a whiff of it occasionally, even though they'd lived there for two years. The unidentifiable smell could usually be attributed to Oliver or Summer though. It was madness to move in when so much work needed doing, but it was the only connection she had left with her mum and she felt safe there.

Even so, it got very big and lonely after Oliver and Summer had gone to bed. And no matter how many times she checked the bolts on the door, she didn't like being downstairs on her own. If Louise and Erica moved in it wouldn't be like that. She wouldn't be lonely. But the downside to not being lonely was that she'd never be alone either and Polly knew it'd never work. She couldn't maintain the façade twenty-four hours a day that everything was ok. It'd be exhausting and there was too big a risk she'd let her guard slip. Then she'd lose everything.

'No, they're not moving in,' she said.

'Why?' Oliver's neck twitched as he swallowed. 'It'd be fun. Louise could make breakfast every day.'

Polly thought that was reason enough for them not to move in. She loved Louise, and wouldn't be where she was without her, but her microwaved scrambled egg left a lot to be desired. Mainly the desire to have as few of the five senses working as possible when presented with the dish that managed to be both raw and rubbery in equal measure.

'The house is a mess,' she said feebly.

'George won't care.' Oliver grabbed her hand. 'Please, Mum. Let them move in.'

Polly didn't look at him. It wasn't because the house was a mess. It was because she was a mess.

'It wouldn't work. I'm sorry.'

'Yeah, right.' His voice wavered and he turned away.

Jumping up, she wrapped her arms around him. His elbows rammed against her, trying to break away, but she held on tight.

'The holiday was fun,' she whispered. 'But it wouldn't be like that if we lived together all the time.'

'But if we lived together all the time...' His voice cracked and her stomach scrunched up in the same way the news-paper article had in her palm. 'If we lived together, then we wouldn't...' Tears coursed down his cheeks. 'We wouldn't be on our own anymore.'

Turning, he tucked his head into her chest and sobbed loudly, like the eight-year-old boy he was, rather than the man he felt he had to be when she was having one of her pathetic panic attacks.

'Please, Mum,' he cried. 'Please let them move in.'

Polly hugged him as tightly as she could, her own tears trickling into his thick hair. She had to get over her anxiety and persuade Louise to move in, for Oliver's sake. It wouldn't be easy, but she had to. Oliver had asked her to and she always did what she was told.

Apart from that one time.

Chapter Three

Louise

'It'd be so nice for the kids,' Polly said down the phone. 'You wouldn't need to pay anything. The life insurance covers bills.'

'Sorry Poll, I can't.' Louise lowered her voice. 'Nick'd hate it.'

'What would I hate?'

Louise jumped as the back door swung open behind her and Nick came in carrying the recycling caddy.

'Nothing, love,' Louise smiled.

Nick looked nervous. With good cause. The last time she'd called him love was when he'd discovered how much her ticket to Take That's reunion tour had cost.

'Got to go,' she said to Polly.

'Will you at least think about it?'

'Ok,' Louise lied. 'Bye.'

She snatched a loaf from the side and posted two slices into the toaster. A notepad sat on the worktop and she double-checked her itinerary.

'Some of the delegates are arriving early evening, so I'll head off after lunch,' she told Nick. 'Be back Tuesday afternoon. Don't forget Erica's dropping Jasmine round before school.'

'Have you told George you won't be here for his match Monday night?'

'He'll never notice I'm not there.'

'He notices every time.' Nick pushed his glasses up. 'He got man of the match last week. It'd be nice if you could—'

'We can't all sneak out of work and make up the time later.' Louise dipped a finger into the jam jar. 'How are you going to go back to the office on Monday when I'm not here?'

'Rachel said she'd help.'

The jam clogged in Louise's throat. 'When did you speak to that cow?'

'Bumped into her the other day. She said she needed some practice before the baby arrived so—'

'So you thought you'd let her loose on the twins?'

'She is their aunt.'

Louise's neck wobbled. 'She doesn't have a clue how to look after them.'

'She only has to sit here while they do their homework and watch TV.'

'She won't sit here. My sister's a typical Aquarius – she'll be poking her nose in everywhere, checking for dust and dirt and tins that have gone past their expiry date. Any excuse to criticise me.' Louise started making another list. As if she hadn't got enough to think about, now she had to ensure the house was show-home standard. 'You'd better put that shelving unit up,' she snapped. 'Get the kids to tidy their rooms. And replace the potpourri in the cloakroom.' She added a note to hide all her underwear. No point handing her ammunition. Louise still cringed about the time Rachel had whipped her greying bra off the radiator and placed one of the G-cups over her head. She couldn't resist flaunting the fact she was skinny and Louise wasn't.

'I'll do what I can, but I've got some homework for my writing class on Wednesday. We're talking about narrative voice.' Nick pushed his glasses up. 'Not sure I've got one yet.'

'Shame you didn't have one when you saw Rachel.' Louise tutted. 'Where's that asparagus kettle she got us for Christmas? She'll have something to say if it's not on display.' She gripped her pen. 'She'll have something to say about everything.'

Nick stood behind her and slipped his arms around her waist. 'Don't get stressed about it.'

'Don't talk to me about stress.' Louise tapped her notepad. 'This is the biggest conference I've ever organised. There's so much to think about – speakers, caterers, lighting, how many toilet rolls 300 delegates might get through.'

Nick kissed the top of her head. 'Maybe I can take your mind off it.' His hand crept inside the pocket of her dressing gown. 'The twins aren't up yet.' There was a rustle as his fingers encountered a Curly Wurly wrapper. It didn't deter him. 'Fancy going back to bed?'

Louise felt her heart rate increase. She wished it were as a result of heightened desire. When they'd met fifteen years ago, she'd been the seducer. Nick, a shy, red-faced reporter from the local paper, was covering the Safety in the Work Place conference she'd help organise. His eyes had been as large as the lenses on his glasses when he'd seen her on her knees, her V-neck blouse gaping open, taping cable to the floor so no one could trip over it on their way to the stage. After a few glasses of cheap fizz, she'd led Nick to the conference centre's pokey storeroom where she'd ripped her blouse open, grabbed the back of his head and pinned him to her chest while undoing the clasp on his belt. It was the best sex she'd ever had – an intoxicating mix of power and adrenalin, fuelled by the slight concern someone would walk in and catch them at it on a box of lanyards.

'How about it?' Nick whispered now, leaning down to rub his cheek against hers.

She really should. It had been months. She tensed as his fingers edged towards the waistband of her pyjama bottoms. She missed his touch and longed to kiss him, but that would lead to sex and their thin bedroom curtains didn't block out the sun streaming in. Nick would see every roll, dimple and crease slipping over the sides, like porridge bubbling over a pot and plopping onto the hob. When she'd lost weight, they could resume the 'active sex life' she'd boasted to Erica about.

She slapped his hand gently. 'Better not. The twins will be up any minute.'

Nick's arms slipped away from her waist.

The toaster pinged and she turned to it, grateful for the distraction. She'd make it up to him when she was thinner.

'It doesn't occur to you to ask if I want any, does it?' Nick said.

'You never eat first thing.'

'It'd still be nice to be asked.' His shoulders slumped. 'It'd be nice to be asked anything.'

'Like what?'

'Like, shall *I* make the coffee? Would you like *me* to take the dog out?' Nick paced up and down the narrow galley kitchen. 'Would you like a day off from ferrying the twins to football and drama? Do you want to watch something other than *EastEnders*?'

Louise nibbled at the toast as his words and pacing gathered speed. He did this every now and then. Had a bit of a rant, then everything went back to normal. Once he'd stopped, Louise held out a piece of toast. He shook his head.

'Why are you moaning if you don't want any?'

'It's the principle.' He gave her a sideways look. 'What's my novel about?'

Louise hesitated. Nick had told her the plot of the book he was writing but she couldn't remember the details. Possibly because she hadn't actually listened. She'd meant to but had been mentally calculating whether she could afford a gym membership. Not that she'd admit that to Nick. Better to work out secretly and do a tah-dah reveal when she'd shed the two stone she'd put on in as many years.

'Did you read any of those chapters I printed off for you?'

She shoved a corner of toast into her mouth. Should she be honest? Tell him she'd taken them into work to read at lunchtime, but in her haste to get to the birthday buns someone had brought in, had accidentally put them on the 'to be shredded' pile on her desk? Would it comfort him to know that the junior who'd put them through the shredder enjoyed reading them so much he'd asked for the next instalment? She suspected not.

Nick gave up waiting for her to answer. 'What about my email then?' he asked quietly.

Her neck grew hot.

'Did you read that at least?'

The heat crept up towards her face. Yes, she'd read the email that he'd sent six weeks earlier. The email that threatened to tear her life apart. He'd been unhappy for a year, he'd written. They never talked, laughed, had sex. He couldn't remember when they'd last done anything as a couple or she'd shown him any interest. He loved her, but something had to change if they were going to stay together.

She put her toast down, no longer hungry. Why had he said *if* they were going to stay together? They *had* to stay together. She loved him so much. Couldn't bear to be without him. She'd thought long and hard about how to react to the email and had eventually decided to pretend it didn't exist. It worked with his receding hairline and her expanding waistline.

'What about my email?' Nick repeated.

She hesitated, wondering how to tackle this without admitting that she was avoiding him 'til she'd lost weight. Should she pretend she'd never got the email? No. He'd witnessed her lying many times over the years – swearing blind she hadn't thrown away the papier-mâché pig one of the twins had made, that she hadn't got her sister's message about meeting up, that she hadn't polished off the Garibaldis. He'd know if she lied now.

She decided to brazen it out. 'Oh, that.' She swiped the air. 'We all need to let off steam after a bad day. I knew you didn't mean it.'

'Didn't mean it?' Nick's spine straightened, making him appear even taller than his six-foot, five inches. 'I poured my heart into that email and you ignored it. Just like you ignore the twins half the time.' He shook his head. 'You don't think about anyone but yourself.'

Louise swallowed, regretting it instantly as her throat made an unattractive rasping noise. 'I do think about other people.'

Nick gave her a look of disdain. 'Colin Firth doesn't count.' He turned and left the room, closely followed by Woody, the scraggy Westie Nick had brought home from the kennels after writing a feature on abandoned dogs.

Uncertainty gripped Louise. Nick was never confrontational. He was a typical Cancerian – steadfast, loyal and predictable. She followed him into the hall.

'I'm taking Woody out,' he said. 'Won't be long. Tess wants to run through her lines before drama. Unless...?' He looked at her questioningly through his glasses.

Louise smiled apologetically. 'I would, but I've got to pack for this conference.' Finding three days' worth of outfits in her wardrobe that still fitted was a major concern. She needed to have a trying-on session while Nick was busy, so he wouldn't walk in on her when she was trying to do up a zip with a coathanger or fasten a waistband with masking tape. 'I'll test her next time.'

Nick shook his head. 'Sometimes it seems as though you can't be bothered with the twins. Or me.'

Louise opened her mouth, but Nick interrupted her. 'If you were bothered, you'd have come to bed.'

Louise clasped the neck of her dressing gown. 'The twins—'

'That's an excuse. You've always got an excuse.'

'It's not an excuse.' Her double chin rested on her hand. 'It's life. We're busy and tired.'

'Well it comes across as though you don't care.'

'Of course I care,' Louise said defiantly. 'I'd move into Polly's with Erica if I didn't.'

'What do you mean?' Nick asked.

'Nothing,' she said quickly.

He stared at her. 'Don't treat me like an idiot. Why is Erica moving into Polly's?'

Louise waved a hand through the air dismissively. 'She's got some silly idea about us moving in together for a month.

29

Helping each other with childcare in the week and coming home at weekends.'

'What's silly about it?'

'It's not normal.'

'Is our marriage normal then?' Nick's eyes searched hers through his glasses.

'Course it is. Erica's bloke's never around and poor Polly hasn't got one. Kind of makes sense for them, but not us.'

'I said something had to change,' Nick said softly. 'Maybe this is the answer.'

'No.' Louise crossed her arms. 'I don't want to.'

'It's not just about you.'

Louise's heart hammered beneath her folded arms. She needed to get them off this subject. Add it to the list of things they never talked about. Woody sat at Nick's feet looking hopefully at the lead in his hand.

'You'd better take him out,' she said. 'Want me to get the poo bags?'

Nick exhaled loudly. 'Not sure I can keep doing this.'

Louise patted his arm. 'Won't be for much longer. He can't have long left.'

He jerked away. 'I'm not talking about clearing up after the dog.'

There was a thud above them and George squinted down as he passed the top of the stairs on his way to the bathroom. Like Nick, he was tall and thin. His gangly frame was growing faster than he could adjust to, resulting in an inability to move without tripping or knocking something over. On cue, his feet tangled around themselves and his knees buckled.

He steadied himself on the bannister. 'Can we go to the park later to practise penalties, Dad?'

'Course, mate.' Nick smiled up at him, the tension on his face easing.

George gave a thumbs-up and went into the bathroom.

Louise tried to return Nick's smile, but he took his glasses off and rubbed his eyes. His hand was so large it covered his whole face. It reminded Louise of the game he played with George and Tess – sliding his hand down to reveal one facial expression, then sliding it back up to reveal another. A grin, then a pout. A sneer, then a gurn – which she feared was how she looked normally.

Nick replaced his glasses. 'I think you should move in to Polly's. Give us some space to think.'

A chill ran through Louise. 'But we've got enough space here.'

'I don't mean physical space.' Nick gripped her shoulders. 'Go to Polly's for a month. See how we feel then.'

Louise shook her head. 'I know how I feel. Moving out won't change anything.'

Nick's hands dropped to his sides. 'I really hope that's not true.'

Her throat burned. She mustn't cry. She looked like Miss Piggy when she cried. Miss Piggy without the make-up, wig and glamorous clothes. So, a standard pig really. The thought made her want to cry even more. She pulled herself up as tall as she could and wished she wasn't still a foot shorter than him.

'You can't kick me out,' she said, more authoritatively than she felt. 'I own half this house.'

'I'm not kicking you out.'

'What do you call it then?' She glared at him, choosing anger to mask her fear. 'What about the twins? Don't you care about them?'

'Course I do. If it wasn't for them—' Nick stopped himself and glanced up the stairs. 'If we break the cycle, get out of this rut, maybe we stand a chance.'

'It's not fair to uproot them. They'll hate living at Polly's.'

'We both know that's not true.'

Louise shook her head. 'I'm not leaving,' she said, with a forcefulness she didn't feel. Inside, she was falling apart.

'Then I will.' Nick's own forcefulness seemed genuine and Louise's knees went weak.

'What?' she whispered. This wasn't typical Cancerian behaviour. What had happened to steadfast, loyal and predictable? Louise desperately tried to think of a strategy to resolve the situation. What did she offer clients who were being wooed away by other events organisers? She frowned. Fifteen per cent off his next booking plus free leaflet distribution wouldn't help this situation.

'I'll rent somewhere.' Nick clipped Woody's lead on. 'The paper's full of ads for flats to let.'

'No.' Bile rose in Louise's throat. 'You can't do this.'

Nick sighed heavily, his eyes full of sadness. Louise seized her chance.

'You're right. I haven't paid you and the twins enough attention. I haven't read your book. Not because I don't care. It's because...' she faltered. Admitting it was down to overeating wouldn't elevate her in his eyes. He'd add greed to her list of faults. 'I'm sorry. I'll change.' She would. She'd lose weight and be back to her old self in no time.

'Trouble is, Lou, I'm not sure I believe you.' Nick's voice wobbled. 'Taking a short break, having time to assess things, could be the way to save us.' He turned away and her heart twisted as he rubbed his eyes. She reached out to touch him. The flab on her arm wobbled and she whipped her hand back again.

'If you don't want to go to Polly's, I'll look for somewhere to rent short term.' He took a deep breath and turned back to face her. 'Most contracts are for six months though.'

'No,' Louise shouted. They both looked nervously up the stairs and she lowered her voice. 'Six months is too long. We'll go to Polly's.' She couldn't believe she was agreeing to this, but the alternative was far worse. 'Just for a month,' she added. 'And we'll come back at weekends.'

Nick nodded. 'It's the kindest way to do it for the twins.'

What about the kindest way to do it for her?

Nick opened the door, letting in the hum of lawn mowers and the smell of freshly cut grass. He strode down the path, Woody jerking ahead on his lead, opened the gate and was gone. Oh, hang on, he was coming back. Her heart soared. He'd realised this was ridiculous and was rushing back to tell her he didn't want her to leave.

'Forgot the poo bags,' he said grimly.

He snatched them up and Louise watched him stride away again, a cruel déjà vu unfolding before her, except that this time he didn't come back.

Louise closed the door and leant up against it. The bravado she'd tried to display vanished and tears erupted from her. How could she have been so stupid to let slip about the house share? If she hadn't, this would have been an ordinary argument that would be forgotten about by the time she got back from her conference. Now her life was changing for the foreseeable future. She wouldn't be seeing her lovely Nick every day. Instead, he was being given the opportunity to realise he was better off without her. And she was going to have to move out of her home. She was going to have to live in a rundown B&B and use a bucket to flush the toilet. She dropped her head back and wailed.

'Mom?' Tess ambled down the stairs in too-tight pyjamas. 'Has Dad deleted *Come Dine with Me* again?'

Louise wiped her face hurriedly. 'No. I'm alright, love.'

'What are we doing today?' Tess's cheeks were creased from the pillow, her light brown hair damp and knotted around her shoulders. 'Can we see Jasmine, Oliver and Summer?'

Louise sighed. Nick was right. The twins would love the shared house. On holiday there hadn't been any arguing or moaning about being bored. Instead they'd played and had fun.

Louise smoothed her bobbed hair in the hall mirror. Silly to get so upset. It was only for a month and she'd be back every weekend. She'd use the time to lose weight and prove

33

to Nick that they belonged together. She wiped a smudge of yesterday's blue eyeliner away and gave herself a steely glare. It would be fine. They'd had a laugh when they were away, and she could keep an eye on Polly. She seemed to be ok these days, but sometimes Louise caught a glimpse of the anxiety that had haunted her when they'd first met.

Louise would never forget how lost and alone Polly had looked, standing at the school gate, hugging Oliver as though afraid that if she let him enter the school gates he'd never come out again. It had taken several weeks of enforced conversation before Polly had said anything more than guarded, monosyllabic answers, and even longer to persuade her to allow Oliver and George to have a play date. These always had to be at the B&B, which suited Louise fine – no clearing up the mess they made.

It was on one of these play dates that George had fallen over and bloodied both knees. This was such a common occurrence that Louise didn't bat an eyelid, but Polly had crumpled to the ground, clawing at her throat and gasping for breath. Louise had applied her extensive first aid training, putting Polly in the recovery position while she breathed deeply into a paper bag. Mortified, Polly had blamed the episode on a sleepless night and they'd never mentioned it again, but Louise worried there was more to it.

Living with Erica wouldn't be so bad either. She'd get all the latest backstage gossip from the show and could wind her sister up by hinting at it but not telling her what it was. Rachel couldn't believe that Louise was friends with someone in showbiz. The only claim she had was that her mother-in-law had appeared on the *Antiques Road Show* in 2003. And that was hardly something to brag about. The vintage teapot she'd presented turned out to have been made in Taiwan.

Louise tried to smile but couldn't quite manage it. No matter how much she sugar-coated it, it wasn't fine. She had a whole month of not knowing where Nick was, what he was doing or who he was doing it with.

A beep came from the kitchen.

'Dad's left his cell.' Tess appeared in the doorway, Nick's mobile in her hand. Her newly acquired American drawl was extremely annoying, not least because it gave Nick another outlet for his technophobia – the Disney channel.

'Go and stick the telly on. I'll be through in a minute.' Tess shuffled past and Louise went to put Nick's phone back in the kitchen. As she lowered it onto the work surface, she remembered there was an app that pinpointed the exact location of consenting friends. Making sure Tess couldn't see her, she unlocked the keypad, downloaded the app and synced his mobile with her own before replacing it on the worktop. She might not be with him for the next month, but at least she'd know exactly where he was.

Chapter Four

Erica

A chicken? Really? Erica looked at the photo from the au pair agency in disbelief. Why would someone applying for a responsible position send a picture of themselves holding a chicken? She deleted the email without even reading the profile. The next applicant had submitted a photo of herself in an inflatable sumo wrestler suit. Delete. The woman could have the caring nature of Princess Diana, the playfulness of the cast of *Friends*, and the healing hands of Christ, but she wasn't getting near Jasmine with that dress sense.

Dan climbed into bed next to her, put in his earbuds and opened Netflix on his iPad. Erica rolled over to study him. Although almost fifty, he still had a thick head of hair, albeit grey, and there was no sign of the stocky build he'd apparently had at school, thanks to a dedicated gym regime and the 5:2 diet. He was so grumpy on his fasting days that had his job not required overseas travel, Erica would have insisted he find one that did. A long-term posting on an international space station sounded about right.

Thankfully, today wasn't a dreaded fasting day. She pressed herself up against him.

'Jasmine's asleep.' She ran her fingers down his chest. 'So we could…'

Dan grabbed her hand and eased it away. 'Not tonight, eh? The China trip's taken it out of me.'

'Oh, ok.' Erica retreated to her side of the bed, trying not to feel rejected. She couldn't really take umbrage when she'd forgotten he was coming home until he'd walked through the door that evening. She hadn't thought about him at all while he'd been away. Replacement childcare was consuming all her thoughts. She'd barely had time to fantasise about Ryan Gosling.

Picking up her own iPad, she placed a Waitrose order for the following morning. Given their financial situation, she should look into shopping elsewhere, but didn't have time. Jasmine wouldn't have had tea that night if it weren't for M&S's thoughtful placing of the food court near the lingerie department, enabling Erica to nip in when buying control pants for a client. Guilt coursed through her as she thought about how crap this week had been for Jasmine. She'd been to every after-school club going, coming home with all manner of items, from a macramé bag made in textiles to a bruise from tag rugby. Without any decent au pairs available, things didn't look set to improve.

Erica tugged at her dark, cropped hair. Louise had raised a valid point when they were away. Instead of struggling to resolve this by herself, why shouldn't Dan get involved? His usual argument was that he hadn't wanted children and had only caved because she'd threatened to leave him if they didn't at least try. Even so, he should help out.

'I can't find an au pair,' she said.

'Why are you looking at au pairs? Get another nanny.'

'We can't afford it.'

He patted her thigh through the sheet. 'Won't be for much longer. As soon as the big accounts start coming in we'll be rolling in it.'

'What do we do 'til then? Jasmine's in after-school clubs and Louise takes her to school, but the summer break's only a few weeks away.'

Dan took one earbud out. 'You haven't told Louise about our financial situation, have you?'

'Course not, but I can't keep asking her to help. Next week will be easier because you're home, but—'

'I'm not doing the school run.'

'You'll have to on Monday. Louise is away and I've got a meeting at nine.'

'So have I.'

His dismissive manner set Erica's teeth on edge. 'Change it then.'

Dan looked at her as incredulously as if she'd suggested he go to work wearing only his vest and pants.

'You're her dad, for fuck's sake.' Erica threw her hands in the air. 'I'm not being unreasonable. You should want to take her – you barely see her.'

'It's not that I don't want to, but when you're a partner people have certain expectations.' He couldn't resist a smug smile at the word 'partner'. Erica only just resisted punching him.

'Come on, Dan. I'm desperate. I even considered something drastic.'

'I've been saying for years boarding school is the answer.'

Erica glared at him. 'Not that fucking drastic.'

'What then?'

'You know my friend Polly?'

'The widow?'

'Don't call her that,' Erica said defensively. She was a huge fan of labels, but on materialistic items, not people.

'How do you know her again?'

An image of Polly pulling Jasmine out of the road flashed through Erica's mind and her stomach clenched. 'School,' she said noncommittally. She was too ashamed to tell Dan exactly how they'd met.

'Can't understand why you hang around with her and Louise. They're nothing like your other friends.' He frowned. 'You even went on holiday with them. What happened to your cool city breaks with Zoë and Tonya?'

'A little thing called money,' she said. 'The Airbnb was free. Jasmine got a holiday – which we can't give her right now – and I could work.'

She added the dig about a holiday to offload some of her own shame onto Dan. Guilt was her standard setting – she constantly beat herself up for not being around enough for Jasmine – but the guilt she felt over what had happened two years ago was on a whole other level. How could she have been so preoccupied with a work call that she hadn't noticed Jasmine running out into the car park to meet her? She shouldn't have even been on the call. Praising Jasmine for her part in the Christmas show should have been the priority. Even if her time onstage had been so minute it made the part of the lowly cattle seem like a leading role.

She swallowed hard, remembering that awful moment of turning around to see what had caused a car to screech to a halt and realising that the child screaming as she was hauled to safety was Jasmine. She'd sprinted over, dropped to the ground and hugged Jasmine so tightly she'd squealed loudly again. Tears streaming down her face, Erica had spluttered thanks to the woman who'd saved her over and over again.

The woman was Polly. And next to her was Louise, who Erica had met at the New Parents' Support Group. She'd been the one who had an opinion on everything and liked to voice it. Sometimes her comments were funny, but mostly she came across as a know-it-all prick. Erica had ignored her invitation to meet up when the formal sessions ended and pretended not to see her at school events by engrossing herself in a phone call. Just as she had then.

To Louise's credit, she never mentioned Erica's snubs. Instead, she seemed thrilled to see her and eagerly introduced her to Polly, who barely spoke. She didn't need to – Louise did all the talking, telling Polly about Erica's glamorous job styling TV stars and filling Erica in on her own busy schedule juggling her twins with a high-flying career in event management. She seemed to think that being working mums made them soul mates and that fate had brought them back together.

When Louise had invited her and Jasmine to Polly's for a play date the following Saturday, a combination of guilt and gratitude had forced her to accept, even when every instinct screamed *fuck that*. Somehow this became a regular date. Erica wasn't sure how, as Dan was right; Polly and Louise couldn't be more different to her friends from St Martins and her years of living in London. But they'd all splintered off to commuter towns, as she and Dan had to Hazelworth in Hertfordshire. They still met after work for cocktails and Erica relished the conversations that didn't revolve around the children or McDonald's latest meal deal – popular topics with Polly and Louise – but their various careers prevented them meeting very often.

When work started on *Sing to Win* and Erica couldn't make the Saturday play dates, Polly insisted Jasmine come anyway. Erica would bring a bottle of wine afterwards as a thank you, which Polly and Louise (who always hung on to get the insider info on the show) insisted they open there and then and share with Erica.

And so, as a result of her neglect and Polly's vigilance, she now saw Polly and Louise more often than her real friends. Even if Jasmine didn't adore playing with Summer, Erica would have felt duty bound to maintain the friendship. Thank goodness Jasmine hadn't been saved by the woman who did the school run on her daughter's scooter and wore papier-mâché jewellery.

She couldn't admit any of this to Dan though. If he knew Jasmine could have been fatally injured while in Erica's care, her argument that he didn't take his parenting role seriously enough would be flimsier than a *Love Island* contestant's swimsuit.

The guilt trip worked. Dan reached out and took her hand. 'When my partnership's secure and we've paid off the loan, I'll make it up to you both. We'll take Jasmine on the holiday of a lifetime.' He squeezed her hand. 'Thank you for encouraging me to go for partner. Couldn't have done it without your support.'

Now was her chance. 'Speaking of support,' she said. 'We're going to have to pull together 'til we get another nanny. I can't

40

do all the childcare and run the house on my own; you know how busy I already am.'

Dan nodded. 'I'll look at my diary in the morning. Not sure I can do any more than I currently do though.'

The self-control Erica had to exert to stop herself asking what it was he currently did would have made Gandhi look weak-willed.

'What was the drastic idea you had?' Funny how Dan was much more receptive to hearing it now he might have to pull his weight a bit more.

'Don't know if I told you, but Polly's got a huge house. Used to be her grandparents' B&B.'

Dan's eyes wandered back to his laptop. 'Booking a twin room for you and Jasmine, are you?'

'Course not.'

'Thank fuck for that.'

'We'd have our own rooms.'

Dan's head jerked round. 'What? In some shitty B&B?'

'It's not a B&B anymore.' It was shitty, but Erica decided not to mention that. 'If we moved in during the week, Polly, Louise and I could share childcare and housework. Polly could pick Jasmine up from school with her son and Louise's twins, and I'd help out when I was around.' She was deliberately forgetting that she was never around. It wasn't happening anyway.

'What about us?' Dan raked a hand through his hair. 'When would I see you both?'

'You're in China half the time,' Erica said. 'And we'd be back at weekends.' She winked. 'We could have date nights in the week.'

Dan looked as though he was struggling to breathe. 'You can't do this. What would everyone think?'

'We wouldn't tell anyone.'

'But if they found out? How would it look?' Dan lowered his voice as though worried someone would hear. 'Like I can't afford to support my partner and child and they've had to move into a slum.'

'It's not a slum.' It was a bit. 'And who's going to find out? Why would they care?'

Dan's jaw clenched and Erica gave him a reassuring smile.

'You haven't seen those dicks for thirty years. If you don't post it on Facebook they'll never know.' She sighed. 'It's not happening anyway. Even Polly's not as desperate as me.'

Dan's face relaxed and he exhaled loudly. 'Don't scare me like that.' He went to put his earbuds in and hesitated. 'How did her husband die?'

'Some sort of accident. She won't talk about it; says it's too painful. She was pregnant with Summer when it happened. He didn't even know.'

'Fuck.'

'I know.' Erica felt guilty again for getting worked up about something as comparatively trivial as a work meeting.

'I like the sound of date nights, though.' Dan tapped his nails against his teeth. 'Maybe it's not such a bad idea.'

'Polly and Louise don't want us to, remember?'

'Probably just as well. You wouldn't really rather live in a B&B than here, would you?'

Erica looked at the door leading to her built-in wardrobe and the art deco dressing table and matching freestanding mirror. It had been a wrench to leave her apartment in London and move to a grown-up, family-friendly area and house, but the character, space and luxury decor they'd been able to afford had compensated. No, she wouldn't rather be at Polly's. She loved her house. Apart from Dan's collection of creepy theatre masks that hung in the hall. She could live without those.

Dan kissed her forehead. 'We're in enough debt as it is; a few more hundred pounds isn't going to make much difference. Find a nanny and forget about this commune nonsense.' He turned his attention back to his tablet.

Erica sighed and looked at her own iPad. Dan was deluded if he thought a few hundred pounds would secure them a nanny;

not now they expected their own property, car and holidays in the Algarve. She reread the applications from the au pairs. Surely there was one who would do? She shook her head. No. Desperate as she was, she couldn't leave Jasmine with a stranger she didn't trust. Her stomach tightened, as she saw the career she loved unravelling before her. She turned to voice her concerns to Dan, but he was asleep, slumped over his iPad. She eased it out of his hands.

'I was watching that,' he grumbled, before admitting defeat and falling back on the pillows.

She put the iPad on the bedside table next to her phone and noticed a voicemail message from Polly.

'I've been thinking about your idea of moving in.' Polly's voice was quiet. 'I know I said no, but if you're still up for it, we'd love you to. Let me know.'

Erica listened to the message again. This was brilliant. With Polly looking after Jasmine, her career was saved. She snuggled down under her Egyptian cotton sheets and tried to identify the nagging feeling in her stomach. This was exactly what she'd hoped for. So why was she wondering what the fuck she'd done?

Chapter Five

Polly

Polly had been cleaning all weekend and was exhausted. For the last two years she'd worked on the principle that it was much easier to apologise for the mess than it was to clear it away. But if she used that line every day Erica and Louise might smell a rat. Or worse, find one.

She walked along the passageway from the kitchen to the entrance hall, pausing to check Summer in the den on her way. She lay on the sofa watching a cartoon, her cheeks twitching as she sucked her dummy. She was so beautiful – dark brown curls and eyes that were such a startling bright blue they took Polly's breath away. She'd only ever seen one other pair of eyes that vibrant before. Her throat tightened and she put a hand to her pendant and gripped it. Was she doing the right thing letting the others move in? Was she capable of pretending that everything was ok?

'When are they getting here?' Oliver called from the hall. The excitement in his voice reassured her that she was. She'd find a way to make it ok.

The crunch of gravel in the car park at the back of the house answered his question and he bolted down the passageway to the kitchen. Polly kissed Summer before following him. Louise came through the back door, clasping the strap of her brown bag tightly across her bosom as though afraid someone might pinch it if she put it down. Tess stood next to her clutching a bag of Haribos equally protectively. Oliver and George nudged each other, clearly excited, but reluctant to blow their cool and show it. Although both eight, George was a head taller than Oliver and about half his weight. 'Lanky streak of piss' Ian would have called him. He'd not had much of a way with words.

'Hi.' Polly stepped forward to hug Louise, then remembered Louise didn't do displays of affection, so wiped a speck of dust from the cooker instead. Louise hadn't explained why she'd changed her mind about moving in and Polly didn't want her to change it back on account of an ill-judged embrace. 'How are you, Tess?'

'Cool,' Tess replied. Polly found her American accent cute, though Louise said that would change when she heard it 24/7. 'Living here's gonna be awesome.'

Polly smiled. 'It's so great you're moving in.'

'Staying, not moving in,' Louise said. 'Just for a month and only weekdays, remember?'

Oliver elbowed George. 'Let's go upstairs.' They ran out of the kitchen and along the passageway.

'Where's my room?' Tess asked.

'I'll show you when Jasmine gets here,' Polly said.

'Cool.'

'You've got bunk beds.'

'Cool.'

'I got that cereal you like with the choc chips.'

'Cool.'

Polly could see what Louise meant about the accent wearing a little thin.

She turned to Louise. 'Want to see your room?'

Louise shrugged but picked up her suit carrier and followed Polly down the passageway past the doors labelled 'WC' and 'Room 3', which was now a den, and past the optics on the wall that had been a bar when it was a B&B. Tess veered off into the den when she saw the television was on. They reached a door with a brass-coloured, peeling number four on it. Polly pushed it open and watched Louise's face nervously.

45

This was like a VIP room at Claridge's compared with the bedroom upstairs with the damp patches, or the bedroom with the hole in the ceiling, or the bedroom with the damp patches *and* a hole in the ceiling, but it was tiny. There was hardly room for Louise to get round the single bed. A clothes rail was shoehorned into one of the alcoves and a chest of drawers in the other. To brighten the room up, Polly had added a yellow duvet, blind and rug, which was actually a bath mat because she hadn't been able to find a rug small enough. The new additions hadn't exactly transformed the room into an oasis of welcoming warmth. 'You can't polish a turd,' Ian would have said.

Louise stepped into the room. 'Know how Harry Potter felt now,' she muttered.

'Sorry it's so small.' Polly pulled her sleeves down over her hands. 'But there's a shower and toilet next door. You won't have to queue in the morning.'

Louise hung her suit carrier on the rail then sat down with a big sigh. The bed creaked loudly, but she didn't seem to notice.

'What's wrong?' Polly asked, noticing that Louise's eyes were bloodshot and her blue mascara was smudged. She couldn't have looked more fed up if she'd discovered Cadbury's was going into liquidation.

'Nothing,' Louise said sharply. She hauled herself up. 'Let's get the kettle on.' The doorbell rang as she left the room.

'I'll get it,' Tess called. Her footsteps thudded down the passageway followed by the swish of Louise's combats rubbing together.

'Polly,' Louise shouted a moment later from the front door. 'The bolt's stuck.'

Polly hurried after her. 'There's a knack to it.' She jiggled the bolt until it slid across.

'Hi ladies.' Erica's broad smile faltered slightly when her shoes stuck to the carpet. Jasmine smiled shyly beside her.

'Hey. We're roomies.' Tess gave Jasmine a gentle push and Jasmine staggered backwards. Their physiques were at complete odds to one another's, as though they came from different species, not just different families. 'Dibs having the top bunk.'

'Go on up, if you want to,' Polly said. 'You're in room eight.'

'Cool.' Tess dragged Jasmine towards the large, curved staircase in the hall.

'Watch this,' Oliver called from the top of the stairs. He flung one leg over the side of the bannister and slid down. George went to follow.

'Stop,' Louise shrieked. 'You'll break the bannisters. Or your neck,' she added, as an afterthought.

'Come on,' Tess said to Jasmine, who looked nervously at her mum.

Erica gave her a reassuring wink. 'Want me to come up with you, sweetie?' Jasmine nodded.

The three of them started up the stairs.

'Tess,' Louise called.

Tess turned around eagerly.

'Move that fire extinguisher when you get to the top.' Louise shook her head at Polly. 'Never prop fire doors open. That's a serious breach of health and safety.'

Tess looked at Erica holding Jasmine's hand and ran on ahead.

'See you in the kitchen in a minute,' Erica called down. 'I brought champagne.'

'Don't you want to see your room?' Polly asked.

'Let her have a drink first,' Louise said. 'Possibly two.'

In the kitchen Louise sat down at the small round table in the centre of the room. 'Where will we eat? Won't get eight people round this.'

'The old dining room,' Polly said. 'We can push all the little tables together.'

'The girls like their room,' Erica said, joining them. Her eyes darted around the kitchen, as though seeing the peeling units and chipped tiles for the first time. She gestured to the yellowing net curtains at the window. 'Can we take those down? It'd be nice if the light could get through.'

Louise nodded and her heavily hair-sprayed bob flapped like wings. 'Potential fire hazard, those curtains.'

Polly refrained from saying that Louise's hair was probably the most flammable item in the house.

Erica took a bottle of champagne from her bag. 'Glasses?'

Polly took some sherry glasses from the back of the cupboard. They were a remnant from the B&B's glory days, along with fifteen tiny metal teapots, all of which leaked and could only be handled with oven gloves. Erica filled the glasses to the brim.

'Steady on,' Louise said. 'We're here to look after the kids, not get sloshed.'

'But they're so much easier to look after when we're sloshed.' Erica winked. 'Come on. It's our first day.'

'Business before pleasure.' Louise took an A4 folder from her bag. 'I've drawn up rotas for meals, school runs, cleaning and the dishwasher.'

Erica's bangles tinkled as she raised her glass to her lips. 'Who put you in charge?'

'Never said I was in charge, but someone's got to be organised.' Louise looked round the room. 'Where shall I stick them?'

'I've got an idea.' Erica drained her tiny glass.

Louise pinched her lips together. 'Face like a bulldog chewing a wasp,' Ian would have said.

'We don't need rotas,' Erica said. 'We'll figure it out as we go along… shit.' Blood trickled down her finger.

Polly's throat contracted.

'There's a crack in the glass.' Louise went into health and safety mode. 'Hold your hand up.'

A drop of blood splattered onto the table. Polly felt as though her own blood was draining from her body.

'Got any plasters, Poll?'

Louise's voice was echoey. A giant eye flashed before Polly.

'Poll?'

'I've got some nipple daisies in my bag.' Erica sounded as though she were speaking from another room.

Polly struggled for breath. She couldn't do this in front of them. They'd want to leave before they'd properly arrived. But the blood. She gripped the edge of the table, desperately trying to stop herself from slipping under it. Just as everything began to go dark she became dimly aware of a buzzing sound. Its vibration mirrored the pounding in her ears. She forced herself to concentrate on the sound. It was the doorbell. But both her friends were here. She didn't know anyone else.

Only a few seconds could have passed, as Erica was explaining to Louise what nipple daisies were. Louise didn't sound as though she'd be investing in any. Polly blinked hard and both women came into focus.

'Shout if it's another bible salesman.' Louise jerked her head in the direction of the front door. 'I'd like to ask why God only felt the need to create one Colin Firth.'

Polly's throat relaxed as she realised Louise was right. It'd be a sales rep. She occasionally got calls from people trying to flog related supplies, such as bibles, mattress cleaning products and tiny, metal teapots. She made her way shakily along the passageway towards the front door. Summer tottered out of the den, chewing on her dummy, and Polly picked her up, then crossed the hall and looked through the spyhole. A man with shaggy, brown hair stood on the doorstep dressed in jeans and a casual shirt, a black Labrador at his side. He didn't look like a salesman, but he didn't look threatening either. She opened the door a crack and peered out.

'Hi.' The man smiled and gestured to the old B&B sign above Polly's head. 'Do you let rooms out?'

Polly shook her head. She really had to take that sign down.

'Do you know of any others? My ex is coming to visit the kids and needs somewhere to stay.'

'No,' Polly said quietly.

He smiled. 'You've got kids at North Hill, haven't you? I've seen you at the gates. My two go there too.'

Polly nodded politely.

Summer wriggled in Polly's arms and reached down to the dog.

'Do you want to stroke her? Her name's Bess.'

Summer nodded and smiled up at him from below her eyelashes.

Polly stepped back. 'We'd better get on,' she said. 'Got friends round.'

Summer stuck out her lower lip and Polly made a mental note to reinforce the 'stranger danger' message. Rather than being wary, Summer was on the verge of giving this man her phone number.

'Course. Sorry to have bothered you. I'm Alex, by the way.'

'That's ok. Bye.' Polly shut the front door and yanked the bolt back into place. She paused, then looked through the spyhole. Alex was walking away. The curved glass distorted his image, but he wasn't distorted in Polly's mind. For the first time since the accident, she'd looked at a man properly. Enough to notice the colour of his eyes. Alex's eyes were blue. A startling bright blue that took Polly's breath away.

Chapter Six

Louise

Louise eased herself up from the kitchen table. She should have stopped drinking after the first bottle. Or the second. She definitely shouldn't have had any of the third. It was Erica's fault. She'd actually run to the small supermarket up the road when the champagne ran out. Then gone back again later to get another bottle. The own-brand prosecco wasn't a patch on the champagne they'd started on, but no one really cared by that point.

While they'd been drinking and sharing pizza, Louise had tried not to think about what Nick was doing. Would he remember to make his sandwiches for the next day? Should she text and remind him, even though he hadn't replied to her messages telling him to set his alarm and iron his work shirts? Probably embarrassed to admit how much he needed her.

As Erica regaled them with tales of celebrity wardrobe malfunctions, such as the time a singer's chicken fillet had slipped out the side of her halterneck and flopped onto the stage, Louise tried to pretend it was just a nice, fun evening and that she'd be going home soon. Home to Nick.

But when Polly yawned and Erica said she needed to go to bed so she could get up for a run before work, Louise couldn't pretend anymore. She wasn't going home. She *was* home, for the next few weeks anyway. Reluctantly, she followed Erica and Polly along the passageway and stopped outside room four.

'Night.' Erica lurched forward to give her a hug and careered into the optics on the wall instead. 'Shhh,' she said loudly to the rattling glass bottles.

Polly smiled at Louise. 'Sleep well.'

They walked away and Louise stood alone in the passageway, listening to the creak of the stairs and the rasp of the fire door as they made their way to their rooms. Her bottom lip wobbled and she shook herself. This was ridiculous. She stayed in hotel rooms on her own with work. This was no different.

She pushed open her door and it banged against the bed. Ok, it was slightly different. She'd never had to edge into a hotel room sideways. Wouldn't it be better for Erica to have the smallest room, given that her torso was approximately the same width as Louise's upper arm? Polly was skinny too, but she was entitled to a decent bedroom upstairs. Why was Erica entitled to one as well? Louise pressed her lips together, trying not to feel resentful. She should be glad she was on her own down here. No need to worry about snoring – Nick wore earplugs – or farting in her sleep. She hoped Nick's earplugs drowned that out too.

Nick. She missed him already and it had only been one afternoon. Did he feel the same? She took her phone from her hoodie pocket and opened the app she'd set up. '*Locating Nick*' read the message, then a head and shoulders silhouette appeared on their road, an arrow pointing in the direction of their house. He was home. Course he was. Where else would he be on a Sunday night? What was he doing, though? She logged onto his email looking for clues, but the only message he had was from *Men's Health* detailing common myths about haemorrhoids.

Tears pricked her eyes. Would Nick tell her if he had haemorrhoids? She honestly didn't know. Sniffing, she changed into her pyjamas and curled up on the bed. She didn't want to be here. It was horrible. A toilet flushed on the floor above, followed by a loud groan from the hot water tank, which didn't improve the situation. A creaking floorboard outside her room made her start. Swallowing down her tears, she reached out and opened the door. Oliver and George froze, slices of cold pizza in their hands.

She held out her hand and they begrudgingly handed them over.

'Back to bed, you two. You've got school in the morning.'

The boys crept off and Louise shut the door and took a bite of pizza. Then another. And another. She crammed the last piece into her mouth and brushed crumbs from her hands. Enough feeling sorry for herself. She was a Taurus, for God's sake. Resilient and independent. So what if she and Nick were spending a few weeks apart? What was the worst that could happen? She pulled the duvet up and closed her eyes. She didn't want to know the answer to that question.

Chapter Seven

Erica

A loud beeping came from Erica's phone on her bedside table. She groaned and fumbled for it, accidentally knocking over a miniature kettle. It was a wonder she'd managed to set an alarm the night before, considering she couldn't remember going to bed, although she did have a vague recollection of doing the conga to the corner shop.

An hour later, Erica was back from her run and discovering the joys of the mildew-scented shower. Grimacing, she stepped out of the cubicle and reached for her towel. A spluttering noise came from the passageway and she froze, one arm stretched out, her entire body – her entire *naked* body – completely exposed. The bathroom door was wide open and George and Oliver stood on the landing, clutching their mouths and laughing hysterically. Erica snatched the towel up, strode over to the door and slammed it, her face burning with rage. Putting on a peep show for prepubescent boys wasn't quite what she'd envisaged when suggesting the house share.

Twenty minutes later, Erica came down the stairs, a fake smile plastered on her face. She wouldn't let those little sods know how much they'd embarrassed her. Her smile dropped as one of her heels slipped on the worn carpet and her leg plummeted forward, threatening to catapult her down the stair-case. Fucking hell, these stairs were more lethal than a ski slope. Clutching the bannister, she made her way gingerly down the rest and crossed the hallway, wondering why there was such a racket coming from the dining room. It was the children. They sat on assorted chairs around a large table, made up of several smaller tables pushed together. Cereal boxes and a four-litre carton of milk stood in the middle. Jasmine was next to Tess, who was talking loudly while shovelling cornflakes into her mouth. Oliver and George nudged each other when they saw Erica and sniggered. George misjudged the length of his arms and elbowed Oliver in the face. Oliver stopped laughing. Erica wondered if she could get away with doing the same to George. Suspecting it wouldn't go down well with Louise, Polly or social services, she instead dropped a kiss onto Jasmine's head.

'Mummy, I can't find my school bag.' Jasmine's large front teeth dug into her lower lip. 'You did bring it, didn't you?'

Erica thought back to the huge pile of bags by the front door at home. There had been so many it was very possible she'd missed one.

'My homework's due in,' said Jasmine, panic in her voice.

'You're gonna get a detention,' Tess drawled, displaying half-chewed cereal.

Jasmine's chocolate-brown eyes widened with fear.

Erica checked her watch. 'Don't worry, sweetie. I'll drive home now and get it.' If the traffic was on her side, she'd be back in time to do the school run that Louise had scheduled her in for. She turned to leave, just as George reached out for a carton of orange juice. A split second later, the sticky, almost fluorescent liquid was dripping down the sleeve of Erica's white Victoria Beckham blouse that she really couldn't afford and had only worn twice.

'Sorry,' George mumbled, his cheeks bright red.

'Mummy,' Jasmine pleaded. 'My bag.'

'On my way,' Erica said faintly, backing out of the room.

She made her way to the kitchen, holding her arm out in front of her and staring in horror at the orange stain on her sleeve. Was the blouse salvageable or was she going to have to throw it away before she'd even paid the credit card bill?

Polly sat at the kitchen table in a floral robe. Summer was on her lap, squidging bits of banana with her palm before ramming them into her mouth. Louise leant against the work surface in a navy polyester suit, a triangle of toast in her hand.

'Morning,' Erica said, going to the sink to wash her stained sleeve. 'How are you both?'

'Terrible,' Polly said, her bloodshot eyes confirming her hangover.

'I've felt better,' Louise said. 'Got a pitch this afternoon for an alcohol awareness conference. Hope they're not aware how much I've got in my system.' She put the toast triangle into her mouth. 'Don't forget you're doing the school pick-up tonight.'

Erica tensed. 'I can't, I'm in London.'

'I meant Polly. You're doing the pick-up Thursday.' Louise nodded to the far wall.

Erica turned her head and saw several sheets of A4 paper taped to the larder door. The pages were divided into squares and names were written in each box, with highlighted headings. One sheet was devoted to maintenance, detailing how to refill the salt dispenser in the dishwasher and clean the lint filters in the tumble dryer. Erica's earrings rattled as she shook her head. What the fuck was a lint filter?

'About these rotas,' she started. 'I don't remember agreeing—'

'This is a rough draft. I'll get a whiteboard from work and do it properly.' Louise took a wooden spoon from a jar on the side and pointed out Erica's name on the first sheet. 'You're doing school drop-off today and Wednesday.' She moved the spoon to the next sheet. 'School pick-up, Thursday. Breakfast, Wednesday. Dinner, Thursday. Dishwasher, Tuesday and Friday.'

Erica's stomach tightened. She hadn't anticipated such a prescribed schedule. Hitler couldn't have put this much thought into his planned takeover of the British Isles.

'You can't assume I'm available.'

'You are. We synced the calendars on our phones last night.'

'I don't remember that.'

'If you ask me, you weren't paying attention. Too busy demonstrating the doggy position.'

'What?' Erica gasped. How pissed had she been?

'Some yoga move.' Louise slurped her tea. 'It was towards the end of the night.'

'The downward dog.' Erica breathed a sigh of relief.

'Whatever it was, I don't need to see it again.' Louise put her mug in the sink. 'I'm off. Bye all.'

Polly bounced Summer on her knee. 'Kettle's just boiled if you want a cuppa.'

'Thanks, but I'll make a chia smooth—' Erica stopped. 'No, I won't. Forgot my smoothie-maker. Shit, and Jasmine's school bag.' Erica grabbed her keys. 'Back in ten minutes,' she yelled, running out into the car park. So much for the house share making life easier. She'd been up for two hours and not only was she running late, she had to work out what a lint filter was, get her blouse dry-cleaned and buy a lock for the bathroom.

–

Erica walked the length of the Wardrobe room and smiled with satisfaction at the rows of clothes rails ready for the *Sing to Win* contestants.

Pixie, the assistant producer, leaned around the door. 'Delivery for you in reception.'

'Thanks.' Erica sighed to herself as she took in Pixie's dip-dyed pink hair, crop top and skinny jeans. Being a stylist had definitely been more fun before she'd become old enough to have given birth to most of the staff.

'And there's a new Shooting PD on his way up,' Pixie said, consulting a clipboard. 'Rob Mascoll. Head of PD said you was to meet him at the lift and show him where the production office is.'

Were, not *was*, Erica longed to say, but pointing out grammatical inaccuracies wasn't consistent with the youthful image she was trying desperately to convey.

'Why me?' she said instead.

'Cos it's your fault Grant left and dropped us all in it.'

'How?'

Pixie shrugged. 'Don't total the messenger.'

'Has Rob Mascoll worked on the show before?'

'Nah.' Pixie glared at Erica, as though that was her fault too. 'Can't believe Grant's in LA. Lucky sod.' She hurried off in another direction.

Erica wasn't sure how lucky he was – she'd sampled Phoebe's cooking – but the sod part was definitely accurate. Not only had he absconded with her nanny, she was now going to be stuck hand-holding some pimply, young graduate who didn't know a thing about working in TV and would probably get a hard-on every time one of the young wannabes twerked on stage. Erica checked her watch as she hurried along the corridor towards the lift. She really didn't have time for this.

The lift doors opened and she stopped and turned. And turned. And turned. She was stationary, but her stomach was swivelling. Fuck, he was gorgeous. Late-thirties she guessed, about six-foot with broad shoulders, smooth, dark brown skin, jet-black hair and a clean-shaven, square jaw; so much more attractive than the bushy beards many men sported these days. It didn't matter how much beard oil they massaged into them, there was no dressing up the fact that they were pubes on a chin. Air kisses had never been so popular.

She held out her hand. 'Hi. Erica Perera, consultant stylist. You must be...' A pasty young man in his early twenties slouched out of the lift and Erica faltered. If it turned out he was the new recruit and this perfect specimen of a man was destined for another department, there was no justice in the world.

'Rob Mascoll, the new shooting PD.'

Erica mentally grabbed a fistful of air.

Rob shook her hand, his long fingers firmly clasping hers. 'Nice to meet you, Erica.' Creases appeared at the edges of his dark eyes as he smiled. It was a proper smile, one with warmth and feeling, not politeness or obligation.

'Perera?' he said. 'Unusual name.'

'My parents are from Sri Lanka,' she explained, returning his firm handshake and wide smile. Maybe she wouldn't mind the hand-holding after all.

Chapter Eight

Louise

Louise's phone beeped and she grabbed it, desperately hoping for a message from Nick. They were halfway through their third week at the B&B and for Louise, that was two-and-a-half weeks too long.

Perhaps Nick was wondering what to have for tea. They usually had chicken kievs on a Wednesday. A whole box was too much just for him though. Maybe he was texting to invite her to join him? She eagerly checked her message, disappointment flooding through her when she saw it was from Erica.

> How's Jasmine? Thanks for babysitting. Is Polly ok? Feel a bit guilty about having a date night. As though I'm flaunting the fact I have someone when she doesn't. x

> They're both fine. Stop worrying x

Louise replied, then tucked the phone into a pocket in her combats. It beeped again and she fished it out eagerly. Erica's name flashed up alongside three kisses. Louise sighed heavily.

'What's up?' Polly asked from the sofa, Summer asleep in her arms.

'Just Erica checking on Jasmine.' Louise opened her magazine and reread Nick's horoscope.

'Why don't you and Nick go out one night?'

Louise's neck flushed. 'He's working late.'

Even if Nick did want to take her out, he'd change his mind when he picked her up and saw Erica. She'd looked stunning, all long, slim, brown limbs in a clingy green dress and heels, her full lips in a dazzling smile at the prospect of a fun night out with Dan. Louise, with her chubby, mottled limbs in bobbly jogging bottoms was the polar opposite. You couldn't get a starker contrast between two people if you lined up Rihanna and one of The Hairy Bikers. No wonder Nick didn't want to see her.

'I'm hungry,' Tess said from where she was lying on the floor in front of the TV.

'How about a biscuit?' Polly said. 'I'll put Summer to bed, then get you all some.'

The flush on Louise's neck travelled up to her face. She'd polished off the last pack in bed the night before.

'I'll get them.' She'd nip to the shop over the road while Polly was settling Summer.

In the kitchen, George and Oliver were peering into the larder.

'What are you up to?' Louise asked.

They jumped and turned. After two-and-a-half weeks of living together the pair were inseparable and George was morphing into a mousier, lankier, clumsier version of blond, sturdy Oliver.

'Nothing,' George said.

Louise crossed her arms.

'Just getting some crisps,' he mumbled, his gangly arms hanging by his sides.

'Crisps?' Louise strode over to the larder. 'Where?' That'd take Tess's mind off biscuits.

She retrieved a large multi-pack from the vegetable rack and tore it open. George and Oliver surged forward, bringing with them the scent of sweat and school dinners.

61

Louise grimaced. 'When did you last wash?'

Oliver snatched up two bags of crisps. 'Let's finish our game.'

Louise grabbed George's arm. 'Homework first.'

George looked anxiously at the door as Oliver scampered away. 'Doesn't have to be in 'til next week. I'll do it at the weekend?'

Louise nodded. If he did it at the weekend, Nick could answer the awkward questions, such as what partitioning was or how subordinate clauses worked. It was embarrassing having to admit she didn't know, with the added humiliation of Jasmine explaining the answer.

'Alright, but have a shower.' She stuffed a packet of prawn cocktail crisps into the pouch pocket of her hoodie.

George shot out the door and up the passageway after Oliver. Louise made herself a tea while listening out for the inevitable sound of George tripping over or running face-first into a wall.

'Want a cuppa?' she asked Polly, who'd come into the kitchen. She'd taken her hair out of its customary ponytail and her long red curls fell around her shoulders.

'No, thanks.' Polly's phone beeped and an alert from Louise flashed up on the screen.

'Ignore that,' Louise said, reading the message. 'I'd scheduled a house meeting, but we need Erica to be here.' She passed the phone to Polly. 'You've got two missed calls. Someone called Becky.'

Polly's face paled.

'Old friend of yours?'

'Kind of.'

Louise frowned. Polly had said she wasn't in touch with anyone from her hometown.

Polly turned her phone face-down on the table. 'Wish she'd stop texting.'

'If you ask me, Facebook's what you need. Easier to ignore than texts and you don't have to accept people. I've ignored my sister's friend request for years. I'll set you up.'

'No,' Polly said sharply.

Louise choked on her tea. She was only trying to help.

'Sorry.' Polly clasped her pendant. 'Didn't mean to snap. It's just,' she hesitated. 'I don't trust the Internet. Who knows who can see what, when it's up in the Cloud.'

Louise opened her mouth to explain why the Internet was safe and how the Cloud worked, then realised she didn't have a clue. Besides, more importantly, she also realised she hadn't checked Nick's email that day.

She stood up. 'Got some work to finish off. I'll do it in my room, so I'm not in your way.'

'You're not in my way.' Polly gave a small smile. 'It's not even been three weeks but I'm already used to having you all here. It'll be horrible when you leave.'

Louise paused at the door, desperate to check up on Nick, but reluctant to leave Polly. 'Be nice to get your house back, have Oliver and Summer to yourself.'

Polly didn't say anything. She looked so fragile. Perhaps this move had done more harm than good, giving her a taste of what it was like to have another adult to talk to.

Louise sat back down. 'It's been lovely, but we always said it was only for a month. You'll still see us all the time.'

'Erica hasn't got a nanny yet. I heard her on the phone to Dan.' Polly leaned forward, her green eyes wide. 'I'm going to ask if she wants to stay on. Bet she will with the school holidays coming up. Why don't you stay too?'

'Wouldn't be fair on Nick,' Louise said quickly. 'It's been great for him to focus on his novel, but he misses us.'

Polly leant back in her chair and ran her pendant back and forth along its chain. 'That's sweet.'

'Yes.' Louise avoided Polly's eyes. 'Give me five minutes to get this work done and we'll watch that new drama. Tom Hiddleston's in it and there's brief nudity. His, hopefully.' Picking up her tea, Louise ambled along the passageway to her room and flopped down on her bed.

Opening her laptop, she took the crisps from her pocket and logged into Nick's email account. The rainbow circle whirred on the screen and she watched it anxiously, dreading the day he changed his password. Reading his emails was the only contact she had with him. At the weekends he spent his time taking the twins to their various clubs, helping with homework and playing in the garden. Louise watched from the window as he played Simon Says with Tess or football with George or hosing the garden became a water fight. In the evenings he worked on his novel in the dining room. Hunched over his computer, he'd push his glasses up and type for hours. Louise would lie on the sofa, trying to focus on the TV, but listening to the click of keys through the glass frosted doors dividing them. When she peered round the door to tell him she was going to bed, he'd say a polite goodnight, and in the morning she'd come down to find him asleep on the sofa. On Sunday afternoons, when they got ready to head back to Polly's, he'd fuss over the twins, telling them how much he'd miss them, then wave them off, having avoided any contact with Louise at all.

The whirling rainbow vanished and Nick's email account opened up. A new message sat in the inbox. *Sender: Rachel Fisher.* Louise choked on the crisp she'd just crammed into her mouth. Why was her sister emailing Nick? She gripped her mug. She had to read it. It wouldn't be wrong; she was just taking an interest in his wellbeing. Glancing furtively at her bedroom door, as though afraid Nick might burst through it, she clicked on the email.

> Hi Nick. Just wanted to check you're ok after the other night. Don't be disheartened, you've never had that problem before and it happens to everyone at some point. As for your size being an issue – many men would love to be as big as you!

Louise clamped a hand to her mouth and her wedding ring chipped against her tooth.

Don't let it stop us. I know you're worried about
Louise finding out but she won't. I know where
we can go so she won't see us. Call me. R x

Bile rose in her throat. Surely not? Not Nick? Words, not
women, were his passion. He must be the only straight man
alive who wished the sexy *Countdown* presenter would get out
the way of the word board. But her sister's email – '*Don't let it
stop us. I know where we can go.*' The proof was in the pudding,
as they said, and she'd had enough puddings in her time to
recognise one. There was no mistaking the words. He was
having an affair – with her sister.

Gritting her teeth, she read the email again. It must have
been going on for some time. Long enough for Rachel to know
that he didn't suffer from impotence usually. The fact it had
never happened with Louise didn't bring any consolation, nor
that he'd ever complained about being too big to her. No doubt
her sister was tighter down there. Even her fanny had to be
superior. Louise gagged at the thought. Nick was *her* husband,
not Rachel's. Why did she want him when she had one of her
own? Nick couldn't compete with a cosmetic surgeon on a
six-figure salary with a red Jag and five-bed house. What was
he thinking? Rachel was pregnant, for God's sake. A whimper
escaped her. Pregnant. What if Nick was the dad?

The mug slipped from her hand and fell to the floor. The
baby couldn't be his. It couldn't be.

She stood up to get her phone and lukewarm tea squelched
beneath her feet. She had to see Nick and find out. Oh God.
How would she cope if it was his.

Her phone app searched for Nick, the *Locating* message
flashing for an agonisingly long minute. Louise's chest rose and
fell. Where was he? At home with his chicken kiev or at work
covering a last-minute news story? The screen cleared, then
opened out a map showing Nick's whereabouts. He wasn't at
home or work. He was in the neighbouring town about ten

miles away. On Maple Avenue, part of a new estate with paved driveways and hanging baskets and camouflaged wheelie bins. The app didn't say which house number he was at, but Louise knew. He was at number three. Rachel's house.

She only just reached the bin before throwing up. He was with her sister right now. Eager to compensate for his short-comings last time, no doubt. Louise heaved again into the wicker basket. The last time she'd been at Rachel's house had been two years ago for an official launch party of her new kitchen. She and Nick had stood awkwardly by the revolving corner unit away from everyone else, pretending to enjoy the caramelised onion and goat's cheese tartlets. On their way home they'd taken the piss out of Rachel's descriptions of intelligent storage systems and ergonomically designed flap fittings. Louise retched over the bin. She couldn't bear to think about Rachel's ergonomically designed flap fittings.

Wiping her mouth with the back of her hand, she looked at the app on her phone again. The silhouette showing Nick's location was moving. It edged out of Maple Avenue and turned onto the road leading to the neighbouring village. Louise's hand shook. Where was Rachel taking him? To the Hungry Horse they sometimes took the twins to as a treat? Or to that cosy little bistro out of town, with shaded nooks and candles in jam jars and a ridiculously overpriced menu that called gravy 'jus'? Were they racing towards it in the Jag, his hand on her knee, laughing at how clever they were? Maybe they were discussing baby names.

'Let's get those biscuits,' she heard Polly say from the den.

The silhouette was still moving on her screen. He'd gone past the Hungry Horse and the bistro and was nudging along the road towards... towards home. He'd be there in fifteen minutes – she could be waiting when he arrived. She hauled herself up and looked in the mirror. Her hair stuck up like wings, but a generous squirt of hairspray smoothed it down. She ringed her blood-shot eyes with blue liner, preparing herself for battle.

Sliding her feet into a pair of crocs, she crept out into the passageway, past the den to the kitchen and out of the back door. She couldn't deal with explanations as to where she was going and why. She'd text Polly when she got home. In the car she gripped the steering wheel tightly. She wasn't sure what she was going to say or do, but she knew one thing. Nick wouldn't be bragging about how big he was when she'd finished with him.

Chapter Nine

Polly

'Anyone seen the biscuits?' Polly asked, rifling through the cupboard. 'I know I bought some.'

'Mummy says biscuits are *a minute on the lips, a lifetime on the bum,*' Jasmine said.

Tess frowned. 'Why does your mom put cookies up her butt?'

The landline phone rang in the passageway and Polly froze. Her therapist, Becky, was the only person who used that number.

'Let's leave that,' Polly said. 'It'll be a cold call.'

Jasmine ignored her and ran to answer it. 'Mummy's going to ring to say goodnight.'

George side-stepped Jasmine, fell against the table and knocked a pile of laundry onto the floor. His flurry of apologies drowned out what Jasmine was saying on the phone.

Moments later Jasmine reappeared, looking disappointed. 'It's Becky,' she said. She bit her lip when she saw Polly's face. 'Is that bad?'

Polly forced a smile. 'Course not.' She walked slowly into the passageway where the phone sat on a little table below the optics.

'Hi, Polly,' Becky said warmly. 'Sorry to ring so late, just wanted to make sure you're ok. You cancelled your last session.'

'I'm fine.' Polly glanced nervously at Louise's door, hoping she couldn't hear. 'Don't think I need to come anymore.'

'It's great that you're feeling so positive, but it's important to keep coming. You've been through so much and you'll be going through it for a long time. Our sessions will help you on your journey.'

Polly reached for her pendant. 'Honestly, I'm ok.'

'We have to continue the conversation,' Becky said softly. 'Or you'll never be able to move on.'

'I'll call the office and make an appointment,' Polly lied. She'd had enough of the conversation. Talking about it didn't change anything. He was still dead.

'Let's make one now. I can do—'

'Got to go. It's the kids' bedtime.' Polly hung up and yanked the lead out of the wall. She couldn't stop Becky ringing, but she could stop her getting through.

'Mamma,' Summer called from upstairs. Polly hurried to the hall and up the stairs to her bedroom, her pendant thumping against her chest as she ran. Summer stood in her cot, chewing on her dummy.

'Hi, poppet.' She lifted Summer out and hugged her tightly. 'I'm sorry you never got to meet your dad. He'd have loved you so much.' Summer's bright blue eyes gazed into Polly's and for a moment it was as though she were looking into *his* eyes. Polly's heart ached as she remembered how they used to light up when he saw her. How he'd made her feel safe and valued. How he'd kissed each scar and stroked her long red curls and told her over and over how much he loved her and would always look after her. She fought back tears. How different their lives would have been if he'd lived. 'Let's go downstairs and see what the big kids are up to,' she managed to say.

The big kids – apart from Jasmine, who watched nervously – were taking it in turns to slide down the bannister.

'There's no cookies,' Tess said, landing heavily in the hall.

'How about some toast?' The children followed Polly back along the passageway to the kitchen as though she were the Pied Piper. Polly flipped the bread bin open. A solitary crust nestled at the back. 'Cereal?' She opened the fridge. A centimetre of milk swished around the bottom of the four-pint carton. Was it her turn to buy more? She didn't think so, but so many of Louise's messages and reminders pinged up on her phone it was hard to keep track.

Polly shifted Summer onto her other hip. 'I'll go and get some biscuits from the shop if you four get ready for bed while I'm gone.'

The children nodded and ran out of the kitchen.

'Just popping to the shop, Louise,' Polly called. 'Won't be long.'

Inside the shop, Summer grabbed a lollipop from a stand by the door and bounced up and down in Polly's arms. Polly put milk and bread into a basket, then deliberated over the biscuits. Which kind would the children like best? Which would make them so happy they'd convince their mums to stay on instead of leaving at the end of the month? Balancing the wire basket on her knee, she scooped several packets in. Summer reached over to grab one and upended the basket so that it tipped up. The milk carton flipped onto its side and teetered on the edge.

'Oh no,' Polly gasped.

'Here, let me.' A tanned hand reached out for the plastic-rimmed handles and caught the milk before it fell to the floor.

Polly looked up gratefully. 'Thanks.'

'You're welcome.' Bright blue eyes smiled at her. 'Alex. Don't know if you remember. I asked about rooms at your B&B a couple of weeks ago.'

Polly smoothed her curls behind her ears. Alex. Yes, she remembered.

Chapter Ten

Louise

Louise let herself into her house and dropped her bag at the foot of the stairs. The house felt strange without Tess's chattering and George's football banging against the side wall. Woody barked in the garden. Ignoring him, Louise walked into the living room. Her glass swan Conference Organiser of the Year award was at an angle on the mantelpiece. She straightened it and went through to the dining room. The table was covered in printed out pages from Nick's novel, some with handwritten notes on. How could such neat writing come from such enormous hands? What else had those enormous hands been up to?

Anger coursed through her. Snatching the pages up, she scrunched them into balls. The previous day's post was stacked neatly at one end of the table, a letter reminding Nick to give blood on the top. She swiped them onto the floor. Half a chocolate bar sat on the computer desk in the corner of the room. What kind of freak only ate half a bar? Louise crammed it into her mouth and glared at the computer. Now that she thought about it, things had started to change when the computer arrived. Nick had bought it second-hand from work when the newspaper upgraded its system. Instead of writing in a notebook in the living room, he'd worked at the computer in the dining room. She'd encouraged him too. 'That novel won't write itself,' she'd said when he looked like he might want to talk over her programme. And off he'd go into the dining room, sliding the glass door shut behind him and sinking into his chair. Yes, the computer was definitely partly to blame.

Through the net curtains she saw Rachel's red Jag pull up outside the house. Heat flushed up her neck and she stormed out into the hall to confront Nick. She'd deal with her sister separately; it would be too painful to see them together. And Nick would probably stop her if she tried to maim Rachel.

The front door swung open and Nick walked in backwards, waving goodbye.

'You're home late.'

Nick jumped and banged his head on the doorframe. The look on his face downgraded itself from sheer terror to slight alarm when he saw Louise standing in the hall.

'What are you doing here? Are the twins ok?'

'Where have you been?' she snapped.

'Went for a drink with the news team.'

'The news team?' Louise pursed her lips.

'Yes.' He couldn't meet her eyes. 'Just a thank you for putting another issue to bed.'

Anger exploded inside Louise. He'd been putting something to bed alright, but it had nothing to do with the newspaper.

'Liar.' She pushed him and he fell against the coats.

'What the...?' He turned round, his glasses skew-whiff.

She'd never felt so betrayed. With her ex, Dave, she'd been disappointed and upset, but not surprised. This was so much worse. She'd trusted Nick.

'I know you were with Rachel.'

Nick opened his mouth and closed it again.

'Tonight wasn't the first time, was it?'

He swallowed hard, his Adam's apple bulging and retracting.

'Think you've been really clever, doing it behind my back, don't you?'

'That's not how I meant it to be.'

'Even bragging about how big you are. When did you get so full of yourself?'

Nick shook his head. 'I wasn't bragging. I *am* big and some-times it makes getting into the right position tricky.'

An image of Nick lying on top of Rachel flashed through Louise's mind. Of Rachel's peroxide blonde hair spread out on the pillows, her mouth at his ear, coaxing him into that tricky right position. Bile burned the back of Louise's throat.

'You're disgusting,' she spat. 'How could you? With my sister, of all people?'

Nick grabbed Louise's shoulders. 'I'm sorry, I—'

Louise pushed his hands away. 'How long?'

'About three weeks.'

So the baby wasn't his. Thank God. But it meant that the affair had started as soon as she'd moved out. Had Rachel been waiting on the corner when she drove away or had they had the decency to give it a couple of hours?

'Is that why you made me leave?'

'Course not.' He pushed his glasses up. 'It wasn't planned. I wasn't even thinking about it. Rachel drove past when I was walking back from my writing course one evening and picked me up. She suggested it and I thought I might as well give it a go.'

'Give it a go?' Her legs felt weak. 'She's pregnant. Doesn't that mean anything?'

'She said we might have to stop near the due date, but not to worry about it for now.'

Louise whimpered. 'How can you be so blasé about it?' Gripping the dado rail she lowered herself onto the stairs. 'My sister,' she whispered.

'Is that what you're upset about?' Nick crouched down. 'Would it have bothered you if I'd gone to a professional?'

Shrieking, she launched herself at him, her fists pummelling his shoulders, knocking him backwards.

'Stop.' He raised his hands to protect himself. 'Get off!'

But she couldn't stop. She wanted to hit him again and again and again. Make him know how much he'd hurt her. 'I hate you,' she hissed, swiping at him with her palms. 'I hate you both.'

Nick grabbed hold of her wrists. Louise struggled for a minute before giving up. Her shoulders slumped and tears coursed down her cheeks.

'Lou?' Nick scrambled up and held her. She tried to pull away, but his long arm was wrapped around her. 'I'll stop,' he said firmly. 'I'll tell Rachel I don't want to do it anymore.' He rocked Louise back and forth. 'I wasn't any good anyway. My stupidly big foot got stuck under the clutch the other day and I stalled at a roundabout. Almost caused a pile-up.'

A loud sob caught in Louise's throat. 'What?'

'A pile-up. It was only my fourth lesson.'

Louise lifted her head. 'Lesson? As in driving lessons? Rachel's teaching you to drive?'

He nodded. 'Isn't that why you're—?'

'Oh, Nick.' Relief flooded through her. 'I thought you were having an affair.'

'No! Things have been bad, but I'd never cheat on you. Especially not with…' Nick looked as nauseous as she'd felt just moments earlier. 'Bloody hell, no wonder you were so upset.' He pressed his lips to her forehead. 'How could you think that?'

Louise stretched up, relishing the feel of his lips on her skin. 'Her email didn't say anything about teaching you to drive. It sounded as though you were, you know, doing it.' She laughed at the absurdity of it.

'What email?'

Louise snorted. 'I thought she meant you couldn't get it up, but you'd stalled at a roundabout.' Her laughter was hysterical now. 'And going on about your size not being an issue.' Her shoulders shook. 'She meant your height, not your…' She jerked a thumb in the direction of his groin.

Nick said something, but she was laughing too loudly to hear.

'What was that?' she managed to say in between splutters.

'Why are you reading my emails?' His voice was cold.

74

Suddenly she didn't feel like laughing anymore. 'I…' She searched desperately for an excuse. 'I logged onto your account by accident.'

It was a ridiculous lie and he gave her a withering look.

Louise's face burned. 'You don't talk to me.' She looked up at him pleadingly. 'How else can I find out how you are?'

'Ask me?'

'I shouldn't have to. Why didn't you just tell me you were having driving lessons?'

'It was supposed to be a surprise.' Nick shook his head. 'An affair? Do you think so little of me?'

'I'm sorry.' Louise wrapped her arms around his waist. It was like hugging a plank of wood. 'Blame that cheating ex-husband of mine. It's his fault I can't trust anyone.'

Nick tried to extract himself from her grip, but she held on tightly.

'I'll try harder,' she said quickly. 'But you have to tell me stuff.'

'You don't listen when I do.'

'I will, I promise. I'll make more of an effort.'

Nick stopped pulling away. 'Really?'

Louise nodded enthusiastically. 'I'll help teach you to drive.'

Nick gave a small smile. 'Not sure I want to learn anymore. Rachel saw me tonight when I was walking back from work and asked if I wanted another go. I drove to hers ok, but Stuart came back with us and I didn't have the bottle to drive with him in the car too.'

'So that's why you were at Rachel's house.' It all made sense now.

Nick stiffened. 'How do you know I was there?'

Louise swallowed hard. Her throat rasped loudly as though she were trying to swallow a fly. 'Don't be cross,' she said, her voice quivering. 'I signed you up to an app that shows me where you are.'

'What?' Nick pushed her away. 'Is that even legal?'

'I did it on your phone and authorised it on your behalf,' Louise said quietly.

'What the hell? You're spying on me, as well as reading my emails?' He put his hands to his head. 'This isn't a marriage. It's a bloody trial.'

'It's only because I love you. I don't know what I'd do without you.' Her neck and face felt as though they were on fire. 'I couldn't handle it if you went off with someone, like Dave did.' She reached out, but he sank down onto the bottom step.

'I'm sick of being punished for what he did.' He took his glasses off and rubbed his eyes. 'I'm sick of it all. You put me down, take the piss, expect me to do everything. All those bloody lists you write, as though I'm incapable of thinking for myself.'

'They're meant to be helpful. Running the house is a big job. Makes sense for me to project manage and you to be a...' she hesitated, wondering how to dress up the word 'minion'.

'A minion?' Nick finished for her.

'No!' She assumed a horrified expression. 'Course not. We're a team.'

'Have you any idea how patronising you are?' His voice cracked. 'I don't need instructions on how to do everything. I know what time school starts, what fillings the twins have in their sandwiches, which pants can and can't go in the tumble dryer, without you writing it down.' A tear trickled down his cheek.

'Don't cry.' Louise hoped it wasn't the thought of her pants that had caused such distress. She dropped to her knees and placed an arm awkwardly around his neck. 'Everything will be alright.'

'No, it won't.' He uncoiled her arm from around his neck and stood up. 'It's gone.'

'What's gone?' she whispered.

'Everything.' He wiped his eyes. 'The trust. The hope. Any chance we can get back to who we used to be. It's all gone.' His voice cracked.

'No.' Louise grabbed his arm. 'It's not gone. We love each other. I just made a stupid mistake.'

His eyes looked smaller and more vulnerable without his glasses on. 'No, Lou. You've pushed me that one step too far. I justify almost all your actions, but spying on me, not trusting me...' He blinked and looked away. 'I can't justify that.' He slid his glasses on. 'Go back to Polly's. I'll be in touch about seeing the twins.'

'No,' she whimpered. Nick took her arm and led her to the front door. 'I'll change,' she said twisting her head round to look up at him. 'I'll stop writing lists.'

Nick opened the door.

'I'll read your novel, I promise.'

A firm hand in her back pushed her out onto the doorstep.

'Please, Nick.'

'Goodbye, Lou.'

The door shut. She stood and stared at it for a moment before stumbling down the garden path, tears rolling down her cheeks. This couldn't be happening. He couldn't have thrown her out. Their marriage couldn't be over. She looked back and saw Nick watching her from the window. Maybe he was regretting what he'd said. Maybe he was going to come rushing out and tell her he didn't mean it. He turned away. Louise sank to the ground. This *was* happening. He *had* thrown her out. Their marriage *was* over. And it was all her sister's fault.

Chapter Eleven

Polly

Polly looked away as soon as her eyes met Alex's. She stared down at Summer's head. She had Weetabix in her hair. It must have been there since breakfast. She hoped it wasn't in her hair too.

'Any more shopping to do?' Alex asked. Polly shook her head and he gestured to the till with his head, his brown hair flopping into his eyes. 'Shall we?'

He stepped aside and followed Polly to line up behind the other customers. Summer chewed noisily on her dummy. Polly desperately tried to think of something witty or scintillating to say.

'Did you find another B&B?' she asked, failing abysmally in both the witty and scintillating departments.

'Your hair looks nice down,' Alex said at the same time.

Polly felt her cheeks redden. He'd said her hair looked nice!

Alex coughed into his fist. 'A budget hotel on the edge of town. It did the job.' He looked around the shop before settling his gaze on Summer, who was staring at him quizzically. He tweaked her lollipop. 'Is that for me?'

Summer held out the lollipop and whipped it away when Alex reached over for it. She repeated the action and grinned coquettishly at him. As coquettishly as someone can with a dribbly dummy hanging out of their mouth.

'Don't let my two see your lollipop; all they're getting is boring milk.' Alex nodded towards the door. 'They're waiting

78

in the car.' He raked his hair out of his eyes. His forearms were very tanned beneath his rolled-up shirtsleeves. 'What about your son? Is he with his dad?'

Polly swallowed hard. 'No, they don't have a…' she trailed off.

'Ah.' Was it her imagination or did Alex look pleased? He wouldn't if he knew the truth.

Polly's phone rang in her bag and she adjusted Summer in her arms so she could answer it.

'Hola!' Erica's voice was slightly slurred. 'Where are you?'

'The shop over the road. Louise is at home.'

Erica's earrings rattled down the phone. 'Can you ask Jasmine to call me when you get home so we can say goodnight please?'

'Ok. Bye.' Polly hung up and noticed a message from Louise. Probably a reminder to get milk and bread. For once, she was ahead of the game.

> Had to pop out. Not sure how long I'll be.

Polly stared at the message in disbelief. Louise wasn't at home? The children were on their own? But she'd told Louise she was going out, she knew she had. She thought back. Yes, she'd told her, but she hadn't checked Louise had heard her. She'd just assumed she had. Her throat tightened. Oh Christ. The children were at home on their own. She struggled for air. How could she have let this happen? At the till, a customer was trying to wedge a large box of washing powder into a small bag. Polly felt as though someone was doing the same to her lungs. She couldn't have a panic attack. Not here, when she had to get home.

'Everything alright?' Alex asked.

Polly was too disgusted with herself to speak. She shouldn't be here, chatting with Alex. She should be at home, keeping the children safe. She ran to the door and yanked it open.

'Your shopping,' Alex called. 'Can I—'

Polly didn't hear the rest of his sentence. She was running along the pavement. Summer waved over her shoulder, but Polly didn't look back. The children were on their own. Anything could happen, anything. As her own history proved.

The road was busy. Polly searched for a break in the traffic so she could dart across, but there wasn't one. She had no choice but to stop and wait at the pelican crossing, her eyes fixed on the lights, silently urging them to change. She reached into her bag for her mobile. Her hand shook as she rang her landline number. Oliver or Jasmine would answer and she could keep them on the phone until she got home. It wasn't as good as being there, but she'd know they were safe. Except that she'd unplugged the phone. Her despair grew, as lorries and cars thundered past. She could see her house, but was trapped on the other side of the road, helpless to do anything but wait. A police siren sounded in the distance. Summer stretched across to press the button, throwing Polly off-balance. Her foot slipped out of her espadrille and a sharp stone dug into her sole, propelling her back to *that day*. She'd been outside barefoot then, a heavy child in her arms, a siren in the background, urgency and fear twisting her stomach. Her chest tightened, pressing down on her lungs. She was dimly aware of a shrill beeping noise and car horns. An eye flashed before her. A blade dug into her wrist.

'Are you crossing or what?'

A shout from the nearest car brought her back to the present. Her heart pounding, she ran across the road, down the drive, along the side of the house and round to the back door.

'I'm back. Is everyone ok?' Clasping Summer to her, she ran through the kitchen, along the passageway, past the empty den and out into the large, open hall. 'Where are you?' she shrieked.

'Here.' The children appeared at the top of the stairs in their pyjamas. 'You told us to get ready for bed.'

Polly's legs gave way and she sank to her knees. Thank Christ. They were alright. Oliver ran downstairs and placed a hand on her shoulder. She clasped it tightly. She was never letting them out of her sight again.

'What cookies did you get?' Tess asked.

'I'm so sorry,' she started. 'I—'

A loud knock at the front door made them all jump. Tess screamed dramatically and Polly instinctively reached for Summer, her heart racing.

'Hello,' a voice called through the door. 'I've got your shopping.'

Shakily, Polly got to her feet and looked through the spyhole before opening the door. A car was pulled up on the kerb, its indicator flashing. A boy and girl peered out of the back window.

Alex held out a carrier bag. 'Are you alright? You worried me, running off like that.'

'Yes, I'm fine.' Her hand trembled as she took the bag. 'Thank you. How much do I—?'

'My treat.' Alex raked his hair out of his eyes and it flopped straight back into them again.

'That's really kind.'

'No worries. I'm just glad you're alright.' He stepped away, then turned back. 'Sure you're ok?'

Polly nodded. 'Just been one of those days. Thanks again.'

Summer grinned and waved as Polly shut the door.

'Who was that?' Oliver asked.

'A man,' Summer giggled.

Oliver frowned.

'He brought my shopping over.' Polly handed him the bag. 'Help yourselves.'

She turned and gripped the bannister. The children were safe, but what would Erica and Louise say if they knew she'd left them? They wouldn't stay until the end of the month, let alone beyond it. It wouldn't matter what type of biscuits she bought the children, they'd be straight out the door and she'd be on her own again. A sob caught in her throat. She didn't want to be on her own anymore.

Chapter Twelve

Erica

'Do you think they want us to go?' Erica asked. The waiting staff were noisily placing chairs upside down on the empty tables around them.

'Possibly.' Dan drained his tequila and stood up, clutching the edge of the table.

A waiter steered Erica towards the door. A vibrant mural of peasants carrying calla lilies caught her eye.

'Beautiful.' She ran a hand delicately across the mosaic tiles, admiring the colours and textures. The picture came off its hinges and swung back and forth across the wall like a pendulum. The waiter covered his eyes.

'Sorry,' Erica squeaked, her face hot.

Dan put an arm around her shoulders and lurched sideways. 'Thank you and good night.' He tipped his fingers to the side of his head at the waiter who held the door open for them.

Erica closed her eyes as the night air hit her face. Everything started to swirl and veer from side to side.

'Think I might have drunk too much,' she said. 'It's been lovely though – the food, the cocktails, the wine, the shots.' Tequila swirled around the back of her throat. Perhaps not the shots.

She opened her eyes and noticed a homeless man asleep in the doorway of a neighbouring shop. Fumbling in her bag, she took ten pounds from her purse and tucked it under his makeshift pillow.

Dan pulled her away. 'Don't give him money. You're fuelling his drug habit.'

Erica didn't respond. She and Dan had very different views and she didn't want to end such a lovely evening with an argument. Instead, she let him lead her away. They turned down a side road and her heel slid away beneath her. She stumbled into a lamp post, pulling Dan with her. Their faces were millimetres apart. Parting her lips slightly, she gave him a meaningful stare. He returned the look. She gasped. Rather than telling her he needed to send an urgent email or was too tired, he was looking at her with real passion. There was a pinging noise above them and the light went off, plunging them into darkness.

'Guess that means it's midnight. Not going to turn into a pumpkin, are you?' Dan bent his head and kissed her. His mobile vibrated in his pocket and he ignored it. Erica would have toppled off the pavement in shock if he wasn't holding her up. This was a big deal. He was showing how much she meant to him. The closest he'd got to such a grand gesture before was not eating the hotel chocolate on her pillow while she was in the bathroom. Erica kissed him back, wishing they were somewhere slightly more private than the middle of the high street. A beer can rattled up the road and they both jumped.

Dan took Erica's hand. 'Come on.' He led her down a side road to a shaded, woodland area and kissed her hard, one hand grabbing her arse, the other trying to find a way into the neckline of her dress.

'Don't rip it,' she murmured, as they lay down.

Dan gave up his quest and compromised with a quick squeeze of each breast through her dress before tugging it up. He pulled his chinos down and thrust into her. Twigs and lumps of earth dug into her, but she didn't complain. Dan didn't usually do spontaneity and she wasn't going to put him off by suggesting they find a leafier dell to bunk down in. When had he last been spontaneous? He'd refused to sneak off to their hotel room during a corporate event a few months earlier and on their wedding anniversary she'd worked herself up into a frenzy, gyrating on top of him like a bucking bronco before realising he'd fallen asleep. Maybe it was as far back as their first holiday, when they'd had sex in their private sauna. Even then Dan had been hesitant, worried the steam might bring on a yeast infection.

Dan grunted, reminding her to focus on the job in hand. She thrust her hips forward, driving him deeper into her. He moaned softly, a look of satisfaction on his face. Yes, this was all their relationship had been missing – some quality time to rekindle the passion. Quality time. Such an American expression. Tess's Disney channel drawl must be filtering into her, like osmosis. Tess was an odd kid. Very domineering and opinionated. Though Louise could be too and the apple didn't fall too far from the tree. Dan moaned again. Focus, Erica told herself. Thinking about Louise wasn't exactly conducive to an orgasm. She dug her heels into his thighs and circled her hips in a figure of eight. That was better. Yes, she could feel things warming up now. If she could just get Dan to move slightly to the left…

'Are you alright, madam?'

A bright light shone in her face and she screamed and turned her head away. Dan froze, his head buried in her shoulder.

'Madam.' The voice was stern and low. 'I'm a police officer. Are you being attacked?'

'No.' Erica's voice was shrill. 'This is my partner.' Dan lifted a hand. There was a soft thud by Erica's head as it dropped back to the ground.

'We had a call from one of the houses opposite about some potentially dangerous activity.' The officer's torch was directed on Erica's face. Fuck, suppose he was a parent at Jasmine's school?

'Thank you for checking, officer, but I'm fine.' She cleared her throat and Dan's penis slipped out of her.

'So you're not in any danger? This is a voluntary act?'

'Yes, voluntary,' she said, her face hot with shame.

The officer exhaled loudly. 'Did you know you can get two years under the Sex Offender Act for having sexual relations in a public place?'

Erica tried to sit up, but Dan's body was tense and motionless on top of her. His warm, damp breath in her ear was the only indication that he was actually alive. She wanted to hit him. Had he heard the policeman? They could get two years. Did that mean two years in prison? Just for having a shag? That couldn't be right. She hadn't even come.

'We're very sorry, officer. We didn't realise anyone could see us.' Stones dug painfully into her back, as Dan's cadaver-like body pushed her into the ground.

The police officer grunted. 'I'll let it go this time, but if I catch you again, I'll have to take you in.'

'Thank you,' Erica said. 'I guarantee there won't be a next time.'

'Get dressed and go home.' The officer's footsteps grew faint as he walked away.

Dan rolled off Erica, yanking his trousers up in a single motion. Erica pulled her dress down and stood up.

She glared at Dan. 'Thanks for your input.'

'You handled it perfectly.' Dan pushed himself up off the ground. 'Whatever I said would have made him angry.'

'You could have tried.' Erica wrapped her arms around her trembling body. They were supposed to be a team, working together, supporting each other. He'd been so full of bravado to start with. So cocky, so gung-ho. That had all changed when the Old Bill turned up. No sign of any balls then. Although that was probably a good thing or they'd be facing a charge of indecent exposure as well.

Dan zipped his flies up. 'Come on. Let's get you home.' He put an arm around her shoulders and they walked back towards town. She was too cold to push him away.

'We'll laugh about this one day,' he said.

Erica rolled her eyes. He already was, inwardly at least. There was a definite swagger in his step. She supposed it was different for men. Being caught at it in public was a bit of an accomplishment. There was probably an award for it in some lads' mag; the playboy's equivalent of a Scout badge for outdoor pursuits. For her, it was the most humiliating experience of her life.

Dan squeezed her shoulder. 'You were certainly right about getting the spark back.'

Erica rubbed her hands up and down her arms, desperately trying to generate some warmth. 'Don't get any ideas. We're never doing that again.'

'Course not.' Dan tapped his nails against his teeth. 'We'll go to a hotel next time. Book a room in the name of Mr and Mrs Smith.'

'We can't afford it,' Erica snapped.

They reached the main road and Erica flagged down a taxi. Dan went to kiss her and she turned her head away.

'Let's take Jasmine out at the weekend,' he said.

Erica's head snapped back round. Had she heard him right? 'Don't you have to work?'

Dan took her hand. 'A chap in the office said that his teenage children never want to spend time with him. Said he envied me. Made me realise I've only got a few years left before Jasmine's more interested in her friends than me. I don't want to waste that time.'

He'd never spoken so sincerely and Erica felt a surge of affection for him.

'Book something up and message me the details.' He helped her into the taxi. 'Let's make the most of her while we can.'

Erica grinned at him through the window. At last, here was the support she'd been craving and the answer to her problem. The month at Polly's was almost at an end and she hadn't found an au pair she'd trust with Jasmine. If Dan wanted to get more involved, then with the help of summer clubs, they could juggle the childcare between them.

'This is great,' she said. 'The school holidays start in two weeks. You could take some time off to spend with Jasmine while I'm at work.'

Dan grimaced. 'Wish I could but I'm up against it at the moment.' He tapped the roof of the taxi. 'See you at the weekend.'

So he wanted to be more involved with Jasmine, but only when it suited him. The car pulled away. Erica didn't wave goodbye.

Chapter Thirteen

Louise

Louise stormed out of the downstairs cloakroom. 'Whose turn was it to get toilet rolls?' she bellowed up the stairs.

The lively chatter stopped abruptly and the only sound was the tap running in the main bathroom. If they had toilet roll in there, there'd be trouble. Scowling, she stomped down the passageway to the kitchen. Looked like it was down to her to sort it out. Like bloody always.

In the kitchen, she flicked the kettle on. The jar they kept their housekeeping money in sat on the windowsill, a handful of change nestled in the bottom. She frowned. There had definitely been a five-pound note in there the day before.

The back door opened and Erica came in, her face shiny from her run.

Louise thrust the jar at her. 'Have you taken some money out?'

'No.' Erica pulled her damp t-shirt over her head and wiped the sweat off her face. Not a smidgen of flesh hung over the top of her shorts or moulded itself around the straps of her sports bra. She clearly wasn't normal. Louise tried not to think about how obscene she'd look in that outfit. The overspill from the shorts would be more gateau than muffin-top.

'Maybe Polly spent it,' Erica said. 'That's what it's for, isn't it?'

'Well she hasn't spent it on toilet rolls.' Louise plonked the jar down.

Erica's phone beeped and she slid it out of a little holster contraption strapped to her arm. 'Can we set up a direct debit and pay our share into your account instead of putting cash in every week?'

'So I'm lumbered with buying everything?' Louise snorted. 'Don't think so.'

'Mom.' Tess came into the kitchen and thrust a book and pen at Louise. 'You have to sign my homework journal.'

Louise signed the book without looking at it.

'Who's taking us to school?' Tess asked.

Louise turned to the whiteboard and inhaled sharply. The grid that she'd carefully measured out and painstakingly filled in with that week's rotas had been rubbed out.

'Who's done that?' She looked to Erica for a response, but she was engrossed in her phone.

'Jasmine was in here earlier,' Tess said, before slipping out of the room.

'Jasmine, eh?' Louise turned to Erica.

'Shit.' Erica looked up from her phone. That had got her attention.

'Yes,' Louise snapped. 'What are you going to do about it?'

'Don't know. Nothing like this has happened before.' Erica looked crestfallen and Louise felt a flicker of sympathy. It was hard hearing your child wasn't as perfect as you thought they were. Not that she was under much illusion with the twins. Tess's dream of being an international pop star had been dashed when she was told she could only stay in the school choir if she promised to mime, and the less said about George puncturing the football in the end of season qualifying match the better.

'Tell her not to do it again,' Louise said. 'Luckily I've got a copy of the rota, but still.'

Erica followed Louise's gaze to the whiteboard. 'Oh good, you've got rid of the rotas. They were a right pain in the arse.'

Louise's flicker of sympathy was replaced with rage. 'No, I haven't got rid of the rotas. Your daughter rubbed them off.'

'Sorry,' Erica said dismissively.

Louise shook her head in disbelief. Erica wasn't even pretending to take this seriously.

'Got a crisis at work,' Erica said. 'I put one of the *Sing to Win* judges in the same dress Katie Price is wearing on the cover of *OK!*'

'And that's more of an issue than Jasmine's vandalism?'

'The judge is fuming.' Erica's phone pinged and she scanned her message. 'Fuck. *This Morning* is doing a segment on it. I've got to get to work.'

'What about—' Louise started, but Erica was gone. Louise glared at Erica's departing pert bottom. Why should Erica get a derrière that the phrase *arse like a peach* had been coined for, while she had to haul an onion sack's worth of peaches around behind her? With the added insult that her skin was also the texture of the onion sack.

To torture herself further, she pushed her hands against her stomach. The waistband of her navy skirt shunted down a centimetre and she gasped at the novel sensation. She'd been on the verge of going up a size, but now there was actual movement in her clothes. Could the stress of the break-up have caused her to lose weight?

She hurried along the passageway to look in the mirror behind the optics. Turning her head from side to side, she ran her hands over her face and pulled the neck of her non-iron blouse open. Was there the faint trace of collarbone showing beneath the fat? She hadn't seen that for years. She smiled at her reflection and her cheek muscles resisted, no doubt baulking at the strange sensation. She hadn't had cause to smile since Nick had told her to leave the previous week.

Tears filled her eyes. A whole week of keeping it secret from everyone because she couldn't bring herself to say the words out loud. A whole week of not knowing where he was or what he was doing or who he was doing it with. A whole week of feeling sick and not being able to eat. But, miraculously, during that excruciating week, her body had been slowly shrinking. At last something was on her side. She ran her fingertips over her collarbone. If she could get back to being curvy rather than fat, then maybe she could get Nick back too.

—

The receptionist at the *Herald* smiled at Louise. 'Can I help you?'

'Nick Capon please.'

'Who shall I say is here?'

'His wife.'

'Sorry. Only been here a few days. I'm Karen.' The woman smiled and Louise was pleased to see that she had lipstick on her teeth.

Louise peered through the glass wall behind reception into the editorial office, but couldn't see Nick. He'd been appalled when a refurb had taken place and he'd been placed in what he called a fish tank. 'We're hardly Woodward and Bernstein. No one's going to be riveted at the sight of us at our computers,' he'd moaned. 'How am I going to eat my Bombay mix with people watching?'

'The editorial team's in a meeting,' Karen said. 'Can I take a message?'

Disappointment flooded though Louise. Nick had to see her to appreciate the weight loss.

'It's important I talk to him in person.'

'I'm sure he won't mind being interrupted then.'

Karen entered a security code into the door keypad and walked across the office, past a ceiling-high cheese plant, to a meeting room at the far end of the office. There he was, standing in front of a flip chart covered in his neat writing. His long arms moved animatedly as he talked to his team, who looked up at him, nodding and making notes. He was so authoritative, so in control, so dynamic, so... so sexy. Louise caught her breath. He was. He was sexy.

He pushed his glasses back up his nose and her heart pounded. How could she have thought that habit was geeky? That those willowy limbs were lanky? His height freakish? Her heart rate quickened. She was seeing him properly for the first time in years. He wasn't boring, he was uncomplicated. He wasn't annoying, he was methodical. He wasn't clumsy, he was – no, actually he was clumsy. But that aside, he was a truly wonderful man. And she was head over heels in love with him.

Karen knocked on the door of the meeting room and leant in. Nick stopped what he was saying and looked across the office to where Louise stood. She smiled and waved, her chest rising and falling dramatically. Could he feel that chemistry surging between them? Their eyes met and his shoulders slumped. No, just her then.

Moments later he was in reception. Taking Louise's elbow, he steered her towards the front door. 'Are the twins ok?'

She nodded.

'Then why are you here?'

Louise's heart sank. On the drive over, she'd imagined him being overwhelmed by her new, svelte physique and lifting her up for a long, lingering kiss. Well, not svelte perhaps, but less rotund. And he couldn't exactly lift her up, on account of the rotundness. And she might skip the long, lingering kiss too as, despite the lack of privacy, he'd clearly been snacking on Bombay mix. But, even without all that, he could show some enthusiasm.

'Call me at home if you've something to say.'

'You won't talk to me at home,' she said defensively. 'You only want to talk to the twins.'

'That's because we're separated.'

'Don't,' Louise whispered. 'It might get back to the twins.'

'Hardly think they're going to hear it from Karen.' Nick pushed his glasses up. 'Anyway, we've got to tell them some-time.'

She shook her head vigorously.

'We have to explain why we're not going on holiday together.'

Bile rose in her throat. 'But the villa in Spain's booked.'

'You can still go. I'll take George and Tess somewhere another week. Surfing in Devon perhaps.' His eyes lit up. 'It'll be good to introduce them to new experiences, away from that God-awful Brits Abroad place we go to every year. May as well be in the middle of Essex for all the Spanish culture they get.'

'You weren't complaining when we stumbled on the naturists' beach,' Louise snapped. 'You were very happy to spend a few hours soaking up that particular bit of culture.'

Nick stared glumly at his shoes. 'Think we've veered off the point a bit. What did you need to tell me? Were the twins nervous about their maths test? They didn't need to be; we revised loads at the weekend.'

Louise's neck flushed. She didn't know they had a test. 'I came to tell you...' She could hardly admit to the long, lingering kiss scenario. 'Some of the housekeeping money's missing,' she said instead. 'Possibly stolen.'

'What's that got to do with me?'

'Thought you should know what kind of environment the twins are being forced to live in.' She put a hand on Nick's arm. 'They need their dad. All the time – not just at weekends. They miss you.'

'I miss them too,' Nick said. 'In fact, I've been thinking—'

'That we should move back?' Louise looked up at him hopefully.

'No,' he said softly. 'That you shouldn't come home with them at weekends anymore.'

Louise almost gagged. This wasn't why she'd come to see him. What could she say to convince him to give her another chance? To show him how well they worked together?

'What about the Tesco delivery?' she asked. 'You need me there to check off the Best Before dates.'

Nick sighed. 'I run a newspaper. I think I can cope. You need to stop doing the weekly order for me anyway. How many chicken kievs do you think I eat?'

Louise ran her thumb across the soft cotton of his blue, striped sleeve. 'Best I do. Remember what happened before?'

Nick's cheeks flushed slightly. He'd decided to try a different supermarket recently. It had taken the best part of an afternoon to set up the online order and the food hadn't arrived for ten days because he'd clicked on the wrong date. And the apples were bruised.

He prised her hand off his arm. 'We've got to tell the twins it's over.'

Louise felt as though he'd karate-chopped her in the throat. 'We can't,' she croaked. 'It'd ruin their end-of-year tests.'

Nick nodded. 'Ok, we'll wait 'til the end of term. I want to have them on my own at weekends though. We'll say you've got to work.'

'But, but…' Her words caught in her throat, unable to work their way past the large lump that had formed.

He placed a hand in the small of her back and opened the door. 'I'll call them tonight.' The door closed behind her and Nick walked away. Karen watched him as he went back into the office. Get your eyes off my man, Louise thought, gulping hard. But he wasn't her man. Not anymore.

Chapter Fourteen

Polly

It was Saturday morning and Polly and Jasmine were at the kitchen table playing Snap. This was the fourth week of their stay – their last week, although no one had said anything – and for the first time, Erica and Louise were staying for the weekend.

The twins had gone home without Louise, as she had to prepare for a conference the following week. She'd been in her room all morning, only surfacing to shuffle to the loo or make herself a tea. Apparently she was working on her laptop, but Polly was sure she'd heard the *Pride and Prejudice* theme tune playing. Erica had hired a freelancer to go into the studio on her behalf so she could spend the day with Jasmine, but had been catching up on emails all morning. Every now and then she popped into the kitchen, dropped a kiss onto Jasmine's head and promised she wouldn't be much longer. Jasmine nodded agreeably each time, but Polly could see that the smile was slipping.

'Sorry, sorry, sorry.' Erica came into the room, looking stunning in a short, green shift dress, a gold, multi-strand necklace and wedge sandals. This was her off-duty, casual attire. Polly glanced down at her own faded skinny jeans, long-sleeved tee and espadrilles. She didn't care how she looked as long as her arms were covered and she didn't smell of anything too sinister. Provided the aroma of baby wee didn't count as sinister.

Erica's phone rang. 'Shit, it's the freelancer. She can't have a problem already.' She blew a kiss to Jasmine. 'Sorry, sweetie. Just be a minute.' She strode out of the kitchen, her phone clamped to her ear.

Polly turned to Jasmine. 'Your turn.'

Jasmine looked down at her cards. It took a few moments for Polly to realise she was crying.

'Oh, poppet. What's wrong?' She smoothed Jasmine's dark fringe out of her eyes.

Tears streamed down Jasmine's face. 'Mummy's always working.'

'She's got a very important job,' Polly said loyally, even though in her mind there was no job more important than being with her children. Her mum had always made her feel valued and loved and she intended to do the same for Oliver and Summer.

'She never plays with me.'

Polly opened her mouth to defend Erica, but it was true. The little time Erica was there, she spent on her phone or laptop. She pulled Jasmine onto her lap.

'Mummy's very busy, but I can play with you anytime.'

Jasmine smiled and leant her head on Polly's shoulder. Polly rocked her back and forth and stroked her hair.

'What are they?' Jasmine asked. Polly's sleeve had worked its way up revealing a row of angry red marks on her lower arm.

'Nothing.' Polly pulled her sleeves down over her hands. 'Shall we go and find Mummy?'

Jasmine bit her lip. 'Can we stay here a bit longer?'

Polly looked out of the door to see if Erica was coming, but the passageway was empty. 'I'd like that.' She pulled Jasmine close and hugged her tightly.

'I wish Mummy was home all the time, like you,' Jasmine said.

Polly leant her forehand against Jasmine's. 'You can pretend I'm your mummy when she's not around, if you like?'

Jasmine smiled. 'Yes please.'

They stared into one another's eyes, each understanding that they could provide what the other needed.

'I'm glad we moved here,' Jasmine whispered.

'So am I, poppet. So am I.' Polly began to sing softly, rocking Jasmine back and forth. It was an old ABBA song, 'Thank You For The Music', that her mum had sung to her when she was little. Jasmine wrapped her arms around her. Polly felt high at Jasmine's response to just a small amount of attention. All the children could do with this – that little bit extra that their mums didn't have time to provide, but she did. It needn't be a big deal; Erica and Louise didn't even have to know. She'd just quietly step in when they weren't around. For the first time in a long time, she felt excited. It fed into her singing, giving her energy and confidence, until her voice filled the room.

'Go, Polly!'

Polly jumped and eased Jasmine off her lap.

'Don't stop, you've got a brilliant voice.' Erica knelt down and hugged Jasmine. 'Sorry about having to take that call. The freelancer I hired to go to the studio today has appendicitis. Either that or she got last-minute tickets to Glastonbury.' She sighed. 'Not sure what to do now. Bit tricky to dress the contestants via Zoom.'

'Go in, if you want to,' Polly said. 'I'm happy to look after Jasmine.'

'It's not that I *want* to go in.' Erica took Jasmine's hands. 'I'm so sorry, sweetie. I don't have a choice. Everyone will have to perform naked if I'm not there and no one wants to see that, do they?' She pulled a face and Jasmine giggled. 'I'll make it up to you tomorrow, I promise.' She gave Jasmine another huge hug. 'Will you be alright with Polly?'

Jasmine nodded. 'Promise you'll be home in time to brush my hair for bed. And find my *Frozen* nightie?'

'Definitely.' Erica stood up. 'You haven't seen Jasmine's nightie, have you?' she asked Polly. 'The Shanghai Disneyland one? I can't find it anywhere.'

Polly shook her head. She knew the one Erica meant. It was covered in shimmering crystals and was the kind of nightie every little girl dreamed of owning. She'd wear it herself if it came in an adult size.

'I'm sure it'll turn up.' Erica took a lipstick from her bag and slid it across her full lips. 'Thanks for this, Polly. I owe you.'

Polly wondered whether it was a good time to suggest extending the house-share arrangement. After all, here was a perfect example of how well it worked. Or would highlighting it remind Erica that the month was almost at an end? An idea came to her.

'Can you get some wine on your way home?'

Erica nodded approvingly. 'Like your style.'

'We could have it tonight, with a takeaway.' Polly tugged her sleeves down. It'd be easier to broach the subject of them staying on, at least for the summer holidays, after a few glasses of wine.

'Great idea.' Erica hooked her bag over her arm and slid a large pair of sunglasses on. 'I meant it about your voice. You should audition for *Sing to Win*. Bet you'd get on.'

Polly's throat tightened and she shook her head. Being on TV wasn't an option. Because then they'd be able to find her.

Chapter Fifteen

Erica

'Erica.'

Erica turned round. There, among the manic shoppers charging around King's Cross and tourists tripping everyone up with their cases, was Rob Mascoll, the new PD, smiling at her with his chocolate brown eyes and full lips. He radiated warmth. Erica cleared her throat. Some parts of her were feeling very warm right now.

'Hi,' she said. 'Just on my way to the studio.'

'Mind if I join you?'

'Sure,' Erica said casually, but her stomach folded in on herself. What was going on? Why was she reacting in this way? She was a happily not-married woman.

'Great.' He held up a coffee cup and paper bag. 'Can I get you one?'

'Thank you, but no.' She didn't want coffee breath. Not that having minty-fresh breath was relevant.

'Can you give me thirty seconds? Just need to do something.' He hurried off.

Erica hoped he hadn't gone to fetch one of those annoying fold-up bikes. His attractiveness rating would plummet if he did. Not that his attractiveness was relevant, of course.

She watched Rob hand the drink and bag to a dishevelled man holding a sign saying *I'm hungry. Please help*. They exchanged a few words, then Rob jogged back to where Erica stood. She waited for him to recount his good deed – Dan still bragged about the time he'd given a Second World War veteran a two-pound coin for a poppy when he'd only been asked for a pound – but Rob didn't. Instead, he thanked her for waiting.

'How long have you been on *Sing to Win*?' he asked, as they walked towards the tube station.

'Since it started.' In her peripheral vision she could see the curve of his upper arms under the sleeves of his racing-green t-shirt. 'Just as well it's only on for a few months a year or I'd be burnt out. How are you getting on?'

'It's a good gig. I freelance, so I'm usually all over the place. Nice to be in London. Closer to home.'

Erica allowed herself a sideways glance and took in his strong profile. 'Where's home?'

'Cambridge. You?' he asked.

'Hertfordshire. So yes, London's great. Just thirty minutes on the train. Easy to get in and not so far I can't go for a drink after work.' Her cheeks grew warm. Did that sound as though she was asking him out? 'I mean professionally. Networking or discussing work. All above board. Just if I'm thirsty.' Erica cringed. *Just if I'm thirsty?* What crap was she spouting?

A ringing came from her bag. 'Sorry. Might be to do with my daughter.' She checked the screen to see if it was Polly, but it was a supplier she'd left a message for earlier. She went to answer the call, but lost the signal as they entered the tube station. 'I'll call back,' she said. 'It's a work thing.'

'How old's your daughter?' Rob asked.

'Eight. My friend's looking after her for me.'

'She's not with your husband?'

'He's in China. Jasmine's dad, that is. I'm not married.' She prepared to give him her usual spiel about how they didn't feel a ceremony and certificate would add anything when they already lived together and everything was in joint names, when her phone rang again. She must have walked through a pocket of reception. It was the supplier calling back, suddenly eager to speak to her now she'd added the words *prime time TV show* to her message after having ignored her for days. Erica went to answer the call, but her phone cut out again.

'Sorry,' she said. 'Been trying to get hold of a particular brand of tit tape all week. Hopefully this supplier's got some for me.'

Rob rubbed his chin with the back of his hand. 'Tit tape?'

Erica cringed again. 'It's nothing.'

'No, I'm intrigued.' Rob looked questioningly at her, a sparkle in his deep brown eyes.

Erica cleared her throat. How had she ended up talking about tits? 'It's a clear, double-sided tape that holds a low-cut top in place so it doesn't gape open, or sticks a backless bra to the body.'

'Could be just what I need to keep my medallion central.'

Erica laughed. 'I'll send some your way.'

The tube pulled into the station and everyone headed to the doors. A shoulder rammed against Erica, knocking her to the side. She lost her footing and stumbled into Rob, landing face-first in his chest with a squeal. Mortified, she tried to step back but more commuters had surged forward, filling every available space so she had no option but to remain pressed against him, her forehead millimetres from his chin. Not having coffee breath was now a definite advantage.

The train doors opened and in the mayhem of people piling on and off she managed to unpeel herself from Rob and board the tube.

'So,' she said, pretending nothing had happened. 'Do you have children?'

'A six-year-old daughter, Daisy. I'm divorced too,' Rob said. 'She lives with her mum, which is tough. I have her a couple of evenings in the week and every other weekend and school holidays. Must be hard for your ex, not seeing Jasmine very often.'

Ex? Divorced too? Erica opened her mouth to explain the mix-up, but caught sight of her reflection in the tube window and realised her long, multi-strand necklace had hooked itself around one of her breasts. Crap. First tit tape, now this? How was she going to unhook herself without looking as though she were suggestively inviting him to ogle her chest?

'What time is it?' she asked, hoping that the gadget on Rob's wrist was a watch, not a fitness tracker. Dan took great delight in telling her how many steps he'd done that day and what his resting heart rate was. Thankfully, Rob's was a traditional watch and Erica was able to free her breast while he checked it, without suffering a monologue on the number of calories consumed versus the number burned. Pleased with herself for her quick thinking, she jauntily swung her bag over her shoulder. The sudden movement caused her necklace to swing across her chest and hook itself back over her breast. Oh, for fuck's sake. She was wearing a choker in future.

–

Erica's phone beeped as soon as they left the station. She rolled her eyes at the text instructing her to buy bread and milk. How did Louise think she was going to rustle up fresh produce from the confines of a television studio? She wasn't even sure the canteen served fresh produce.

'Everything ok?' Rob asked.

She nodded and he smiled. She couldn't help but smile back. He was so unbelievably sexy. She shook herself. She shouldn't be thinking like this. It was unprofessional. And disloyal to Dan. Which reminded her, she needed to put him straight on that one.

'Jasmine's dad,' Erica started. Her wedge caught on the pavement and she yelped and grabbed Rob's arm to regain her footing. 'Sorry,' she said, letting go immediately. What was wrong with her? She managed to behave normally around other people – why not Rob? It wasn't as if there was anything special about him. She glanced up at his tall frame, full lips and chocolatey eyes. Ok, perhaps there was something a bit special, but that was no reason for her to turn into Mr Bean.

'Are you alright?' Rob asked.

'Fine, thanks. I should know not to wear heels on the commute.'

'Happens to me all the time too.'

They smiled and for the brief moment they held one another's gaze, a charge of electricity coursed through Erica. Feeling her cheeks flush, she looked down, only to discover that her necklace had swung back into its new favourite position.

They reached the TV studio and Rob pushed the door open and stood aside to let her pass. Trying to reclaim some of her usual poise, she walked through as elegantly as she could with a necklace wrapped around her left tit.

A poster on the wall in the entrance caught Rob's eye. He stopped to read it and Erica took the opportunity to detangle herself.

'What's that?' she asked, holding the strands of her necklace firmly in place.

'Crisis is organising a charity run – The Square Mile – to raise money for the homeless.' Rob slid his phone from his back pocket and took a photo of the poster.

'Are you going to do it?' Erica asked, scanning the details.

'Why wouldn't I?' Rob said. 'It's only a couple of hours after work and I'm in London already. Any way to raise some money and increase the charity's profile is worth doing.'

Erica nodded thoughtfully.

'Do you run?' Rob asked.

'Yes.' Erica took her phone from her bag and took a photo herself. 'If I can get a babysitter for Jasmine, I'll do it too.' The run wasn't until August and the four weeks at Polly's was almost up. She had no idea who was going to look after Jasmine day to day, let alone for an evening so she could do the run, if Polly asked them to leave.

'Great.' Rob grinned at her and Erica felt her heartbeat quicken. Caused by concern for her childcare situation, nothing more. Although that didn't account for the pulsing between her legs.

'I'd better get to Wardrobe,' she said, suddenly eager to get some distance between her and this gorgeous man before she did something that could be deemed inappropriate. Such as licking him.

Rob nodded. 'I'm headed to the studio floor.' He touched her waist briefly as he stepped round her and her body quivered. He started to walk away, then stopped and turned round.

'Erica.'

'Yes.' She pressed her thighs tightly together, both delighted and horrified by the sensations he was causing.

'Let me know if you get thirsty later.'

Chapter Sixteen

Louise

Louise pushed her chicken korma around her plate. Usually she loved Indian food but she couldn't face it tonight. Not when the twins were home with Nick and she wasn't. She'd hoped he'd invite her in, but he'd shattered that dream by closing the front door on her so quickly he actually shut his foot in it.

'Are you alright?' Polly asked.

Louise nodded. She needed to make more of an effort or they'd keep asking. She turned to Erica.

'How's *Sing to Win* going? Any heart-throbs this year?'

Erica rolled her eyes. 'I wish. All the male contestants are about twelve.'

'Don't you have to be sixteen to apply?'

'They probably are, but the acne takes years off.' Erica nodded at Polly. 'You should enter. You've got a beautiful voice.'

'No.' Polly's voice was strained and anxious rather than beautiful. 'It's not for me.'

'Shame, but I understand.' Erica drained her glass. 'Let's open another bottle. I need to drown my sorrows. School finishes in a week and I still haven't found an au pair.'

'I'll get it,' Louise said. She needed to get away for a moment. Erica didn't have any sorrows to drown, she was being dramatic. Dan hadn't risked amputating his foot in his haste to get rid of *her*. She took the wine from the fridge and walked back up the passageway past the den. Jasmine and Summer were in bed and

Oliver was lying on the sofa watching a film. Louise's throat burned. What were Nick and the twins doing right now? Were they lying on the sofa together? She frowned. No. Even in her melancholy state she couldn't romanticise that – the three of them would never fit; not with Nick and George's height and Tess's girth. A corner sofa was what they needed. They'd all fit on one of those. She would too, if Nick let her.

'Not having date nights isn't healthy,' Polly was saying as Louise came back into the dining room.

'If you ask me, you shouldn't jump to conclusions,' Louise snapped. 'You don't know anything about it.'

Erica took the bottle from her. 'I just said how busy Dan is. We only managed one date.'

'Oh.' Louise sat down. 'That's the trouble when two water signs get together. Too independent for their own good.' She twisted her wedding ring around her finger. 'Me and Nick are earth and water, the perfect balance. Cancer and Taurus. The crab and the bull.'

Erica's expression indicated that she felt Louise was talking bull. Louise willed her to say it. She could do with a good argument to vent her frustration. Instead, Erica refilled their glasses and checked her phone. 'I've got a bid on eBay ending in eight minutes.' Her gold bangles rattled as she waved her phone in the air. 'It's a limited edition Swarovski figurine of Elsa for Jasmine, to make up for her missing *Frozen* nightie.'

Louise's jaw dropped at the amount Erica had bid. She could put a down payment on a corner sofa with that. 'If you ask me, it'd be a lot cheaper to buy another nightie.'

'Dan got it from China and it's gone out of production.' She refreshed her phone. 'I have to win this.'

'No one's going to top that bid,' Louise said. 'It's in the bag.'

'Basket,' Erica said.

Louise's neck wobbled. Pedantic cow.

'While I think of it,' Erica added. 'Would you two sponsor me? I'm doing a 10k run next month to raise money for the homeless.'

'Of course,' Polly said.

Louise sniffed. Charity began at home, as far as she was concerned. Except that she didn't have a home, thanks to her bloody sister. Rather than asking for sponsorship, Erica should be giving the money she raised to her.

As if she'd read her mind, Polly spoke. 'I know you only planned to live here for a month, but we love having you all here.' She looked at Erica and Louise hopefully. 'You're welcome to stay as long as you like.'

Erica whooped and grabbed a fistful of air. 'I know I've got to stop doing that,' she said, 'but this calls for an air grab. Jasmine and I would love to. Thank you.' She clinked her glass against Polly's.

Polly's eyes filled with tears and she raised her glass.

Louise sat quietly, wishing she could turn down Polly's kind offer. But she couldn't go back home and she didn't have anywhere else to go.

'Cheer up, Louise. We'll carry on using your rotas.' Erica winked. 'It'll be like you're still here.'

'Actually, I will still be here.'

'Really?' Polly and Erica stared at her.

Louise nodded, fighting back tears of her own. Should she tell them? It was so hard carrying on as normal. But saying it meant admitting it was real and she wasn't ready for that yet.

Instead, she shrugged. 'It'd be unfair on the twins to move out when everyone else is staying.'

'But won't Nick—'

'He'll survive,' Louise said shortly.

'This is wonderful.' Polly clasped her hands together. 'I was sure you'd all go and I'd be on my own again.'

'Given the calibre of au pairs out there, you could be stuck with us for some time.'

'Fine by me,' Polly said. 'This house share is the best thing that could have happened.'

Erica grinned. 'It's great, isn't it? Everyone should do it.'

What's great about it, Louise wanted to scream. Having a bedroom carpet that could go in the washing machine did not compensate for giving Nick the opportunity to discover he preferred life without her.

Erica jumped up and her necklace flew across her chest, hooking itself around one of her breasts. 'We should write a book about it.' She thrust her glass in Louise's direction. 'Get Nick to do it.'

'What?' Heat spread across Louise's chest and up her neck.

'One of those success story, self-help things. It'd be a best-seller in no time.' Erica drew an arc in the air with her glass, scattering wine. 'I can see it now – book signings, television appearances. I know a great production director.'

Louise glared at her. Was she insane? Staggering about with that stupid necklace caught up on her stupid, microscopic boob, suggesting that Nick, *her* Nick, write a book about the thing that had caused their break-up? She was so angry she couldn't speak.

Even in her drunken state, Erica was astute enough to pick up on Louise's negative vibes. 'Ok, forget the book. Getting a bit carried away.' She flopped down into her chair. 'But you have to admit, we've got it sussed.' She raised her glass. 'Here's to supporting each other.'

They were both so happy. Polly eager and relieved, Erica pissed and confident and beautiful and perfect and everything that Louise wasn't. It wasn't fair. Nothing was fair. She wanted to scream and shout and throw things. Erica preferably. She must only weigh eight stone. Louise could easily pick her up and hurl her across the room. But then she remembered Erica pressing two tickets to last year's *Sing to Win* final into her hand at the school gate, and humouring her relentless requests for backstage gossip. Erica wasn't the bad guy. She didn't deserve to be Louise's scapegoat. If she knew what Louise was going through, she'd be the first to sympathise and distract her with laughter and freebies from the studio.

Louise forced a smile and picked up her glass. 'Here's to bossing you around for a few more weeks.' She swigged some wine, then picked up her phone. 'Right, if we're going to do this, let's do it properly.' She opened up the calendar. 'One week 'til school finishes. One week 'til all five kids are home all day, every day, for six whole weeks.' She leaned back in her chair. 'Any bright ideas?'

'Summer camp?' Erica said.

'Any others?'

'I can't wait,' Polly said. 'No dashing around and worrying about being late. No making them do homework when they've been stuck in a classroom all day.' She smiled. 'They're free.'

'Childcare isn't,' Louise said. 'Usually costs us an arm and a leg.' Not as much as two separate holidays would though, she realised with a jolt. A lump formed in her throat and she took a large mouthful of wine. She couldn't think about that now. 'Holidays,' she said. 'We're in Spain the fifth week. How about you two?'

'We're away the fifth week too. Staying with Dan's mum in Bath.'

'Bit of a come-down from last year's trip to Mauritius,' Louise said. 'Thought you'd be going somewhere flashier.'

'No need,' Erica said. 'I love Bath. It's his mum I'm not so keen on.'

'How about you, Poll?'

'No plans.'

Louise patted Polly's arm. It was all too easy to forget Polly's situation until something like this came up and it belted you forcefully round the head.

Polly ran her pendant along its chain. 'It's ok. I'm getting the flat roof on the extension updated. When you're both away will be a good time to get it done.'

'That's one week taken care of then.' Louise frowned. 'Still leaves another five. I'm away with work fifteenth and sixteenth of August.'

'August sixteenth is Madonna's birthday,' Erica said. 'She's amazing. Hope I look that good when I'm her age.'

Louise tapped her on the head. 'Never mind Madonna. Unless her namesake's son steps in and helps out, we're stuck without childcare for most of the holiday.'

Erica threw her hands into the air. 'This is crap. Men don't have to worry about any of this. They go to work and come home. We go to work, come home, then sort out everything to do with the house and the children. We haven't *got* it all – we *do* it all.' She shook her head so hard it was a wonder she didn't knock herself out with her earrings.

'But I'm here,' Polly said. 'I can look after them.'

Erica's earrings rattled some more. 'There are too many children for one person to look after. It's not feasible and I can't take any time off. I can't afford—' she paused. 'I can't afford to be unavailable at such a busy time.' She tugged at her hair. 'I haven't had any luck with an au pair, but maybe we could find a childminder to come and help out.'

'No.' Polly put her hands up. 'I'd rather do it myself.'

'It's too much. I couldn't handle the guilt of leaving it all to you.'

Louise nodded. 'Erica's right. It's a lot for one person.'

Polly tucked a red curl behind her ear. 'The leisure centre does activity days. We could sign the kids up to a few things and I'll have them the rest of the time.' She nodded enthusiastically. 'I'd like to do it.'

Erica smiled gratefully. 'That'd be great, if you're sure. But you must say if it gets too much.'

'It won't. It'll be fun.'

Louise patted her arm. 'Thanks, Poll.'

The twins would be happy when she told them they were staying. Nick would be ecstatic. The only one who wouldn't be happy was her. She blinked back tears. She wouldn't ever be happy again.

Chapter Seventeen

Erica

'So we're going to stay a bit longer, get through the holidays, then I'll look properly for a nanny or au pair. Do you mind?'

'No, as long as no one finds out.' Dan didn't look up from his MacBook Air. 'Makes my life easier, actually.'

'Really? You said it was a stupid idea when I first suggested it.'

Dan typed into a spreadsheet on his screen. 'That was before I realised how distracting you and Jasmine are when you're here. I can just get on with what I need to do now without being interrupted.'

As far as Erica could see, he got on with what he needed to do when they *were* there. What else did he have to be getting on with? She was tempted to ask, but it would lead to an argument and this was date night.

Getting up, she strode around the living room, enjoying the plush, cream carpet beneath her feet. She never went barefoot at Polly's. The floor was coated in a layer of crumbs or plaster or other substances that she couldn't – and didn't wish to – identify. She couldn't complain though when Polly was generously inviting them to stay indefinitely and look after Jasmine. Erica would be screwed if she hadn't.

'Sit down,' Dan said. 'You're making me nervous. Put the television on.'

'This isn't much of a date night,' Erica grumbled. She flicked through the channels but couldn't find anything she wanted to watch. 'We should get some of the subscription channels.'

'Not really essential purchases, are they?'

'Feels pretty essential right now.' She tossed the remote control onto the sofa. 'When do you think your bonuses will start coming in?'

Dan tapped his nails against his teeth. 'Hard to say. The board's making redundancies so I'm keeping my head down. Wouldn't be a good time to ruffle feathers.'

Erica sighed. 'I daren't look at my credit card bill.'

Dan closed his laptop and took her hand. 'I'm sorry you're having to make sacrifices. Just a few more months, then we'll have more money than we know what to do with.'

'I'll know what to do with it.' Erica started listing things on her fingers. 'Shoes, handbag, luxury holiday, Mary Poppins.'

Dan laughed and put an arm round her.

At last. Now their date could begin. She'd been feeling randy all day at work and was looking forward to a release, without being arrested halfway through. Slipping a hand inside his shirt, she stroked his chest.

'Steady on.' Dan put his hand over hers. 'I've just finished work. I'm not ready to jump straight into bed.'

'Who said anything about bed?' Erica swung a leg over his so that she was straddling him.

'You're insatiable.' Smiling, he levered her off and walked to the mini fridge in the corner of the living room. 'Let's have a drink first.'

'I'm driving.'

Dan got himself a bottle of beer, sat back down and jabbed the remote control at the television, flicking through the channels until he reached a game of darts.

Erica rolled her eyes. 'Really?'

Dan patted her thigh, his eyes on the screen. 'You said there was nothing you wanted to watch.'

'That statement still stands.'

'Just this game,' Dan said. 'Then I'll turn it off.'

'You better had.' She put her feet on his lap, the way loved-up couples did in films. He rested his cold beer bottle on them and her toes spasmed involuntarily, jabbing into his groin.

'Ow.' Dan pushed her feet away.

So much for romance. Picking up her phone, she opened her photos. She'd taken a lovely picture of Jasmine that evening to show Dan. She'd just finished brushing Jasmine's hair – their bedtime routine that she hoped Jasmine would never grow out of – and her dark bob shone around her face.

'Look.' She held up the phone.

Dan smiled. 'That's a good one. Send it to me and I'll post it to Facebook. I'll fudge her piano exam result, though. No need for anyone to know she hasn't got her grade three yet.'

Erica forwarded him the picture and scrolled through her album. A photo of the poster she'd taken at the studio came up.

'I'm doing the Crisis Square Mile 10k run in a few weeks,' she said. 'Raising money for the homeless. Fancy doing it with me?'

Dan pulled a face. 'Why would I?'

An image of Rob sprang into her mind. 'Why wouldn't I?' had been his reaction when they'd talked about it.

'To help other people less fortunate than ourselves,' she said. 'Why do you think?'

Dan shook his head. '10k's not impressive enough to shout about.' He tapped his bottle against his teeth. 'Tough Mudder or Iron Man's more me. For a higher profile charity, too. Home-lessness isn't really my thing.'

Erica gritted her teeth. 'It's no one's *thing*,' she said. 'No one chooses to be homeless.'

Dan clenched his jaw, but wisely didn't launch into his usual rant about how the homeless were a bunch of dossers who needed to pull themselves together and get a job.

Erica took a deep breath and forced herself to let it go. This was date night, after all. She came across some photos of Jasmine, grinning broadly as she patted a goat.

'Jasmine loved Willow Farm,' she said. 'We should go again this weekend.'

'No, we shouldn't,' Dan grunted. 'My backside can't take another tractor ride.'

'The new butterfly park then?'

Dan shook his head. 'Probably have to work.'

Looked like the honeymoon period was over. It was back to business as usual – she and Jasmine being the family unit with Dan as an added extra when he had the time or inclination. Even their mid-week date nights had regressed from an evening of conversation and fine dining to a ready meal and watching darts. Irritation coursed through her.

'What happened to wanting to make the most of her while you still can? Your colleague envies you and you're throwing it away.'

'Who?' Dan frowned. 'Oh him. He's gone. One of the redundancy casualties.' He turned back to the television. 'Good shot.'

'Jasmine thinks we're doing something together.'

'I'll buy her a hamster. That'll take her mind off butterflies and farms.'

Erica threw her hands into the air. 'And who's going to look after this hamster? It won't be you mucking out its shit and being kept awake all night by a squeaky wheel, will it?'

Dan rubbed his eyes. 'Don't be like that. I've had a hard day.'

'I've had a hard day too,' Erica snapped. 'Should have appreciated it more, as it's the only hard thing I'm getting at the moment.'

Dan gave her a sympathetic smile. 'Is it that time of the month?'

'Fuck off.' Erica picked up her bag and strode out of the door. She was quivering with rage as she slipped her heels on in the hall. Why was it that when men stood up for themselves they were seen as principled and strong, but when women did they were accused of having their fucking period?

'Erica,' Dan called through the door.

She took a deep breath. She should give him the opportunity to apologise. For Jasmine's sake she would rise above this and behave like a grown-up. She went back into the living room and Dan smiled sweetly.

'Couldn't put the recycling out, could you? I can never remember what goes where.'

Erica slammed the door behind her.

Chapter Eighteen

Polly

Polly waved as the children disappeared through the turnstile into the leisure centre. It was only nine a.m., but she was exhausted. Summer had woken her at six by hurling a sodden nappy out of her cot, then hurling herself out. Shortly afterwards, Jasmine had burst into her bedroom screaming because her new hamster, Olaf, had escaped from his cage. After an hour of searching, clearing up the vase George broke during the search, and convincing Jasmine that this wasn't a police matter, they'd found Olaf curled up asleep in the cup of one of Louise's bras on the clothes airer in the den. Then came the usual resistance to getting dressed and out of the house when there were Xbox games to play, TV programmes to watch and a hamster to coax out of a bra. Polly wished Louise and Erica hadn't signed the children up to so many activity days at the leisure centre. Instead of helping her out, it created more stress.

Her phone rang in the hood of Summer's buggy as she pushed her through the park. Her therapist's number was on the screen. Polly switched the phone to silent.

'Ork, ork.' Summer wiggled out of the buggy harness and prepared to launch herself off the footrest. Polly stopped and Summer slid out and toddled away, slurping loudly on her dummy. A dog barked to their left and Summer ran after it at a pace that would impress Usain Bolt.

'Wait!' Polly ran after her, bumping the buggy over the grass. Summer continued her sprint, her nappy forcing her to run with a waddle, so she resembled an over-eager penguin. She reached the dog and crouched down next to it.

'Careful, poppet.' The black Labrador looked friendly, but when seemingly docile pets were capable of gnawing off their sleeping owners' faces – if the stories in Louise's magazine were to be believed – biting off a toddler's hand would be as consequential to them as picking their teeth.

'It's ok, she's harmless,' said a voice she was starting to recognise.

Alex smiled at Polly and she instinctively pulled her cuffs down and folded them around her hands. He wore jeans and a blue shirt with the sleeves rolled up to the elbows, revealing tanned arms. His fine, brown hair fell to just above his shoulders.

'We're going to the swings,' she said.

'I'll help push, if you like.'

Before Polly could object – though she wasn't sure what she could object to; being kicked in the crotch every time Summer swung forward should be something she was happy to hand over to someone else – Alex had tied his dog to the railings surrounding the play area and was leading Summer to the swings. So much for Polly's 'stranger danger' talk. Summer had clearly paid as much attention to Polly's warning to be wary as Pandora had about the box.

''Gain, 'gain,' Summer said, as she swung high into the air.

Polly looked at Alex. 'You don't have to.'

Alex smiled and his eyes crinkled until they almost disappeared. 'I don't mind. Bess needs a rest. She's due to give birth in a couple of weeks.'

Polly looked at the dog's swollen stomach in alarm.

'Don't worry. We had a scan at the vet's yesterday and she's not going to drop just yet.'

Polly nodded, then stood awkwardly, not knowing what to say.

'Are you a nanny?' Alex asked.

'No. Why?'

'You usually have loads of kids with you. Looks like you've got your work cut out.'

'Three of them are my friends'. I help out with childcare. I don't have a proper job.'

'I'm a landscape gardener. Lot of people wouldn't consider that a proper job either.' Alex glanced across. 'Were you ok the other week?'

'When?'

'In the shop. You were in a hurry to get out.'

Polly put a hand to her pendant. 'Yes, sorry about that. All sorted now. Thanks for dropping my shopping round,' she added. 'And for pushing Summer.'

'You're welcome. I remember how knackering it is from when mine were this age.'

'How old are they now?'

'Maisie's eleven. Going up to secondary school in September and very excited. Mostly about her new pencil case. Max is eight – same as Oliver. He said they play football together at break time.' Alex pulled a silly face at Summer as she swung towards him. She looked up at him through her lashes. She was such a flirt.

'I run a football club at weekends and during the holidays,' Alex continued. 'Here in the park. Why don't you bring Oliver along?'

The swing creaked loudly, as Alex continued to push it, stepping forward to put his full weight behind it. Summer squealed excitedly and leant her head back.

'I'll ask him,' Polly said. 'Can his friend George come too?'

'Bring the girls too. The more the merrier.' Alex gave the swing an energetic push. 'You could even join in yourself.'

Polly laughed. 'Don't know about that.'

Alex's arm brushed against Polly's as he stepped back and she edged away, alarmed by the alien tingling cascading through her body.

Alex looked at his watch. 'I don't need to be anywhere for a couple of hours. Might go and find a café in the sun.'

He looked directly at Polly. His eyes were such a vivid blue. They shone out against his tanned skin. They were exactly the same colour as...

Her breath caught in her throat and she turned away abruptly. 'Don't let us hold you up.' She stepped forward and caught the swing.

'I meant, maybe we could all—'

'We need to go.' Polly lifted Summer from the swing and backed away.

'Hang on.' Alex reached into his back pocket for his phone. 'Let me take your number and I'll text you the details of the football club.'

Polly hesitated. Very few people had her number and she wished a couple of them didn't. Then she thought about how much Oliver would love the football club.

She rattled off her number, said goodbye and walked quickly to the gate, her stomach churning.

Summer waved to Alex over Polly's shoulder. 'Nice man,' she said.

Yes, Polly thought, strapping Summer into her buggy. But so was your dad and look what happened there.

Chapter Nineteen

Erica

Rob tore Erica's shirt open. 'Christ, you're gorgeous.' He kissed her hard, then lowered his mouth to her breasts, massaging her smooth skin with his lips, tugging gently at her nipples with his teeth. She gasped and gripped the back of his head. He undid the tie of her wraparound skirt, letting it fall to the ground, pushed the flimsy fabric of her thong to one side and eased a finger inside her. She moaned loudly. She'd never been so wet.

Rob gripped her arm. 'Mummy.'

'Yes,' she whispered. 'Come to Mumma.'

'I can't sleep.'

'What?'

'Wake up.'

Erica's eyes snapped open. Jasmine was shaking her arm. Erica swallowed hard. It was a dream. Of course it was. She might still be furious with Dan but she'd never cheat on him. Or wear a wraparound skirt.

'Can I sleep with you? Tess is snoring and she smells.'

Erica tugged her negligee down under the covers. Usually she'd happily let Jasmine in, but what if her dream continued when she went back to sleep? It'd take some pretty inventive storytelling to explain why she was crying out 'take me now, big boy'.

She cleared her throat. 'Olaf would miss you if you weren't there.'

'We could bring him in here.'

'Better not. It might confuse him.' No way was she sleeping with a rodent. Predictably, Dan had elevated himself to hero status by buying the hamster, but was having nothing to do with the handling of urine-soaked sawdust or being bitten when topping up its food and water. Erica's only comfort was that hamsters didn't live very long. She was hoping Olaf wouldn't make it to the weekend.

She climbed out of bed. 'Come on. I'll tuck you in.'

Sleepily they made their way along the passageway. Erica pushed Jasmine's bedroom door open and a dark, squat shape loomed towards them. Both she and Jasmine sprang back.

'Wassup?' Tess drawled. Even at three in the morning she sounded as though she'd stepped out of an American teen movie.

'Nothing. Jasmine's going back to bed.' Erica stepped forward and a soft tentacle wound itself around her ankle. She shrieked, kicking her foot wildly to the side.

Jasmine screamed and gripped Erica's arm. Tess grabbed the other one, pulling Erica so she was bent double, Jasmine hanging off one side, Tess the other. Erica fell to her knees, desperately trying to free her foot from whatever was wrapped around her ankle. Logic told her it had to be something plausible, but logic also told her that open-toe boots were a ridiculous invention and she still wore them.

The light snapped on.

'What's going on?' Polly's voice was full of panic.

'Mummy saw a scary monster,' Jasmine cried.

Tess tightened her grip, forcing Erica into an arm lock. Resisting the urge to headbutt Tess away, Erica rolled to the side to escape her clutches. Shakily, she examined her ankle and found a pink, leopard-print dressing gown belt wound around it.

'A scary monster?' Polly said warily.

'No.' Erica held up the belt. 'A scary pattern choice.'

Footsteps sounded along the passageway and Oliver appeared at Polly's side. 'Who screamed?'

'Me,' Jasmine said, with a hint of pride. 'Mummy thought she saw a monster.'

'I screamed first,' Tess drawled sulkily.

'What's going on?' Louise hollered up the stairs.

'Nothing,' Erica called back.

'Then keep it down. Some of us are trying to sleep.' Louise's bedroom door slammed beneath them.

'Sorry we woke you,' Erica said.

'It's ok. Summer and George slept through it.' Polly yawned and rubbed her eyes. The sleeves of her pyjama top slipped down to her elbow, revealing a row of scars along her inner arms. Erica's stomach tightened. She'd seen scars like that on one of the *Sing to Win* contestants a couple of years ago. Polly saw her looking and quickly lowered her arms, tugging the sleeves down and wrapping them around her hands. 'Oven burns,' she said. 'Took over the cooking when my mum died and was always burning my arms lifting things in and out of the oven.'

A feeling of intense sadness swept over Erica. Polly had only been fourteen when her mum died. When most teenagers were sulking because they'd been asked to make their bed, she'd been running a household. It was very possible she'd brushed against the inside of the oven while sliding hot trays off the shelves. But that wasn't what had caused the scars on the *Sing to Win* contestant's arms and they looked very similar.

A whirring noise from the corner of the room made them all jump, then exhale with relief when they realised it was Olaf racing around the wheel in his cage.

Polly took Oliver's hand. 'Back to bed.' She smiled good-night and they wandered back up the passageway.

Tess and Jasmine were bickering over whether there really was a monster.

'Mummy says there's no such thing,' Jasmine said, although she didn't look convinced.

'You won't be able to hear what Mommy says when the monster's chewed your ears off.' Tess clambered up the ladder to the top bunk, the rungs groaning under her weight.

Jasmine's large front teeth bit into her lip.

'She's only teasing.' Erica hugged Jasmine. 'Tess wouldn't want to sleep in here if she thought there really was a monster.' The way Tess was acting, Erica doubted a monster would want to sleep with her.

A scratching sound came from Olaf's cage. Erica watched him urinate in his bed of sawdust and roll around in it. No wonder the room stank. Although, she realised, as she looked around, it wasn't all down to the hamster. Worn clothes and damp towels were strewn across the floor. Empty beakers lay on their side. Sweet wrappers and tissues spilled over the edge of the bin. Her guilt mingled with shame as she realised she hadn't cleaned Jasmine's room the whole time they'd been there. She was so used to having the nanny do everything, it hadn't occurred to her.

She hugged Jasmine. 'Sleep with me tonight.' Any accidental cries of 'big boy' could be blamed on a dream about monsters. 'We'll tidy your room at the weekend and make it nice again.'

A snuffling noise came from the far wall. But this time it wasn't Olaf. It was Tess, watching them from her bunk.

—

'How do you work this thing?'

'We've been here six weeks and you don't know how to use the washing machine?' Louise looked up from the kitchen table, an uneaten slice of toast in front of her. 'That explains why your pants, if you can call them that, are always in the sink.'

'They have to be hand-washed and it's only been a few times. I wash everything else at home at the weekends.'

Louise tutted. 'There isn't enough time in the day to list all the hygiene implications involved with mixing soiled under-garments with serving items.'

Erica bristled. 'My undergarments are *not* soiled.' She dropped Jasmine's bedding onto the floor and began to feed a sheet into the washing machine.

Louise nodded her head in the direction of the white board. 'It's my turn to use the washing machine today.'

Erica rolled her eyes. 'Not another rota.'

'So you are aware of them, then?'

'Yes. I've just made breakfast for everyone.' Erica's bangles tinkled as she swiped an arm back and forth. 'Been up and down that passageway five times carrying all the boxes and bowls and drinks to the dining room.'

'In other words, you're doing what Polly and I do every day,' Louise snapped. 'If you ask me, you're lucky Polly steps in for you so often.'

Patronising as Louise was, she had a point. 'I know I need to do more, but my hours... it's hard.' Erica looked down. There was a long, shiny mark on the floor tiles, leading out from beneath the sheets to the back door. No doubt a smear left by an escaping meatball or some other such delicacy. Now wasn't the time to criticise the menu though, not when she wasn't contributing. Although, perhaps there was a way she could.

She smiled at Louise. 'I'll pay for a takeaway on the nights I can't get back to cook.'

Louise slammed her magazine shut. 'Typical bloody Aries. Think you can throw money at every problem. Someone's still got to order the takeaway, collect it and clear up afterwards.' She picked up her toast, glowered at it and put it down again.

Erica turned away, biting her lip so she didn't scream at Louise to give her a fucking break. Upstairs, footsteps and thuds rang out as the children raced around. She could hear a faint cry of 'Liar, liar, pants on fire. Knickers went up the telephone wire!' Better hope they weren't soiled or Louise would be slapping a health warning on them. Why was she constantly in a bad mood? She'd always been direct and bossy, but she used to be a laugh. Now she was just bossy, firing out instructions on what to do and when to do it. She ruled over them with an iron fist and that fist had a very tight grip. Must be from opening all those jars of chocolate spread.

Erica clutched the edge of the sink. Something sticky squelched beneath her fingers. She didn't want to know what it was. Swearing to herself, she turned the tap on and scrubbed her hands. Water ricocheted off yesterday's dinner plates, swirling baked bean juice down the tea-stained plughole. Limescale clung to the tap. Some sort of green slime grew between the back of the sink and the wall. Why was she living in this shit hole, letting Louise talk to her like shit? No amount of childcare was worth this. The edge of the sink dug into her arms and she looked down at the angry red creases left behind, not dissimilar to the scars on Polly's arms. Had Polly been telling the truth about them or had she done them herself? And if she had, what had driven her to it?

There was a heavy sigh behind her. 'Sorry for snapping,' Louise said. 'Got a lot on at the moment, but I shouldn't take it out on you.'

Erica's bad mood dissolved instantly. It took guts to apologise, and now that she looked properly, she could see Louise's eyes were ringed with dark circles and her usually ruddy cheeks were pale.

'What's wrong?'

To Erica's alarm, Louise's eyes welled up.

'Nick and I—'

'Mom.' Tess trudged into the kitchen. 'I'm bored.'

Louise blinked and looked away. 'Don't you have lines to learn for drama club?'

'Learnt them already.' Tess's voice changed from whiny to eager. 'Can you test me?'

'Not now, love,' Louise said quietly.

Tess's face fell. 'Dad would. He does different voices for all the characters too.'

'I'm no good at accents.' Louise thrust her toast at Tess. 'Here, take this and stick the telly on. I've got to get to work.'

Tess snatched the plate and stomped out of the room.

'What where you going to say?' Erica asked softly.

'Nothing.' Louise avoided Erica's gaze. 'Use the machine,' she said. 'I can't be bothered to do any washing today.'

'Thank you.' Erica bent down and scooped up the sheets. The mysterious shiny trail came to an end at her feet. A long, fat, slug clung to one of the pillowcases. Shrieking, she threw it to the ground, her hands springing to her chest. She kicked the bedding in the direction of the back door, where it nestled by a bin liner full of dirty nappies. 'That is fucking disgusting. How did it get in?'

'Through the floorboards, probably,' Louise said. 'It's an old house.'

'My house is Georgian and we don't get slugs.' Erica swept a hand around the kitchen. 'Or mouldy taps or overflowing bins or crumbs all over the floor.'

'You would if you didn't have a cleaner.'

A cleaner. Of course. Why hadn't she thought of it before? Sod the expense; it was a drop in the ocean compared to the rest of their debt and it'd make life at Polly's so much more bearable.

'That's how I'll contribute.' She grinned at Louise. 'I'll pay for a cleaner. There'll be less work for you and Polly and I won't feel so bad about not being here to help.'

Louise crossed her arms tightly across her chest and Erica prepared herself for a lecture on the banality of such a frivolous lifestyle. Instead Louise shrugged.

'Guess I was wrong,' she said. 'Some problems you can throw money at.'

Chapter Twenty

Polly

'Morning.' Erica stepped into the den where Polly was changing Summer on the sofa. Erica clocked the contents of the nappy and stepped back again.

Polly fastened the sticky ties of the fresh nappy, rolled the soiled one into a ball and went into the kitchen, leaving Summer watching TV. Erica sat at the table.

'Aren't you late for work?' Polly crammed the dirty nappy into the already full bin.

'My first appointment's been put back an hour. I'll get the nine o'clock train.' Erica fiddled with her earring. 'Does Louise seem ok to you?'

'Yes. Why?'

'She was a bit flustered earlier, but if you think she's alright…' Erica cleared her throat. 'What about you? Are you ok?'

Polly pulled her cuffs down over her hands. 'Course. Why wouldn't I be?'

'It's just that…' Erica broke off. 'Sometimes it seems like…' She paused again. Polly grew increasingly nervous. Erica couldn't have found out, could she?

Erica leaned forward. 'There's no easy way to say this so I'm just going to blurt it out. I'm worried about you. Whenever you get a call from your friend Becky you ignore it, but you look shaken. Who is she? Why don't you tell her to fuck off and leave you alone if you don't want to talk to her?'

Polly felt as though her lungs were contracting. She wanted to put her hands over her ears the way Summer did when she didn't like what she was hearing.

'It's not as easy as that,' she managed to say.

'I'll tell her to fuck off then. I'd find it very easy,' Erica said. 'And why are you so against seeing Ian's parents? Surely it'd be nice to have some help now and then? Dan's mum has too hectic a social life to help me, but most grandparents live for that shit. Couldn't you—'

'No.' The trapped air in Polly's lungs came shooting out with force, making her sound more aggressive than she'd intended.

Erica placed a hand on Polly's arm. 'I know it's nothing to do with me, but I'm saying this because I care.' Erica eased one of Polly's sleeves up. 'I've seen scars like this before.'

Polly snatched her arm away, pulling her sleeve down to cover the tell-tale red lines.

'You don't have to go through this on your own,' Erica said softly. 'You've got me and Louise.'

Tears filled Polly's eyes. Could she confide in them? Tell them some of what was going on? Not all of it of course, but enough to ease a little of the weight that was constantly pressing down on her, squashing her lungs, squeezing the life out of her. She looked at Erica, who nodded encouragingly.

'They're not burns,' she whispered. 'I used to cut myself.' She put a hand to her necklace and squeezed the pendant tightly. Erica put an arm around her and Polly felt tears coursing down her cheeks. After three years of hiding the truth, the desire to talk about it was so strong. Some of it anyway.

'After my mum died, my dad worked constantly. He had his own plastering firm. I was at home on my own most of the time.' She pulled up her sleeve and ran a finger across a silver, feathery scar. 'That one really is an oven burn. Knocked my arm against the side taking a baking tray out. The pain stopped me thinking about how lonely I was.' She waited for gasps of horror from Erica, but she sat quietly, her large brown eyes full of compassion.

Polly took a deep breath and continued. 'I tried burning my arm on purpose, but it got infected and I had to get it treated at the doctor's, so I cut myself instead. Not badly, just enough of a sting to distract me. I worked at a hairdressers' and always had scissors on me. I could do it whenever I wanted.' She ran her pendant back and forth along its chain. 'My dad had lung cancer and wanted someone to look after me when he died. He took Ian on and brought him home, encouraging us to get together.' She closed her eyes. 'He died a few weeks after we got married. Everything happened so quickly – my mum, dad, Ian. Everything was a blur 'til I had Oliver, then it all clicked into place. It wasn't about me anymore. I stopped cutting myself then. I couldn't risk anything bad happening.' Her voice wobbled. 'But something bad did happen. Something really bad.' She couldn't say any more. Her throat was contracting, her lungs trapping the air trying to escape. A large eye flashed in front of her, propelling her to that horrific day.

'Oh, Polly.' Erica's voice brought her back to the present and she blinked. The eye disappeared. 'I'm so, so sorry.'

Polly took a deep breath. She'd answer one of Erica's other questions.

'Becky,' she said. 'She's a therapist. I've been seeing her since Ian…' she stopped. That was enough sharing.

'Does talking to her help?'

'Yes,' Polly lied. No one could help her.

Erica took her hands. 'I'm so sorry,' she said again.

'It's ok.' Polly wiped her cheeks. 'Well, not ok, but better than it was. Having you all living here is a big help.'

'I understand.' Erica squeezed her hands. 'You were there for Jasmine when she needed you and now we're here for you.'

Polly's throat contracted again and she fought back another wave of tears. Erica wouldn't be so understanding if she knew the full story. She wouldn't understand at all.

Chapter Twenty-One

Louise

Louise listened, shocked, as Polly told her about her self-harming and therapy. Why had Polly felt she had to keep it to herself? And why had she opened up to Erica, not her? Erica sat across the kitchen table, an arm around Polly, nodding gravely. That should be her arm around Polly, not Erica's.

'Oh, Poll,' Louise said. 'Is there anything I can do?'

'No, but thank you.' Polly smiled. 'I feel better for having talked about it.'

To Erica. Even though Louise had known her longer and been the one to take Polly under her wing when she'd moved to Hazelworth. It was like being picked last for teams at school again. She pressed her lips together and looked away. Her eyes fell on the housekeeping jar on the windowsill and she seized the opportunity to vent her hurt.

'Another fiver's gone,' she snapped. 'Have either of you taken it?'

Polly and Erica shook their heads.

'Speaking of money,' Erica said. 'You haven't sponsored me yet.'

'Money going missing is more important than that.' Louise took a notebook from her bag and turned to a page covered in writing. 'Yet another thing to add to the list.' She might not have any control over her marriage or Erica and Polly's burgeoning friendship, but she was bloody well going to have control over this house.

'What list?' Erica asked warily.

'This one.' Louise turned to a page in her book and added a note at the bottom. 'As we're all here, may as well go through it now.' She looked at Erica. 'When's the cleaner starting?'

'Haven't had time to find one yet.' Erica smiled apologetically. 'Don't suppose you could ring round a few agencies, could you?'

Louise scratched her head, shocked into silence by Erica's cheek.

'Obviously I'll pay,' Erica added.

Louise ignored her and read from her list. 'Item one, rotas. They're not being followed properly. Almost every week the shifts have to be rearranged, because people,' she glared at Erica, 'aren't following them. Item two, bins have to be emptied. Item three, the dishwasher needs unloading twice a day. Item four, the filter in the tumble dryer has to be cleaned after each use or it becomes a fire hazard. Item five – ties in with the missing housekeeping money – we need to start listing what we're taking out and spending it on.' She paused to catch her breath and looked up. Polly was massaging her scalp through her curls, a vacant look on her face. Erica was reading something on her phone.

Louise slammed her notebook on the table. 'Are you even listening?'

Polly looked guilty.

'Sorry.' Erica put her phone down.

'Item six, the whole house needs a bloody good clean.' Louise pointed at the wall behind the bin, which was covered in tea stains and encrusted scraps of food. 'The Food Standards Agency would close this place down if they saw the state of it.'

Erica grimaced.

'Soon as you've done it, it needs doing again,' Polly said. 'Worrying about it won't change that.'

Erica smiled. 'We won't need to worry about it when Louise finds a cleaner.'

A burning sensation gathered in Louise's stomach. It coursed through her body, firing hot splinters of irritation and frustration and anger. She slammed her fists down on the table. A glass of water tipped over and smashed to the floor.

'*You* were supposed to get a bloody cleaner,' she shouted. 'I organise people all day at work. I shouldn't have to do that here too.' She covered her face with her hands. She didn't want to be here. She wanted to be home watching TV with Nick. She wouldn't even mind if one of those Scandinavian dramas were on. She wouldn't mind about anything again, if only he'd have her back.

She was vaguely aware of movement – chairs scraping, broken glass being swept up, a bottle of wine being unscrewed, an odd wailing noise. Someone was rubbing her back. Water gathered in her cupped hands. The wailing noise grew louder. It was coming from her.

Now that she'd started crying, she couldn't stop. She'd spent so long holding it in. She cried and cried until, exhausted, her body stopped shuddering and her tears reduced to panting. Slowly, she lowered her hands. Erica and Polly sat quietly. A glass of wine was on the table in front of her. Louise tipped her head back and drained half the glass.

Erica refilled it. 'Sorry for being crap. You're doing a great job.'

'It's not that.' Louise's chest rose and fell. She had to tell them. She'd go mad if she continued this façade. 'Nick and I have split up.' She took a tissue from the waistband of her combats and blew her nose. 'I read his emails and accused him of having an affair with my sister. He says I betrayed his trust and doesn't want to be with me anymore. The twins don't know yet.' Her voice wobbled. 'She was only teaching him to drive.'

'Shit.' Erica scratched her head. 'When did this happen?'

'Four weeks ago.'

'Four weeks?' Polly looked as though she might cry herself. 'Why didn't you say?'

'I thought I could talk him round, but he won't listen.' Louise pressed the tissue to her eyes. 'He hates me.'

'No, he doesn't,' Erica said. 'The dynamics have flipped and you need to flip them back again.'

Louise glared at Erica. How could she be so blasé about it? 'He says our marriage is over. There's no flipping involved, apart from the fact it's flipping shit.'

Erica shook her head. 'Up 'til now, you've had the control in the relationship. Now he has. You've got to get that control back.'

'How? He won't let me go home at weekends.' Louise looked at Polly. 'Is that ok with you, if I stay? I know we originally said only during the week…'

'I'd love you to.'

Louise sniffed. She'd been hoping Polly would say no, so Nick had to let her go back.

'Good,' Erica said.

Louise was starting to really dislike Erica. 'How is this good?'

'Give him some space and he'll start to wonder where you are. Don't answer the door when he collects or drops off the twins for a while, then make sure you look amazing when you do see him.'

Was she having a laugh? It was easy for Erica to say 'look amazing', with her long, slender limbs, brown flawless skin and designer wardrobe. She wouldn't look quite so amazing if she was five-foot, two-inches tall with mousey brown hair, a ruddy complexion and what her mum used to kindly refer to as 'big bones'.

'How?' she grunted.

'A makeover.' Erica's eyes travelled down Louise's body to her waist, before peering under the table to look at her lower half.

Louise instinctively clamped her knees together. 'We're not in one of Tess's American teen dramas,' she tutted.

'First thing I'm going to do is burn those combats. Don't mean to be rude, but they're a man-repellent if ever I saw one.'

'What's the point?' Louise sighed.

Erica actually winced. 'Your clothes represent you. They lift your spirits and show the world how you feel and want to be viewed. You'd feel so much better about yourself in an outfit with a nipped-in waist that makes the most of your hourglass figure. You've got curves that most women envy. Do some exercise to tone up, get a new hairstyle and you're sorted.'

Louise scratched her head through her heavily lacquered hair. Erica may have hit a nerve – with all the delicacy of a sledgehammer – but she was right. She'd let herself go so much that some parts were in another time zone. One that fashion hadn't been kind to. She sat up straighter. Erica's makeover could be the answer to getting Nick back.

Erica looked appraisingly at Polly. 'You could do with an overhaul too. Does that long-sleeved tee come off or does it need to be surgically removed?'

Polly tugged the cuffs down. 'I don't like showing my arms.'

'I understand.' Erica gave Polly a sympathetic smile. 'Don't worry, you can be stylish and covered up. We'll just add some colour and interest to your wardrobe.'

Louise's shoulders slumped. Typical. Erica's caring had lasted all of two minutes and now her attention was on the slimmer, prettier doll she could dress up. Still, she didn't need Erica's charity. She'd do this herself.

She stood up. 'I'm going to bed.'

'Why?' Polly asked.

'You two are busy. We'll finish the house meeting another time.'

'Stay,' Erica said. 'You haven't finished your wine.'

Louise sighed dramatically. She'd stay, but only for the wine. She plonked herself down and picked up her notepad.

Erica took it out of her hand. 'Relax. We'll sort it out later.'

'When?' Louise huffed.

'This weekend. Dan's away so Jasmine and I may as well stay. We'll get pissed and do some serious online shopping. Are you in?'

Polly nodded eagerly. 'I'd love that. It's very quiet when you're not here. Going to be odd when you're all on holiday.'

Louise looked at Polly thoughtfully. They were both going through a tough time. Why not go through it together? 'Come to Spain,' she said. 'Without Nick there'll be plenty of room.'

'But there's one of him and three of us.'

'He's so tall, he's practically the equivalent of all three of you. The beds aren't that big, so he always sleeps in the other room anyway.' Her voice wavered. If they ever got back together, she'd never let him sleep apart from her again.

Polly looked as though she couldn't quite believe what she was hearing. 'We've never been abroad.'

'Make sure you get passports and flights sorted asap.'

Polly beamed and warmth flooded through Louise. She'd done something nice and it felt good. It was an alien feeling. When was the last time she'd done something nice, other than tweeting Colin Firth on his birthday? The warmth travelled up to her scalp making it tingle. She dug her nails in and scratched at the roots of her hair. Her head felt as though it was on fire and she clawed at it manically.

'Stop.' Erica thrust her hands into her own hair. 'You're making me itch.'

Louise prised her hands away from her head. 'No wonder that shampoo was on offer. The twins were complaining about it too.'

Erica let out a long, low whimper. Her eyes were wide. 'Don't move,' she ordered, rising slowly from her chair and backing away from the table.

Louise shook her head. 'What are you talking about?'

'I said, don't move,' Erica shrieked. 'You've got nits.'

Chapter Twenty-Two

Erica

Erica gripped the strap of her Hermès bag and prepared to jostle for one of the vacant seats. The smell of the nit solution should be enough to warrant her a carriage to herself. Her phone rang as the train pulled into the station and Polly's name flashed up on the screen.

'Mummy.' Jasmine's voice wobbled. 'I need my bike. It's orienteering day.'

'I'm on my way to work, sweetie.'

'Please, Mummy,' Jasmine cried.

'Sorry,' Polly said into the phone. 'Didn't realise they need their bikes today.'

Erica boarded the train. 'Does the leisure centre have one she can borrow?'

'No. Don't worry – she can spend the day with me and Summer.'

'But I'll miss the treasure trail,' Jasmine said in the background.

The train doors began to slide shut. Erica's mind raced. Getting Jasmine's bike from home and to the leisure centre would delay her by at least an hour, even in a cab. She'd never get to her meeting on time. Guilt coursed through her. She couldn't let Jasmine down. She had to get that bike.

Thrusting her arm between the closing doors, she forced them to open. 'Tell Jasmine I'll get it.'

In the cab, having secured a deal for a ride to her house, to the leisure centre, and back to her house again, and having rearranged the format of her meeting to a Zoom call, she sat back, pleased with herself. She hadn't let Jasmine down or had to cancel her meeting. They pulled up and, assuring the driver she'd only be a few minutes, she let herself into the house. Dan's briefcase was inside the door. He must be running even later than her.

'Only me,' she called out, heading straight to the garage. She wheeled the bike outside and went back in to tell Dan.

He wasn't in the living room, but clearly had been. The TV was paused, there was a pile of tissues on the arm of the sofa, and the remains of an Egg McMuffin sat on a plate on the coffee table. Erica rolled her eyes. Dan must be the only member of the human race who ate McDonald's with cutlery. He'd even got the stainless-steel salt and pepper pots out.

There was a flush from the downstairs toilet and a minute later Dan emerged, wearing silk, spot pyjamas. He was only one step away from a smoking jacket and cravat. He jumped when he saw her.

'What are you doing here?'

'Hello to you too,' she said stiffly. She was still pissed off about being asked to put the bins out.

He put a hand up. 'Sorry. Wasn't expecting to see you.'

'I'm not supposed to be here. Jasmine needs her bike. I'm about to drop it off at the leisure centre.'

'Oh, ok.'

They stood in awkward silence. Dan's eyes flitted to the TV screen and back to Erica.

'Why aren't you at work?' Erica asked.

'Sorry?'

'Work?' Erica repeated.

'Because,' Dan said slowly, elongating the word. 'I'm not feeling great.' He patted his stomach. 'Yellowtail teriyaki wasn't a wise menu choice on the plane.'

Now that Erica looked at him properly, she could see that his face was flushed and his complexion dewy.

'Why are you eating McDonald's if you're ill?'

'Thought it might bung me up, but it didn't.'

Erica knew he must be mortified. Discussing bodily functions made him very uncomfortable. He claimed to never pass wind, but it was impossible to consume that much airplane food and not let the odd one go during the night.

'You poor thing. Do you need me to get you anything? Water? Bananas? Imodium?'

Dan shook his head.

She pointed to the pile of tissues on the sofa. 'How about tissues?'

Dan's face turned crimson.

'Or toilet roll? Have you got enough toilet roll?'

'Yes, thank you.'

'Ok. I'd better get Jasmine's bike to her.' She didn't feel right leaving him when he was ill, but knew he'd prefer to be alone. 'Hope you're better soon.' Smiling sympathetically, she blew him a kiss. She wasn't sympathetic enough to actually kiss him.

'It's sweet of you to worry about me.' Dan smiled. 'We should have another date night. A proper one, where we go out, like we did before.'

'Not *exactly* like before.' She winked. 'No, I'd like that.' She meant it. The rare conversations they now had always led to an argument, usually about Dan's lack of involvement with childcare and Erica's subsequent frustration. 'Frustration' being code for massively pissed off. A fun evening out would remind her why they'd got together in the first place.

She picked Dan's plate up to take to the kitchen, glancing briefly at the TV as she did so. Dan stared at her in horror. She swivelled back and looked properly at the image. The couple frozen on the screen were completely naked. 'Is that a porn film?' she spluttered.

Dan nodded.

Erica looked him up and down. 'Are you really ill?'

'No.' Dan said quietly. 'I've taken the day off.'

A whoosh of anger erupted from her stomach. 'When I ask you to take time off to help with Jasmine, you're always too busy.' She pointed at the screen. 'And when I instigate sex you never want to.'

'It's not that I don't want to. You ask me when I'm tired or in the middle of something.'

'Whatever.' She thrust the plate at Dan and barged past him into the hall. 'I'm going. Don't you dare get spunk on the suede sofa.' She realised that was what the mound of tissues must have been for and shuddered.

There was a loud crash behind her. Dan's plate was in pieces on the floor.

'It's only a film!' he shouted. 'A harmless release from my stressful job. You should be grateful all I do is watch it. There are plenty of men who'd go and get it.'

'Grateful?' Erica gasped. 'Grateful that you're jerking off rather than screwing someone else? Is this what our relationship has boiled down to?'

'Looks like it.' Dan clenched his jaw. 'And you're to blame.'

'How?'

'All you do is witter on about how hard your life is and put more pressure on me by asking when I'm going to have paid the loan off. You have no appreciation of how hard I work to give you and Jasmine this house.'

'You chauvinistic git,' Erica snapped. 'I pay my share.'

'Doesn't count for much when you're not even bothering to live here,' Dan shouted.

'I didn't want to move out. I had no choice. It's alright for you. Your life hasn't been affected by Phoebe leaving. Mine's turned upside down. I've even had nits.'

Dan grimaced and took a step back.

Erica threw her hands in the air. 'I can't go anywhere or do anything without making sure someone's around to look after Jasmine. And then I have to help with Polly and Louise's children to keep it fair, while making sure I'm on top of things at work. You can go to the office, go out whenever you want, leave the country without a moment's thought.'

'I don't like going away all the time. I'd rather be at home.'

'You wouldn't if you were the one responsible for childcare. I'd give anything to have a few nights in a hotel with room service. You have no idea how easy your life is. You don't have to think about anyone but yourself.' She was shaking from head to toe, every nerve in her body taut, every part of her skin ablaze. 'I don't care that you're watching porn. What I care about is that you've taken a day off to do it when you should want to spend any free time you have with your daughter.'

'Give me a break,' Dan bellowed. 'It's one fucking day.'

His hands curled into fists. Erica had never seen him so angry. She'd never felt so angry herself. She wanted to punch him. Channel all her fury into her fist and hit him as hard as she could.

Dan clearly felt the same. Baring his teeth, he raised his arm. Howling, he spun round and punched the wall. Erica flinched. His howl turned to a whimper.

'Fuck, that hurts.' He dropped to the floor. 'Think I've broken my hand.'

That put paid to his morning's entertainment then.

The front door swung open.

'How much longer are you going to be? Got another ride booked in—' The cab driver stopped and looked down at Dan kneeling on the floor surrounded by broken crockery and a half-eaten Egg McMuffin. 'Everything alright?' he asked warily.

'Fine, thank you.' Erica smoothed her dress down. 'How much to add a trip to A&E to your route?'

–

Erica leaned against the wall of the studio corridor and sighed. Should she phone Dan? Make sure he was ok? The purple lump on his knuckle had looked pretty sore. No, she decided. He didn't deserve her sympathy when he wouldn't take a day off to spend with Jasmine, but he would to have a wank. Which, it seemed, he'd rather do than have sex with her. She blinked hard, refusing to let herself cry. This was nothing compared to what Polly and Louise were going through. She couldn't believe they'd both harboured such deep secrets. No wonder Louise had been so snappy since they'd moved in and Polly wore that awful long-sleeved tee.

'Are you ok?'

Erica's stomach flipped over when she heard Rob's voice. Heat rushed to her cheeks, as she recalled the most recent dream she'd had about him. The positions they'd got themselves into made Dan's viewing choice look suitable for the Disney channel.

'I'm fine, thanks.' She brushed away the tear that had ignored her instruction not to cry.

'Sure?' Rob wouldn't be looking at her with such concern if he knew what she'd been dreaming. He'd be asking for a restraining order. 'You look like something's worrying you.' He touched her arm lightly, and a tingle shot through her. 'I was about to get a coffee from round the corner. Fancy one?'

Erica hesitated. She'd love to, but was that a bit like a date?

'If you're worried about time, I need to be back in twenty minutes, so it'll have to be a quickie,' Rob said.

Her dream flashed through her mind again. She shouldn't go.

'We can discuss our charity run training. How can you refuse?' Rob grinned and gestured towards the door.

Erica decided it was safe to go. If Rob was anything like Dan, a protracted analysis of his training schedule would soon obliterate any erotic feelings she had towards him.

It transpired that Rob was nothing like Dan. Instead of describing his progress in minute detail, with graphs on his Fitbit or, as had happened, spreadsheets, Rob instead asked Erica how she was getting on.

'I feel a bit guilty asking for money when 10k is an average run for me,' she admitted. She thought back to Dan's comments. 'It's hardly Iron Man.'

'Those things are for show-offs,' Rob said. 'They just do them for the t-shirt.'

'Have you ever done one?'

'No.' Rob laughed. 'Too much of a wimp. I'd wear the t-shirt all the time if I had.'

Erica smiled. His laugh was infectious and his self-deprecation endearing. Even if he was full of shit. That body was made for challenging workouts.

'You could always try and beat your PB, your personal best,' he suggested. 'That way you'd be pushing yourself and training harder.'

'That's a great idea.' Erica didn't know what her PB was, but she could time herself the next morning and aim to improve on that. 'Problem solved. Thank you.'

They reached the café and Rob insisted she sit out in the sun while he went inside to get them a coffee. Erica usually had a green smoothie but didn't want to risk getting spinach in her teeth. Her phone beeped with a text from Dan. It was a photo of his bruised fist. His middle finger was the most prominent and Erica doubted this was down to the bandaging method used.

Rob returned with their drinks, sat down and squinted across at her, shielding his eyes with one hand. His smooth, brown arm glistened in the bright sunshine beneath his t-shirt. Erica distracted herself by rummaging in her bag. It was the safest way to ensure she didn't lean over and stroke him.

'Everything ok?' Rob asked softly. 'You looked a bit fed up earlier.'

Erica found her sunglasses, slipped them on and nodded. 'Just a bit of friction at home,' she said.

'Want to talk about it?'

This was the perfect opportunity to explain the situation with Dan. But she was so pissed off that she knew she'd end up moaning about him and that would be disloyal.

'I'm in a slightly unusual living arrangement at the moment,' she said instead. 'Not too unusual,' she added quickly. 'Not in a religious sect or the back room of a knocking shop.'

Rob smiled. 'I'm intrigued.'

'Jasmine and I are living at my friend's at the moment. I was finding it impossible to juggle childcare with work and keeping on top of the house, life admin, any sort of social life, going for a run, even.'

Rob nodded. 'Must be really tough. Especially if you're not getting any support from Jasmine's dad. Is he still in China?'

Erica nodded, glad he couldn't see her eyes behind her sunglasses. Dan was only in China half the time, but he may as well live there permanently for all the help he was.

'Rather than us all struggling, Jasmine and I, and another friend and her children, moved into Polly's a few weeks ago. It used to be a B&B so there's loads of space. We share the childcare, cooking and housework between us.' Erica bit her lip guiltily. She wasn't exactly doing her fair share. She hoped Louise found a cleaner soon.

'Sounds like a great idea,' Rob said. 'Bet loads of people would do that if they could.' He picked up his coffee cup. 'Must be hard having three separate viewpoints of how things should be done though.'

Erica thought of Louise's rotas and militant scheduling. Thank God Polly was so compliant and didn't try to incorporate her own systems or it'd be unbearable.

'It's not too bad,' she said. 'Jasmine and I go home most weekends, so we get our own time too.' That would have to change with *Sing to Win*'s live shows taking place on Saturdays from now on. If Dan was away, Jasmine would need to stay with Polly.

'What happened this morning?' Rob asked.

'Jasmine needed her bike, so I had to jump off the train, go home and get it, drop it off to her and reschedule a meeting. All before nine a.m.'

'The joys of parenthood, eh?' Rob smiled. 'My time with Daisy is just as chaotic. Sounds to me as though you're doing an amazing job. It's not easy maintaining a successful career with being a successful mum.'

Erica gave a small smile and sipped her coffee. She was probably coming across as modest. The truth was, she was ashamed. She wasn't being a successful mum at all. She was barely being a mum. A quick kiss in the morning, often before Jasmine was properly awake, then dashing through the door to brush her hair before putting her to bed wasn't what she'd had in mind when she'd fought so hard with Dan to have a baby, threatening to leave him if he wouldn't at least try. What had she done it for if she wasn't spending any quality time with her longed-for daughter?

Her only consolation was that Louise was even more crap than her. She might physically be at home more, but she didn't pay the twins any attention. George falling headfirst into a stacked pile of dinner plates – which he'd managed to do the night before – barely got an acknowledgement. Louise was going through a painful break up though and her behaviour didn't excuse Erica's. Jasmine deserved so much more than she was currently giving her.

'Don't be so hard on yourself,' Rob said, as though reading her mind. '*Sing to Win* is mentally and physically exhausting. Doing that while raising a child is phenomenal, so don't underestimate what you're achieving. And it's short term. The show finishes in September, which should take some pressure off.'

Erica sat up straight. Rob was right. There were only a few weeks left and then she'd be back to her usual, much more manageable, workload. She'd make it up to Jasmine then.

'Thank you.' She smiled over at him. 'I needed to hear that.'

'You're welcome.' Rob smiled back and held her gaze. Her body quivered.

'We'd better get back.' She stood up quickly. 'How's Daisy?' Talking about their children would put an end to the quivering.

'She's great, thanks.' Rob's smile was broad and proud, like a teenager owning up to his first crush. 'We're going punting in Cambridge next week.' They reached the studio entrance and he stopped. 'You and Jasmine could come if you like?'

Erica hesitated. Jasmine would love it. But it felt wrong to arrange to meet Rob outside of work, even for a play date. The coffee they'd just had was bad enough.

'Sounds fun,' she said carefully.

'So you'll come?' Rob rubbed his jaw with the back of his hand, looking almost shy.

Erica cleared her throat. She needed to make her relationship status transparently clear. When Rob knew the situation, *maybe* they could take their daughters out on a purely platonic basis with no misunderstandings or guilt involved. Or thoughts of falling into the river and Rob giving her mouth-to-mouth resuscitation.

'The thing is, Jasmine's dad—' she waved her hand casually through the air. Her bag slipped off her arm and fell to the floor. The contents scattered in different directions – lipsticks, pens, tissues and, mortifyingly, a tampon. She dropped to the ground, scrabbling to scoop everything up. Rob knelt down to help her. Their fingers and arms brushed against each other's as they gathered safety pins and mints and tissues. Each touch triggered a stirring between her legs. They both reached for her compact mirror. Erica got to it a split second before Rob and his hand closed around it over hers. He didn't release his grip. Slowly, she looked up. They were so close she could see the different flecks of brown in his irises. Their eyes met and his pupils dilated.

'Did you see what she was wearing?' The studio door slid open and Pixie, the third assistant, and another young woman sauntered out towards them. 'Talk about Whitney dressed as Britney.'

Rob sprung up and held a hand out to Erica. She clasped it tightly, allowing him to help her up. Pixie grinned up at Rob and exaggerated the swing of her hips. It was hard not to stare at the cheeks of her smooth, pert arse beneath her high-waisted, very short shorts, as she walked away and disappeared around the corner.

Rob shook his head. 'When did underwear become outerwear? Or am I showing my age?'

Erica gave what she hoped was a nonchalant shrug. 'You don't think she's sexy?'

Rob laughed. He had a deep throaty laugh that made Erica's toes wiggle inside her shoes.

'Hardly. She's closer to Daisy's age than mine.'

Erica suppressed the urge to grab a fistful of air.

He opened the door for her. 'Let me know about punting. If you're free, it'd be great to see you both.' He smiled and walked away.

Erica sighed. It would be great to see him too. Which was exactly why she couldn't go.

Chapter Twenty-Three

Polly

Polly's pendant thumped lightly against her chest as she pushed Summer's buggy through the park. Jasmine held one of the handles, Oliver and George walked slightly ahead, Tess trailed behind. Summer almost gave herself whiplash when she saw the swings and squawked indignantly at the injustice of being wheeled past.

'Over there, Mum,' Oliver shouted, pointing to some children dribbling balls in and out of orange cones. He and George sprinted towards them. Polly winced as George tripped up and tumbled to the ground. His face crimson, he sprung up and bolted after Oliver, pretending the fall had never happened.

Alex had his back to them, his tanned arms moving through the air as he explained something to the children.

They reached the group and Alex high-fived the children and gestured to a bag of footballs. 'Help yourself.'

Tess pouted. 'I'm a girl.'

'You're probably a natural then.' Alex smiled at Polly. 'Glad you could make it. You can stay and watch or have an hour to yourself. Up to you.'

'We'll stay,' Polly said. Given the choice, she'd always stay with her children.

She and Summer settled themselves beneath a tree a few metres away. The children listened to Alex's instructions and they improved before her eyes, especially Tess, who had a strong kick. Polly watched her flush with pleasure when Alex called out 'Great pass!' and felt a swell of pride. Parents and childminders gathered around them towards the end of the hour, clapping when goals were scored, groaning sympathetically when they were missed. Jasmine and Tess's team were replaced with another. Jasmine looked relieved, preferring not to perform in public. Tess plonked herself down heavily on the grass, muttering that it wasn't fair. There were a crucial few seconds left and it was down to a penalty kick. Everyone was quiet, waiting for the deciding goal.

'Polly,' Tess said loudly. 'How do babies get in their moms' tummies?'

Laughter erupted around them.

'Well?' Tess demanded, clearly enjoying the audience.

'Ask your mum,' Polly whispered.

'Can I use your cell?'

'Not now – tonight.'

'Why won't you tell me?' Tess asked. 'Dontcha know?'

There was more laughter.

'I know,' Jasmine said.

'Yeah, right,' Tess said. 'You don't even know how to slide down the bannisters.'

Jasmine blushed. 'I don't know how they get in, but I know how they get out.'

'Everyone knows that.' Tess pulled a d'uh face. 'Out your butt.'

'Shhh,' Polly said, but they took no notice.

Jasmine looked confused. 'Mummy says they come out your bellybutton.'

'Butt,' Tess said. 'I saw my mom put a tube up there once to stop them falling out. It was gross.'

A few people moved away.

'This isn't the time to be talking about it,' Polly whispered.

Everyone around them clapped and she realised with relief that the game had finished. Oliver and George ran over and flopped down on the grass. George had grazed his knee and Polly's throat tightened as a drop of blood ran down his shin. She squeezed her eyes shut.

'George,' Tess said. 'Babies come out your butt, not your bellybutton, don't they?'

George looked at his sister with disgust. 'Not *my* butt, they don't.'

Polly forced herself to breathe deeply. A giant eye flashed before her as she fumbled in her bag for baby wipes and thrust them in George's direction, her head turned away from him.

'Here, George. Clean your knee,' she said shakily. She couldn't look until she knew the blood was gone.

'Thanks, Polly,' George mumbled.

Deep breath in, then breathe out for five, Polly said to herself, hoping George would be done quickly.

A minute later, the pack of wipes hit the side of the head and her eyes snapped open.

'Sorry.' George pressed his hands to his flaming cheeks. 'Was trying to get them in the bag.'

'It's ok.' Polly put the wipes away, avoiding looking at George. 'All clean now?'

'Yes, thanks. Sorry.'

She smiled at him. He looked so distraught. 'Don't worry,' she said. 'Accidents happen.' They did to George, anyway.

He thrust his used, bloody wipe at her. 'What shall I do with this?'

Her breath caught in her throat. 'Put it in the bin,' she managed to say, pointing to one nearby.

'Ok.' He scrambled up and loped away, his long legs covering the distance quickly, then doubling back to retrieve the wipe he'd dropped en route.

'Maybe Alex will tell us,' Tess said.

'Tell us what?' Polly asked.

'How babies are made.'

'Don't ask him,' Polly said quickly. The prospect of Tess commanding Alex to explain the facts of life was so mortifying it distracted her from George's knee.

'Only if you pinky promise to tell us later.'

'I don't think your mums would—'

'Alex,' Tess called out. 'Do you know—'

'Ok,' Polly said quickly. 'Pinky promise.'

Tess held out her little finger for Polly to shake.

'Thanks, Polly,' Jasmine said, clearly eager to find out whether it was her bellybutton or butt she should worry about in the future.

'Great job, guys,' Alex said, coming over. 'Have you got time to meet Max and Maisie?' He gestured to a dark-haired girl and fair boy, who were gathering up balls.

'We can't, Polly,' Tess stage-whispered. 'We need to go have our baby talk.'

Alex laughed. 'I won't ask. Same time next week? Unless I see you in the park before?'

'Look forward to it,' Polly said.

To her surprise, she meant it.

Chapter Twenty-Four

Louise

Louise's alarm went off and she groaned. Six o'clock was too early to get up, especially on a Sunday. But it was the only way to get the den to herself and she had to do this to try and get Nick back. She picked up her newly purchased DVD. *Thirty Days to a New You*, the strapline stated, beneath a photo of a nubile young instructor. Clutching the DVD, she crept quietly down the passageway towards the den, stopping off to go to the loo. The last time she'd exercised, eight years ago at an antenatal exercise class, she'd wet herself while attempting a jumping jack. She wasn't going to make that mistake again.

In the den, she shut the door, put the DVD in the machine and started the 'gentle warm-up'. Within minutes she was sweating profusely. Her breasts were also taking a battering, swinging alarmingly up and down and side to side beneath her pyjamas. She clamped them to her chest with both hands and looked desperately around the room for a solution – ideally Colin Firth, who could hold her breasts in position. He was nowhere to be seen, but luckily one of her bras was on the clothes airer. Grabbing it, she put it on over her pyjama top, then continued the warm-up in comfort. Or less discomfort, at any rate.

The gentle warm-up led to a beginner's level workout. Sweat poured down her face and her pyjamas clung to her underarms and crotch as she performed squats, lunges and other inhuman exercises. This is for Nick, she told herself, gritting her teeth through something called a mountain climber. Who climbed mountains on all fours while thrusting their knees into their chin? She was never going hiking with them.

'Almost there,' the instructor said. 'Just another twenty seconds to go.' Twenty seconds? That wasn't almost there. That was miles from the cable car, which any normal person would use to scale a mountain of this terrain. She closed her eyes and pictured Nick's face. Was it wrong that she quite wanted to punch it?

'Louise?' Erica stood at the door in her running gear. 'You're exercising.'

'Talk about stating the bloody obvious,' Louise said. Well, she tried to say it, but instead omitted a low groan. Her arms gave way beneath her and she slumped to the floor, every muscle in her body aching.

'Good for you.' Erica's voice wobbled slightly. 'Original workout gear.'

Louise didn't respond. She wasn't sure she'd ever be able to respond to anything ever again.

'I've got something for you.'

Erica disappeared and Louise rolled over onto her back. The instructor was still on the screen, extolling the virtues of exercising multiple muscle groups.

'Here.' Erica returned and held open a copy of *Vogue*. 'This hairstyle would look great on you.' She smiled in what she probably thought was an encouraging way. 'Much more flattering than that pudding-bowl bob you've got.'

She left the room. Louise's multiple muscle groups didn't have the strength to respond.

–

Later that afternoon, Louise leant against the landing window and watched the traffic below, waiting for Nick's car to appear. The twins had told her about their dad's new purchase. Nick hadn't even told her he was taking a driving test. A week earlier she'd watched from the same window when he'd picked George and Tess up for their adventure holiday. He'd laughed good-humouredly when they'd asked where the DVD players were. 'We can play I-Spy,' he'd said. It was a wonder the twins had still gone.

While they'd been away, Louise had tried to distract herself with work, but her thoughts were on what Nick and the twins were doing, and if they wished she were doing it with them. Not that she'd wanted to go – camping in Wales and taking part in aerial adventures, kayaking and gorge walks was not her idea of a holiday. Tess hadn't been keen either. The only gorging she liked to do on holiday involved ice creams. Hopefully she'd moaned enough to spoil the holiday and Nick would abandon his rose-tinted vision of a character-building, bonding break and realise that a week on a sun lounger in Spain wasn't so bad after all. Maybe, after a week away, he'd think she wasn't so bad after all either. She could only hope.

Polly came out of her room with Summer on her hip and Jasmine at her side. Jasmine was cradling something in her palm, a large smile on her face.

'Careful you don't lose it or the tooth fairy won't come,' Polly said. She looked at Louise. 'Sure you want me to answer the door?'

Louise nodded. She longed to see Nick but had twenty-nine days of the 'New You' DVD to get through first.

'Silly question,' Polly said. 'You'd have changed out of your PJs if you were going to see Nick.'

Louise looked down in surprise. She hadn't realised she was still in her pyjamas. She even had the bloody bra on over them too.

A car door slammed and she spun back round to the window. Nick's burgundy Scenic was parked outside at an angle, one tyre up on the pavement. And there was Nick, unfolding his long limbs from the car. He opened the back door and Tess and George jumped out and ran to the house. They were back.

Her lovely family was back. Nick linked his fingers together and stretched his arms up above his head, then from side to side, jutting his hip out in the opposite direction. Louise pressed both palms against the windowpane, craning her neck to see more. Shaking his arms loose, Nick walked to the back of the car to get the twins' bags. His blue, check shirt rode up as he reached into the boot, revealing the waistband of his boxer shirts. Louise's fingertips squeaked against the glass.

The doorbell rang. Ignoring every instinct to run downstairs and hug them all to her hammering chest, Louise eased the fire door open, crept to the top of the stairs and peered down. Tess and George came into view in the hall below.

'Don't I get a goodbye?' Nick's voice carried up the stairs. Louise's stomach turned into a Slinky.

The twins hugged their dad, then ran across the hall and down the passageway.

'Would it be ok to come in please?' Nick asked Polly. 'I need to speak to Louise.'

Louise gripped the bannister tightly.

'Sorry, she's out,' Polly said.

'Out?' Nick sounded horrified. 'She hasn't seen the twins for a week and she's gone out?'

Polly looked up to where Louise was hiding at the top of the stairs. Louise shook her head frantically. Polly turned back to Nick and smiled weakly.

'She, er...' She trailed off.

Come on Polly, Louise urged. Think of something. Polly looked over her shoulder at Louise again, a helpless expression on her face. Thankfully, before she caved under the pressure and shouted, 'She's right there', Erica came out of the dining room, her phone in her hand. She saw Louise hovering at the top of the stairs and winked.

'Hi, Nick,' she smiled. Louise frowned. There was no need for her to smile at Nick *that* much.

Polly looked at her with relief. 'Nick wants to see Louise. I told him she's not here, but she wouldn't have gone out when she hasn't seen the twins for a week, would she?'

'Of course she wouldn't,' Erica said smoothly. 'But she can't come to the door right now.' She patted her stomach. 'Tummy upset. Been in and out of the loo all day and doesn't want anyone else to get it.'

Louise put a hand over her eyes.

'Oh. Sorry to hear that.' Nick shuffled on the doorstep. 'Tell her I hope she's better soon. Please.'

'Will do.' Erica closed the front door.

'That was awful. I hate lying,' Polly said.

'Yes, it was awful.' Louise stomped down the stairs. 'Couldn't you have come up with something else? Me on the toilet isn't exactly the image I want to leave him with.'

Erica threw her hands in the air. 'Would you rather he thought you were so heartless you didn't want to see the twins? Or worse – saw you in that outfit?'

'Course not, but diarrhoea? You could have said I was on a conference call and couldn't be disturbed or something. Anything but the trots.'

'Look on the bright side,' Erica said. 'You'll look amazing when he next sees you in comparison to how he thinks you look right now.' Her phone rang and she darted into the dining room to answer it.

George came back through the passageway. 'What are you wearing?'

'Never mind that. Come here.' Louise hugged him. 'Missed you.'

'Can we go to the park?' George asked. 'Dad and I played football every day and I'm getting better. He says if I practise I—'

'Sorry, love, I can't.' Louise was in agony after that morning's workout. If she bent down to put her crocs on, she might not get back up again. 'We could play a board game?'

George shook his head. 'I'll ask Polly.' He ran up the stairs, tripping twice before reaching the top.

'Where's your sister?' Louise called after him.

'Dunno.' The fire doors shut behind him.

Louise lumbered down the passageway, each step a feat in overcoming the pain barrier.

Tess was in the kitchen, eating a packet of crisps. 'Hi, Mom.'

'Hi, love.' Louise enveloped Tess in a huge hug. 'How was the holiday?'

'Ok, I guess.' Tess nestled her head into Louise's chest. 'Mo-om.' She elongated the vowel. 'Can we go shopping?'

'What for?'

'Wanna get some new clothes. I've got holiday money left over from what Dad gave me.'

'What's wrong with the clothes you've got?'

'They're babyish. Jasmine's are real cool.'

Louise snorted. 'Probably cost a lot more than what Dad gave you.'

'Please Mom. Can we look at least? When you've got changed,' she added.

'Sorry, love. I can't today.' Leaving the house would involve washing and dressing and Louise ached too much to do either.

'I hate you.' Tess stomped her foot. 'Wish we lived with Dad all the time.'

She pulled away and knocked into Jasmine, who was coming in the door with Polly. Jasmine's hand flew up into the air and she cried out in anguish.

'My tooth.'

'Tess,' Louise said sharply. 'Help Jasmine find her tooth.'

'Why?' Tess sounded on the verge of tears. 'Only jerks believe in the tooth fairy. Jerks who wear dumb, show-off clothes.' She turned and ran up the passageway. Moments later her feet thundered up the stairs.

Louise grimaced at Jasmine. 'Sorry about that. Probably tired from her holiday. Take no notice.' She'd let Tess cool down, then go and talk to her.

Polly took Jasmine's hand. 'You believe what you want to believe, poppet.'

She led her out into the garden and Louise lowered herself carefully into a chair at the table and picked up the copy of *Vogue* Erica had given her. She turned the glossy pages, wincing as her biceps announced their distress at having to perform so arduous a task. The magazine didn't seem to have a horoscopes page. It was mainly pictures of skinny women bent awkwardly to show off their shoes or holding fancy bags that were bigger than they were. So this was Erica's world. She remembered Erica's excitement one evening when she'd brought home a new bag – a Herpes, was it? She frowned. No, that couldn't be right. Whatever it was, she'd had her name on a waiting list for months. Louise had spluttered into her tea when Erica revealed it cost £1,300. 'It has a coordinating passport sleeve,' Erica had said defensively, stroking the soft leather, as though that justified the expense.

Louise reached the page Erica had earmarked for her and studied the model's choppy, jaw-length bob. Her hair looked glossy and natural. Bet she'd never had nits. She ripped the page out, folded it in half and pushed it into her pyjama pocket. She put the magazine down and was getting up to look for Tess when there was a knock at the front door. Louise ignored it, but a minute later there was another, louder knock. Grumbling, Louise hauled herself up and ambled down the passageway to answer it. With any luck it'd be a Jehovah Witness. She could do with slamming the door in someone's face.

Picking her way through assorted shoes that had been kicked off in the hall, Louise reached the door and opened it. Nick towered above her, holding a scruffy, blue rabbit that Tess slept with. Louise gasped and her hands flew to her chest. She was still wearing the bloody bra over her pyjama top. And it wasn't even her good bra.

'Tess left this in the car.' Nick pushed his glasses up. 'Sorry you're ill. You look terrible.'

Louise pressed her lips together. She couldn't deny the diarrhoea without admitting that she looked this terrible voluntarily.

'We need to talk when you're better.' Nick thrust the toy rabbit at her. 'Call me when you're up to it.'

He turned and left, tripping down the steps in his haste to get away. Louise shut the door. She'd blown it. Avoiding him until she'd transformed into a new and improved model had been her last chance to win him back. There was no hope left for their marriage now. Hugging the toy rabbit to her chest, she trudged across the hall, back down the passageway to her room, climbed into bed and pulled the covers over her head.

Chapter Twenty-Five

Erica

Erica had never been to a sewage works, but she suspected this was what one would smell like. On a bad day. She stared in horror at Polly changing Summer's nappy on the kitchen table.

'Won't be a sec,' Polly said, one hand clasping Summer's ankles so that her bottom was suspended in mid-air, the other cleaning her with some premium exfoliating wipes Erica had got from the make-up studio.

Erica wrenched the back door open and wafted it back and forth. Summer twisted round to watch her and put a hand into her soiled nappy.

'Careful, poppet.' Polly tugged another five-pounds-a-pop wipe from the pack and ran it across Summer's hand before adding it to a mound of brown wipes on the table.

Erica gagged. 'We eat off that table.'

'Don't worry, I'll clean it when I'm done.'

'Clean it? You need to burn it.' Erica turned away and gulped in fresh air from the outside, trying to ignore the squelching and scraping noises going on behind her. Where was Louise to issue a health warning when Erica needed her?

Jasmine skipped into the kitchen. 'The tooth fairy came!'

'Told you she would,' Polly said.

'Tess was wrong and you were right.' Jasmine held up a five-pound note. It was more than Erica usually left, but she'd spent half the weekend at the studio and guilt had loosened the tooth fairy's purse strings.

'Lucky you.' Polly slid a clean nappy under Summer's bottom. 'We can go shopping later, if you like?'

Erica tensed. Shopping was her thing, not Polly's. 'I'll take you,' she said quickly.

Jasmine grinned.

'Not today, though, sweetie, I'm working.' Jasmine's smile dropped and guilt coursed through Erica. 'We'll go another time soon, I promise. What do you want to buy?'

Jasmine's large white teeth dug into her lower lip as she considered the question. 'Definitely not tampons.'

'I should think not.' Erica gave Polly a where-the-fuck-did-that-come-from? look.

'There's something I need to tell you.' Polly looked embarrassed. 'The other day they asked where babies come from.'

Erica laughed. 'Bet that wasn't awkward.' She hugged Jasmine. 'I'll tell you all about it tonight.'

'Polly told us everything,' Jasmine said. 'Did you know the real word for a twinkle is a vagina?'

Heat surged through Erica. 'You told her?' How dare Polly? Explaining the wonder of how new life was conceived was one of the rites of passage. Not that there had been much wonder about Jasmine's conception. Erica had discovered she was at the optimum temperature for ovulation about three minutes before she had to leave to catch a flight to Milan. Dan hadn't even had time to remove his trousers.

Polly lifted Summer down from the table. 'They kept asking. In the end I thought, what's the harm? They need to know.'

'Yes, but it's my job to tell Jasmine, not yours.'

Polly smiled apologetically. Erica swallowed down her anger and forced herself to remember how indebted she was to Polly. If it wasn't for her pulling Jasmine away from the oncoming car that night, Jasmine might not be around to be given ad hoc sex education lessons.

'I've thought of a question.' Jasmine looked up at Erica through her dark fringe. 'How long does it take?'

'Nine months,' Erica said quickly before Polly could answer.

'Not that. The bit when the man…' Jasmine thrust her hips to and fro like an out-of-sync body-popper.

Erica tensed. How graphic had this sex education lesson been?

'We didn't talk about that,' Polly said, her cheeks red. 'I think the children have been embellishing amongst themselves.'

Erica crouched down and hugged Jasmine. 'We'll talk about this properly tonight.'

'Do you have to go?' Jasmine's brown eyes were like saucers. 'I never see you. Please stay.'

Talk about tugging at the heartstrings. Meryl Streep's daughter had given her less grief in *Sophie's Choice*.

'Sorry, sweetie, I have to.'

Jasmine's lower lip wobbled.

'But I'll get back early and take you to the Italian where they let you put your own toppings on the pizzas. Sound good?'

Jasmine gave a resigned nod and Erica kissed her goodbye and stood up.

Polly held a hand out to Jasmine. 'Fancy watching a film?'

'What did you have in mind?' Erica asked, unable to keep the sarcasm out of her voice. '*The Joy of Sex*, maybe?'

'About the sex thing,' Jasmine said thoughtfully. 'Do you have to kiss while you're doing it?'

–

'All set?'

Erica's stomach tightened at the sound of Rob's voice. She nodded and felt her pulse quicken when her eyes met his. Her phone beeped and she welcomed the opportunity to look away, until she read Louise's text stating it was her turn to put the recycling out. Why did everyone think refuse collection was her responsibility? Rob held the door to the minibus open for her. He was such a gentleman. Bet he wouldn't ask her to put the bins out.

They had a whole day together, out on location filming VTs for the remaining *Sing to Win* contestants. She took a seat and Rob sat next to her. The seats were narrow and she could feel his shoulder and thigh against hers. Pressing her own thighs together, she tried to ignore the sensation building between her legs. Her pelvic floor seemed to be doing an intensive aerobics workout. A few more journeys like this and she wouldn't have to worry about bladder control when she was older. The rest of the crew chatted, but for once she and Rob were silent. Was his lack of conversation down to boredom, or disinterest... or was he worried she fancied him? But he had sat next to her. Maybe he fancied her? If he did, surely there'd be some tell-tale sign. She glanced casually at his lap. A newspaper lay across it. Did it just happen to be there or was it concealing his ardent desire?

'Want a closer look?' Rob asked.

She inhaled sharply. Was this another of her smutty dreams? Was he going to whip the paper away to reveal an enormous hard-on? He passed the newspaper to her. No hard-on. She was ashamed to realise that she was disappointed.

'Thanks.' She shook the paper out and held it up to hide her flaming cheeks. How was she going to get through an entire day when she was fantasising about his penis before they'd even got out of the car park?

The minibus started up. 'First stop, London Eye to film a VT for the boy band's version of "Love is All Around",' Pixie shouted.

'Nice to get out,' Rob said. 'Most VTs feature the contestant pacing their dressing room, taking deep breaths and saying, "Oh my God, I can't believe it".' He pressed his fingertips to his cheeks and widened his eyes in the exact way the wannabes did and Erica laughed. 'They're all the same.'

'I know.' Erica put a hand on his arm without thinking. 'I'm sure there's a factory churning out identikit wannabes somewhere.' His arm was warm and firm. She snatched her hand away and gripped the newspaper. 'Remember, some of their outfits are held together with safety pins,' she said. Much safer if she kept their conversation professional. 'Don't let them be filmed from the back. Or below the waist when the girls are clambering out of the limos. Their legs tend to go akimbo. Deliberately, I'm sure.' A vision of her own legs deliberately going akimbo beneath Rob flashed through her mind and she ran a hand across her hot brow. So much for keeping it professional.

'Got it,' Rob said. 'Why do they get to travel in limos while we're stuck in this shitty minibus?'

'I'd rather be in this shitty minibus than listen to them moan about their outfits all the way. I've packed three choices each but they'll still complain.'

'Good point.' Rob smiled and his eyes went to her hairline. 'You've got newsprint on your—' He ran his thumb over her forehead. Erica's pelvic floor performed several star jumps. She folded the newspaper up carefully and resisted the temptation to rub it over her entire body.

'Sorry Jasmine and I couldn't make it to Cambridge,' she said. It was time to straighten the mix-up about her and Dan. 'Jasmine's dad—'

'Listen up,' Pixie shouted. 'Skylar's singing a number from *The Lion King* so we was going to film her with the cast at the theatre.' *Were* going to film her, Erica thought. 'Change of plan,' Pixie continued. 'They was at a do last night and Simba's got food poisoning, so we're going to head to Trafalgar Square and get footage of Skylar with the lion statue thingies.' Erica rolled her eyes. They were lion statues. Why add the word 'thingies' to the sentence? Although, she realised guiltily, she managed to add Rob's thingy to many of her own internal musings.

'You were saying,' Rob said. 'Jasmine's dad…'

'Yes.' She cleared her throat. 'He's—'

'Erica.' Pixie leaned over the seat in front, propping her breasts up on the headrest to ensure maximum exposure. 'Hope we're not going to have any tantrums from Skylar about her outfit today. Got a lot to fit in and can't afford to lose time 'cos you wasn't prepared.'

'*Weren't* prepared,' Rob said. 'And Erica is.'

Pixie sucked her cheeks in, reversed her breasts off the head-rest and turned back.

Erica giggled. 'Glad I'm not the only one left who appreci-ates the correct use of grammar.'

'Youngsters today.' Rob shook his head exaggeratedly. 'I blame social media.'

'Me too.' Erica's hand was on his arm again. 'They think LOL is an actual word. They say it instead of laughing.'

'No way.'

'Way.'

'We must sound well old.'

'What–ev–uh.'

'Just keepin' it real.'

'Soz.'

'Shall we stop now?'

'Yes, please.'

They grinned at one another and their eyes locked. Erica looked away hurriedly. He was a work colleague, nothing more. She wouldn't exchange lingering looks with Pixie, so she mustn't with Rob. Not that Pixie's Snapchat-influenced attention span would allow for anything as long-lasting as a linger.

'How's the house share going?' Rob asked.

Erica reflected on the discovery that Polly had told Jasmine the facts of life, tried to take her shopping and used the kitchen table as a changing mat.

'Has its ups and downs,' she said. 'I wouldn't be able to do this job if it wasn't for Polly and Louise's help, but it's challenging at times.' She used the word 'challenging' loosely – really, she meant 'shit'.

'In what way?' Rob asked.

Erica looked at him in surprise. Dan never asked more than one question. That ran too great a risk of leading to a conversation. After talking to clients and colleagues all day, he was too tired to face a discussion on something he had no views on, or had a conflicting view on, resulting in yet another argument.

She batted her hand through the air. 'Boring stuff. You don't want to know.'

'Yes, I do,' Rob said. 'But we can talk about something else if you want to take your mind off it.'

Erica thought for a moment. He didn't need to hear about the petty who's-left-the-ironing-board-out? arguments that drove her mad, but it'd be good to get a different perspective on the childcare element from someone who wasn't involved.

'When we had a nanny, Jasmine was fine with me working the hours I do,' she said. 'But since we moved into Polly's, she doesn't want me to leave. I've explained that I have to work, that my career's important, but she doesn't seem to understand in the way she used to.'

Rob nodded. 'Living at Polly's is new for her. Maybe that's why she's a bit clingier.'

'But she loves Polly, and Polly loves her.' A bit too much for Erica's liking.

'You know you're leaving her in safe hands then. You shouldn't feel bad.'

'I do, though.' Erica fiddled with her hoop earring. 'And I worry Jasmine will give up on me and start to prefer Polly.' A lump formed in her throat and she stared out of the bus window. She sounded so pathetic and needy. Just as well Dan didn't delve into her innermost thoughts if this was what happened when someone did.

'Jasmine's never going to love Polly anywhere near as much as she loves you,' Rob said warmly. 'It's your guilt making you think she does. Not that you should feel guilty,' he added. 'But I know it's part of being a parent. I feel guilty constantly for not being there every morning and evening for Daisy. But me and her mum weren't right together. I have to remind myself that an unhappy home would be worse for her mental wellbeing and make sure I see her as much as possible. You're there a lot more for Jasmine than I'm able to be for Daisy, so please stop being so hard on yourself.'

Erica bit her lip to stop herself crying. She hoped Rob was right and that she was over-reacting to Jasmine's attachment to Polly. It wouldn't be for much longer anyway. As soon as the show was over, she'd have more time for her daughter. They just needed to get through the next few weeks.

–

The minibus drove into the studio car park and suggestions of an after-work drink were touted. After a day of pandering to the wannabes they were all in need of alcohol. On the whole, the VTs had gone well, although filming Skylar atop one of the lion statue 'thingies' had taken longer than planned, as each time she clambered on and off, she provocatively flashed a hot pink thong. Erica had watched Rob's carefully concealed frustration grow as he asked yet again for her not to give away all her secrets with each dismount.

'You up for a drink?' Rob asked. After their earlier chat, he'd seemed to sense she was feeling more emotional than she let on and had changed the conversation to a lighter subject – mocking his attempts to get sponsorship by livestreaming a training run. He claimed people had withdrawn their donations when they saw him in action, which Erica very much doubted. She'd look him up on Instagram when she got a chance. Purely for running technique tips. For the rest of the day, they'd chatted and laughed in between shoots. It was the most fun Erica had had at work for a long time. 'I owe you one for all your help today,' Rob added.

'I didn't do anything,' Erica said lightly, her tone belying the quivering in her abdomen at the thought of spending more time with him.

'Yes, you did. I'd still be trying to film Skylar if you hadn't intervened.'

Telling Skylar that everyone could see her panty-liner had got her to snap her legs together quicker than a Venus flytrap. Erica looked at her watch.

'I can't. Promised Jasmine I'd take her for a pizza and I'm already running late.'

'Maybe some other time?'

Erica followed Rob off the bus, pretending not to hear his invitation or notice his outstretched hand. She regretted the latter when she lost her footing on the step and one leg plummeted to the ground at a much quicker pace than the rest of her body. Shrieking, she clasped the door.

'You ok?' Rob steadied her and she nodded. He tucked his fingertips into the pocket of his jeans and looked down. 'Daisy and I might go for a picnic at the weekend. Shall I take your number and let you know, in case you and Jasmine want to join us?' He looked almost bashful. Not a trace of Dan's cockiness or swagger. She put Dan's cock out of her mind. She had bigger things to think about, such as how she was going to get across London and home in time to take Jasmine out when it was already six o'clock.

'Sure.' She reeled off her number. 'Sorry, I've got to run.'

Rob nodded. 'Bye, Erica. See you soon.'

He walked away towards the row of bars around the corner from the studio. For a moment she was tempted to join him. Everyone was going; it was a harmless drink. But she couldn't let Jasmine down. She'd be late back, but at least she'd be back.

Forty minutes later, after an excruciatingly slow tube ride, Erica boarded the train home. Polly hadn't replied to the text she'd sent explaining the delay and there was no answer on her mobile or the landline. Erica fidgeted in her seat, worrying that her lateness might create abandonment issues for Jasmine. Her phone beeped and she snatched it up eagerly. But it wasn't a reply from Polly, or a random demand from Louise. It was a text from an unknown number.

Erica's inner thighs contracted. She fancied a lot more than just the picnic.

Guiltily, she forced herself to think about Dan. They'd barely spoken since their fight but needed to get past it. Jasmine must miss him. Erica certainly missed her mildew-free, monsoon shower and walking across a floor without having to scrub the soles of her feet afterwards. But did she miss Dan? She shook herself. Of course she did. Just because she didn't think about him didn't mean anything was wrong with their relationship. She was busy, that was all. And these fantasies about Rob were merely a side effect from not having had sex with Dan for a while. Nothing more.

She'd text Rob later saying they couldn't come to the picnic and send Dan a message now instead. She stared blankly at her phone. She couldn't think of a single thing to write.

–

Erica dropped her bag inside the back door and hurried through the house to the den where they were all watching television. Erica stiffened when she saw Jasmine. She was sitting at Polly's feet and Polly was brushing her hair. That was Erica's job. She always brushed Jasmine's hair.

'Hi,' she said, fighting the urge to lunge across and wrestle the brush out of Polly's hand. Usually Jasmine jumped up, threw her arms around Erica and gave her a huge, toothy smile. Today she didn't even look round. Erica crouched down beside her. 'Sorry I'm late, sweetie. Let's get to the restaurant and have dinner.'

'We've already eaten,' Polly said.

Erica forced a smile. 'We can still have pudding. I hear their gelato's amazing.'

'Not hungry.' Jasmine leaned back against Polly.

'Can we go, Mom?' Tess said. George looked round hopefully.

'No,' Louise replied, her eyes fixed on the screen.

'I'm so sorry.' Erica tucked a strand of Jasmine's hair behind her ear. 'Work over-ran.'

'That's ok. We had fun, didn't we, poppet?' Polly kissed the top of Jasmine's head.

Erica went cold. What the fuck was going on? Yes, she owed Polly big time, but she should be the one kissing Jasmine, not Polly. She stood up and held her hand out.

'Let's go upstairs, sweetie.'

'Don't want to.'

'I've got you a present.'

Jasmine's head turned slightly. 'What is it?'

Good question. The make-up girl had given her a freebie earlier, but she couldn't lure Jasmine away with a cream that promised to banish liver spots.

'It's a surprise,' she said, trying to remember how much cash she had in her purse. Not a lot, thanks to the overly generous tooth fairy.

'Is it an iPod?' Jasmine asked.

'No fair.' Tess stuck her lower lip out. 'I wanna iPod.'

'Be thankful you've got a duvet cover,' Louise said.

Erica groaned. How had she managed to forget again? Poor Jasmine had been sleeping with her single duvet inside a double cover since a slug slimed her original one.

'I hate my bed. It's scratchy.' Jasmine's brown eyes widened innocently. 'I'll come if I can sleep in your bed.'

Erica would have frowned if the Botox allowed it. Why was Jasmine behaving this way? She'd never been defiant before.

'She can come in with me and Summer,' Polly said.

Jasmine beamed. 'Epic.'

'No!' Erica exclaimed. Polly was taking looking after Jasmine too far now. If she wasn't so desperate for childcare, she'd tell her so. She turned to Jasmine. 'Of course you can sleep with me. Let's go up now.'

'Mom—' Tess started.

'Don't even think about it,' Louise said. 'There's barely room for me in my bed.'

Jasmine deliberated for a moment. 'And you've got me a present?'

Erica nodded. She didn't know how else to get Jasmine away from Polly. She'd look at the Apple store online, see how much iPods were and try and buy back some loyalty. One of her cards must have some credit left. Jasmine hugged Polly goodnight and walked out of the room, ignoring Erica's out-stretched hand.

'It's no trouble for her to sleep with me, honest,' Polly said.

'No, thank you,' Erica said stiffly. '*I'm* here now.' She turned and followed Jasmine upstairs, gripping the bannister tightly. She'd never felt jealous of the nannies. They were employed by her to look after Jasmine in a caring, but professional way. This was different. This was intimacy. This was nurture. This was what it felt like to be replaced.

Chapter Twenty-Six

Polly

'Hi there.'

Polly jumped at the sound of Alex's voice. 'Oh, hi.' She held up a loaf of sliced bread. 'Just getting the kids' lunch. They're at home. With Erica,' she added. 'Not on their own.' She'd double-checked this time. 'How about you?'

Alex grimaced. 'Bess is in labour.'

Polly inhaled sharply. 'Is she ok?'

'Think so. I've been watching YouTube clips and apparently dogs just get on with it, unless there's a problem.' He scraped his hair off his face. 'I'm a bit nervous. What if something goes wrong?'

'It'll be fine.' Polly surprised herself by how calm she sounded, considering she could barely deliver a sentence some days, let alone a litter. 'Just follow Bess's lead.'

Alex didn't look convinced. 'I'd better get back. Was hoping to get some latex gloves, but they don't do them here.'

'I've got some.' Erica had bought them the week she was on toilet-cleaning duty. 'I'll pay for this, then get them for you.'

Five minutes later she handed the gloves to Alex, who'd been pacing up and down the pavement outside her house, wringing his hands, like an expectant dad.

'You're a life saver, thank you.' He hesitated. 'Don't suppose you want to help, do you?'

'What? With the puppies?' Polly's earlier calm strapped on a pair of running shoes and shot off into the distance.

Alex nodded. 'It'd be nice to have someone there in case Bess needs help.'

Polly's throat tightened. 'I'm not good with blood.'

'There won't be any. It's unbelievably clean. The pups come out individually wrapped in little sacs.'

She clasped her pendant. 'I can't, sorry.' She couldn't take the risk. 'Wouldn't be fair to leave the kids without any notice.'

'No worries. I shouldn't have asked. Thanks for the gloves.'

Polly saw the look of concern on his face before he walked away. Guilt gnawed at her. She didn't know Alex very well, but felt sure that if their positions were reversed, he'd help her. And if there wasn't going to be any blood, what was stopping her? She took a deep breath.

'Alex, wait,' she called. 'Give me two minutes.'

He grinned. 'Thank you,' he said, his blue eyes sparkling.

Polly ran down the passageway to where Erica sat at the kitchen table on her laptop.

'Sorry to ask, but can you have the kids for a couple of hours?'

Erica's head snapped up. 'What?'

'It's an emergency or I wouldn't ask.' Polly pulled her cuffs down. 'I've promised to help deliver some puppies.'

Erica shook her head. 'What?'

'A friend's asked me. I need to go now.' Polly laughed nervously.

Erica did not laugh. She looked petrified.

'Don't forget Louise is here,' Polly added.

Erica looked as comforted as someone who'd been told that they had six weeks left to live instead of five. Louise had been holed up in her room for the last few days, only emerging for essentials such as using the loo or getting a drink. Judging by the stale aroma wafting from her pyjamas, washing wasn't considered an essential.

'Can you make them sandwiches for lunch?' Polly pointed to the bread she'd just bought. 'And get Summer up from her nap in an hour. She'll be confused, but tell her I'll be back soon.'

Erica nodded numbly.

'If you want to get out of the house—'

'I *do* want to get out of the house,' Erica said eagerly.

'—you could take them to the park,' Polly finished.

'Oh, you mean with them.' Erica's voice shook.

'I'll be back as soon as I can.' Polly ran to the car park where the children were playing football, explained what was going on and kissed them goodbye. Erica sat trance-like in the kitchen. Polly faltered. What was she doing? She couldn't just dump the kids on Erica. How would Summer react when she woke up and her mamma was gone? She wouldn't go, she decided.

'Polly,' Alex called from the hall. 'Don't mean to pressure you, but I need to get back to Bess.'

'Is that a man's voice?' Erica sprang up. 'Your friend's a man?'

Polly felt her cheeks redden.

'Well, go on then.' Erica ushered her towards the passageway.

'Maybe I shouldn't. The kids—'

'Will be fine,' Erica said firmly. 'Go and play with his puppies.' She winked theatrically.

'It's not a euphemism.' Polly's face was on fire now.

'Polly,' Alex called again, a note of urgency in his voice.

'She's coming,' Erica called back, pushing Polly out of the kitchen. 'Don't do anything I wouldn't do,' she whispered. 'Or would like to do,' she added wistfully.

–

'Here it comes,' Alex said.

He and Polly knelt by a huge box that Bess was nestled into. She whimpered and a pup slithered out onto the towels.

Bess licked the puppy, breaking it free of the sac it was encased in, and chewed through the thin umbilical cord, both of which she swallowed. Alex was right about it being clean. Disgusting, but clean.

Within an hour another four pups had been born.

'Just one more to go.' Alex refilled Bess's water bowl. 'Well done, girl.'

Polly watched the puppies in wonder, as they suckled at Bess's belly, feeling their way with their noses, their eyes glued shut.

'It's coming already,' Alex said.

They watched as the final puppy slid out without any fanfare or even a whimper this time. Polly couldn't help but feel envious at the ease with which it came out. No thirty-five-centimetre-head crowning, followed by shoulders so wide they made eighties shoulder pads look slimline. Bess was so blasé about the experience, she didn't seem to have noticed the last delivery.

'She should have torn the sac open by now,' Alex said a minute later. 'It won't be able to breathe.'

Polly's throat tightened. 'What do we do?'

'Tear it open ourselves, then rub it to get it breathing.' Alex handed a pair of latex gloves to Polly. 'Ready?'

She nodded and they reached into the box and lifted the puppy out. The sac was lubricated – Polly chose not to think about what with – and it slipped around in their hands. Alex gently broke open the sac and wiped the puppy's nose and mouth. Polly wrapped it in a towel and massaged its damp fur. The puppy lay lifeless in her lap.

She and Alex looked at each other nervously.

'Stillbirths are quite common in litters,' he said sadly.

'Come on, poppet,' she said, rubbing more firmly. 'You can do it.'

The puppy didn't move. Tears pricked Polly's eyes. The puppy couldn't be dead, not before its life had even begun. That wasn't fair. Although, as she knew from experience, life often wasn't fair. She gave the puppy a final, enthusiastic rub. *Please wake up*, she begged it silently. *Don't let another life be wasted.*

Alex put a hand on her arm. He looked shaken too. 'Sorry, Polly. I think it—'

The towel squirmed and the puppy let out a tiny cough.

'It's breathing,' Polly exclaimed, holding it close. The puppy wiggled in her hands, slowly at first but growing in strength by the second. She placed it next to Bess's belly and within moments it was suckling, along with its siblings.

She and Alex grinned at each other, laughing with relief. It took Polly a minute to realise that Alex's hand was gripping hers. She also realised that she didn't mind.

–

'Hi, I'm back.'

The children were sprawled across the floor in the den watching TV. Erica was slumped in a chair, one hand over her face.

Summer ran over and wrapped her arms around Polly's legs.

'Mamma stay,' she said.

'I will, poppet.' Polly picked her up and covered her face with kisses.

Erica looked up. 'Is it really you?' Her eyeliner was smudged and her usual sheen-free face shiny. 'You're not a mirage, are you?'

Polly laughed. 'Has it been that bad?' She hugged Oliver, blew a kiss to Jasmine and waved at the twins.

'Bad?' Erica sprung out of the chair and strode to the kitchen, heading straight for the fridge. 'No, it hasn't been bad.' She took out some wine, unscrewed the cap and swigged from the bottle. 'It's been fucking awful.'

'What happened?' Polly took two glasses from the cupboard.

Erica's hand shook as she filled them. 'They don't listen. They just demand things. Food mainly.' She took a long drink from her glass. 'We went to the café in the park and George got his arm trapped in the vending machine. The manager had to get him out. Don't know how you do it every day.' She shuddered at the prospect. 'Tell me about your man. I need a distraction.'

'He's not *my* man,' Polly said. 'He's just a friend. His son's in Oliver's class.'

The kitchen door opened and Louise trudged in. Her hair, which was usually lacquered to within an inch of its life – and the life of anyone passing – hung lank around her face and her skin was waxy.

'Feeling better?' Polly asked.

Louise shrugged and plonked herself down at the table. 'Any wine going spare?'

Erica inhaled sharply, got a whiff of Louise and exhaled immediately. 'You've been in bed all day, leaving me on my own to look after the kids. How come you're suddenly well enough to have a drink?'

'Oh, give me a break.' Louise poured herself a glass and took a large, loud slurp.

Grimacing, Erica rolled the foil from the wine bottle into a ball and tossed it into the bin. The ball ricocheted off the mound of rubbish already in there and landed on the floor. 'For fuck's sake. Who's on bins this week? It can't be me again.'

'I'm bathrooms,' Polly said. She hadn't actually done them yet, so to compensate, she opened the dishwasher to stack the plates from lunch.

'It needs unloading,' Erica said.

'Why didn't you unload it then?' Despite her melancholy, Louise couldn't resist getting involved.

Erica bristled. 'I've been slightly busy today. While you've been lounging around in bed.'

'I wasn't feeling well,' Louise protested.

Polly sighed. 'If you can see it needs unloading, surely it makes sense to unload it.' If she could manage some basic jobs when at home, why couldn't Erica?

'You didn't empty the bin when you saw it was full this morning,' Erica said.

It was true. She'd had to cram Summer's nappy in, but if Erica wasn't prepared to unload the dishwasher, why should she empty the bin?

Erica turned to Louise. 'When's the cleaner starting?'

'Don't look at me,' Louise snapped. 'You're supposed to be finding one.'

'I haven't got time with work and the charity run next week. I'm going to pay for it. Isn't that enough?'

Were they seriously arguing about housework? 'Let's not fight,' Polly said.

Erica took a deep breath. 'You're right. Sorry.'

Louise grunted and took another slurp of wine. Erica shot her a look of pure disgust.

'Another fiver went missing the other day.' Louise nodded in the direction of the housekeeping jar on the windowsill. 'Did either of you use it?'

Polly and Erica shook their heads.

Louise crossed her arms. 'One of the kids must be taking it then. About forty pounds have gone missing now.'

Erica stiffened. 'I hope you're not calling Jasmine a thief.'

'I didn't say it was Jasmine.' Louise paused. 'But I noticed a load of sweet wrappers in her room.'

'Forty pounds on sweets? She'd be the size of a fucking house,' Erica snapped. 'Tess is in that room, too, remember?'

'Are you saying Tess is the size of a house?' Louise spat.

'If the extra-wide shoe fits…'

'Stop.' Polly put a hand up. 'No one's stealing money to buy sweets. I get them at the leisure centre.'

'You what?' Erica couldn't have looked more horrified if Polly had admitted to buying them crack. 'Jasmine's been off with me lately and now I know why. She's stuffed full of sugar and E numbers.'

'It's just a little treat,' Polly said. 'To make up for you being at work so much.'

Erica's face hardened. 'I have a successful career. I'm a role model – proof that being a woman doesn't mean staying at home and doing the dishes. That shouldn't require compensation.'

Polly chose not to point out that Erica *hadn't* done the dishes on the one day she was home.

'Hate to go back to it,' Louise said, not looking as though she were hating it at all. It was the most animated she'd looked for days. 'But we still don't know where the money's going.'

'It's not gone on sponsoring my run, that's for sure,' Erica said pointedly to Louise.

'Someone must be taking it,' Louise continued, ignoring Erica's thinly veiled hint. 'Tess said that Jasmine always has new clothes.'

'How dare you?' Erica's hands tightened into balls. 'They're freebies from suppliers and, before you say it, I bought her iPod.'

'I'm not talking about big purchases, like iPods,' Louise said. 'Something smaller, like clothes or a toy.'

Polly tugged her sleeves down over her hands. None of the children would steal, she was sure of it. Someone must have taken the money to buy something and forgotten. It could even have been her.

Polly delved into her bag for her purse. 'Just remembered, I borrowed it. I'll put it back now.'

Erica turned to Louise. 'Hope you're going to apologise.'

Louise frowned. 'What about all the other money that's gone missing?'

'I'm sure there's an explanation.' Polly pushed a five-pound note into the jar. 'Let's put it somewhere safer though.' She opened the cupboard above the kettle and the door swung off on one hinge, almost decapitating her.

'George had an incident with the door.' Erica glared at Louise. 'Haven't noticed you bringing his vandalism up in the house meetings.'

Louise tutted. 'He doesn't mean to break things.'

Polly put the jar on the highest shelf and wedged the door back into place.

Erica stood up and looked down at Louise. 'Jasmine didn't take that money.'

'No?' Louise pursed her lips. 'Well, someone did.'

Chapter Twenty-Seven

Louise

The back door opened and the sound of thudding feet and voices poured into the house. Louise pulled the covers up over her head. She should have used the time Polly and the children were out to draw up the rotas for the following week, but as no one else gave a toss about them, why should she? She'd get up and help Polly in a minute.

'When you do a number two, does it go down the pipe and back out the tap?' one of the children asked from the kitchen. Louise closed her eyes. Or she'd stay where she was.

After a few minutes their chatter moved out into the court-yard and the house was quiet again. Her phone beeped on her bedside table. She considered ignoring it. Nick wasn't due to call the twins until later. But it might be from HR, asking when she'd be back at work. She honestly didn't know. For the first time in her career, she had no enthusiasm for her job. Strange, given that telling people what to do was her hobby and being paid to do it was even better.

Sighing, she pulled the duvet down and looked at the phone. It was her daily horoscope. *Venus and Neptune come together. This is a good time to let go and forgive others*, she read. Forgive others? The astrologer was having a laugh. She'd never forgive her sister. If it wasn't for her, she and Nick would still be together.

Louise sat up. Her head spun with the sudden movement combined with lack of food. She couldn't remember the last time she'd gone any length of time without eating; she'd even managed to wolf down a ham sandwich during labour. She'd sneak into the kitchen while Polly and the children were outside so she didn't have to speak to anyone.

Louise opened her bedroom door and caught sight of her reflection in the mirror behind the optics. Her hair was stuck to her head with grease and the jogging bottoms and baggy t-shirt she'd been wearing for days smelled like a school locker room. She really should shower and change, but what was the point? A bang came from the kitchen. She ducked back into her room, then realised what the noise was. It was the broken cupboard door. The housekeeping money was in that cupboard. Louise hurried along the passageway to the kitchen. Which one of the little sods was it? She hoped it was Jasmine. That'd teach Erica to judge her.

Wrenching the door open, Louise looked across to see the broken cupboard door hanging off its one remaining hinge. A figure knelt on the work surface, one hand in the housekeeping jar, the other holding a five-pound note. A strange gulping noise came from Louise's throat and the girl turned. When she saw Louise, her small brown eyes widened and her cheeks turned crimson.

Heat surged up Louise's chest and neck. 'What the bloody hell do you think you're doing?'

Tess's bottom lip wobbled.

'My room, now,' Louise hissed. Tess clambered down from the work surface, sniffing loudly. Louise snatched the money from her hand, shoved it back into the housekeeping jar and wedged the cupboard door back before leading Tess along the passageway. Her neck and face felt as though they were on fire. Erica was going to have a field day with this after Louise had practically accused Jasmine of stealing. More than a field day – she'd have a week-long agricultural convention with talks from the Farmers' Union and televised sheepdog trials.

Louise shut the bedroom door and glowered at Tess. 'How could you? I've been accusing everyone else when it was you.' Tess hung her head. 'What are you doing with it all?'

'Saving to buy a *Frozen* nightie, like Jasmine's,' Tess said in a small voice.

'The Disneyland one that disappeared?'

Tess nodded miserably. 'That's why I wanted to go shopping. So I could buy her another one.'

'Why?' Louise's patience was running out and she hadn't had much to start with. 'It'll turn up.'

'It won't.' Tess twisted the hem of her t-shirt. 'I ripped it. I was only trying it on, but it was too small. I hid it in your gym bag at home.'

Louise frowned. She had a gym bag?

'If I get another one, no one will know.' Tess's eyes filled with tears. 'Why didn't it fit? It's not fair.'

Life's not fair, Louise thought bitterly. If it was, chocolate would count as one of your five-a-day, her sister would be the fat one and she and Nick would still be together.

'What you gonna do?' Tess whispered.

Louise didn't know. She should speak to Nick about a suitable punishment, but he'd insist they told the twins about the separation.

'What possessed you to try the nightie on?' she snapped. 'You must have known it wouldn't fit.'

Tears poured down Tess's face. 'I thought if I wore it, I'd look pretty too.' She swiped at her cheeks. 'But it tore. 'Cos, 'cos…'

She was crying so much it was hard to distinguish her words. Louise was too angry to care what she had to say.

''Cos, 'cos…' Tess sobbed.

Louise pressed her lips together. How the bloody hell was she going to face Erica?

''Cos I'm fat,' Tess wailed.

Fat. That hideous word had plagued Louise all her life. From her sister, school friends, her first husband, work colleagues – not to her face of course, but she could tell they were thinking it every time she helped herself to a biscuit during a meeting. Her whole life had been a vicious circle of seeking comfort in food, feeling ashamed and eating more. She'd never got any support growing up. When she'd come home crying, her mum had given her a bar of chocolate, which just fuelled the problem. Instead of offering advice on how to stand up for herself, she'd accepted that that was the way it was for people like them. Nick was the only one who'd never made her feel ashamed. He'd embraced her curves, especially the two frontal ones, but she'd still felt ugly. Why? She wasn't sure.

Louise looked at her daughter. She didn't want her to suffer the same way she had and still did. Empathy and love and shame cancelled out all her earlier frustration and self-pity. It was up to her to break the cycle and give Tess a chance to be something other than the victim.

She knelt down and stroked Tess's hair. 'I was like you at school.' Tess took her thumb out of her mouth and looked up. 'I'd have done anything to be one of the popular girls, rather than the fat, ugly one that everyone teased.'

Tess clamped a hand over her eyes. 'Even you think I'm fat and ugly,' she wailed.

'No! I didn't mean it like that.' Louise prised Tess's fingers away to reveal her soft, fresh, tear-streaked face. 'Don't ever think that. You're beautiful.' Her voice wavered. 'You don't have to be the same as everyone else to be beautiful.'

Tess's eyes slid round to meet hers. 'But I wanna be the same.'

Louise blinked hard. 'So did I. But I've just realised that being thin and having cool clothes doesn't make you prettier.' She stroked Tess's cheek. 'Being you is what makes you pretty. Being a good person, who's kind and honest and fun. And you're all those things.' Louise put an arm around Tess and she snuggled into her. It felt warm and comforting and right. 'What you did was wrong, you know that.' Tess nodded. 'But you did it for a nice reason – to make up for a mistake you made. Next time, tell the truth. People will think a lot more of you than if you lie. Be yourself and everyone will like you.'

Tess's eyes grew wet again. 'I get so mad at everyone for being better than me. It makes me do mean things.'

Louise braced herself. 'What kind of things?'

'I make fun of Jasmine for being too scared to slide down the bannister,' Tess said.

'That's not too—' Louise started.

'And I let her hamster out of its cage.'

'Maybe the catch wasn't done—'

'And hid her school bag on our first day here. And rubbed your writing off the whiteboard so she'd get in trouble. And called her names.'

Guiltily, Louise acknowledged that Tess had probably learned that behaviour from her. She wasn't backward in coming forward when it came to having a moan about people. For years the twins had thought her sister's first name was Bloody. Louise hugged Tess tightly. Erica was going to be furious when she heard all this. Unless, of course, she didn't hear it. Louise kissed Tess's forehead.

'If you ask me, we should forget any of that happened and start again. Both of us. I don't always treat people the way I should, either.' Especially Nick, she thought with a heavy heart. 'If we're nicer to them, then they'll be nicer to us.' She kissed Tess's cheek. 'And stop thinking you're fat and ugly, because you're not.'

'You're not fat and ugly either, Mummy. Just a bit squishy.'

'Squishy, eh?' Louise tickled Tess, who squealed with delight. Louise couldn't remember the last time she'd hugged Tess or George or played with them or even paid them any proper attention. The thought filled her with shame. 'Well, you're not squishy. You're beautiful, and I'm not going to stop telling you that 'til you believe it.'

Tess stopped wriggling and snuggled into Louise's chest. 'I love you, Mummy.'

It took Louise a moment to realise that Tess wasn't using an American accent.

'I love you too,' she whispered.

Hot tears trickled silently from Louise's eyes as she wrapped her arms around Tess. This was what it was all about. Looking out for the twins and helping them grow into decent adults who other people wanted to spend time with. From now on that was going to be her priority. It might be too late to repair her marriage, but it wasn't too late to improve her relationship with the twins. Starting now.

Chapter Twenty-Eight

Erica

Erica double-checked the locker door, tucked the key into the side pocket of her Lycra shorts and smoothed down her red Crisis t-shirt. She was glad they weren't running in aid of the RSPCA. The electric blue singlet was a tough look to pull off.

Rob was putting his things in the locker next to hers. It had made sense to travel to the event together as they were both going straight from work. Several other people from the studio were also taking part, including Pixie, but it made no sense at all to travel with her because she was an annoying twat.

Rob wore the same red t-shirt, but with loose black shorts. It was the first time she'd seen his legs and it took great strength of mind not to give them a once-over. Unfortunately, her eyes didn't have the same strength – she blamed the weight of her lash extensions – and her gaze dropped to his thighs. She swallowed hard. They were muscular, without being comically exaggerated turkey-drumstick proportions. His calves were toned and covered with soft, dark hair. Not so fine her own would make his look effeminate if they were ever allowed to grow, or so hairy they could be shorn and made into blankets for every homeless person in London. No, they were just right.

'Ready?' Rob asked.

Erica tore her eyes away from his legs and nodded, unsure why she had butterflies in her tummy. She wasn't running any further than she had before, so didn't need to worry about crumpling to the ground with exhaustion and Rob having to drag her over the finishing line as though they were the Brownlee brothers, or being carted off by a kindly OAP in a St John's ambulance. Rob's arm brushed against hers as they joined the throng of other runners. The butterflies flapped their wings harder.

'Where's the starting line?' Erica asked, as she was jostled from either side by people in the crowd striding confidently forward. Every few seconds she was nudged into Rob, which, although far from unpleasant, wasn't an efficient way to travel. If it was going to be like this all the way round it'd take them all night. Again, a night with Rob wasn't exactly a hardship, but in her dreams there hadn't been quite so many spectators.

'Starting times are staggered.' Rob pointed into the distance at banners positioned high up that specified different running speeds. 'To do it in fifty minutes, we need to head to the five-minute kilometre marker. Have you ever done an organised run before?'

Erica shook her head.

'Thanks for doing it today then.'

'Why wouldn't I?' Erica echoed his words. 'As you said, it's a great cause. There's a man who camps out near the studio. Used to have his own business but lost everything in the recession. It's a disgrace when we have so much and he has so little.' She shook her head. 'Worst thing is, I'm a hypocrite. Instead of donating every spare penny I have, I kid myself that buying Pete a coffee and sandwich every day makes up for splashing out on clothes and cocktails and all the other materialistic crap I buy. Makes me feel guilty every time I think about it.'

'I know Pete,' Rob said. 'I drop him off a flat white and BLT every day.'

'That's what I get him too,' Erica said. 'Hope he likes them and didn't ask for it the first time because he couldn't think of anything else.'

They laughed and Erica realised she had her hand on Rob's arm. She quickly let go. She had to stop being so tactile.

Although, being so penned in by the other runners that she was practically nestled into Rob's chest didn't exactly help with that.

'The crowd will thin out when we reach the starting points,' Rob said.

Erica cringed. He didn't think she was using it as an excuse to press herself up against him, did he? She tried to move away.

'It's not you,' Rob said in a low voice. 'The man to my left keeps treading on my foot. I'm not going to be able to walk, let alone run, if he carries on.'

'Don't worry. I'll give you a piggyback if it comes to that.' Any excuse to get her hands around those thighs.

Rob laughed. 'I can tell by your toned arms that you're strong, but I'm not sure you want fourteen stone on top of you.'

His smile froze as he realised what he'd said. 'I didn't mean—' he began.

'I know.' Erica smiled. 'Don't worry.'

They walked in silence for a moment, Rob no doubt kicking himself for his choice of words, Erica contemplating how it would feel to have Rob's fourteen stone on top of her. Bloody nice, that was how.

'This is us.' Rob pointed up at the five-minute banner and they stepped to the side, allowing the faster competitors to go ahead.

Erica realised that there were a lot more people behind them than there were ahead of them.

'What happens if I can't keep up the five-minute pace all the way?'

'You'll be tasered by one of the marshals,' Rob said. 'It only hurts for a minute.'

'Ooh, let's steal one to keep the wannabes in line.'

Rob grinned. 'Wish they really did have them now.'

A crackling came from loudspeakers positioned around them and a spokesperson for Crisis thanked them all for supporting the charity, explained the evacuation procedure and safety points and wished them well. A buzz of excitement carried through the crowd, as they waited to start.

'Everyone's smiling now,' Rob said. 'Half of us will be crying in an hour's time.'

Erica laughed. No way would Rob be struggling. Not with those thighs to propel him along. And no way she was going to lag behind. There had been a note of admiration in his voice when he'd said she was strong. She wasn't going to ruin this image by dawdling.

'Not us,' she said, running up and down on the spot. 'We'll be having a celebratory drink in an hour.'

'Fighting talk. I like it.'

They grinned at each other and joined in the chant, counting down from ten to one. Then they were off. Not exactly in a *Chariots of Fire*-type sprint, more a gentle jog while apologising to various people around them as their elbows knocked against each other or they accidentally cut someone up while trying to overtake the person in front. Erica sighed. They'd never hit their fifty-minute target with all these people in the way. It was busier than the cut meats aisle in Waitrose on Christmas Eve. Frustrated, she scanned the crowds, surprised to see so many people had turned out to support the event.

'Got anyone cheering you on?' Rob asked.

'No.' It was too late for the children to be out and Dan was in China. Not that she thought he'd have come if he was in the UK. Dan's hand was still sore and Erica was convinced he was milking it. He'd told everyone it was a sporting injury and judging by the way he wore his sling with pride, he seemed to have convinced himself that was how it had happened. Unless the Olympic Committee was now chaired by Hugh Hefner, Erica was pretty sure masturbating wasn't a sporting discipline.

As Erica watched runners around them waving at the onlookers, she wondered if she should have invited her London friends. But they had busy lives and it made more sense to meet up when she could actually speak to them.

'I felt guilty enough asking people to sponsor me, without them having to come and watch too,' she told Rob. A gap opened up in the runners and they picked up their pace. 'Any friends coming to see you?' Her stomach turned at the thought of a special friend enveloping him in a congratulatory smooch at the finishing line. She'd be beautiful of course, with glossy hair and a shine to her skin that couldn't be more dissimilar to the unattractive sweat currently forming on Erica's face. Nor would she have wet patches under her arms. Erica could feel hers spreading across her non-absorbent charity t-shirt. Perhaps the RSPCA singlet would have been a better look after all. It was irrelevant though; she couldn't compete with Rob's siren girlfriend. Not that she needed to, she reminded herself firmly. She was with Dan. Her stomach turned again.

'Past Daisy's bedtime and I don't have any friends.'

Erica laughed. 'Ah, I feel bad for you now.' She didn't feel bad at all. She felt elated.

Now that the runners were more spaced out, they were able to pick up speed and they ran in companionable silence for several kilometres. Erica pushed herself hard, determined to prove to Rob that she was worthy of the moniker strong.

'We're making great time,' Rob said when they passed the 7k marker. 'If we carry on like this, we'll definitely do it in fifty minutes.'

'What's the fastest time you've done before?' Erica asked.

'Fifty-four minutes.' Rob wiped his forehead with the back of his hand. 'Hadn't appreciated quite how fit you are. I'm having to work hard to keep up.'

Erica resisted the temptation to say that she'd been appreciating how fit he was since they first met.

'Want me to slow down?' she teased. 'I feel bad for over-exerting you.'

Rob returned her smile. 'Let's see how we go. If I'm not holding you back.'

Erica waved her hand. 'I'll take a hit for the team.'

They ran in silence for another kilometre before Rob spoke.

'Can I make an observation?' he asked. 'I know you were joking about feeling bad just now, but you say it about a lot of things. Not being around enough for Jasmine, spending money instead of donating it all to charity, asking your friends to sponsor you. You carry a lot of guilt on your shoulders and you shouldn't.' He paused to catch his breath. 'We may not know each other that well yet, but I get the sense that you're a kind, thoughtful person. You shouldn't keep beating yourself up.'

They didn't know each other that well *yet*. That implied he assumed they'd be spending more time together, getting to know each other better. Lovely as that sounded, it was no good. She had to explain the situation with Dan. Not the entire situation. Not that they were barely talking and she was increasingly wondering what the hell she was doing with him. They'd been here before: when Jasmine was a baby and Erica was too exhausted with work and night feeds to give Dan the attention he needed; when a styling job in New York overran and she'd got home twenty-four hours later than planned, meaning Dan had had to cancel some meetings to – shock, horror – look after his own child; and the time she'd eaten the last of the guacamole, not realising he'd planned to have it with smoked salmon and scrambled egg for lunch. Each of these times there had been a period of avoidance and annoyance and they'd got over it. They'd get over this too. She just had no idea when.

She took a deep breath. 'Been meaning to tell you this for a while. I think I accidentally gave the wrong impression about—'

A searing pain shot up her calf and she cried out.

'Erica.' Rob's voice was full of concern. 'What's wrong?'

The muscles in Erica's calf contracted again and she stopped. 'Cramp,' she whimpered. She'd had it before, but never to this extent. Before, it had been a mild tightening that she could shake off. This time it felt as though the inside of her leg was twisting itself into knots. And it fucking hurt.

Rob put an arm around her.

'Lean on me,' he said. 'Then try and stand on the leg. If you can bend your knee and put some weight on it, the muscle will loosen up.'

Erica did as he asked, gritting her teeth as her lower leg spasmed. Rob dropped to his knees. Keeping one arm around her waist, he massaged her calf with his free hand, firmly kneading the sore muscle and working into a knot, which pinpointed the pain. Erica leant forward, resting both hands on his shoulders, bending and straightening her sore leg until the muscle relaxed and the pain ebbed away.

'I'm ok,' she murmured. 'Thank you.'

Rob took his arm away from her waist – Christ, she must have been in a bad way not to have appreciated that more – and continued to massage her calf, this time with both hands. Erica closed her eyes, now fully aware of every sensation his touch was creating. His fingers were firm and deft, manipulating the muscle to relax it further. She bit her lip to stop from crying out, with pleasure this time, rather than pain. If only the cramp had been higher up.

'What seems to be the trouble?' A man's voice broke through her thoughts and her eyes snapped open.

'Nothing,' she said automatically.

'Cramp,' Rob said at the same time, releasing his grip on her leg.

Erica hoped her disappointment didn't show.

'Let's take a look at you.' The older gentleman, wearing a St John Ambulance uniform with the name 'John' on his ID tag, gestured to them to move to the side of the track. Erica briefly considered asking if he was *the* St John, but suspected he'd been asked before.

'No need, thanks.' Erica held a hand up. 'My friend's magic fingers sorted me out.'

Oh, how she wished they would.

'No harm in applying a heat pack,' John, possibly St John, said. 'Best to be on the safe side.'

191

'Honestly, I'm fine.' Erica took a step forward and winced.

'You don't look very fine,' Rob said.

'It's just a bit tender. I can run it off.'

Rob frowned. 'You don't want to tear the muscle.'

'Have some water,' John said. 'Could be dehydration.' He took two bottles from a coolbag and handed them to Rob and Erica. If he could turn them from water into wine, then he'd earned his sainthood.

He didn't – just 'John' it was, then – but Erica drank gratefully anyway. She'd been so busy at work that afternoon, she'd barely drunk anything. Rob took a few mouthfuls, then tipped the rest of the bottle over his head. The water cascaded down his chest, soaking his t-shirt so that it clung to him. Erica's legs trembled and she knew it was nothing to do with the cramp. Rob shook his head and a few droplets of water landed on Erica. She was never washing again.

'Try some stretches,' John said. 'Lunges and toe-touches to stretch out the calf. If you feel better after those, you might be alright to carry on if you take it easy.'

'Ok. Thank you.' Erica extended her leg back and leant into the stretch, holding it for a couple of minutes before doing the same the other side, then finishing up by touching her toes. Nearby spectators watched with mild interest. This was so embarrassing.

'How does it feel?' Rob crouched down and wrapped a hand around her calf again.

Amazing, Erica thought.

'As I said, take it easy.' John hoisted the coolbag onto his shoulder. 'And have a hot bath tonight with Epsom salts if you've got them.'

'Will do,' Erica lied. Nothing would entice her to have a bath at Polly's, with its mouldy slip-proof mat and permanent ring of grime around the tub. She'd end up dirtier than she had been before she got in. 'Thanks for all your help.'

John nodded and wandered off, looking around for the next casualty to give saintly care to.

Rob gave her a leg a final squeeze. Every atom in Erica's being tingled.

'The muscle's relaxed, but it could be sore for a while.' He stood up. 'Sure you want to go on? There's no shame in finishing early due to injury. You've done 8k.'

'No way,' Erica said. 'My leg's never felt better, thanks to your massage.' She could only begin to imagine how the rest of her body would feel if Rob paid it the same attention.

'Ok, but say if it seizes up again.'

They began to run. It only took a few steps for Erica to realise that her calf was tender and she couldn't go anywhere near as fast as she had before.

'Are you ok?' Rob asked.

'Yes, but I'm going to slow you down.' She gave Rob a regretful smile. 'You go ahead. I've held you back enough.'

'No way. Never leave your buddy behind. It's the law.'

'But you were on target to hit your PB.'

'I don't care what time I get.' Rob grinned. 'I only mentioned PBs to make you feel better about asking people for money.'

'Really?' Erica was astounded. Dan viewed every scenario as an opportunity to demonstrate he was better now than he'd ever been. That philosophy served him well at work where success was judged on his most recent accomplishments, but wasn't so great in the bedroom where he strived to make Erica come quicker each time they had sex. Just as well they hadn't done it for a while as he probably expected her to orgasm before he'd even entered her by now.

'Really,' Rob said. 'Won't make any difference to the amount we raise and that's what this is about.'

'Thank you,' Erica said. Despite his assurance that he didn't care what time he made, she still pushed herself, ignoring the burning in her calf, until she felt Rob's hand on her arm.

'We're not soldiers in the field,' he said gently. 'No one's going to die if we get there later than we'd aimed to.'

Reluctantly, Erica slowed down to a gentler pace. 'I feel like a failure.' She bit her lip. 'I pride myself on my resilience and determination. I don't want to be this pathetic wimp who can't run a few kilometres without causing a fuss.'

'I've never seen anyone create less of a fuss. You'd have tried to carry on if your leg had broken.'

'A broken leg's a decent excuse to stop. Cramp isn't. That's just embarrassing.' She'd never be able to tell Dan. He'd probably blame it on her period.

'Good to see you took my advice to give yourself a break on board.' Rob nudged her with his elbow. 'Getting cramp doesn't make you any less resilient or determined. It makes you human.'

'But you could still—' Erica started.

'Stop,' Rob said. 'If I was injured, would you sprint off or hang around to make sure I was ok?'

'Hang around, of course.' Erica answered without thinking. She'd crawl around the course if it meant spending time with him.

'There you go then,' Rob said. 'We're a team. We can call ourselves "Roca".' He laughed. 'Sorry – crap name.'

Erica smiled up at him. Usually she preferred to operate alone, both in her job and her personal life. Team Roca, however, was something she'd very much like to be a part of. Her smile wavered. She wasn't sure she felt the same about team Dan and Erica.

Chapter Twenty-Nine

Polly

'Just the two of you? I was expecting the whole gang.' Alex opened the gate and Summer hurtled through and wrapped her arms around his legs.

'They're at an activity day at the leisure centre.' Polly tugged the sleeves of her new floral dress down over her hands and checked that the skirt hadn't got rucked up at the back. She'd protested that it was too short, but Erica insisted her legs were too good to be hidden away. That had been before Polly had said Jasmine could sleep in her bed. Now Erica behaved as though she'd like all of Polly to be hidden away.

Alex picked Summer up. 'Want to see some puppies?' Summer grinned through her dummy and nodded. Polly made a mental note to advise the children to scream very loudly if a man invited them to look at his puppies under normal circumstances.

Polly followed them along the path, past the brightly coloured flowers and well-kept lawn. The garden couldn't have been more different to hers. Fortunately, Summer's vocabulary wasn't developed enough to ask where the tarmac and rusting appliances were. Alex paused to point out a butterfly to Summer. Polly smiled, watching the way his dishevelled brown hair caught on the collar of his red, faded shirt when he moved his head. Her inner thighs tingled, rekindling feelings she hadn't experienced for a long time. What was happening to her? It was as though helping with the puppies had released something.

And that something was in danger of being her knicker elastic. Alex glanced over his shoulder, his blue eyes bright against his tanned, slightly lined face. The tingle in her inner thighs moved up an inch.

'You ok?' he asked, registering her flaming cheeks.

She nodded. 'Just a bit hot.'

'Maisie's homemade lemonade will cool you down.'

'Your kids are here?' Polly's hot flush cooled instantly. She'd assumed they'd be at some sort of holiday club, like hers were. 'We can come back another time. Don't want to be in the way.'

'Don't be daft.' They reached the house and Alex stepped back to let Polly pass. 'The six puppies might be in the way, but you're not.' Alex put his hand on the small of her back to usher her through the door. His palm was warm through her dress. 'They're in the utility room. Follow your nose. As soon as I clear one puddle up, another appears.' His eyes crinkled. 'Can I tempt you to have one? I'll do a deal – buy one, get five free.'

Polly laughed, but her throat felt tight. What if Alex's kids didn't like her? What if she said something stupid that made Alex not like her? What if… She stopped herself. What Ifs belonged in her past, not her future. She took a deep breath for courage, regretting it instantly as the stench of dog hair and urine flooded her nasal passages. Alex hadn't been exaggerating. But some of the aromas Summer released weren't exactly pleasant.

Alex's daughter, Maisie, knelt on a blanket stroking Bess. Six tiny black Labradors suckled at her belly, their eyes closed contentedly. Summer crouched down and watched the puppies feeding. She took her dummy out and turned to Polly.

'Boobies,' she breathed in wonder.

Alex and Maisie burst out laughing and Summer grinned delightedly at her audience.

'Polly, Summer, this is Maisie,' Alex said. 'Max is playing football in the garden.'

Maisie smiled shyly. She had Alex's floppy brown hair and blue eyes. Polly returned the smile and knelt down on one of the few pieces of newspaper that wasn't yellow. The puppies wriggled and nudged each other with their paws. One was smaller than the others. Polly guessed it was the one she and Alex had saved and felt a surge of affection for it.

Alex fussed over Bess, topping up her water and food, and Polly felt a surge of affection for him too.

'Boobies,' Summer said again. Everyone politely ignored her this time, so to regain their attention, she took it to the next level. 'Boobies,' she said louder, turning to Polly and patting her breasts as though warming up a couple of juggling balls.

Alex clapped his hands together. 'Maisie, why don't you show Summer the garden?'

'Ok.' Maisie kissed Bess's head, then sprung up and led Summer out of the room.

'A man,' Summer exclaimed loudly from the kitchen. 'Mummy needs a man.'

Polly froze.

'Sounds like they've found the gingerbread men,' Alex said. 'Don't know about you, but I definitely need one.'

In the kitchen, Polly perched on a bar stool. She hadn't paid much attention on her last visit, but now admired the oak worktop and Quaker-style units, each with a slightly different coloured wood door. She followed a knot in the wood with her fingertip.

'Perk of the job,' Alex said. 'I get to keep the wood if a tree's got to be cut down.'

'You made it?' Polly gasped. 'It's beautiful.'

Alex grinned. 'You think so? My love of carpentry drove my ex mad. Although I was often in my workshop to get away from her.' He grimaced. 'Sorry, too much information. Don't want to bore you.'

Hearing he didn't like his ex-wife was definitely not boring. 'When did you break up?'

'Five years ago. She ran off with my business partner.'

'That's horrible.'

'Hurt at the time, mainly because of the kids, but we got over it. There's a much better atmosphere in the house without her.' Alex handed Polly a glass. 'What happened with you?'

Despite the cold of the frosted glass in her hand, a bead of sweat trickled down her spine. If she told him she'd never hear from him again. What sane man would want that baggage on top of two kids and six puppies that were on a mission to turn his house into a water feature?

'Long story,' she said. 'But we got over it too.' She took a sip of lemonade, hoping the tart juice would mask the bitter taste of bullshit. She'd never be over what happened.

'Lovely garden,' she said, to change the subject.

'Won't be once those dogs get out there. They can't leave 'til they're eight weeks old. It'll be a cesspit by then.'

'Are you trying to put me off having one?'

'No, please do.' Alex raked his hair out of his eyes. 'I think the tiny one's got a soft spot for you.'

'The kids'd love one, but we haven't got a garden; just a courtyard and huge car park from when it was a B&B. It's a waste of space really.'

'Why don't I take a look? Bet it wouldn't take much to turn it into a garden. It'd be great for the kids, as well as a dog.' He pointed to where Maisie was pushing Summer in a swing. Max chased a football, his blond hair flopping around his face. He was much fairer than Alex. More like his mum, Polly supposed, surprised by the dull ache in her stomach this thought created.

'Oliver's a great footballer,' Alex said. 'Be even better if he had somewhere to practise at home. Maybe we could talk about it over dinner one night?' he added softly.

A pocket of heat exploded in Polly's stomach. Did he mean just the two of them or did his invitation extend to their combined artillery of four children and seven dogs?

Alex seemed to read her mind. 'I was thinking just us, if you can get a babysitter.'

Polly put a hand to her necklace. Dinner without the children was a date. A date was betraying the man she loved. She couldn't brush him aside, as though he didn't mean anything. She clutched her pendant. But he was dead. No matter how hard she wished he wasn't, it wouldn't bring him back. Turning a date down wouldn't either. And he'd want her to be happy. She was only thirty. There was a lot of life left ahead of her and it'd get pretty lonely when the children got older, started hanging out with their friends more and, eventually, left home. What would she do then? Sit in the house on her own, only stirring when a rep came round selling miniature kettles? She let go of her pendant. No, that wasn't what he'd want for her.

Alex raked a hand through his hair. 'I'll see if the kids want a drink. Think Summer would like the lemonade?'

'That'd be really nice, thank you.'

'Sure it's not too sour? I can put more sugar in.'

Polly smiled shyly. 'No. I mean dinner would be really nice.'

–

Erica strolled through the back door. Polly didn't look up from the hob, where she was stirring a bolognaise sauce. Even if she hadn't seen Erica pass the window, she'd know it was her. Living together these past two months had made their movements, mannerisms and habits almost as familiar as her own. Erica was instantly recognisable by the click of heels, tinkling jewellery, a regular vwoop sound as a text was sent or received and the occasional swear word when she stumbled. Well, more than occasional. And not just when she stumbled.

Louise's arrival was heralded with the click of the kettle and a heavy sigh, closely followed by a lengthy off-loading of whatever was making her sigh. This could range from the injustice of Poundland charging more than one pound for its school uniform, to how ridiculous Nick's horoscope was that day – 'What does it mean there's an unwelcome noise in his life? George brought his fart gun with him.'

'Hi,' Polly said.

'Hi.' Erica made no effort to start a conversation.

'I'm making spaghetti bolognaise,' Polly said, desperate to instil some normality.

'With ingredients?' There was disbelief in Erica's voice.

Polly nodded. She couldn't take umbrage when all her previous meals had come straight from the freezer or a tin.

'It's my turn to make dinner.' Erica sounded put out, even though she'd rolled her eyes that morning when Louise had reminded her. 'I *am* capable of providing a meal.'

'I know. Just trying to help.' Polly didn't add that she was trying desperately to get their friendship back on track.

There was silence for a moment, then she felt a hand on her arm. 'Sorry,' Erica said. 'It's really nice of you. I hadn't even thought about what to order in.' She tugged her hair. 'Where's Jasmine?'

'They're all in the den.' Polly paused. 'Do you think you'll stay again this weekend?'

'Don't know yet. Depends on Dan. Why?' Erica's phone pinged and she fished it out of her bag.

'A landscape gardener's coming over on Saturday to look at the car park.'

'We won't go out there if we're here.'

'It'll be easier if there aren't any cars.'

'I'll park in the lay-by.' Erica giggled at the message on her phone. 'Roca,' she said quietly.

'What?' Polly asked.

'Nothing. Private joke.'

The sound of her nails tapping against the screen set Polly's teeth on edge. Irritation coursed through her at Erica's inability to even feign interest.

'It'd be nice if you asked first.'

Erica looked at her blankly. 'Asked what?'

Polly banged the spoon against the side of the saucepan. 'About staying at the weekend, rather than just assuming it's ok. It is *my* house.'

'Yes, it is.' Erica had a strained expression on her face, not dissimilar to the one Summer used when filling her nappy. 'You said we should think of it as our home too, but you're right that it isn't.'

'I didn't mean it like that.'

'I thought you liked having us here.' Erica crossed her arms. 'Or is it just Jasmine you like having?'

'Course not,' Polly said quickly. 'I want you all here, but I'd prefer it to just be me, Oliver and Summer on Saturday when the landscape gardener comes.'

Erica's eyes widened. 'Is the landscape gardener the "friend" with the puppies?'

Polly pulled her sleeves down over her hands.

'Fan-fucking-tastic!' Erica grinned. 'Tell me everything.'

Polly returned her smile, relief that Erica was talking to her cancelling out her irritation. 'He's divorced and his kids go to the school. He runs the football club at the park.'

'What's his name? What's he like?'

'Alex.' It felt good to say his name. 'He seems really nice.'

'Nice?' Erica looked disappointed.

Polly nodded. 'He's kind and funny and great with Summer. It's good for her to be with a man.'

'It'd be good for *you* to be with a man.' Erica winked. 'Is the car park thing a ruse to get him here and then you can—?'

'No.' Polly's stomach lurched. She hoped Alex didn't think that was her intention. 'He really is looking at the garden.'

'Oh.'

'But...' The lurch turned into a flutter. 'He invited me out for dinner.'

Erica grabbed Polly's hands. 'When? Where? We need to plan your outfit.'

Polly grinned, grateful that the earlier friction had passed.

'Tomorrow night. Only thing is, I've never left the kids in the evening before.' She felt guilty just thinking about it. Summer was used to falling asleep in her arms.

Erica's face took on Summer's surreptitious-poo expression again. She was clearly tussling with her conscience, knowing she should offer to babysit, but really not wanting to.

Louise appeared in the doorway. She'd showered and changed at last, which was a relief, both for Louise's dignity and everyone's nasal passages.

'Louise,' Erica exclaimed. 'Polly's got a date tomorrow night. Will you be here?'

'Where else would I be?' Louise sighed, then visibly shook herself and forced a smile. 'That's great, Poll. Who's the lucky guy?'

'Alex. A divorced dad from the school,' Erica said before Polly could answer. 'So you'll definitely be here tomorrow? I will too, so I'll take care of Jasmine.'

Louise nodded. 'Probably best you settle Summer first, Poll. The others can watch TV 'til they conk out.'

'They like watching films in bed. Mine's big enough.' Polly smiled at Erica. 'Jasmine loves it when we all snuggle up.'

Erica stiffened. 'What do you mean *we*? You get in bed with them too?'

Polly wasn't sure why, but the atmosphere had changed again. 'Yes,' she said cautiously.

'I think the sofa's a more appropriate place to watch films than your bed.' Erica stood up abruptly. 'I'm going to find Jasmine.' She picked up her bag and strode out of the kitchen.

Polly watched her go. How had they gone from excitedly discussing her date to Erica walking out?

'Don't mind her,' Louise said. 'Tell me about this Alex. What's his star sign?'

'Don't know,' Polly said. 'I'll try and find out tomorrow. I'm taking the kids to meet his puppies. They're only a few days old and so cute.'

'You'll have to count the twins out,' Louise said. 'I've got the day off so we can do something.'

Polly knew it was irrational, but she didn't want Louise to take the twins out. They were part of her unit. 'You don't need to do that. Save your holiday.'

'It's ok, Poll.' Louise patted her arm. 'You've done more than your bit. They're my kids after all, not yours.'

Polly wrapped her hand around her pendant, disappointment sweeping through her. No, the twins and Jasmine weren't hers. But she'd begun to feel as though they were.

Chapter Thirty

Erica

Erica ran a garment steamer over a top one of the contestants had chosen to wear in that week's show. The word 'top' was a generous description for such a flimsy item of clothing. Erica's earrings jangled as she shook her head. Maybe she was getting too old for this job. Everything seemed revealing and she'd caught herself pondering the logic of cropped jumpers the other day, temporarily forgetting that fashion had no logic.

Erica picked up the next outfit and blasted it with the steamer. There was a dull ache across her shoulders, perhaps caused by the tension that had formed between herself and Jasmine. They'd always been so close, but Jasmine was increasingly defiant, shunning her in favour of Polly, and refusing to let Erica brush her hair. Jasmine hadn't even said goodbye that morning when she'd left for work, but had gazed moodily into her bowl of cereal like a teenager.

Putting the dress back on the clothes rail, Erica reached her free hand over her shoulder and kneaded the top of her back to try and relieve the pain.

'Have you got yourself in a headlock or is this a new dance craze I don't know about?'

Every part of her tensed at the sight of Rob, including her trigger finger. A large hiss of steam burst out of the nozzle.

'Just attempting a DIY massage. Feeling a bit stiff.' If this were one of her sordid dreams, he'd bend her backwards over the clothes rail and tell her he had the same condition.

Rob stepped towards her and she gripped the steamer tightly. Another hiss of steam blasted out. She put it down before she gave herself third-degree burns and opened her mouth to speak, but couldn't think of anything to say. Since the charity run they'd been exchanging texts regularly. Only about work, of course. And funny things that had happened at work. And at home. But it was just light-hearted banter. It definitely wasn't flirting. So why, when their virtual conversations flowed so easily, was she now struggling for words?

He weaved in and out of the clothes rails towards her. Oh crap, he wasn't going to massage her, was he, like the love interest did in films, revealing a previously unknown tender side? He reached her and crossed his arms. No massage then. Erica wasn't sure if she was relieved or disappointed.

'How's your calf?' Rob asked.

'Fine, thanks.' She smiled. 'How are you?'

'Great.' He prodded the base of the clothes rail with his foot. 'I've realised I've been going about this the wrong way. All that pretence of a casual drink after work, or a play date with Daisy and Jasmine...' He looked up, uncertainty in his eyes. 'What I really want to say is, can I take you out for dinner some time?'

Erica's stomach folded in on itself. This gorgeous man was inviting her on a date. She didn't think people did that anymore. The wannabes only met people on Tinder, the concept of which had stalker/slasher movie written all over it. But she'd just been asked out properly. What a lovely position to find herself in. Given the variety of positions she'd imagined them in, it was a wonder there were any left.

He was waiting for her answer, his deep brown eyes nervous and unsure. A wave of sadness crashed over her. She had to say no. Lovely as it'd be, going to dinner could be viewed by some people – Dan, for example – as bordering on adultery. Unless, of course, she'd misinterpreted his invitation and it was just as a colleague.

She took a pair of silver hot pants off the rail and fiddled with the hanger. 'That's really kind, but, honestly, you don't have to. I'm happy to give advice about the show any time.'

'I mean on a date. Nothing to do with work. Just you and me.'

The hanger shot out of Erica's hand. No room for misinterpretation there. He fancied her. And she fancied him. It was very straightforward. How easy it would be to say yes. To go out to dinner, fall into bed afterwards, keep her two lives separate. People did it all the time. But she wasn't one of them. Her relationship with Dan had reached a stalemate and she couldn't work out how they were going to get past it, but dating another man was unlikely to help the situation. And she didn't want to deceive Rob. She had to be honest and tell him she'd love to go to dinner, but it could only be as friends, as she was still with Jasmine's dad and she was sorry if she'd unintentionally misled him.

She cleared her throat. 'Thank you. I'd love to go to dinner—'

'Erica, someone in reception for you.' Pixie appeared in the doorway.

'Could you ask them to give me a minute, please?' Erica said. She had to finish that sentence.

Pixie glowered. 'I'm not your messenger.'

'Do you know who it is?'

Pixie flicked a pink-tipped tendril over her shoulder. 'Dan Ford, I think he said.'

Erica's stomach hit the floor. What the fuck was Dan doing here? He was supposed to be in China. She looked at Rob, who was smiling at her, presumably in anticipation of the date she'd just said she'd love to go on, and blissfully oblivious as to who Dan Ford was. She had to put him straight on that point, but she'd prefer to do it in a more tactful way than introducing them to one another.

'I'd better go. Catch up with you later.'

'Look forward to it.' Rob grinned and her stomach scissor-kicked. Why did he have to be so sexy?

Erica hurried down to reception.

'Erica.' Dan pulled her to him and hugged her tightly. He smelled of stale coffee and sweat.

She pulled away. 'Why are you here? You're not due back 'til Friday.'

Dan grimaced. 'The company's undergoing a major reshuffle, which means redundancies. We're being called in in turn. My slot's at four o'clock.' His eyes were bloodshot and ringed with dark circles. His usually pristine, white shirt was crumpled and there were damp patches beneath his arms. 'It doesn't look good.'

'Maybe you're part of the reshuffle,' Erica said, not mentioning that he didn't look good either. 'They might want to move you back to the UK.'

Dan shook his head. 'It'd be a massive demotion unless they made me a member of the board, which I can't see happening.' He ran his fingers through his grey hair. His hands were trembling. 'How's it going to look if I lose my job?'

Guilt coursed through Erica. She hadn't given him any attention lately. He might be a selfish git at times, but he had a vulnerable side and right now he needed her.

'Let's go and get a coffee,' she said softly.

Dan nodded. 'I passed a place on the corner.'

Erica couldn't risk going to the café she and Rob had been to. 'There's a better one near the station.'

–

Ten minutes later they were sitting at the back of a greasy spoon.

Dan frowned into his polystyrene cup. 'This is the better one?'

Erica cleaned the table with a wipe. 'Hard to believe I know, but their...' she scanned the menu, 'bubble and squeak burgers are legendary.'

'I'll take your word for it.' He took a mouthful of instant coffee and grimaced. 'Got half a mind not to go to the meeting.'

'You've got to.'

'Why? I don't owe those fuckers anything. I've devoted my career to the company, taken out a massive loan to help fund it, and now they're going to shaft me. And what have I done it for?' He took Erica's hand. 'I'm never here. My daughter hardly knows me. I rarely see you.' Tears welled up in his eyes.

Erica wasn't sure how to react. He'd never cried in front of her before. Perhaps a bubble and squeak burger would perk him up. She offered him a menu but he shook his head.

'No point panicking 'til you've heard what they have to say,' Erica said. 'It might be good news.'

Dan continued as though she hadn't spoken. 'I'll never get that money back. I'll lose the car, the private health care, my vintage cellar plan through the Wine Society. Everything. I'll be a laughing stock.'

Despite his despair, Erica couldn't help but roll her eyes. 'Vintage cellar plan?'

'You have to spend a certain amount each year to keep your membership. I can't commit to that if I'm not working.' His voice broke. 'I was only a month away from the premier cru Côte d'Or.' He pulled her to him, pinning her arms to her sides and forcing her neck to tilt at an awkward angle to accommodate his head, which was nestled into her chest. 'At least I've got you.' His sobs intensified, oblivious to the stares and nudges from the other clientele. Erica tried to ignore them, but Dan clung onto her so tightly, she was unable to manoeuvre and was forced to peer helplessly over his shoulder at the group of men who, without wishing to stereotype, Erica suspected weren't as in touch with their emotions as Dan was right now.

She wiggled her shoulders until he released her. 'This might not be a bad thing.'

He gave a hollow laugh. 'How?'

'You could become a contractor. You'll get paid a fortune and won't have the pressure of being a partner or the long hours and travel. Jasmine will love having you around more.'

'You're right.' Dan wiped his eyes. 'Contracting carries a lot of prestige. I'll tell everyone I fancied a change.' He thumped the table. 'Fuck the company. I'll screw them for as much redundancy as I can get, pay off the loan and take a few months off to recharge. You can move back from Molly's.'

'Polly's.'

'I'll base myself in London and make you and Jasmine my priority,' Dan continued. 'Being with you two is more important than anything else.' He kissed her forehead. 'I'll show those fuckers that they can't bring me down.'

Erica smiled. This was what they needed. Something to reunite them and mend the rift that had caused them to live side-by-side rather than together for months. Instead of operating alone, they'd be team Eran. Or Daca. Hmm. The name needed work, but that was ok. The important thing was that they'd be a family. And while he was taking a break, she wouldn't need help with childcare. They'd move back into their clean, comfortable home, free of shitty nappies, mildew showers and rust-lined toilets – she hoped it was rust – and Jasmine would go back to being her placid, happy self. Happier in fact, as Dan would be there all the time.

All the time. Every morning when she woke up. Every evening when she got home. Every weekend. A sudden tightness formed in her stomach. Must be the aroma of the bubble and squeak burgers. Couldn't be anything else because this was perfect. Absolutely fucking perfect.

Chapter Thirty-One

Louise

'Morning,' Louise said to Polly, who was pulling clothes out of the washing machine. 'Getting ready for the holiday?'

'We're not going for almost a week,' Polly said.

'Well, don't leave it 'til the last minute.' Louise was planning to do hers that night. Much better to be prepared than risk leaving something. She still had palpitations when she recalled the time she'd invited a delegate to take the podium at a conference, only to realise she'd forgotten to bring the podium.

Louise slid a ten-pound note under the coffee pot. 'Sponsorship money for Erica. Better late, than never.'

'So you don't think someone's stealing money?' Polly put a hand to her chest. 'I'm so relieved. Can't believe any of the children would do that.'

Louise turned away so Polly wouldn't see her cheeks flush crimson. 'No, my mistake. Found the cash in another jar at the back of the cupboard. Sorry, should have said.'

Tess thudded into the room and Louise put an arm around her and kissed the top of her head, pleased for the distraction and to see Tess. How had she ever thought her lovely children were an inconvenience?

'Mummy.' Tess's American drawl had gone completely. 'Can we go swimming?'

Louise's heart sank. She hated swimming with a passion. It was mortifying walking around in what was basically underwear, praying she didn't see anyone she knew. It didn't get much more inconvenient than that. But she couldn't say no, not when she had eight years of being a decent mum to catch up on. Nine if you included the twins' gestation period when she'd ignored advice to consume iron-rich figs and eaten lorry-loads of Snickers bars instead, despite the midwife's peanut ban. As it happened, expectant mothers were now encouraged to eat nuts to ensure the baby *didn't* get an allergy, so she'd been doing them a favour really. They'd never have thanked her for a tolerance to figs.

'Please,' Tess begged.

'Go on then.'

'Epic!' Tess threw her arms around Louise. 'I'll tell George.'

'I can take them after we've been to see the puppies, if you like,' Polly said. 'I know swimming isn't your thing. Make up for you looking after Oliver and Summer tonight.'

Louise fought against every instinct to begrudge Polly a night out when she was stuck at home. A home that wasn't even her own.

'No, you're ok.' She took a grapefruit from the fridge, which was, regrettably, her breakfast. Placing it on a chopping board, she thrust a knife into the flesh. A squirt of juice hit her in the eye. Eating it was bad enough. It didn't need to torment her in the preparation stage too. To remind herself why she was going through this ordeal, she focused on the fact that for the first time, in a long time, she was a size sixteen. Her size twenty, threadbare, navy swimsuit was in the bin. In its place, she had a black, scoop-back, one-piece with discreet tummy panels.

She'd buy the twins some holiday clothes today, she decided. And let them choose what they wanted this time, rather than rummaging through the discount rail, ignoring Tess's grumbles that the reason the clothes were in the sale was because they were 'totally gross'.

'I'm meeting Alex at eight tonight,' Polly said. 'I'll make sure Summer's asleep first.'

Louise pushed her bowl away. Did Polly have to keep going on about her date? She'd often thought that meeting someone would help ease Polly's pain and loneliness, but it had been easy to think that when she was with Nick. Now *she* was the one on her own. Who was she going to watch *EastEnders* with? Not Erica. Since Louise had intimated that Jasmine might be stealing the housekeeping money, Erica spent the rare evenings she was at home in her room. Louise's neck grew hot at the thought. She'd tell Erica tonight that she'd made a mistake, apologise and hope it'd be forgotten about.

'We're going to the Mexican restaurant Erica recommended,' Polly said, picking up the laundry basket.

Bitterness nibbled at Louise's insides and she battled against it. The old Louise was bitter. She didn't want to be that person anymore. She wanted to be someone worthy of being a friend. Someone others liked. Someone *she* liked.

She smiled at Polly. 'Have a great time. Alex sounds like a nice bloke.'

'He is.' Polly stared into the basket. 'You don't think it's bad of me? To go on a date?'

'No,' Louise said firmly. 'Enjoy yourself.' And she meant it.

—

Louise switched her phone to silent and took a handful of popcorn before passing the tub to the twins. They'd had a full day of swimming, shopping, the hairdressers', dinner at Nando's, and were now at the cinema.

'Thanks, Mummy.' Tess wrapped her arms around Louise. She smelled of chlorine and sun cream.

'Yeah, thanks,' George mumbled. 'That waterflume was epic.'

Louise's neck flushed and she smiled at them both. 'Glad you had a good time.' She patted Tess's hand. 'This time next week we'll be in Spain and can go swimming every day.'

She used the term 'swimming' loosely. For her it consisted more of sitting on the edge of the pool while Tess and George splashed about. But it was more involved than she'd been before and they'd seemed happy just for her to be there. Very happy, if the enthusiastic cries of 'watch me, Mummy' and waves from the top of the slide were anything to go by. And she'd been happy too. She'd always been scornful of Nick's love of playing before, but now she understood. It wasn't that he particularly enjoyed throwing a frisbee back and forth for hours on end, or playing hide and seek in a three-up, three-down, or being kicked in the goolies during a gymnastics demonstration. It was that he enjoyed seeing the twins having fun and being a part of it. And so did she, now.

Chapter Thirty-Two

Erica

Dan answered the phone straight away. 'Have you finished work?'

Erica walked briskly towards her platform. 'Yes. I'm at King's Cross. Be with you by seven. What happened in the meeting?'

'It's still going on. I just stepped out.'

'Why's it taking so long?'

'Because I *am* part of the reshuffle. They're promoting me.'

Erica gasped. 'That's fantastic.'

'I know. Can't wait to update my LinkedIn profile,' Dan laughed. 'We're finalising my new contract now, then going out to celebrate.'

'Shall I come and meet you?'

'Best not. We'll be talking business.'

'Ok.' Guiltily she realised she wasn't disappointed. 'What's the promotion?'

Dan paused for dramatic effect. 'I'm head of food and beverage for the Middle East.'

'Wow! Well done.' She mentally worked out the time difference. 'How will you do that from London?'

'I won't.' He exhaled proudly. 'The job's based in Dubai.'

Erica stumbled in her heels. 'I thought you wanted to be in London, so you could spend time with me and Jasmine.'

'I did. I do. But I can't turn this down – it's too big.'

Erica floundered momentarily. 'What about everything you said this morning?'

'That was before I knew about this job. We're talking mega bucks. My bonus will pay off the loan. You can get a nanny again. I'll come back every weekend and you and Jasmine can come out during the school holidays.'

Erica shook her head. 'What about my work? I can't disappear every few weeks.'

'Let's not worry about that now. It won't happen for another couple of months; I need to wrap things up in China first.' He laughed again. 'And to think those shits at school called me a loser. Marc Hennesey's still on the base management level at his firm. Who's the loser now?' A popping noise followed by a cheer rang out in the background. 'I'd better go.' He lowered his voice. 'Thanks for this morning. You really came through for me when I needed you.'

'What about Jasmine needing you?' Erica snapped.

'Don't spoil it for me. This promotion is what I've been working towards.' Someone said his name in the background. 'Got to go. Don't stress about this. We'll sort it out.'

He hung up and Erica stared at her phone in disbelief. Everything he'd come out with that morning had been bullshit and she'd fallen for it. So much for team Eran or Daca or whatever crap name she'd tried to come up with. He didn't want to be with her and Jasmine. He wanted prestige and money. The vulnerability he'd shown was merely damage to his pride and image when he'd thought he was losing his job. Angry tears pricked her eyes. She and Jasmine were nothing more than props in his life that he picked up and discarded at will. Well, if that was how he felt about them, he could go fuck himself.

Her phone beeped with a text.

Short notice I know, but are you free for dinner tonight? I've reserved a table at Brasserie Zedel, just in case. Meet for drinks in the wine bar opposite first? Rob x

Brasserie Zedel. She'd told him how much she loved the art deco restaurant when they'd driven past on their day out filming VTs and he'd remembered. He'd shown more attentiveness in that text than Dan had shown in the last few years.

A last call for her train came over the tannoy. She'd have to run to catch it and what exactly would she be running to? Another frosty reception from Jasmine. Watching *EastEnders* with Louise. Trying not to gag while Polly changed Summer's nappy on the sofa. All while Dan celebrated his responsibility-free promotion.

She read Rob's message again. She wouldn't go for dinner, but where was the harm in a drink? Dan was out with his colleagues. She'd do the same. A flicker of guilt reminded her that this wasn't the same at all. But, she reasoned, it was the perfect opportunity to explain to Rob that Dan was still in her life – although the way she felt right now he might not be for much longer. She'd have one drink and go home afterwards. Her fingers trembled as she typed back a message.

Sounds great. I'll be there in 20 minutes. E x

She followed it with a text to Polly saying she was delayed with work and would be late home, then turned her phone to silent and headed back towards the tube.

Chapter Thirty-Three

Polly

Polly pulled on the pale green dress Erica had picked out for her date. Again, it was far shorter than she'd have chosen, but the strappy chiffon overlay had sleeves to her wrists, which was Polly's main requirement. Her phone beeped as she smoothed the dress down. It was a text from Erica.

> Held up at work. Won't be in til later. Please give Jasmine my love. E x

Polly swallowed down her disappointment. Erica had seemed so excited about the date. Now, not only was she not bothering to come home and help with her outfit and make-up, she wasn't even wishing her luck. Was she still angry because Polly had let Jasmine into her bed a couple of times? Polly checked the time. She was meeting Alex in half an hour, but it only took ten minutes to walk to the restaurant, so there was no need to panic that Louise wasn't home yet.

Fifteen minutes later, Polly rang Louise's phone. The phone went straight to voicemail. Polly tried again. Her throat tightened. Something must be seriously wrong, if Louise wasn't able to contact her or answer her phone. Shaking, Polly tried Louise's number one more time, then phoned Alex.

Ten minutes later, Alex was in her kitchen.

'I'm sure they're fine,' he said. 'She probably forgot.'

Polly shook her head. 'We talked about it this morning. She said we'd have a lovely time.'

Alex's blue eyes crinkled at the edges. 'And we will. We'll go as soon as she gets back.'

'Something bad's happened, I know it.' Polly's voice broke. 'She'd be here by now if she could be.'

'What bad thing's happened?' Oliver appeared in the kitchen doorway.

'Nothing, poppet.' Polly forced a smile. 'Just wondering where Louise and the twins are.'

Alex smiled reassuringly at Oliver. 'How many keepie-uppies can you do now?'

They started talking tactics and Polly walked out into the courtyard to get some air. Should she phone the hospital? The police? The thought made her legs buckle and she sank down onto the disintegrating steps. She didn't want to involve the police. It might lead to some questions she'd rather not answer.

Alex came to the back door. 'I could drive through town, see if I can spot her car, if you like? Did you say they were going swimming and shopping?'

Alex set off with the details of Louise's car. Luckily Oliver knew the make, model and registration number, as all Polly could remember was that it was blue. When it was actually grey. She paced the passageway and stairs, alternately checking Oliver and Jasmine in the den, Summer in bed and trying Louise on her phone. After twenty minutes, Alex rang.

'Found it,' he said.

'In one piece?' Polly asked nervously.

'Yes. She's parked in the cinema car park.'

'What?' Had Louise's car been stolen and abandoned? But that didn't explain why she wasn't answering her phone. 'I don't understand. Why is her car in the cinema car park?'

'I may be speculating wildly,' Alex said, 'but I suspect she's watching a film.'

'She can't be. She knew she needed to babysit. She wouldn't forget.' There was silence on the other end of the phone. Alex was clearly too polite to disagree with her. Polly hesitated. Maybe she hadn't mentioned it to Louise this morning. Maybe she'd imagined it. 'Cocked up again, have we?' Ian would have said. Polly shook her head. No, they had talked about the date, she knew they had. Which meant Louise had forgotten. But it was so out of character. What could have distracted her so much everything else slipped her mind?

A thought struck her. 'What films are on?' she asked.

'Some horror and the latest Colin Firth.'

Colin Firth. Yes, that was enough to distract Louise to the extent that she forgot everyone else on the planet existed; even her best friend, who was waiting for her to come home so she could go out on the first date she'd dared consider since...

'Shall I come back?' Alex asked.

...since the accident.

Cocked up again, have we? Ian whispered.

'I could get a takeaway and some wine?' Alex said. 'Not the meal out I wanted to treat you to, but it'd still be nice.'

'No,' she said quietly. 'Thank you, but it's a bit late now.'

'No worries.' Alex sounded disappointed. 'I'll call you tomorrow.'

Polly hung up. She clearly wasn't meant to go. This was a sign that it would be wrong of her to move on.

She wrapped her hand around the cool metal of her pendant. *Yes, Ian. I've cocked up again.*

Chapter Thirty-Four

Erica

Erica drained her glass and put it down on the bar. She'd arrived before Rob and had ordered them both a margarita, but had drunk hers already. And his. It hadn't taken the edge off her anger yet. How could Dan have done this to her and Jasmine?

'Hi,' Rob said behind her. How could a voice have so much impact? That one simple word had transformed her mood from angry to aroused. 'Sorry I'm late. Tube's playing up. What can I get you?' He spoke quickly. He was nervous. Erica smiled and kissed his cheek, as she would with any friend.

'A margarita, please.'

His eyes widened and he kissed her cheek in return. His lips were warm, smooth and firm. Her pelvic floor donned its leotard and began another energetic workout.

'Productive day?' he asked, signalling to the barman.

Erica nodded. 'All the final acts' outfits are sorted. Until they change their minds at the last minute, that is.' Just like Dan had. He had more in common with the wannabes than she'd realised: narcissistic, self-centred, slightly orange. Anger flared within her.

'Can you make that a large margarita, please?' she said to the barman.

'How large?'

'As large as they come. I'm very thirsty.'

Rob laughed and added a beer to the order. Erica studied his profile. Fuck, he was handsome. Just looking at him made her tingle and tremble and want to nibble his lower lip.

'That large enough for you?' he asked, nodding at a goldfish bowl brimming with margarita on the bar.

Erica gave a nervous laugh. 'Hadn't meant quite that large.' She took a tentative sip. Tequila hit the back of her throat and she coughed.

'Let's find a table.' Rob picked the bowl up and led her to a dimly lit corner of the room. He placed their drinks on a high table and Erica climbed up onto a bar stool.

'Cheers.' He clinked his beer bottle against her vat of margarita.

'Bottoms up,' she said, taking a long sip. Why had she mentioned bottoms?

'Can't believe there's only two weeks of the show left,' Rob said. 'Although it's so full-on now, we'll all need a break.'

Erica nodded. 'The end is always stressful. The wannabes are petrified they'll cock it up and not make it to the final.' Great, now she'd said the word cock. What next? Penetration? She sucked her straw and watched the level of the goldfish bowl lower at alarming speed.

'So they tell me in the after-show interviews. At length. Some nights I don't think I'll get out of the studio.'

Erica rolled her eyes. 'Tell me about it. I have to wait 'til they've finished the interviews, then help them get changed.'

'Can't they dress themselves?'

'Sometimes I have to unpin their costume, or make sure they don't rip it in their excitement, or go home in it. And they're so hyper, they want to talk. I become a kind of big sister during the show. Listening and looking after them is part of my job. I draw the line at helping them into their pyjamas though.'

'Should hope so. Bet some of those lads would like nothing more.'

'Hardly. I'm old enough to be their...' She winked. 'Let's stick with big sister, shall we?'

Rob grinned. 'Sophisticated older woman. They must love that.'

'You can talk. Good-looking production director.' The cocktails were taking effect and her earlier tension had eased away, leaving her feeling warm and fuzzy and maybe a tiny bit flirtatious. 'Someone must have made a pass at you.'

'Not that I've noticed.'

'Come on.' Erica nudged him with the toe of her shoe. Her already short dress rode up. Rob developed a sudden fascination in the label on his beer bottle.

'I'm not into those identikit women with tattooed eyebrows and hair extensions,' he said. 'The woman I like is naturally beautiful.'

Erica gripped both sides of the goldfish bowl and sucked manically on her straw, praying a false eyelash wouldn't choose that precise moment to work itself loose.

He looked into her eyes. 'You must know it's you.'

Her stomach folded in on itself. This was everything she'd dreamed of. Rob's eyes were dark and intense. This was everything she wasn't allowed.

'Alright, mate.' A man appeared behind Rob and slapped him on the shoulder.

'Oh, hi.' Rob held out a hand. 'Steve, this is Erica. Erica, Steve. We used to work together.'

Steve nodded in what Erica thought was a polite, disinterested way. It was hard to be sure because the room had starting spinning.

Steve turned back to Rob. 'I hear you landed the renovation show. Any chance they need someone else?'

'I'll find out and let you know.'

Erica drank steadily, her eyes darting between Rob and Steve, both of whom seemed to have developed an identical twin. She reached the bottom of the bowl and the straw squeaked against the glass.

Rob reached for one of Steve's four hands and shook it. 'Have a good evening. I'll catch up with you later.'

'Don't forget to let me know about the job,' Steve said, walking away.

Erica sucked on a wedge of lime to try and soak up some alcohol.

'What's this renovation job?' she asked, hoping she wasn't slurring.

'A new show being produced by Clare Wright.'

Erica had worked with Clare before. Pleasant enough, in a mumsy way. Not a threat.

'Starts in September,' Rob continued. 'I've got to view some potential houses for the show before then, but it won't take up much time. I'll have a couple of weeks free when *Sing to Win* finishes.' He smiled, almost shyly. 'Maybe we could get together if you've got some time off too?'

Right. Enough of this. She must tell him about Dan. She opened her mouth, but the words didn't come out.

Rob reached over and took her hand. He opened it up and massaged her palm gently with the pads of his thumbs. It was akin to being treated by a reflexologist where every point of the foot relates to a different part of the anatomy. In this case, all points led to one very specific part of her anatomy. She shifted in her seat.

Rob intensified the pressure on her hand and heat surged between her legs. 'At the risk of sounding like a teenage boy, I really like you, Erica. You're fun and intelligent and bloody sexy.'

The hairs on her arms stood up. She stared at them in disbelief. The judges often claimed theirs did after a rendition of some tear-jerking ballad on the show, but she'd thought it was showbiz bullshit.

'I'd like to spend more time with you. Get to know you better.' Rob's fingers tightened around hers. 'What do you think?'

What did she think? She had so many thoughts, it was hard to know where to begin, not least because of the effect his hand was having on hers. If just touching her palm sent crackles of heat around her body, what would happen if he put that hand somewhere else? How much stimulation could one person take? Erica gazed into his deep, brown eyes. She *had* to tell him about Dan. It wasn't fair to deceive him. She liked him too much to do that. Alcohol and adrenalin coursed through her. But if she told him, this moment would be over before it had even begun.

'I want to get to know you better as well.' Sliding off the bar stool, Erica grasped the table to steady herself and sidled between Rob's legs. 'A *lot* better.'

Pressing her body up against his, she wound her arms around his neck, clasped the back of his head and lowered her face to his. He hesitated, then slipped his hands around her waist, and pulled her close. The kiss began gently, cautiously, but within moments intensified. Their mouths parted, their tongues explored one another's. Her lips burned and the room span around her. She couldn't remember the last time she'd been kissed with such intensity. Perhaps she never had.

'Christ, Erica.' Rob pulled back. 'I'm going to explode.'

They stared at one another, panting slightly. She knew it was wrong to be disloyal to Dan, but what did he expect? That he could mess her around and she'd put up with it? She'd been doing that for ten years and she'd had enough. Equally, she knew it was wrong to deceive Rob, but couldn't help herself. He was her dream man. Fun, hot, thoughtful, kind... had she mentioned hot? Everything she could ever want from one person. The show would finish in two weeks and she'd never see him again. The thought made her want to cry. She had to make the most of this opportunity or she'd always regret it. This would be a one-off. One magical night away from reality. And as they only had one night, she wasn't stopping now. Dragging her eyes away from Rob's, she scanned the room.

'In there.' She gestured to the disabled toilet.

'Really?' Rob glanced at the throng of people around them. His eyes flitted back to hers and he nodded. 'Ok, let's go.'

Holding hands and giggling like naughty children, they put their heads down and ran into the disabled toilet. The light was bright and garish compared to the dimly lit bar. The scent of Toilet Duck filled the room. Hand soap dripped from a dispenser on the wall. There could have been a tramp in the corner and it wouldn't have put Erica off. The moment Rob locked the door they fell on each other. There was nothing cautious about this kiss. It was all-consuming and demanding. Weeks of pent-up frustration tore away the layers of coyness and restraint. She pulled his t-shirt over his head and ran her hands over his chest. Rob unzipped her dress and let it fall to the floor, then unhooked her bra, sliding the straps off her shoulders and freeing her body.

He stepped back to look at her. 'Fuck, Erica.' He cupped her breasts with his hands, massaging her nipples with his thumbs. 'You're so beautiful.' His mouth bent to her chest and she tilted her head back, gasping as his teeth gently tugged at her. Greedily, she pulled at the fly on his jeans, wiggled his waistband down and reached into his boxer shorts. He groaned as she ran her hand up and down his erection. She wanted to see him, marvel at his size, but couldn't wait any longer.

'Have you got a condom?' she asked breathlessly.

'No.'

They looked at each in dismay, then Erica spotted a machine on the wall. They grinned with relief and Rob tugged his jeans off and dug in the pocket for some change.

Erica pulled her thong down and when Rob was ready, wrapped one leg around him and guided him in, gasping as he thrust deep inside her.

'Erica.' He kissed her hungrily, wrapping his arms around her and leaning her against the wall behind them. Erica's heel pressed against his buttock, moving back and forth with him. His hands were in her hair, on her back, gripping her thighs, as though desperate to touch every part of her. Her head knocked against the cool wall tiles, but she was barely aware of it. All she was aware of was how good it felt to have him inside her.

His lips left hers fleetingly and a low moan escaped her. She grabbed his chin and forced his lips back to hers, not caring that her actions were so primal. Her knees trembled and her supporting leg threatened to buckle. Rob moved his hands to her buttocks and lifted her, taking her weight so she could wrap both legs around him. He edged even deeper inside her and she cried out, thrusting her hips back and forth in time with his, digging her nails hard into his back. A force within her was building, getting hotter and hotter, stronger and stronger, nearer and nearer, until, 'Yes, that's it, yes!', it exploded, firing red-hot sparks through her. Rob tensed and she gasped as he came, holding her tightly and rocking her to and fro until he came to a standstill. They clung to one another, panting and breathless.

'That was amazing,' Rob said eventually. 'Even better than I'd imagined it would be.'

'So you've imagined it then?'

Rob smiled. 'Usually somewhere slightly more scenic.'

Erica ran her lips along his shoulder blade. 'We could have been on top of the Eiffel Tower and I wouldn't have noticed.' She kissed him again. Their mouths worked against each other's, tenderly to begin with, but growing in passion with each passing minute. Rob hardened against her.

'There were two in the pack,' he murmured.

Erica grinned. 'Then what are we waiting for?'

—

'Do you think anyone knew what we were doing?' Erica asked, as they walked through Leicester Square. They'd missed their table booking at Brasserie Zedel, but Erica wasn't hungry.

'Nah. Plenty of people share a cubicle to save time.' Rob's arm was warm around her shoulder. 'We should introduce it at work. Although, it'd be nice to try it in a bed some time.' Pulling her close, he kissed her. The beeping cars and passing footsteps around them drifted away. Erica felt as though they were in a 1950s romance until a dishevelled-looking woman with several cold sores asked if she could borrow their phone, then spat on the pavement when they said no.

Rob looked at his watch. 'We'd better head to King's Cross. Much as I'd love to book into a hotel for the next twenty-four hours, I've got to pick Daisy up at nine tomorrow.'

'I hadn't realised the time,' Erica sighed. It had been quite a night. Sex with Rob had surpassed expectation. Her lurid fantasies hadn't factored in emotions. She'd naively written them off as unnecessary, but Rob's tenderness elevated the experience from basic sex to something much richer, like adding a dash of amaretto to a black coffee.

'We've crammed quite a lot into one evening. Think how much we could achieve in a weekend.' They stopped at a pelican crossing. 'Maybe when the show's finished?'

Erica concentrated on the traffic lights. She didn't want to think about the evening finishing, let alone the show ending. Because it had to end after tonight before Rob or Dan found out. Guiltily, she realised she was more worried about hurting Rob than Dan.

'This might sound a bit full-on,' Rob said. 'But Daisy and I are going to my sister's Airbnb in Brighton next Monday and Tuesday, if you fancy it. Jasmine could share with Daisy and you could go in the guest bedroom, to save any awkward questions.' He gave her a cheeky grin. 'I can't guarantee you wouldn't get a visitor in the middle of the night, though.'

Erica laughed. 'I can guarantee *you* would.'

'You'll think about it, then?'

He was serious. He wanted them to go away. She could already envisage it: sunny walks along the pebbled beach, paddling in the sea, and, at the end of each day, after Daisy and Jasmine had gone to bed, she and Rob would follow suit. She'd finally get to wear that Agent Provocateur basque Dan had bought her.

Her idyllic, imaginary movie came to a screeching halt. Shit – Dan. Rob took her hand. It was strong and firm and, as she now knew, very, very capable. Oh God, what was she going to do? The evening had been everything she'd fantasised about, but a fantasy was precisely what it was. She couldn't embark on a full-blown affair and go on mini-breaks, using Jasmine as a decoy. Aside from the moral implications, of which there were at least three, Jasmine would be bound to mention her dad, which would dampen any ardour, even one as fervent as Rob's. No, going to Brighton wasn't an option and she'd left it a bit late to introduce Dan into the conversation.

Erica cleared her throat. Much as it pained her, she had to turn him down, but in the kindest way possible. 'It sounds lovely, but I'm not sure I can.' She could see the disappointment in his eyes. 'I've got some other work on the days I'm not at the studio.'

Rob wrapped his arms around her. 'Forgot you're a high-flyer with your fingers in lots of pies. Maybe another time?'

She closed her eyes and leant up against him. There wouldn't be another time. This would be the last time he held her. The last time she felt his chin resting on the top of her head, his arms around her.

'We should go,' Rob murmured, but instead of letting her go, his arms tightened their grip around her.

She squeezed him back, desperate to hold onto him for as long as she could. *Sing to Win* finished in two weeks. She'd have to make excuses to avoid him 'til then. It'd be hard and cruel, but she had no choice. Then that'd be it. Their paths had never crossed before and unless the renovation programme he was moving onto needed some seriously stylish carpenters, they were unlikely to ever see each other again. Her eyes filled with tears at the thought and she buried her head in his chest. He misinterpreted her actions and she felt him smile into her hair.

'Oh, Erica,' he sighed. 'You don't know how long I've been hoping this would happen.'

Guilt coursed through her. She was a bitch for leading him on. If she was the kind, thoughtful person he thought she was, she wouldn't be doing this. She swallowed hard, as a sudden realisation hit her. She *wanted* to be that kind, thoughtful person. And with him she could be. The more time she spent with him, the more she despised the materialistic, greedy part of her life. Not all of it – she could never harbour bad feelings about the Louboutin Mary Janes she'd got in the January sale – but a large part of it. The largest part being the bit with Dan in it.

She swallowed hard. Perhaps she did have a choice after all.

Chapter Thirty-Five

Polly

Louise and the twins breezed through the back door clutching shopping bags. The twins were wearing new clothes that actually fitted. Louise's usual philosophy was to buy everything two sizes too big so they could grow into them – a philosophy that really didn't work with underwear. Tess's hair was now shoulder-length with a side parting and George was sporting a quiff. They looked relaxed and happy and completely oblivious to the anxiety their spontaneous trip to the cinema had caused.

'Hi, Poll.' Louise dropped her bags inside the back door. 'We're having a hot chocolate. Fancy one?'

No, she didn't fancy a sodding hot chocolate. She wanted to know why Louise hadn't come home when she'd promised she would. Louise poured some milk into a glass jug and put it in the microwave, then the three of them sat at the kitchen table laughing at a strip of photos. Over their heads Polly could see that they'd squeezed into a booth and pulled various faces in each picture.

'Look, Mummy,' Tess giggled, pointing to one of Louise sticking her tongue out.

Polly watched in disbelief. It was as though she wasn't there. They were living in her house, rent-free, and they couldn't bring themselves to involve her. The past two months of child-minding, cooking and caring meant nothing to them.

A ball of heat grew in Polly's stomach. They had no idea what she was going through, what she went through every day, and they didn't care. All the emotions she had experienced that evening, from the initial anxiety, followed by confusion and hurt that Louise had let her down, to questioning whether she should even be going on a date, were fizzing into something else – rage.

'Nice day out?' she asked shakily.

'Smashing, thanks.' Louise put her arms around the twins. 'If you ask me, it was the best day we've had for a long time.' Tess and George grinned at her. It was sickening.

'That's nice,' Polly said. 'My evening didn't go exactly as planned.'

'No?' Louise said absently. 'Why's that?'

'Why do you think?' It was the first time Polly had ever raised her voice and Louise's head jerked up.

'There's no need—' Her words faltered as she took in Polly's dress and make-up. 'Oh, Poll.' Red blotches coursed across her chest and up her neck. 'I'm so sorry. I completely forgot.'

'I thought you'd had an accident. Couldn't think of any other reason you'd let me down.' Angry tears pricked Polly's eyes. She didn't want to cry. She wanted to be strong and commanding and let Louise feel the full force of her fury. Not easily achieved when wearing green chiffon.

'Where's Erica?' Louise spluttered, her face scarlet.

'Working late,' Polly snapped. 'At least she messaged to say she was letting me down.'

'I—' Louise started.

'I rang so many times,' Polly shouted, tears streaming down her cheeks. 'Didn't know whether to phone the police or the hospital.' Her crying intensified to the extent that not even she could understand what she was saying. Summoning all her strength, she slammed her palm down on the table. 'Selfish,' she cried. 'Selfish.' Sinking down into a chair, she covered her face with her hands and wept.

–

'Why didn't I get a diary alert?' Louise said for the twentieth time. She patted Polly's arm. 'I'm so sorry.'

Polly wasn't sure what was distressing Louise more; that she'd let her down or that her fail-proof scheduling skills had failed.

'It won't happen again,' Louise said determinedly. She looked at her watch. 'Bloody hell. We'd best get those kids to bed.'

The children were watching a film in the den. Miraculously, Summer had slept through it all. Usually the rustle of a crisp packet opening was enough to rouse her.

'Time to go up.' Louise clapped her hands together. 'See who can get ready for bed the quickest.' Her words brought out the competitiveness in Oliver, George and Tess and they charged out of the room and along the passageway.

'Just popping to the loo,' Louise said, ducking through the door labelled WC.

Jasmine took Polly's hand. 'I'm already in my pyjamas,' she said.

'You win then,' replied Polly. Jasmine beamed up at her, making it impossible for Polly to stay angry.

In the hallway, the twins and Oliver had abandoned any notion of going to bed and were instead racing up the stairs and sliding down the bannisters.

Polly's throat tightened. 'Careful,' she said, watching George lean to one side as though taking a bend on a racetrack. Just as well Louise was in the toilet – she'd cordon off the stairs with hazard warning tape if she saw what they were up to.

'Don't worry,' George said. 'I hardly ever fall off anymore.' He reached the foot of the stairs, misjudged his dismount and landed in a crumpled heap on the floor.

Tess squealed with delight as she slid down behind him. 'You should try, Jasmine,' she said. 'I'll help you.'

A warm feeling replaced the tightness in Polly's throat. Tess was being nice to Jasmine.

'I don't know.' Jasmine looked up the staircase cautiously.

'Start near the bottom,' Tess said. 'That's how we learnt.'

Jasmine nibbled her lower lip. 'Mummy says I can do anything I put my mind to if I believe in myself.'

Polly reached for her pendant. That adage might work for people like Erica, but it didn't for her. He was dead because she'd tried to put her mind to something.

'You're supposed to be going to bed,' she said, feeling exhausted all of a sudden.

'Polly,' Louise called from the toilet. 'Can you get me some loo roll? There's none in here. Again,' she added with a tut.

Polly put a hand to her mouth. She'd forgotten to buy any. They were out upstairs too.

'Will kitchen towel do?' she asked.

'No!' Louise shouted. 'It'll block the drains.'

Polly's mobile rang in the kitchen and she hurried away from Louise's lecture to answer it.

'Hi,' Alex said. 'Just calling to see if you're alright.'

'I'm fine, thank you.' Polly made sure she kept any warmth out of her voice. She couldn't see him again. It clearly wasn't meant to be.

'Sure?' Alex sounded concerned.

'Yes. Look I've got to go.' She hung up and blinked back tears.

Louise came out of the toilet, drying her hands on her skirt. 'It's ok. I found a tissue. Just as well it was only a—' She stopped when she saw Polly's face. 'What's wrong?'

'I just hung up on Alex.'

'Why? I thought you liked him.'

'I do, but it's too complicated.' Polly wiped a tear away. 'I'm not ready.'

Louise frowned. 'If you ask me, you should give it a go. Take it slow and see what happens.'

'Really?' Polly felt a flutter of hope.

Louise nodded grimly. 'Don't make the same mistake as me and push away a decent man. There aren't many around.'

Polly nodded. Louise was right. She should try and move on. She'd call Alex back to apologise and rearrange their date.

There was a triumphant cry from the children in the hallway.

'Well done, Jasmine,' Tess called. 'You're doing it.'

Louise and Polly looked at each other with alarm and hurried down the passageway in time to see Jasmine sliding down the bannister – not from just a few steps up, but from much higher. She saw Polly and lifted one hand to wave. Her face transformed from ecstatic to petrified, as she realised she no longer had control over her balance. The next few seconds were a blur of flailing limbs and a piercing scream. Polly watched in horror as Jasmine slipped over the side of the bannister. Her arms doggy-paddled through the air, as she tried desperately to grab hold of something to save her. Polly wanted to help her. She wanted to run forward and catch her. But she couldn't move. All she could do was stand and watch in horror as Jasmine's little body hit the floor.

Chapter Thirty-Six

Erica

Erica lowered herself carefully onto the train seat, wincing at the tenderness between her legs as she made contact.

Resisting the urge to mentally replay how she'd incurred the pain – in technicolour with surround sound – she instead forced herself to focus on the question that had presented itself and was refusing to go away. Could she really leave Dan? Her partner of ten years. The father of her child. The man who had told her that morning how much he wanted to be with her, and then, mere hours later, announced he was leaving the country.

She closed her eyes. Yes. Yes, she could. It was so obviously the right thing to do that she couldn't believe she hadn't thought of it before. He didn't make her happy. He hadn't really since she'd had Jasmine and the basis of their relationship had changed. Their first couple of years had been fun. Instead of being needy and suspicious, as previous boyfriends had been, he'd understood how important her career and independence was. He never resented the time she devoted to work or for herself and her friends. It suited him, as he had the same ethos. They worked hard, maintained their individual social lives and, when together, dined out and went to the latest shows and on fabulous holidays.

Dan wanted to maintain this lifestyle when Jasmine arrived and, for the most part, he'd succeeded. His work and leisure activities were unaffected – it was the time with Erica that changed. Too eager to get home to Jasmine after work, the fancy meals and theatre trips dwindled down to the occasional birthday treat. And holidays weren't exactly fabulous when they included a child who wanted her parents to play with her every waking moment – of which there were many, as Jasmine was awake by six a.m.

Over the years, they spent less and less time together, a situation which only intensified when Dan was promoted to oversee the business in China and was away two weeks out of four. They barely spoke when he was away, other than to relay essential information or instructions. Erica didn't miss him when he was gone and he'd never given any indication that he missed her. That lack of interest couldn't be a greater contrast to the pain she felt at the prospect of not seeing Rob again.

It wasn't just lust she felt for Rob, she knew that. It was love. Full-on, shout it from the rooftops, run barefoot through meadows, hug complete strangers in the street love. Erica wrapped her arms around herself excitedly. She loved Rob. She *loved* him. She truly did. Although, while she'd happily run through a meadow, she'd draw the line at hugging strangers in the street. Especially the ones who looked as though they might hug her back.

She sighed contentedly to herself, her mind playing a montage of images of Rob: stepping out of the lift the first time they'd met; laughing when she fell against him at the tube station; squinting in the sun outside the café; telling her not to be so hard on herself; supporting her on the charity run. She loved everything about him. Not just his looks – that went without saying – but much, much more than that. His positivity, his kindness, his generosity, his sense of humour, his devotion to Daisy, the way he looked at Erica with such warmth and encouragement, as though she could achieve anything she put her mind to. With him by her side, she could, too.

Hugging herself, she stretched her legs out in front of her. 'Ow.'

Erica's eyes snapped open. A young, Asian woman sat opposite, rubbing her shin.

'Sorry,' Erica said. 'Didn't realise you were there.'

'It's ok.' The woman tucked her long, black hair behind one ear and turned her attention to a large rucksack on her lap.

Erica reached into her own bag for her phone. Shit, she'd forgotten to message Jasmine again. One of the reasons for buying her an iPod – apart from alleviating the guilt for letting her down countless times – was so they could keep in touch without having to go through Polly. Initially, their messages had pinged back and forth, but the past week or so she'd got out of the habit of checking in. Thankfully, Jasmine hadn't messaged her, so she didn't need to feel guilty about not replying, but she had several missed calls from Louise. What had she forgotten to do this time? It had better not be anything to do with the bins. She went to call her, but the phone vibrated and Rob's name flashed up on the screen. Her stomach flipped over.

'Hi,' she said softly.

'Hi.' His smile was in his voice. 'Just wanted to make sure you were ok.'

'I'm very ok, thank you for asking. You?'

'Couldn't be better.' Rob paused. 'Well, I could, but I'm not sure I should go into details on a busy train.'

Erica ran a finger around the hoop of her earring. 'I'll use my imagination,' she murmured.

'Can I see you tomorrow night?' His voice was low and full of intent.

'Yes.' She'd tell Polly and Louise she had to work late again.

''Til tomorrow then.'

''Til tomorrow.'

'Bye Erica. Sleep well.'

He hung up and she clutched the phone to her chest, replaying the way he'd said her name. He used her name a lot – on the phone, in conversation, when he was inside her.

The phone call erased any doubts she had that leaving Dan was the right thing to do. She couldn't recall a single occasion in the last ten years when Dan had rung to make sure she was ok. Not even when Jasmine was a newborn or her mum had died. She hadn't questioned it. Hadn't considered that it would be nice to know someone was thinking of her. She was an independent, strong woman who didn't need that. But depending on someone else wasn't a weakness. It didn't mean she wasn't independent and strong. It was being part of a team. Maybe team Roca.

Telling Jasmine would be the worst bit, but kids were resilient. She'd soon get used to it and it wasn't as if she saw Dan much anyway. And when Erica felt she was ready to meet Rob, she'd make sure he brought Daisy along. The excitement of another girl to play with would help smooth over any negative feelings of Mummy having a new boyfriend.

'Scusie,' the young woman sitting opposite said with a shaky voice. She'd emptied the contents of her bag onto the seat. 'Can't find my phone.' She held her empty rucksack up. 'Should be here, but is gone.' She gestured to Erica. 'Please, you call number, so I hear ring.'

Nodding, Erica dialled the number the woman gave her. Moments later a loud ringing pulsed from the woman's bag. She turned it inside out, discovered a tear in the lining and pulled the phone out.

'Thank you so much.' She pressed the phone to her lips.

Erica cancelled the call and sat back in her seat. What should she wear tomorrow? Stockings, suspenders and basque perhaps? Excitement bubbled through her. Would he take his time undoing each tiny hook and eye or would he rip it from her body as though stripping an ear of corn? She shivered with anticipation, then jumped as a phone was thrust in front of her face. A young Filipino girl smiled out of the screen.

'This my daughter, Lillibeth.' The woman sitting opposite waggled the phone. 'All photos on here. Terrible if I lose.'

Erica nodded politely. The woman clearly wasn't a regular commuter or she'd know the etiquette was to grant all travellers the same amount of personal space they would give a leper.

'My daughter and mother all I have,' the woman said. 'My husband leave for other lady.'

'Oh. Sorry to hear that.'

The woman made a rasping noise with her lips. 'He bastard. Leave me to raise daughter alone. No money, no job. Philippines not good place for woman to find work.'

'So you moved here?'

The woman nodded. 'I very lucky. Get job as live-in housekeeper and babysitter so can send money home to my mother. She look after Lillibeth while I here.'

'What?' Erica was horrified. 'Lillibeth's still in the Philippines?'

'Yes.' The woman held out her phone again. 'My mother send photos.' She chatted excitedly, describing what her daughter was doing in each picture. Erica's eyes wandered from the photos to the mother. She looked so young.

'What's your name?' she asked.

'Imee.' She selected another photo. 'Fifth birthday,' she said proudly.

'She's lovely.' Erica took in Imee's faded jeans and scuffed boots. 'When did you last see her?'

'Eight month ago. I visit again at Christmas. We FaceTime every day.'

Erica couldn't believe what she was hearing. 'That's not right. A parent shouldn't have to leave their child.'

'Lillibeth life much better than if I stay with no job, no money.'

'But you see her less than once a year.'

'FaceTime good. She remember me and one day she move here.'

The situation was so alien Erica was lost for words.

'I lucky to do this. We are good.'

Erica felt very small. 'I admire you, Imee. You've made such a sacrifice for your family.'

'Children most important thing. All parent make sacrifices.' Imee flattened a hand against her chest. 'It about them, not us.'

Erica nodded. 'It's easy to forget that sometimes.'

'You have children?'

'A daughter.' Erica took her phone from her bag and opened up a family photo they'd had taken professionally a few months before. Jasmine sat between herself and Dan, her large white teeth framed by an even larger smile.

Imee nodded approvingly. 'You lucky lady. Enjoy family. Most important thing.'

Erica's face grew hot.

An announcement echoed around the carriage. 'My stop.' Imee stood up.

'Good luck, Imee. I hope you get your daughter over here soon.' Erica felt ashamed. Imee had given up being with her daughter to provide her with a better life. The biggest dilemma she faced was what underwear to wear for her lover.

Her phone vibrated and Louise's name flashed up.

'Sorry for not calling back,' Erica said, remembering the missed calls. 'Work was manic.'

'Where the bloody hell are you?' Louise snapped. 'I've left three messages.'

Erica bristled. What business was it of hers? 'On the train. I'll be back soon.'

'Go straight to the hospital.'

Erica went cold. 'Why?'

'It's Jasmine. She's had an accident.'

Chapter Thirty-Seven

Erica

Erica sat by Jasmine's bedside, her head in her hands. She was a crap mum. Worse than crap. Crap mums did things like let their kids eat biscuits for breakfast. Missing numerous phone calls informing you that your child was injured because you were getting laid – by someone who wasn't even the child's dad – took the definition of crap mum to a whole new level; one that had to be created just for her. She could almost smell the fresh paint.

The night before had been horrendous. She'd taken a cab from the station straight to the hospital. Jasmine was in a bed on the children's ward, Louise at her side – where she should have been. A nurse explained that Jasmine's humerus was fractured in two places and she'd need an operation to pin the bone back together. Seeing Jasmine in agony from her injury, then vomiting after a shot of morphine, had been heart-breaking.

Erica had sat on an uncomfortable plastic chair all night, turning down the offer of a pull-out bed. She didn't deserve a bed. Every hour, a nurse came in to check Jasmine's temperature and blood pressure. 'She'll be alright,' one of them said, noticing Erica's tear-stained face. Erica had nodded. Yes, Jasmine would be alright physically, but what about emotionally? How much damage had been inflicted as she lay in a strange bed in a strange place with strange noises, wishing her mummy was with her, only to be told by Louise that Mummy wasn't answering her phone? Would Jasmine ever forgive her? And if she did, could

Erica ever forgive herself? Imee's earlier words haunted her. *It's about them, not us.* Imee was completely selfless, thinking only of her daughter; Erica was the polar opposite.

Jasmine stirred and Erica took her hand. Jasmine's other arm lay beside her, wired back together during the two-hour operation that had taken place that morning. She'd been lucky to escape with only a broken arm, the doctor had said. Jasmine had landed on her elbow, but a fall like that could have damaged her spinal cord or caused serious head injuries. Erica pressed Jasmine's hand to her lips, cursing herself yet again for not being there.

Her heart had pounded when she'd phoned Dan, waiting for him to ask where she'd been while all of this was going on. But he hadn't asked. Maybe to prevent Erica asking him, so he didn't have to admit to celebrating his new job with a few lap dances. Erica could hardly criticise though, not when she'd been doing so much worse. And when she'd been about to do the worst thing imaginable. Because the scenario where she and Rob lived happily ever after was imaginary. She couldn't leave Dan now. Jasmine deserved a stable, secure family. Erica owed her that. She was deeply ashamed for thinking that Jasmine wouldn't be bothered about them splitting up. She was eight. All eight-year-olds wanted their mummy and daddy to be together. And what Jasmine wanted was what mattered.

The clatter of a trolley signalled the arrival of dinner, even though it was only four p.m. and the odour from the lunchtime parsnips still lingered in the air.

Erica tucked Jasmine's hair behind her ear. 'Dinner time.'

Jasmine's large brown eyes fluttered open. She looked past Erica. 'Where's Polly?'

Erica felt as though she'd been kicked in the stomach.

'She's with Oliver and Summer. I'm looking after you.'

Jasmine didn't say anything.

'The doctor said we can take you home if you eat your dinner.'

'To Polly's?'

Erica shook her head. Dan was adamant they weren't returning to 'Molly's', which he now branded a place of neglect where the children ran wild, unsupervised and undernourished. While Erica didn't share his views, particularly not the undernourished part – he hadn't seen the mountain of biscuits and crisps Polly bought every week – she agreed that their calm, clean house, with all its comforts, was a much more suitable place to convalesce than a mildew-infested B&B filled with tantrums and shrieking. And that was the adults.

'No, sweetie,' she said. '*Our* home.'

'I want to be with Polly.' Jasmine's large brown eyes challenged Erica's. 'She likes being with me.'

Guilt swept over Erica. 'Sweetie, I like being with you too. I'm sorry work's been so manic lately. I've got a freelancer to cover me while you're recovering so I can look after you 'til you're better.'

Jasmine didn't respond.

'It'll be nice to be back in your own bedroom and be home with me and Daddy.'

Jasmine rolled her eyes. 'Daddy's in China.'

'No, he isn't.' The curtain snapped open and Dan strode over to the bed, laden with a giant helium balloon, comics and puzzle books. 'How's my girl?'

'Daddy!' Jasmine let Dan kiss her instead of turning her face away, as she had when Erica tried. Why was she being punished when golden-bollocks Daddy got a warm reception, despite turning up almost twenty-four hours after the event?

He kissed Erica's cheek and she forced a smile, hiding her irritation. Why was he untroubled by Jasmine's accident when she was racked with guilt? Why had he said they meant everything to him, then accepted a job the other side of the world? Why wasn't he Rob?

She stood up. 'I'll go and freshen up now you're here.' She hadn't showered since the previous morning and two rounds of sex followed by a night in a plastic chair had left her smelling scarily similar to the lunchtime parsnips. In the toilet cubicle she cleaned herself as thoroughly as she could with some wipes and antiseptic gel. As she washed, an image of Rob's deep brown eyes staring intently into her own flashed through her mind. She forced it away. No. She couldn't let herself think about him. Splashing water onto her face she thought instead about Imee's words. *Children most important thing. All parents make sacrifices. It's about them, not us.* Imee's sacrifice was being away from her daughter. It was an enormous sacrifice but one Imee was prepared to make to give Lillibeth a better life.

A lump formed in Erica's throat. Her sacrifice to give Jasmine a better life was Rob. Blinking back tears, she dried her face with a hand towel that disintegrated on contact. Her heart felt as though it were doing the same. This was ridiculous; she'd only known Rob a couple of months. She shouldn't be feeling like this. She picked a shred of paper towel off her forehead. But she *did* feel like this. She loved him and didn't want to hurt him. Telling him she was as good as married was unthinkable. He'd hate her for lying and she couldn't handle that. But if she said she wasn't interested, he'd think he had some terrible character flaw or physical defect, which he definitely didn't. She'd had a good enough look to know.

She unclipped her earrings and dropped them into the inside pocket of her bag. She was too tired to figure it out today. She'd find a way to let him down gently tomorrow when she wasn't so sleep-deprived. Right now, Jasmine was her priority.

She reached into her bag for her phone, to put it on silent in case Rob rang. She couldn't risk that happening with Dan at the hospital. Instead of her phone, her fingers closed around the earrings. That couldn't be right; she always kept her phone in the same inside pocket. She checked again, then went through the contents of her bag. It had to be there, she'd had it just half an hour ago when Dan's mum had rung for a progress report. She thought back. One of the nurses had come in to give Jasmine some pain relief. Erica had hurriedly finished the call and put the phone down on Jasmine's table, just inches from where Dan was now. Her stomach tightened. If it rang, he might pick it up. Grabbing her bag, she unlocked the door and hurried along the corridor. Her heels clicked at double time. Please don't let Rob have rung, she said to herself. Please, please, please.

She reached the ward. A nurse pushing a trolley laden with dinner plates blocked Erica's access to Jasmine's cubicle. Erica stood on tiptoes and peered round to Jasmine's bed. Jasmine was propped up, her dark hair contrasting with the white pillowcase. Dan had his back to Erica, his shoulders hunched slightly, one arm bent at the elbow. Erica's eyes went to Jasmine's table. The phone was gone. She stiffened. Where was it? Erica launched herself past the trolley and into Jasmine's cubicle. Her stomach turned to lead. Her phone was pressed to Dan's ear.

'What?' he said indignantly. 'Of course this is Erica's phone.'

Erica gripped her bag so tightly the handles cut into her palms. She hardly dared look at Dan, but at the same time couldn't tear her eyes away. He must have sensed her watching because he turned to meet her gaze. His eyes narrowed as he spoke.

'I'm her husband. Who are you?'

Chapter Thirty-Eight

Louise

'Bloody hell,' Louise exclaimed.

'Shhh.' Erica pointed to the ceiling. 'Dan's mum and Jasmine are upstairs.'

Jasmine's accident had put their falling out into perspective and the tension between them had eased enough for Louise to visit Erica.

Louise lowered her voice. 'What did you do?'

'The only thing I could do. Lied.'

'But Rob was on the phone. Talking to Dan. Asking to speak to you.' Louise splayed her hands on the marble-top island in Erica's pristine kitchen. 'How did you lie your way out of that?'

'Rob hung up as soon as Dan said, "I'm her husband. Who are you?". Even though technically he's not. I guess the label "husband" has more impact than "long-term, co-habiting partner and father of her child".' Erica tugged at her hair. 'Dan, understandably, wanted to know who the fuck Rob is.'

Louise leaned forward. This was better than any soap. 'What did you say?'

'I came up with some bullshit about being out with work colleagues the night before and everyone being drunk and messing around with each other's phones. I'd got a random number in my call history because I'd had to ring a woman who'd lost her phone on the train.'

'What?' Louise was struggling to keep up.

Erica waved a dismissive hand. 'Long story. Dan spoke to this poor Filipino woman, who hadn't a clue what he was talking about, which kind of backed my story up. So Dan thinks Rob is just some twat I used to work with, who was pissing about.'

Louise waited for Erica to perform a self-congratulatory air grab, but instead she stared blankly at the Aga, dark circles beneath her eyes.

'Why are you so down? You got away with it.'

'At what price?' Erica's voice broke. 'Jasmine could have died.' She covered her eyes with her hand. 'I've been so selfish. Just thinking about what I want. I'm so ashamed of myself.' A tear edged out from beneath her hand and rolled down her cheek. 'Jasmine's arm will always be weak, and Rob won't answer my calls or reply to any of my texts.'

'You're still in touch with him?' Louise widened her eyes. 'If you ask me, you're pushing your luck a bit now.'

'I want to say sorry.' Erica sniffed. 'I'm not going to see him again.'

'Just as well. Even you couldn't get away with it twice.' Louise crossed her arms and tried to convey an authoritative, rational pose, but the contemporary, curved bar stool with a walnut finish – she'd thumbed through the brochure on a previous visit – had a revolving seat and she ended up spinning around so she was facing away from Erica.

Erica was oblivious. 'He must hate me.'

Louise pedalled her toes against the footrest until the stool edged back round. 'I'm sure he doesn't.'

'I'd hate me if I was him.' Erica put her head in her hands. 'I should have been with Jasmine, not Rob. She could have broken her neck.' Her voice cracked. 'Fuck, *I* hate me.'

Louise floundered briefly. Erica had a point. 'You were in shock,' she said carefully. 'About Dan moving to Dubai.'

'There's something else.' Erica raised her eyes, either seeking forgiveness from heaven or checking that Dan's mum hadn't drilled a hole through the ceiling and was listening in. 'To convince Dan nothing dodgy was going on, I...' she spoke so quietly Louise had to lean forward to hear. 'I had sex with him when we got home from the hospital. Less than twenty-four hours after I'd had sex with Rob.' Tears trickled down her cheeks. 'I was awake all night, lying there, disgusted with myself. In the morning I had to pretend everything was normal. It was horrible. And it's going to carry on being horrible. And I deserve it, because *I'm* horrible.'

Louise floundered extensively this time. Sleeping with two different men in twenty-four hours was a pretty slutty thing to do. She couldn't recall an *EastEnders* story line that depraved.

'It's not entirely your fault,' she said, desperately clutching for something comforting to say. 'Aries are the most likely of the zodiac to cheat. Their fiery, impulsive nature makes it harder for them to control their primal urges.'

Erica gave a watery smile. 'Thank you.' She wiped her cheeks and pulled herself up tall. 'Anyway, this isn't about me. The main thing is that Jasmine's alright. Doesn't bear thinking about what could have happened.'

'How is she?' Louise asked.

'Sleeping a lot, but ok in herself, thank God.' She clasped her hands together and Louise noticed that they were shaking. 'Easy to forget how fragile they are, isn't it?'

Louise nodded. She wasn't sure she'd ever admit to Erica the terror of seeing Jasmine falling and landing with a thud. She'd dashed forward and tried to catch her, but wasn't fast enough. Instead she'd called an ambulance, put Jasmine into the recovery position and talked to her until it arrived. She wasn't sure what Polly had been doing, but Summer must have woken up because she was in Polly's arms when the paramedics arrived. They'd decided that Louise should go to the hospital, as it was too late for Summer to be going out and she didn't want to let go of her mum – until she saw the paramedic, then she couldn't get out of Polly's arms fast enough. Polly had to prise Summer off one of the men's legs so that he could help carry the stretcher. That girl was going to have a real thing for men in uniform when she grew up. Or male strippers.

'Can you let Polly know how she is?' Erica picked up her phone and put it down again. 'I should ring her, but she's been acting a bit odd lately. Almost like Jasmine's *her* child. Have you found that with the twins? You know, telling them the facts of life and having them in bed with her and stuff.'

Louise didn't feel right talking about Polly behind her back. 'She means well. And she was really good about us forgetting her date.'

'Her date.' Erica put a hand to her mouth. 'Shit. You forgot too?'

'Yes.' Louise's cheeks burned. 'She had to cancel.'

'Shit,' Erica said again. 'Forget everything I said. I'm probably overreacting. And Polly's not to blame for Jasmine's fall. She wasn't even supposed to be there – you were. Not that I'm saying it was your fault.'

Louise bristled. No, it wasn't her fault. Erica seemed to have conveniently forgotten that she was supposed to be there too.

'I'll call Polly later,' Erica said. 'Explain that we're staying here for now.'

'How long for?' Louise asked. If Erica moved out, it wouldn't be three friends helping each other out with childcare anymore. It'd be more like she was Polly's lodger, especially when the twins were with Nick.

'Not sure,' Erica said. 'Jasmine's arm will be in a cast for a few weeks. I've taken some time off so we'll stay here while it heals. And after that, Dan's bonus and promotion mean we can afford a nanny again, so—'

'Afford?' This was news to Louise. She'd clocked the price of the bar stools with their walnut finishes and it hadn't looked as though Erica and Dan were struggling to get by.

'The decent ones cost a fortune. I...' Erica hesitated, then shrugged. 'Dan took out a huge loan to invest in the company so he could become a partner so we haven't had much disposable income. He didn't want anyone to know.'

Louise frowned. Despite the obvious flaws in Erica and Dan's relationship, she respected him enough not to break a confidence. Would she have done the same for Nick? She recalled the glee with which she'd regaled the story of how his online Tesco order had arrived ten days late. Rather than sympathising, she'd made fun of him. No wonder he didn't want to be with her.

Erica misread Louise's expression. 'Before you bring it up again, Jasmine didn't steal that money. Nor did I. Things weren't that bad.'

'I know. I made a mistake.' Louise's neck and face exploded with heat. Should she admit that Tess took the money because she tore Jasmine's *Frozen* nightie? The news might fade into insignificance compared with Jasmine's accident. Alternatively, Erica might use it to vent her frustration and go ballistic. Deciding not to risk it, she changed the subject.

'How are things with Dan?'

Erica's shoulders sagged. 'Awful. I wouldn't have fallen for Rob if they weren't.' Her voice wavered and she cleared her throat. 'We don't think the same way anymore. But he's Jasmine's dad so I have to make it work. I owe it to Jasmine.' She looked as thrilled at that prospect as Louise had when the midwife had suggested the figs diet. Erica sighed heavily. 'Any word from Nick?'

Louise shook her head. 'The twins are with him tonight, but I didn't go to the door. I can't face telling them yet.' She eyed the contents of the wine fridge. 'Fancy a drink?'

'No, thanks.'

'What?' Louise nearly fell off her stool.

'Jasmine might need me in the night. And, you never know, Rob might call. If I've had a drink there's a risk I'll blurt out how much I love him, instead of calmly apologising.'

Louise frowned. Erica was acting like a lovesick teenager. Usually she was the first to scorn the concept of love at first sight and happy-ever-afters. Watching any kind of romantic film with her was a nightmare. She even accused the prince in *Sleeping Beauty* of thinking with his dick.

'He's not going to call,' she said. 'You have to move on.'

'I will,' Erica said. 'As soon as I've explained the situation to him. I'm making things right with Jasmine and Dan. I'd feel better if I could make things right with Rob too. Or as close to right as they can be.'

'Why does it matter? You're never going to see him again.'

Erica blinked hard. 'It matters because I love him.'

Louise shook her head. 'You hardly know the bloke.'

Erica pressed her hands to her eyes. 'I know it sounds crazy, but I do. He makes me…' she gave a self-conscious laugh. 'This is embarrassingly corny, but he makes me want to be a better person.'

It was embarrassingly corny, but Louise didn't say no. 'This isn't like you. I'm starting to think you bumped your head as well.' Her laugh stuck in her throat when she saw the horror on Erica's face.

'What do you mean *as well*? You told the paramedic that Jasmine hadn't hit her head.'

'She didn't,' Louise said quickly. 'Can't have done. She'd have been unconscious or throwing up.'

Erica gasped. 'She *was* sick. The nurse thought it was a side-effect of the morphine.'

Louise's throat made a rasping sound as she swallowed. 'Well, that's what it was, then.'

'It might not have been. They'd have done other tests if they thought she'd hit her head. How could you be so irresponsible?'

'She didn't hit her head,' Louise said firmly. She'd have seen if she had. Without wanting to be gruesome, she'd have heard it.

'Are you sure?' The veins on Erica's neck were taut. 'Are you sure there's not a blood clot lying dormant, waiting to kill her? Come on, Miss Health and Safety. Can you guarantee me that?'

'Course not. That could happen any time.'

Erica clutched the side of the breakfast bar. 'You think she could die at any time?'

'No!' Louise wished she'd never come round. The gossip about Rob wasn't worth this accusation. 'What I mean is, if she does have a blood clot lying dormant, it probably doesn't have anything to do with her fall.'

'Probably isn't good enough,' Erica said through gritted teeth. 'I need to know for sure.'

Louise had had enough. 'If you wanted to know for sure, you should have been there. You call me irresponsible, but you're the one having an affair.'

Erica put a finger to her lips and raised her eyes to the ceiling. 'It's not an affair,' she whispered. 'It was a one-off with a man I love, who I'm never going to see again. Besides, it wasn't my fault, remember? It's because I'm an Aries.' She rolled her eyes.

Erica had a bloody cheek criticising her beliefs after her behaviour.

'I said Aries may find it *harder* to control their primal urges,' Louise snapped. 'Those with morals manage to resist.'

'You're saying I haven't got any morals?' Erica gave a hollow laugh. 'This, from the woman who spied on her husband and accused him of shagging her sister?'

'Better than shagging some bloke I hardly know.'

'I do know him. I know him better than I know you, right now.'

'Well he obviously doesn't want to know you or he'd have answered your calls.'

Erica flinched. 'Get out,' she said coldly. 'Just get out.'

Chapter Thirty-Nine

Erica

Erica smoothed Jasmine's dark hair away from her face. 'Have a nap, sweetie. It'll make you feel better.'

'Will you stay 'til I fall asleep?'

'Course I will.' Erica leant over Jasmine until she drifted off. Her shoulders ached and her back throbbed, but the delight in Jasmine's eyes when they flitted open to check she was there made it worth the pain. A few days with Erica's full focus and no distractions had given Jasmine the reassurance she needed to trust Erica again and she was all smiles and cuddles. Admittedly, the sedatives may have played a part. Erica made a mental note to squirrel away any leftovers for Jasmine's teenage years.

When she was sure Jasmine was asleep, Erica eased herself back into the chair and watched her, taking in her dark lashes, her pinky-brown lips and the rise and fall of her cheeks. It was like studying a painting that was so familiar she didn't often feel the need to look at it in depth. But she did need to because Jasmine was precious and wouldn't stay like this for long. Time went by so quickly that before they knew it, she'd be off to university and leaving home. And that'd be it. She'd be absorbed into the world with a life of her own. A life which, apart from the odd weekend and special occasion, Erica wouldn't be a part of.

Erica sat up straight. Things were going to change. No more constant early starts and late nights. She'd still work – she'd go stir crazy within days and would miss the fashion industry, plus she'd never suit a housecoat – but she'd pick and choose the projects she took on to fit around Jasmine, so they could spend more time together. She wasn't sure how yet, but she'd figure it out. Because no matter how great the thrill of finding that perfect pair of shoes, the ones that made the whole outfit come together perfectly, would that be what she'd remember on her deathbed? She gazed down at Jasmine, tears filling her eyes. No. No it wouldn't be.

Jasmine's fingers twitched beneath the soft cast, as though making sure they could move, which, mercifully, they could. 'You'll be playing the piano again in a few months,' the doctor had told her. It couldn't all be good news.

Dan opened the bedroom door and gestured for her to come out onto the landing. Erica wiped her eyes and went out to see him. He leant against the bannister, his hands in the pockets of his charcoal suit trousers.

'Why have you changed?' she asked. Even the way he dressed irritated her now. He'd been wearing a white, short-sleeved shirt and brown linen trousers when she'd seen him earlier. Even during a heat wave he refused to lower his sartorial standards and wear shorts. It was like living with the ghost of Sir Roger Moore.

'Just popping into work.'

'Again? You're supposed to be spending time with Jasmine.'

'But you and my mum are here. She'll be back from the shops soon by the way.' He must have registered the annoyance on Erica's face. 'I'll only be a couple of hours.'

'It's an hour each way. And you'll get caught up in a meeting and go for a drink after work and miss Jasmine completely.'

'I'll try not to, but you know how it is.'

Frustration coursed through her. She wanted to push him into Jasmine's room and force him to see what he risked losing if he didn't make an effort.

'I've got to go in. Make sure everything's on track for the China handover.' He sighed. 'It's such an arse working from two sites. Be much easier when I'm based in Dubai and only have to come back every few months.'

'Every few months?' Erica gasped. 'What the fuck happened to coming back every weekend?'

Dan had the grace to look sheepish. 'Been meaning to talk to you about that.'

'I'm all ears,' Erica snapped.

Dan took his phone out of his shirt pocket. 'I'll move my meeting back. Meet me downstairs in five and I'll explain.'

Erica went back into Jasmine's room. Her heart thumped hard against her chest. He'd done it again. Fed her a load of bullshit. He was such a selfish fucker. Thinking of his career, instead of her and Jasmine. He hadn't even discussed it with her. They'd agreed long ago not to bore each other with the minutiae of their work – she really didn't care which baked goods brought in the highest yield per quarter and he certainly didn't give a toss how many Swarovski crystals had been hand sewn onto a contestant's bralette (given the size of the top, Erica estimated about twelve) – but to not even mention that he was emigrating to the other side of the world? She'd have slightly more interest in that than blueberry muffin sales.

She gazed down at Jasmine. How could Dan prioritise work over this gorgeous girl? What sort of parent was he? *If you cared about Jasmine, you'd have been there.* Erica recalled Louise's words and shame enveloped her. She was no better than Dan. Maybe she was worse. He'd never hidden the fact that his career was his main focus. He'd only had a child because she wanted one. She shouldn't think badly of him for the Dubai move. He hadn't changed – she had.

Until recently, if she'd been offered the job of head stylist on the US version of *Sing to Win*, she'd have jumped at it. She'd have felt guilty about being away four days a week for three months and would have spent her entire wages on airport gifts for Jasmine and a nanny, but she'd have gone, telling herself that it was a once-in-a-lifetime career opportunity and that Jasmine would still be there when the three months was up. But Jasmine might not be. Not emotionally. The last two months at Polly's had proved how fragile love was and that if you didn't appreciate and reciprocate it, you risked losing it.

She took a last look at Jasmine before going downstairs. She was never going to take that risk again.

–

Dan sat at the island in the kitchen. Erica perched on the bar stool opposite him. He watched her warily, no doubt readying his defense.

She cleared her throat. 'You have to do what's right for you.'

Dan's head contracted, creating a turtleneck effect along his shirt collar. It wasn't a look she could see catching on.

'Why the change in heart? You were seething upstairs.'

Erica nodded. 'I don't have the right to criticise. Until recently' – about three minutes ago to be precise – 'if I'd been offered my dream job overseas I'd have taken it too. I'd have felt guilty, but I'd have done it.'

Dan relaxed his neck cautiously. 'And you wouldn't now?'

Erica thought of Jasmine asleep upstairs. 'No.'

'Oh, come on. You couldn't resist.'

Erica shook her head. 'I've decided not to do *Sing to Win* next year.'

Dan's mouth dropped open. 'You can't give it all up. What will people say?'

'I don't care what people say,' Erica said calmly. 'And I'm not giving it all up – just that show. It takes up too much time. I've barely seen Jasmine the last few months. This accident has been the wake-up call I needed. Made me realise how important it is to spend time with Jasmine.' She'd hoped her words would resonate, but Dan looked as perplexed as if she'd announced she was going to grow a handlebar moustache. 'I need something with more flexibility,' she continued. 'Where I can keep my hand in, without it taking over my life.'

'Like what? Part-time sales assistant at Top Shop?'

'Of course not,' she said, although the staff discount *was* an attractive prospect. 'I'll find a balance somehow.' She fiddled with her earring. 'I'm at a crossroads. I need to work out what my options are and choose a path.'

'Come to Dubai,' Dan said. 'Be a personal stylist to the WAGs of the rich and famous.' He rubbed his thumb and forefinger together. 'Lot of money out there.'

Erica was too stunned to respond. Dan continued to talk, but she zoned him out. A personal stylist to spoilt, rich show ponies? She'd be bored out of her mind. And where was Jasmine in all this?

Dan laughed. 'Don't look so horrified. They're all of a high standard.'

'What are?'

'The international schools.' Dan said. 'They follow the English national curriculum, so if we ever decide to come back, Jasmine could slot straight back in.'

'*If* we ever decide to come back?' Erica threw her hands in the air. 'You've gone from coming back to the UK every weekend to uprooting us all to the other side of the world permanently.'

'Why not?' Dan said. 'You said you fancied a change.'

He opened the calendar on his phone. 'When shall we go and have a recce? The properties are amazing. We can have our own pool.'

Erica cleared her throat. 'Aren't you forgetting something?'

'Shit, yes. Jasmine's arm. How long before she can fly?' He swiped the screen. 'We need to apply now, so she can start in September.'

'Dan.'

He raised a finger without looking up. 'Know what you're going to say. My new role doesn't start 'til October, but that's ok. We'll get you two set up and I'll join you asap.'

Erica resisted the urge to raise a certain finger of her own.

'We ought to get married,' he said. 'Dubai's a religious country and it'll make the paperwork easier.'

Erica rolled her eyes. Dan had never been overly romantic, but even he could have dressed the proposal up to make it less of an administrative necessity.

'Aren't you going to ask me?'

'Course, sorry.' Dan slid off his stool and dropped down to one knee. 'Will you—'

'Not that.' She motioned for him to stand up. 'You haven't asked me if I want to go to Dubai.'

Dan grabbed the side of the breakfast bar and levered himself up. 'Why wouldn't you?'

'Because I'd hate it. The snobbery, the arrogance, the lack of culture.' Her voice sped up. 'The underlying sexism and racism, the red tape, the lethal roads.' She thrust her hands in her hair. 'I don't want Jasmine growing up in that manufactured, unnatural environment with no grasp on reality; cocooned in a surreal world where people dip in and out, but no one puts down roots or even bothers to learn the national language.'

'But you said your career was at a crossroads.'

'A crossroads, yes. Not teetering on the edge of a fucking precipice.'

Dan crossed his arms. 'Hope you don't expect me to turn the job down and stay here.' He started listing all the reasons he was perfect for the role. In many ways he'd earned the right to be proud. After years of being ridiculed at school for being a geek, his intelligence was now reaping rewards. But at what expense? His determination to prove the bullies wrong, to prove himself a success, had made him almost narcissistic.

She and Dan had nothing in common; she could see that now. Even in the early days of their romance, they hadn't talked with the same intensity that she and Rob did, where conversation flowed and they were genuinely interested in what the other had to say. Rob had taken the trouble to get to know more about her in the past few weeks than Dan had in ten years.

He asked about her aspirations, her fears, her beliefs and values. Dan probably wasn't even aware she had any.

She and Rob might be over, but he'd brought out the best version of her she could be and she wanted to be that person. Dan brought out the worst. She didn't love him. What was the point in eking out the charade and limping on for a few more years? Yes it'd be hard for Jasmine initially, but long-term, living with two parents who weren't right together would surely do more harm than good. Not that it sounded as though Dan would be living with them much of the time anyway.

Dan sighed heavily. 'What *do* you want then?'

Erica bit her lip. She wanted what was best for Jasmine, and a life in Dubai, with parents who didn't get on, was far from that.

Her hand trembled as she placed it over his. 'Not this.' She swallowed hard. 'I'm sorry.'

Dan stared at her fingers and traced the outline of her nails with the pad of his thumb. 'It's ok. For a while now I've known your heart's not in it.'

He was more astute than she'd given him credit for.

'Often wish I hadn't bothered coming home,' Dan continued. 'You've got everything running how you want and I'm in the way.'

'Of course you aren't,' Erica said, not entirely honestly. 'It would have been nice if you'd helped out more, though. Even with a nanny there's still loads to do.'

A pulse went off in Dan's cheek. 'My job's all-consuming. I can't just switch gears in my brain and figure out what chores need doing. Whatever I do you criticise anyway. Move the plate I'd just put in the dishwasher, for example.'

Erica bit her lip to stop herself explaining why plates should be stacked upright in the lower drawer rather than laid face-down in the top drawer.

'When you stopped coming home at weekends I really felt surplus to requirements.'

'You know how demanding *Sing to Win* gets leading up to the final. I don't have time to think. I needed childcare and I could get that at Polly's.' Erica felt a pang of guilt at how much childcare Polly had provided without complaint. Then she remembered her brushing Jasmine's hair and her stomach twisted.

'You could have got a nanny if you'd really tried,' Dan said.

'I did try. There weren't any options.'

'That's never stopped you before.'

Erica opened her mouth to protest and then closed it again. Was Dan right? She'd convinced herself she didn't have time to find a nanny, but she'd have made time if she'd had to, if Polly hadn't agreed to the house share. Had she subconsciously wanted to put some distance between her and Dan to test their relationship? Or to end it?

Dan smoothed his tie with the palm of his hand. 'It's not your fault. We're in different places than we were when we met. Uncoupling is the most logical thing to do.'

The fact he used the pretentious phrase 'uncoupling' reinforced to Erica how right the decision was.

He stood up. 'I'll stay at the company flat tonight. I'm going back to China tomorrow for a couple of weeks, but I'll come over in the morning to say goodbye to Jasmine and my mum. You ok for her to stay 'til the weekend?'

Erica nodded numbly.

He cupped her face in his hands and pressed his lips to her forehead. She suppressed a sob. Separating was the right thing to do, but it still hurt. Shakily, she followed him to the front door. His creepy, theatre masks stared down at her from the wall. Would it be crass to suggest he took them now?

He hesitated at the door. 'Do me a favour. If you ever come across one of those shits I went to school with, tell them we uncoupled because you couldn't keep up with my inexhaustible sexual appetite.'

She forced a smile. 'I'll tell them you've got a massive cock too, if you like.' Dan's face fell. 'Because it's true,' she added hastily, holding her hands apart as though demonstrating how large a fish she'd caught. 'Massive.'

He opened the front door and stepped out onto the drive. 'See you, girl.'

And then he was gone.

Erica closed the door and went back to Jasmine's room. She had to haul herself up the bannister with both hands, the strength in her arms and legs having temporarily abandoned her. People described feeling hollow after suffering a trauma, but she was full to bursting with emotions – shock, sorrow, guilt, bewilderment, relief, which caused more guilt. She could barely move she was so overloaded with them.

She resumed her place by Jasmine's bedside. She was still fast asleep, oblivious to the fact that her parents had just broken up. Erica put her head in her hands. How was she going to break the news that not only were they separating, but that her dad was moving abroad and she'd only see him every few months? Would Jasmine blame her for it? They'd only just got their relationship back on track. Would this change in circumstances derail it again? Oh crap, why hadn't she hadn't thought of that earlier? Should she have gone along with Dan's suggestion of a life styling rich women in silk scarves in Dubai? Erica shuddered. No, she couldn't do that. She'd make it work here with Jasmine. She felt sad that she and Dan were over, of course she did, but the sadness was for Jasmine, not for herself. No longer doing *Sing to Win* would have more of an impact on her life.

Jasmine stirred in her sleep and Erica sprung forward, adjusting the sheet so that Jasmine's bandaged arm didn't get caught in it, then she sat back and drew her knees up. They'd be alright, she and Jasmine. More than alright. She'd make sure of it. She had no idea how yet, but she'd figure it out. And while she was doing that, she'd spend the rest of the summer holidays being a mum. She smiled and closed her eyes, satisfied she was, at last, doing the right thing for Jasmine.

Something was still gnawing away at her though, preventing her from relaxing fully. It wasn't the break-up with Dan; that had been a long time coming. It wasn't the fall-outs with Polly and Louise; they'd both been unreasonable. Her eyes snapped open. It was Rob. The thought of how she'd treated him made her heart ache. She wasn't naive enough to think they could pick up from where they'd left off. Even without Dan in the picture, she needed to focus on Jasmine and no one else, but she couldn't bear to think of Rob hurt and confused. He'd been open and honest with her and she'd lied. She'd betrayed him. She had to fix it.

Making sure Jasmine was fast asleep, she tiptoed to her room and phoned Rob. He wouldn't pick up, he'd ignored enough of her calls for her to realise that, but he might listen to an answerphone message.

Rob answered after just three rings. Her heart jolted.

'I asked you not to call me anymore, Erica.' Her stomach twisted. He sounded so cold. 'You've got to stop.'

'Please don't hang up.' Erica gripped the phone. 'I'm so sorry. Please let me explain.'

Rob didn't speak, but he didn't end the call either, so she hurried on. This was her only chance.

'I behaved terribly, I know. I kept meaning to tell you that I was still with Jasmine's dad, but something always stopped me. And then, that night, I realised that I'm in love with you.'

Rob didn't say anything. Was he still angry? Relieved? Pleased? Maybe he was doing a little victory dance? She dismissed that possibility. Only knobs did victory dances. But why was he so quiet?

'Dan and I have split up,' she continued. 'Not just because of you, there are other reasons. Not other men,' she added quickly. 'I've never cheated on him with anyone else.'

'I'm honoured,' Rob said, his voice heavy with sarcasm.

Erica put a hand to her brow. This wasn't going the way she'd hoped it would.

'It doesn't excuse the way I behaved,' she said quietly. 'But I thought that if I explained, you'd understand. Maybe feel a bit better about it.'

'Understand?'

Erica winced at the anger in his voice.

'You lied to me.' Rob sounded slightly breathless, as though he were pacing up and down. 'You cheated on your husband.'

'He's not technically—' she began, but realised that didn't really matter. 'I'm so sorry. I didn't mean to lie or hurt you.'

'Then why did you?'

'I don't know,' Erica said in a small voice. 'I suppose I was scared to tell you in case you didn't want to know me anymore.'

'Of course I'd have wanted to know you,' Rob said. 'We could have still been friends, but I'd have respected your marriage.'

'I tried to just be friends, but I couldn't resist you. I like you too much.'

Rob muttered something she couldn't hear.

'Sorry?' she said tentatively.

'You're the first person I've been involved with since my divorce,' he said. 'She had an affair, but I was the one who had to move out and leave Daisy. It was shit. It hit me hard.' He sounded sad rather than angry now.

Erica squeezed the phone, wishing she could hug him.

'When we clicked, I thought I'd finally met someone I could try again with. It took me ages to get up the courage to ask you out and when I did…' he exhaled loudly. 'Well, you know the rest. Hasn't exactly restored my faith in relationships.'

'I'm so sorry.' Her voice cracked. She'd never asked what had happened between him and his ex-wife. Now she knew she felt even worse than before. 'Can we meet up sometime, just for a coffee? I'd like to say sorry properly in person.'

'No.' His forcefulness shocked her. It was as though she'd been slammed into a brick wall. 'It wouldn't just be a coffee and a quick chat. It'd be opening everything back up again.' He lowered his voice. She had to strain to hear him. 'I really fell for you Erica. Not seeing you is the quickest way to get over you.'

'I fell for you too.' Sensing the call was drawing to a close, Erica spoke quickly. 'I hurt you and I can't bear the thought of that. Of you hating me.'

'I don't hate you, Erica.'

She held her breath.

'But you're not the person I thought you were.'

Her breath came rushing out. 'But—'

'Goodbye, Erica.'

And then, like Dan an hour earlier, he was gone.

She placed the phone on the dressing table. A burning grew in her chest; an excruciating pressure causing her to cry with such intensity that she tumbled from the stool to the floor. She curled up in a ball and sobbed. So this was love. Not hearts and flowers, as the card shops suggested. Not rainbows and smiley emoticons. It was pain. Torturous pain. Her heart was dissolving like a slug in salt. Slowly, agonisingly, permanently.

Chapter Forty

Louise

The chickens are coming home to roost, so make sure that chicken coop is ready for guests. Louise's brow furrowed, as she read her horoscope. What the bloody hell did that mean? She read on. *The sooner you deal with the past, the sooner you can move on.* Which part of her past was that, then? Nick? Polly? Erica? Things had been strained with Polly since Louise had forgotten to babysit and then there'd been that awful argument with Erica the day before. Louise had said some hurtful things she didn't mean, but so had Erica and Louise wasn't convinced Erica hadn't meant them. Jasmine's accident *wasn't* her fault though. Erica should have been there. She pursed her lips. You wouldn't catch *her* sneaking off for a leg-over in the toilet with someone she worked with. Although, if Colin Firth ever turned up in her office, she'd have him in that disabled cubicle quicker than you could say 'handrails'.

A football thudded against the kitchen window, making Louise jump. She turned to see George sprinting across the car park to retrieve it. It was a wonder any part of the house was still standing with him in it. Only that morning he'd knocked her phone into her mug of tea. To their mutual surprise, she hadn't been angry. She was due an upgrade and, until it arrived, couldn't receive Nick's daily texts urging her to contact him so they could talk. 'Talk' clearly being code for 'tell the twins we've split up.' She knew she had to face him at some point, but was in no hurry to invite those particular chickens home to roost.

'Go, Tess,' she heard George shout outside. 'Wicked right pass.'

She smiled to herself. Since Tess's revelation about how unhappy she was, she'd transformed from – if Louise was brutally honest – selfish and whiny to thoughtful and fun and was getting on better with everyone. Unlike Louise, who wasn't getting on with anyone.

Polly and Summer came into the kitchen, Summer in a pink t-shirt and Hello Kitty sunglasses.

'Someone's ready for the holiday,' Louise said brightly. They were going to Spain in two days. It'd be a bloody miserable week if she and Polly weren't speaking.

'No nappy.' Summer took her dummy out of her mouth and pulled her t-shirt up proudly, revealing chunky, dimpled thighs – not dissimilar to Louise's, but without the thread veins.

'Started potty training today,' Polly said. 'Thought the holiday would be a good opportunity, as we'll be outside most of the time.'

Louise frowned. Yes, the holiday would be a good opportunity, but they had a three-hour flight to get through first.

'Have you packed yet?' she asked.

'No, but it won't take long,' Polly said. 'Mustn't forget to clear out the den before we go. The new roof's going on while we're away.'

Louise vaguely remembered Polly saying some work needed doing. She'd assumed there were a couple of loose tiles, not that the whole thing needed replacing.

Polly's phone beeped. She read the message and smiled. 'Alex is asking if we like chicken. We're going over for lunch.' She hummed to herself as she typed a reply.

Chicken? Louise reread her horoscope. Was the B&B the chicken coop? Would Alex and his children be moving in? Her and her big mouth. Why had she encouraged Polly to make a go of it with Alex? What would happen to her and the twins? Where would they live? Panic and resentment rose in Louise's throat and she swallowed them down. They couldn't taste worse than the grapefruit she had to eat for breakfast.

'Ooh,' Summer said in wonder, as a stream of wee gushed from between her legs and formed a yellow puddle on the floor.

'Never mind,' Polly said, mopping it up with a tea towel. She took Summer upstairs to get changed, leaving the soiled tea towel on the floor.

Louise's hard-wired health and safety training had her twitching in her chair. Although that could also have been caused by the grapefruit. A knock at the front door gave her an excuse to get away from both the tea towel and her breakfast. A man in overalls stood on the doorstep and a white van with the words 'Ron's Reliable Roofing' was parked up on the curb.

The man, who Louise assumed was Ron, looked down at his clipboard. 'Mrs Tomlin?'

Louise shook her head. 'She's busy. Can I help?'

'I was passing and thought I'd stop and ask if we can drop some supplies round before Monday.'

'It'll have to be tomorrow or Friday. We're going away for the week on Saturday.'

Ron nodded. 'Should be able to drop them off before then. Good job you're away. Chrysotile can stay in the air for up to seventy-two hours. You can't be too careful.'

Louise nodded. It was comforting to know that there were others out there as concerned with health and safety as she was. She started to swing the door shut, then froze as the significance of his words sunk in. 'Chrysotile?' She yanked the door open. 'Chrysotile?' she repeated. 'Isn't that...' her body trembled, 'asbestos?'

Ron nodded. 'That's why we're replacing the roof.'

Louise's eyes jerked upwards. 'It's in the roof?'

'Only at the back. The room with the extension. It's pretty standard with these 1970s low-rise add-ons.'

'But asbestos kills.' Louise gripped the doorframe tightly.

Ron gave what was probably meant to be a reassuring smile. He looked as reassuring as Jack Nicholson had in *The Shining*.

'We'll have the whole thing off and a new one meeting safety requirements on before you're back.'

'Does Polly, Mrs Tomlin, know?'

'Yeah, it's why she booked us.' Ron turned away and was in his van and driving off before Louise could question him further.

Louise clamped a hand over her mouth. There was asbestos in the roof. Asbestos – a certified carcinogen. One of the most lethal substances created by man. And Polly knew about it. Louise's mind flitted back to the day they'd moved in, to Polly's tour of the house. To her detailed explanation of how to thump the boiler if the hot water hadn't come on. How to jiggle the bolt on the front door to ease it open. How to pump the toilet handle three times to get the cistern to flush. She hadn't said a word about the asbestos hovering above their heads like an executioner's axe. No, that little nugget of information hadn't warranted a mention. Well Louise knew now and she had to get them out. She couldn't avoid Nick anymore. She had to go to him, despite knowing he'd seize the opportunity to tell the twins that the marriage was over. She had no choice.

Turning, she ran up the stairs to George and Tess's rooms. Their holiday cases stood by their wardrobes and she grabbed them, thankful for her organisational skills. Her case was ready too, and the passports, euros and flight details were in a plastic wallet on her bedside table. Grabbing them, she raced back to the kitchen, pulling her case behind her then going back for the twins'. She stumbled out into the courtyard, exhausted.

'Are you alright?' Polly appeared at the back door, a clean, but bare-bottomed Summer in her arms. Between that and the asbestos, she clearly had a death wish.

Louise pushed the cases out of the gate to where the children were playing football in the car park. 'Why the bloody hell didn't you tell me?'

'Tell you what?'

Louise pointed at the extension. 'The asbestos. We'd never have moved in if I'd known.' She turned to the twins. 'George, Tess, in the car.'

'But we're in the middle of—'

'Don't talk. Don't breathe. Just run.'

They must have sensed the urgency in her voice, as they did what they were told.

'Louise,' Polly called out. 'It's ok.'

Louise hurled the cases into the boot before clambering into the driver's seat. 'Get out,' she shouted before slamming the door. 'Save yourselves!'

Slightly over-dramatic perhaps, but this called for a bit of drama. She headed towards home. She'd done it. She'd got George and Tess away from the danger. They were safe. Except that now she had to do the thing she'd been avoiding for weeks. The thing that would rubber stamp the end of the life she wanted and force her into a new, miserable one. She had to face Nick and sit by his side while he told the twins that they were separated. Her hands trembled on the steering wheel. Suddenly she didn't feel safe at all.

Chapter Forty-One

Polly

Polly pulled up outside Alex's house and wrapped a hand around her pendant. She was reeling from Louise's reaction to the asbestos. And she was missing Jasmine. They'd become so close in the last few weeks and now she couldn't even speak to her. Erica was clearly ignoring her calls and her texted replies about Jasmine were sporadic and to the point. How could Louise and Erica have turned on her after she'd done so much to help them? The checkout girl in the corner shop had shown more kindness than her supposed best friends. Until Summer wet herself in the fresh produce aisle. The checkout girl hadn't been so warm after that.

At least things were good with Alex. He'd dismissed her apologies after she'd been so curt the night of their date and they were tentatively building their relationship.

She unfastened Summer and they got out of the car with Oliver. The smell of roast chicken hung in the air. Bess and some of her puppies bounded over when she pushed the garden gate open. Summer ran up to Maisie, and Polly realised her movements were much more fluid now that she was no longer in a nappy. Fluid being the operative word. In hindsight, this hadn't been the best day to start potty training. She'd be mortified if Summer had an accident at Alex's, but there was no going back now. She'd opened the floodgates. Literally.

'Look. Knickers!' Summer said to Maisie, proudly hoicking her dress up to reveal a pair of white pants with the word

'Wednesday' written across the front. A twenty-four-hour clock emblem would have been more appropriate.

'Well done,' Maisie said, extending her hand. 'Let's go and play.'

They walked up the mosaic path at the side of the house that led to the large back garden. The smell of chicken grew stronger. Within seconds Oliver and Max were playing football and Summer was piling dolls into a toy pram. Alex grinned when he saw Polly. He was wearing a green shirt with loose, long, cut-off denim shorts and his ankles and calves were deeply tanned and coated in fine, dark hairs. He was turning chicken skewers over on a barbecue.

The glare from the sun couldn't prevent a chill running through Polly. Barbecues had been Ian's thing. Every Sunday from May through to September, he'd be out in the garden, a pack of beer at his side, a pair of tongs in his hand. Regardless of the weather, he'd arrange the charcoal briquettes and fire-lighters over the grate. Perching on the wall beside the brick-built barbecue, he'd sip from his can and watch the coals slowly redden then lighten to grey before laying out sausages, burgers and spare ribs. Most weekends Adam and Cheryl from next door came over with their two children. It was always the same: Adam playing with the children or helping Polly set up, then tidy away; Cheryl replying to texts and apologising that she couldn't stay longer but she had a gym class or was meeting friends; Ian resolutely manning the barbecue, making sure every morsel of meat was thoroughly cooked. Every barbecue was exactly the same. Until that last one.

They'd reached the back of the house. A gas barbecue stood on the patio, chicken sizzling on one side, brightly coloured vegetables charring on the other. As barbecues went, it couldn't be more different to Ian's – this one looked as though some arteries would actually remain unclogged – but it was still a barbecue. And to her, barbecues meant one thing. The catalyst to the nightmare beginning.

'What's wrong?' Alex put a hand on her arm. 'You're shaking.'

Polly didn't want to make a fuss. She just wanted to go home. It had been a mistake to come, to think she could move on. She'd never be able to. Ian was too much a part of their life.

She pulled her arm away. 'Sorry. We've got to go,' she managed to say.

Alex's face fell. 'Why?'

Polly's throat tightened. She couldn't tell him why. She couldn't tell anyone.

'Come and sit in the shade.' Alex led her to a wooden seat beneath a tree.

Polly tried to resist, but couldn't summon the breath to speak. Her throat had constricted as tightly as if a hand were around her neck. Alex's face was a picture of concern. His image began to fade until he was completely bleached out. Polly blinked. Alex was gone. Ian was staring at her. His eyes bore into her, as they had at the barbecue that day. Those eyes would stay with her forever. They were ingrained in her. They'd never leave her.

Polly felt her head fall forward. She clutched the fabric of her dress, scrunching it tightly in her fists, as she tried desperately to stop her body shaking, to stop it shutting down, to stop it ruining her life.

'Polly?' Alex's voice grew dull. 'Polly?'

Ian's face drew closer and closer. His eyes grew larger and larger until they were so close they merged into one enormous, unblinking eye, watching her, questioning her, doubting her. She wanted to press her hands to her head and squeeze the image out, but Alex was gripping her arms, restricting her movement. She couldn't hear him, but knew he was talking to her. She could feel vibrations through his hands, could sense the concern in his fingers, the urgency in his grip. He was trying to bring her back, pull her away from the horror of her past and into the possibility of a future. Maybe Alex could save her.

Desperately she listened for his voice. If she could zone in on his words, then she could grab hold of them and let him pull her free. Her ears strained, but she couldn't hear him. The only sound was a low drone from Ian's eye, as it continued to stare.

Her anxiety increased, crushing any remaining air from her lungs. Why was the eye still here? Why wasn't Alex's voice scaring it off? Ian's eye continued to drill into her, its constant hum stealing her oxygen so she couldn't breathe. The eye was growing. It was closing in on her completely now. Its glossy, black pupil reflected her image back at her. She could see herself, limp in Alex's arms, her head hanging low. Alex was shaking her, shouting her name. Oliver was running over. Oliver's mouth was opening and closing. She couldn't hear him, but she knew exactly what he was saying. 'Breathe, Mum. Breathe.'

Alex couldn't save her. It was wrong of her to expect him to. It wasn't his responsibility. And it certainly wasn't Oliver's. No, there was only one person who could save her. And it was about time she let them.

Blocking out the garden scene she'd just watched from afar, she confronted Ian's eye. For the first time, she met its gaze head on and stared back.

'That's enough,' she shouted. 'I've suffered enough. I'm sorry about what happened, I'm really sorry, but I deserve to have a life now. Let me live it. Let me at least try.'

The eye blinked, then narrowed and disappeared.

She was suddenly aware of an acute pain in her lungs and grass beneath her knees. Then everything went black.

Chapter Forty-Two

Louise

'Sorry to just let myself in, but we can't stay at Polly's. It's not safe.' Louise knew she was gabbling, but couldn't slow herself down.

'It's ok.' Nick's voice was calm and steady down the phone. 'I won't touch anything.'

'Don't be silly. It's your house too.' House, not home. 'Stay 'til you go on holiday. It'll be good to spend time with the twins before you go away.' He paused. 'It'll give us a chance to tell them what's going on. They're not stupid.'

Yes they are, Louise wanted to say. They didn't suspect anything. She and Nick could easily get back together and the twins would never know they'd been apart. Or was she being stupid now?

'The paper's just gone to the printers. I'll try and get home early,' Nick said. 'Give the twins my love.'

He hung up. Sighing, Louise trudged out into the back garden. George was poised in front of a basketball hoop. Nick must have put it up in the last few weeks. The ball balanced on the edge of the hoop and fell through the net with a satisfying swish. Louise clapped, astounded that the hoop was still in one piece.

George grinned. 'Want a go?'

'I wouldn't be any good.'

George shrugged. 'I could teach you.'

Louise took the ball he offered her. 'Go on then.'

An hour later, she lowered herself carefully into the bath, wincing, as her calf muscles tensed up in the warm water.

Tess had joined them in the garden and it had turned into a rather energetic game. So energetic that Louise had had to lie face-down on the sofa for ten minutes to garner enough energy to limp and wheeze her way up the stairs. Despite creating a pain in her shoulders and legs so intense she felt as though she'd been among the group dragging Stonehenge from Wales to Salisbury, it had been fun. Although playing Jenga was also fun and used far fewer muscles.

Louise massaged shampoo into her hair, then lay back to rinse it out. Her hands moved down her neck, across her breasts, to her stomach. Everything was definitely smaller than it had been two months ago. She closed her eyes, enjoying the swirl of the water in her hair.

A clonking sound reverberated around the bath. She sat up, raising her arms to smooth her hair away from her face. A gasp to her right made her jump. She turned, her hands still in her hair, leaving her breasts completely exposed. Nick stood inside the bathroom, his mouth open, his eyes wide behind his glasses. They met hers briefly then vanished behind a layer of steam. Louise whipped her hands down to her chest, covering her breasts.

'Sorry.' Nick's voice was higher than usual. 'Didn't know you were in here.' He covered his glasses with one hand and sidled towards the door. Louise's clothes were in a pile on the floor and one of his size thirteen feet got caught up in the strap of her 40DD bra. The combination of high digit appendages worked against him and he stumbled and grabbed hold of the pull cord for the fan to steady his fall. A loud grinding noise filled the bathroom. 'Sorry,' he said again, his voice panic-stricken. He tugged at the cord, yanking it in different directions until it clicked again and the fan stopped whirring. 'Or did you want it on?' He peeked over this hand. The steam on his glasses was clearing. He gulped and whipped round to face the wall. 'I'll let you, er...' He shuffled through the door sideways and pulled it shut behind him.

Louise released her breasts and put her hands over her face. What must he think of her? Sitting there with her hands hooked behind her head as though she were a glamour model.

'I didn't see anything,' he called through the door.

That clearly wasn't true. He wouldn't have been tripping over his feet in his haste to get out the door if it was, or choking at the sight of her pink, blobby form.

His feet banged down the stairs and she clambered out of the bath and wrapped herself in a towel. She caught her reflection in the mirror. Her face was scarlet, either from the hot water or the mortification of what had just happened. Either way, rosacea wasn't an attractive look. She finger-combed her hair around her face. Inspired by the photo Erica had given her, she'd had her hair cut and coloured. Her structured, unmoveable, mousy bob was gone. Now, choppy, chestnut-brown hair fell naturally to her jaw line. The feather cut and colour accentuated the gold flecks in her brown eyes and softened her face. 'It takes pounds off you,' the hairdresser told her. Shame the number of pounds lost didn't equate to what the cut and colour had cost.

Tucking the corner of the towel into her cleavage, she ventured out into the hall. The television was on downstairs and she could hear Tess and George discussing the programme. They sounded happy. Enjoy it while it lasts, kids, she thought miserably. Now that they were all together, there was no hiding from Nick's insistence that they tell the twins they were separated. There was no hiding anything in this towel.

She crossed the landing and went into the bedroom she used to share with Nick. The giant teddy bear he'd bought her one birthday sat in the centre of the bed. Picking it up, she pressed it to her face. It smelled of olbas oil and spectacle cleaner. It smelled of Nick.

'Keep meaning to give that back to you.' Nick emerged from their minuscule en suite. Dropping the bear back onto the bed she looked down and realised her décolletage was bulging perilously over the tightly wrapped towel.

She indicated the wardrobe behind Nick. 'Need to get some clothes.'

He stepped back and she shuffled sideways along the narrow gap between the bed and the wardrobe. Her eyes were level with his chest. Even with her calves pressed up against the bed, she couldn't avoid her breasts squishing against him like rollers in a carwash as she sidled past. Nick's Adam's apple bobbed up and down as he swallowed loudly. After an excruciating few seconds, she reached the wardrobe door and pulled it open. The contents were a succession of navy skirts in varying sizes, white revere blouses and a brown wraparound dress she'd worn to her sister's wedding. She closed the door. Nothing could entice her into those again. The new Louise might have lost the love of her life and be wretchedly unhappy, but at least she wouldn't be dressed in polyester.

'I'll wear something from my case. There's time to wash it before the holiday.' She hesitated, wondering whether to go through the mortifying process of squeezing past Nick again or roll commando-like across the bed. Given that she was actually commando beneath her towel, she'd rather avoid that scenario.

'Before you go downstairs, we need to talk.' His tone was gentle. Did he think that would make her more amenable? Hannibal Lecter had had a similar tactic and his victims weren't exactly pleased with his subsequent culinary choices.

She sank down onto the edge of the bed, her stomach churning. She couldn't stop him delivering the most brutal words she could hear, but before he did, she needed to tell him something.

'I know what you're going to say.' She looked at her hands. 'And I don't blame you. Everything you said was true. I took you for granted. Worse than that, I undermined you and put you down.' Her cheeks burned with remorse. 'I must have been a cow to live with.'

'I wouldn't go as far as calling you a cow, but it has been challenging at times.' Nick sat down next to her. 'You see yourself as Queen Bee and me as the worker ant. Yes, you're a great organiser and your lists of instructions are often invaluable, but you forget that I'm capable too. It would have been fairer to share our roles. Support each other equally and be a proper team.'

Louise squirmed uncomfortably. Support was the very thing that Erica had said was missing in her home when she came up with the idea of the house share. Ironic that Nick had felt the same. It should have been him moving in to Polly's. Louise thought of Erica's brightly coloured thongs on the airer and the way Polly's dressing gown gaped open when Summer thrust her arm down it. No, just as well he hadn't.

'Something else I don't understand is your lack of interest in the twins,' Nick continued. 'You clock off as soon as I walk in the door. What little attention you were paying them goes out the window. They pick up on that.'

'I don't know why I was like that.' She thought of Tess and George's smiles at the pool and in the garden playing basketball. 'I love spending time with them now.'

'What about my novel?' Nick asked quietly. 'You know it's important to me. Why are you so disinterested?'

Louise hesitated. 'I'm afraid,' she admitted.

'That it'll be awful and I'll embarrass you?'

'No.' Louise turned her face away so he couldn't see the tears of shame coursing down her cheeks. 'Afraid it'll be a huge success. Then you'll be going to book launches and film premieres and meeting new, exciting people. You won't want a fat, frumpy wife. You'll trade me in for a young, beautiful trophy wife.'

Nick released what sounded like a muffled laugh. He was mocking her now. But wasn't that what she'd done to him for years? Was this how he'd felt the whole time?

'If I did ever achieve "literary success",' he drew speech marks in the air, 'I'd have taken you to the book launches and film premieres. Not that many debut authors do,' he continued. 'Most have to stick with their day jobs. Even so, I hoped you'd be as proud as I was when you won your award. You're a genuine trophy wife.'

'It's an engraved glass swan, not a trophy.' Louise gave a small smile. For a moment she thought he was going to smile back, but instead he took his glasses off and rubbed his eyes.

'What hurt most was the distrust. The spying. How can I be with someone who's suspicious all the time? Who doubts everything I say and hacks into my emails and tracks my movements? It's not healthy. I can't live like that.'

A pain formed in Louise's chest. This was it. The moment she'd been dreading. When he told her he wanted a divorce. This was the end.

'Why didn't you talk to me?' he said. 'You could have asked what I was thinking and doing. You didn't have to spy on me.'

'But you could lie. Like Dave did.' Her words came out in a childish squeak.

Nick pinched the bridge of his nose. 'I know your ex-husband was a shit, but you can't use that as an excuse every time you screw up. Sometimes you have to accept responsibility for your mistakes.'

Louise sniffed. Should she tell him? Relieve the guilt she'd been carrying for the past eighteen years? It wasn't as if she could sink any lower in his esteem.

'It wasn't all Dave's fault,' she said quietly. 'I didn't love him. I only married him to prove to my sister I could get someone. He certainly didn't love me. I'm not sure he even liked me. If I hadn't been sitting next to him at the cinema when Sharon Stone crossed her legs in *Basic Instinct* he'd never have offered to buy me chips after.' Her chest rose and fell, testing the towel's strength to its limits. 'He was horny. I was grateful. When I told him I was pregnant, he did the decent thing and married me. But *I* hadn't done the decent thing. It turned out my period was just late but I couldn't bear the humiliation of him dumping me. I waited 'til we got married and pretended I'd miscarried.' She covered her face with her hands. She'd done it now. As if the way she'd treated Nick hadn't been bad enough, now he knew she was a serial bitch. 'I've never told anyone that before.'

Nick didn't respond.

'Do you hate me?' She swallowed anxiously. 'Even more?'

Nick was still silent. Why didn't he speak? Was he too angry? Too shocked? Too disgusted? His silence was torturing her. Nervously, she parted her fingers and peered at him. He sat with his glasses in his lap, his elbows resting on his knees while his hands cradled his head. He wasn't angry or shocked or disgusted. He was crying.

'Nick?'

He took a handkerchief from his pocket and wiped his eyes. Louise felt a surge of fondness for him. He was probably the only man in the world who still used a handkerchief. Without looking at her, he rubbed the lenses of his glasses and slid them onto his nose, before folding the handkerchief neatly and putting it back in his pocket. Finally, he turned to face her.

'That's the first time you've confided in me,' he said. 'Trusted me with the truth rather than fobbing me off. You've let me see the real you.'

Louise swallowed hard. The real her was a big, fat liar with puffy eyes and a blotchy face. She wasn't sure where he was going with this.

'Tess told me about the money she stole and said you'd been really good about it. And that you told her you were bullied at school too. She and George have both said how much you've changed. They're happier now; I can see it. You even took them swimming.' He gave a small smile. 'I know underneath your bolshie façade you're insecure. Being bullied and cheated on would make anyone wary. But you've got to stop being suspicious and start trusting people. Especially the ones who care about you.'

Louise hardly dared speak. But she had to. She had to ask him.

'Are you one of those people?' she whispered. 'Do you care about me?'

Nick shook his head. Louise closed her eyes. That was that, then. There was no hope left.

'How can you even ask that? Of course I do. You're my wife.'

Her eyes sprung open. 'After everything I've done? The way I've behaved?'

Nick took her hand. 'Believe me, I've tried to stop loving you.' He laced his fingers through hers. He was still wearing his wedding ring. 'Then I saw the effort you were making with the twins. It made me wonder if you were returning to the old Lou. And now, after everything you've just told me,' he gripped her hand, 'I know I could never stop loving you.'

'Oh, Nick.' This was so much more than she'd dared hope for. 'Are you sure? You could do loads better.'

'Hardly. You look fantastic. Your hair and...' he grinned coyly. 'When I walked into the bathroom earlier—'

'Don't.' Louise put a hand over her eyes. 'I must have looked such an idiot.'

'You certainly didn't.' Nick gently prised her fingers away. 'You looked Rubenesque. Like Venus rising from the water.' He frowned. 'You didn't need to lose weight, though. You always looked good to me.'

'Are you mad?' Louise self-consciously pulled her towel tighter around her. 'I was huge. Especially compared with Erica and Polly.'

Nick shook his head. 'You don't have to be the same build as them to be attractive.' His eyes flitted briefly to her cleavage. 'I want you to be healthy and happy, not stick-thin.'

'Really?' Louise whispered.

'Really.' He cupped her chin in his hand and tilted her head up so she had no choice but to look at him. 'I love you, Lou.' He edged closer. 'And I don't half fancy you.'

'So do I.' She threw her arms around his neck and pressed her lips hard against his. He seemed startled by her enthusiasm for a moment, but quickly regained his composure and kissed her back. Louise closed her eyes. She hadn't realised it was possible to be so completely and utterly happy.

Nick's lips moved to her neck. 'Come home, Lou. I've missed you and the twins so much.'

Louise grinned. 'Yes, please,' she murmured.

'Can I come to Spain?'

Louise nodded eagerly. Polly would understand.

'Oh, Lou.' His mouth was on her collarbone. 'Thank goodness for asbestos.'

Louise gasped. The asbestos. She pulled away and jumped up. Nick tumbled forward on the bed.

'I have to go back and talk to Polly. She doesn't understand how dangerous it is.' She smoothed her damp hair. 'Erica doesn't even know yet.'

'Can't you phone or text them?' Nick was panting slightly.

Louise shook her head. 'George knocked my phone into my tea. I don't know their numbers.' She looked around for her clothes, then remembered her case was downstairs.

Nick reached out and took her hand. 'Any chance you could hold off for five minutes before you go?'

Louise looked at his eager, flushed face, his bright eyes behind his glasses and the triangular arrangement of his shorts. He wanted her. He really wanted her, regardless of her size. He'd seen her naked and it hadn't put him off. Heat swirled between her legs. And she wanted him. She delved into her cleavage where she'd wedged the corner of the towel. Slowly she unwrapped it and let it fall to the floor. 'Let's make it ten minutes.'

Chapter Forty-Three

Polly

The air was thick with the smell of marinaded chicken and roast vegetables. Knives and forks clinked against plates. There was a childish giggle as ketchup squelched, fart-like, out of its bottle. Alex apologised.

Polly laughed. She'd done it. She'd overcome the panic attack. All by herself. Without Oliver urging her, fear and desperation in his eyes. Without Alex, kitted out in shining armour with a joust beneath his arm. Without a doctor or therapist. By herself. She'd never confronted it before, never had the courage, or believed she could. But she could and she had. She wasn't afraid anymore.

'Sure you're ok?' Alex asked her.

Polly nodded. 'Sorry about earlier.'

'Stop apologising. Wouldn't blame you for feigning heat-stroke to get out of eating the kids' pasta salad,' he added with a whisper.

Polly laughed again. Max and Maisie had boiled the pasta until all the water was gone, resulting in a solidified ball of slime cemented to the base of the saucepan. Adding a dollop of pesto hadn't increased its appeal.

'Polly.' Maisie appeared beside her. 'Summer's done another wee.'

Polly's cheeks grew warm. 'Sorry.'

Alex laughed. 'No worries. Less of the garden to water later on.'

Polly reached for her bag and took out a packet of wipes and the last pair of clean pants she'd brought with her. 'We're down to our last accident, then we'll have to go.'

Alex pulled at a patch of grass. 'You don't have to.'

Polly glanced at the top of Alex's bowed head. 'What do you mean?'

'The kids and I are going to camp in the garden tonight. You're welcome to join us. Although I doubt you'll get much sleep.'

Polly's cheeks were on fire now. She liked Alex, but wasn't ready to jump into bed with him. Especially not when it was a camp bed.

'Because we'd all be in together, I mean,' Alex added quickly. 'Be a bit of an adventure. Four kids and seven dogs would stop any—' One of the puppies jumped onto his lap and he fussed over it, welcoming the distraction.

Polly ran her pendant slowly along its chain. What was stopping her? The thrill of a night on her own once the kids had gone to sleep? Clearing out the den in preparation for the roof being replaced next week? Tidying the mess in her bedroom where she'd pulled everything out of her wardrobe that morning searching for her sunhat? Or they could stay and have a fun evening. Just minutes ago, she'd told herself she was moving on. Here was her chance. All she had to do was nip home and get pyjamas and toothbrushes.

'Probably a silly idea,' Alex said, stroking the puppy's ears and avoiding her eyes.

Polly let go of her pendant and it fell back against her chest with a gentle bump.

'It's not a silly idea,' she said with a smile. 'We'd love to.'

Chapter Forty-Four

Erica

Sweat poured down Erica's back. And her front. And her sides. People were actually recoiling as she ran past them. Wiping beads the size of baubles from her forehead before they trickled into her eyes, she finally understood the appeal of big eyebrows.

Running in a heat wave during rush hour wasn't sensible, but she'd had to get out of the house. She'd laid sobbing on her bedroom floor until her tear ducts couldn't physically produce any more liquid. Eventually Jasmine had woken up and called out. Erica had dragged herself up, as exhausted as though recuperating from flu, and climbed into Jasmine's bed where they'd watched the film *High School Musical*. It was perfect comfort viewing, but not even Zac Efron could hold Erica's attention and her mind wandered. More than wander – it had gone on a ten-mile hike with a compass, laminated map and slice of Kendall mint cake.

Over and over she'd replayed everything that had happened since they'd moved into the B&B. How had things changed so much in just two months? When she, Louise and Polly had gone away at the end of May, she'd been in control of her life, with a daughter who adored her, a fantastic, if full-on, career, the partner she'd thought she wanted and secure friendships. Now, her relationship with Jasmine was on parole, Dan was gone, she was in love with someone who didn't want to know her and she wasn't sure if she, Louise and Polly would ever be friends again.

When Dan's mum got back from her shopping spree, Erica seized the opportunity to go for a run, promising Jasmine she'd swing by Polly's to get her iPod.

Erica's legs shook as she sped up. She should have phoned Polly to let her know how Jasmine was, but every time she came close to making the call, she remembered Polly brushing Jasmine's hair or kissing her and couldn't bring herself to ring. Veering off the main road, she ran along a parade of restaurants and wine bars. A sandwich board stood outside one, promoting an offer on margaritas, the cocktail she'd had on hers and Rob's first, and only, date. He'd opened his heart up to her that night and she'd betrayed him.

Rob's words played through her mind, as she ran. *You lied to me. You're not the person I thought you were.* She stifled a sob. That would be his lasting impression of her; that she was a two-faced liar. Admittedly there was an element of truth in that – an element approximately the size of Southeast Asia – but even so, she couldn't bear it. She'd hoped that by hearing her explanation he'd understand. Perhaps even forgive her. At the very least, she'd hoped they'd have an amicable goodbye. Instead, the hurt she'd caused had been evident. His ex-wife had already cheated on him. Now she'd done the same. It'd possibly affect future relationships, create trust issues and damage his good faith in people. He could be screwed up for good. And it was all her fault.

Her breath caught in her throat as she pounded along the pavement. She had to repair the damage she'd done. She had to. She was trying to instill in Jasmine the power of resilience and to never give up. She had to practise what she preached and do the same. But how?

She ran on, her arms almost a blur in her peripheral vision as she sprinted along. Talking to him face-to-face was the only possibility. If he saw for himself how sincere she was in her apology, it might be enough to restore his faith in human kind.

But how could she engineer a meeting? Going into the studio wasn't an option – the costumes for the finals had been approved and fitted in advance and she'd appointed a freelance stylist to dress the contestants for the last week of *Sing to Win*. More importantly, she'd promised Jasmine she'd stay off work until she was better. She wasn't going to break that promise. She'd done too much of that in the past. And she couldn't go to Rob's house because she didn't know where he lived. Disappointment washed over her. It was doubtful they'd ever work together again. He was starting the home renovation show in September, if it happened. He'd confided that very few properties were fitting the show's criteria and the producer, Clare Wright, was worried she wouldn't have enough for the six-episode series. What would Rob do if the show were cancelled? Talented PDs were always in demand, so he'd easily get something else, but she wouldn't know what or where.

Reaching Polly's house, she jogged round to the back, relieved to see that neither Polly nor Louise's cars were in the car park. She wasn't sure what to say to Polly yet and was still pissed off with Louise for her irresponsible attitude towards Jasmine's accident. Worse than that though, had been hearing from Jasmine how Tess had bullied her during their stay at the B&B. Shame enveloped her. She'd been so wrapped up in her own life that she hadn't noticed what her daughter was going through. She was never going to make that mistake again.

Pressing her hands up against the exterior wall, she stretched her left leg out behind her. There was a loud crack, as the ground beneath her gave way and her foot slipped down a hole. Shrieking, she clasped the wall, terrified she was about to be swallowed up by a sinkhole. She'd either plummet straight to her death or land in the sewers below on a mountain of soiled nappies. Death was the preferable of the two options. Petrified, she looked over her shoulder and saw to her relief that instead of a gaping hole the size of a Winnebago, the paving slab she'd been standing on had broken in two. She swiped the slab with her trainer. The B&B was a nightmare. Every bit of it was falling apart, even the garden. It'd take more than a bit of landscaping and DIY to put right. Guiltily, she acknowledged that she never had done any decorating, which had been one of the conditions of moving in. But really, would a lick of paint have made any difference when the plaster was falling off the walls, there were holes in the bedroom ceilings and there was more mould in the shower seals than on a slab of Stilton? What the B&B needed was a complete renovation. With some money behind it, a team of professionals who knew what they were doing, and a ban on wood chip, it could be an amazing house.

She took her key from her pocket and paused. The house was falling apart. It needed a complete renovation. With a team of professionals it could be amazing. She gasped. The answer to her problem was right here in front of her. Excitedly, she unstrapped her phone from her arm, opened up her list of contacts and selected the number for the network's features department.

'Clare Wright please,' she said. 'I've got a property that's perfect for her new show.'

–

Five minutes later Erica hung up and grabbed a fistful of air. Clare Wright had been delighted to hear about the B&B and said it was exactly what she was looking for.

'The PD's based in Cambridge,' she'd said. 'Ok if he comes at ten o'clock tomorrow?'

Erica agreed eagerly, only just remembering to ask Clare to use Polly's name rather than her own. He'd never come if he thought Erica would be there. She hugged her phone to her chest. She was going to see him tomorrow. She could make everything right tomorrow. And if it took more than one conversation to convince Rob, that was ok. When the house was approved for the show – Clare was sure it would be – he'd be there regularly, overseeing the filming for several weeks, maybe months. Surely that would be enough time to prove how sincere and heartfelt her apology was. Maybe even convince him that, despite one mistake, albeit it a massive fuck up, she wasn't a bad person.

Feeling more positive, she unlocked the back door and walked into the kitchen. The house was eerily quiet and smelled similar to the alleyway that ran alongside The Cooper's Arms pub in town. She didn't want to know why. Wrinkling her nose, she headed towards the passageway to get Jasmine's iPod from the den when she heard the back door open and close. Warily she turned round, thankful to see it was Polly.

'Hi.' Erica smiled. Telling Polly about the home renovation programme was more important right now than questioning her attachment to Jasmine. 'I've just been speaking to—'

'How's Jasmine?' Polly asked.

'She's great,' Erica said. 'Listen, there's a new programme—'

'Great?' Polly shook her head. 'She's broken her arm. How can she be great?'

Erica faltered. 'You're right. Great isn't the right word. But she's healing nicely. She says hello,' she added, hoping that would ease the tension.

'Why didn't you answer my calls?' Polly's tone suggested it was going to take more than just a hello.

'Sorry,' Erica said quietly. 'Kept meaning to, but so much has been going on.' She smiled apologetically.

Polly didn't return the smile. 'I've had things going on too, but I called you. Several times.'

'Sorry,' Erica said again. 'I should have done.' She fiddled with her phone case. 'I've got something exciting to tell you about the B&B.'

Polly looked at her watch. 'I can't talk. The kids are at Alex's and I need to get back.' She hurried past Erica and made her way along the passageway to the hallway.

Erica followed. 'It'll only take a sec.'

She was about to launch into details of how Polly's home was to be transformed from a rundown shithole into a luxury residence, but paused. Polly might take offence to the term 'shithole'. Before she could decide if labelling the house as 'neglected' or 'in disrepair' could be deemed insulting, the back door flew open again and Louise hurried up the passageway towards them, one hand clamped over her nose and mouth.

'We've got to get out,' Louise shouted, gesticulating wildly towards the door. She grabbed Erica's arm. 'Has Polly told you?'

Erica jerked her arm away.

'No,' Polly said with an impatient sigh. 'There's nothing to tell.'

'Nothing to tell,' Louise spluttered. 'Asbestos causes cancer. If you ask me—'

'Asbestos?' Erica automatically covered her own nose and mouth. 'Is that what that smell is?'

Polly shook her head. 'You're overreacting.'

'No, I'm not,' said Louise. Despite the severity of her news, she looked triumphant that at least Erica was paying attention. 'Asbestos fibres stay in the lungs for years. If the den roof gets damaged—'

'The den?' Erica's stomach lurched. That's where Jasmine had said her iPod was. That's where Jasmine had been playing the day of her accident.

Chapter Forty-Five

Erica, Louise and Polly

Erica's stomach twisted with fear. What damage had been done when Jasmine was innocently playing on her iPod in the den? Were her little lungs now full of cancer-inducing fibres? Were her own? They might all be infected. And Polly and Louise had known.

'Why didn't you tell me as soon as you found out?' she spluttered through her cupped hand at Louise. 'You message about everything else. Couldn't get the text out fast enough that time I accidentally left the fridge door open.'

'My ham and cheese quiche was ruined,' Louise said angrily into her own hand. With two of her three meals a day consisting of grapefruit, the anticipation of quiche for dinner had been the only thing keeping her going. To come home and discover the fridge door wide open and her evening meal in the early stages of penicillin had reduced her to tears. To make it even more galling, the grapefruits had thrived. Not that she needed to eat those anymore. 'I would have rung,' she added. 'My phone's broken.'

'George got near it, did he?' Erica said.

Polly edged towards the stairs. She needed to get back to Oliver and Summer.

'Polly,' either Erica or Louise said. It was impossible to distinguish between them when their hands were clamped over their mouths. 'What about the asbestos?'

A knot of annoyance formed in Polly's stomach. As if she'd have bought the B&B if there were any danger. The surveyor had assured her that the asbestos was contained. 'More risk of having a wall fall on you,' he'd said, as though that would make her feel better.

'The roof's being removed next week when everyone's away,' Polly said slowly, as though explaining the situation to Summer. 'It's not dangerous unless the asbestos is exposed, which it isn't.'

Erica grabbed Louise's arm. 'You're the health and safety expert. Is Polly right? Is it safe, as it is?'

Louise shook Erica's hand away. She was still smarting over the quiche. She thought back to a training course she'd once organised that covered asbestos. In fairness to Polly, there wasn't any real danger, not when the asbestos was sealed in the roof. If she'd stopped to think about it rationally, she'd have known it was safe to stay. But she hadn't stopped. Why? Had she, subconsciously, welcomed an excuse to go home? Had there been a glimmer of hope deep down that she hadn't been aware of?

'Yes, Polly's right.' She lowered her hand from her mouth, feeling a little foolish. 'But it's good it's being removed,' she added in response to Erica's eye-roll. 'You can never be too safe.'

Erica dropped her hand too, took a deep breath, and grimaced. 'What's that smell, then?'

'Summer's potty training.' Polly tried to squeeze past Erica. 'I need to get some pyjamas and bedding. We're camping at Alex's tonight.'

'You're staying at Alex's?' Erica asked. This was perfect. With Polly out of the house, she'd have the opportunity to talk to Rob openly in the morning.

Polly blushed. 'We're sharing a tent with the children. It's not—'

'No need to rush back.' Erica smiled broadly. 'Make a day of it.' Her eyes met Louise's and her smile dropped, as she remembered what Jasmine had told her. She turned to face Louise square on. 'Did you know Tess has been bullying Jasmine?'

Louise winced. 'She hasn't always acted well,' she admitted. 'But that's because she's insecure. She thinks Jasmine doesn't like her.'

Erica gave her an incredulous look. 'Why would she when Tess is horrible to her?'

Polly watched the exchange with growing frustration. Erica and Louise were stationed at the foot of the staircase and there was no way of getting past them.

'I know it doesn't make sense,' Louise protested. 'But Tess really likes Jasmine. She wouldn't have stolen the money if she didn't.' As soon as the words were out of her mouth she regretted them.

'Tess stole the money?' The expression on Erica's face was indecipherable and Louise had no urge to decipher it. 'The money you accused Jasmine of taking?'

'I didn't accuse Jasmine.' Louise could feel red blotches creeping up her neck. 'Just said that someone had taken it and it could have been Jasmine.'

'So you accused everyone else, but didn't have the guts to admit it was your own daughter. How long have you known?'

The red blotches had reached Louise's face now. 'About a week.'

'Why did she take it?' Polly asked, concern etched across her face. 'What did she need so desperately that she stole to buy it?'

'She was saving to buy Jasmine another Disney nightie,' Louise said quietly.

Erica opened and shut her mouth a few times. 'That's really kind,' she said eventually.

Polly nodded. 'I knew she couldn't have done it for selfish reasons.'

Relief flooded through Louise. 'You're not cross?'

Erica sighed. 'How can I be when she was doing it for Jasmine?'

Louise put a hand to her chest. 'That's why I didn't say anything. She knows stealing's wrong, but she was in such a state when the nightie ripped, she didn't know what to do.'

Erica's head turned slowly.

'She didn't mean to. She was just trying it on and it tore. Jasmine looked so pretty in it that Tess wanted to be like her,' Louise added. 'It's a compliment, really.'

'A compliment is telling someone they look nice, not destroying their clothes.' Erica paced up and down the hall. 'How would you feel if someone admired your shoes then snapped the heels off?'

'That's not a realistic comparison.'

'You're right.' Erica looked at Louise's feet with contempt. 'Crocs don't have heels.'

Erica's pacing left the staircase unguarded and Polly headed towards it. She hadn't even climbed the first step when Erica stopped her.

'Did you know about any of this?'

'No.' Polly checked her watch. Alex would be wondering what had happened to her. 'I'd have said something if I did.'

'Would you?' Erica could still feel the pain of seeing Jasmine snuggled up on the sofa with Polly. 'Or would you have used it to get even closer to Jasmine? You're already putting her in your bed, teaching her the facts of life, brushing her hair. It's as though you're trying to turn her against me.'

Polly flinched. All she'd ever done was care for the children. It had been hard work, but she'd never resented it. And now it was being thrown back at her.

'I didn't turn Jasmine against you,' she said bravely. 'You did that yourself.' Erica's short hair seemed to stand up on end. 'You practically live at the studio,' Polly continued. 'When you're here, you're on your phone.' She swivelled to face Louise. 'You're no better. Always reading a magazine or watching TV. You both take me for granted, like an unpaid childminder.'

'I offered to pay for a childminder,' Erica said. 'But you said you'd rather do it yourself.'

'Yes, I would.' Anger strengthened Polly's voice. 'What kind of person gets a stranger to look after her kids?'

'A working mother, that's who,' Erica snapped. 'A mother who wants to give her child opportunities and be a role model, rather than restricting her life experiences to *Peppa Pig* and spaghetti hoops. It's not much of an existence, is it?'

Louise tutted. 'You can't criticise Polly's spaghetti hoops when you don't cook anything at all.'

'You're not exactly Master Chef yourself,' Erica shot back. 'Those bargain basement pizzas you shove in the oven have as much nutritional value as circles of cardboard.'

'If you ask me—'

'If you ask me, if you ask me,' Erica mimicked. 'I can't recall ever having asked you anything, but you tell me anyway. Well I'll tell *you* something – I've had enough of you controlling us with your meetings and text alerts and rotas.'

Louise inhaled sharply. 'We wouldn't know where we were without those rotas. Not that you pay any attention to them.' She crossed her arms tightly. 'Typical Aries, always out for themselves.'

Unable to form a counter-argument, Erica went off on a different tangent. 'You two need to have a word with your boys.' She waved a finger between Polly and Louise. 'They're noisy and messy and don't have any respect. They even spied on me in the shower once.'

'That's terrible,' Louise said.

'I know,' Erica snapped. 'I was mortified.'

Louise shook her head. 'Terrible for them. They could be traumatised for life.'

Erica stiffened. 'You should teach them to respect people's privacy then.'

Polly stepped forward, her frustration giving her courage. 'You don't have any respect for *me*. Has it ever occurred to either of you to ask me if I mind waiting in for a parcel to be delivered, or getting your washing in if it rains, or looking after your kids or—'

'Don't worry, you won't be lumbered with that job again.' Erica thrust a hand towards her. 'Tell me, if I'm such a crap mum, how come the only time Jasmine's hurt herself was when you two were looking after her?'

Colour flooded Polly's cheeks.

'Think you're forgetting Polly saved her from being run over,' Louise said. 'If you ask me—'

Erica winced.

'You did ask, actually,' Louise snapped.

Erica glared at her. 'Ok, you got me. Happy now, are you?'

'Not as happy as you were the night it happened.' Louise crossed her arms triumphantly.

Erica opened her mouth and closed it again. Louise's reference to Rob had reminded her that she needed to tell Polly about the home renovation show.

Louise pressed her lips together. Her decision to be a better person wasn't going very well. She still had to tell Polly that she couldn't come to Spain. The poor woman would be devastated.

Polly's grip on her pendant tightened. She'd had enough; enough of their accusations, of defending herself, of being treated as though she were irrelevant. Turning her back on Erica and Louise, she began to climb the stairs.

'Polly.' Erica cleared her throat. 'Sorry. Forget I said any of that. There's something else I need to talk to you about.'

'Not now.' Polly carried on up the stairs.

'It'll only take a minute.'

'I've got to get back,' Polly said. 'Give me a break, ok?'

'Er, Poll,' Louise said. 'Speaking of breaks, I need to talk to you about our trip to Spain.'

'I'm not going to Spain. I'm fed up with rotas and lists and being told what to do and when to do it.'

Louise's face fell. So much for Polly being devastated. And what was this vendetta against her rotas? Nick had said they were invaluable at times.

'Polly.' Erica ran up the stairs after her. 'I have to tell you something.'

Heat surged through Polly's body. Why wouldn't they sod off and leave her alone? 'No,' she said. 'I'm getting my stuff and then going. Is it too much to ask to be left alone under my own roof?'

'A roof that's full of asbestos,' Louise muttered.

'Forget the asbestos,' Erica said. 'And the plastering and the damp and the wonky toilet seat.' She beamed at Polly. 'I'm getting the whole place renovated.'

'What?' Polly stared at her.

'A professional team's going to do up the house,' Erica said. 'They're coming tomorrow to do a recce. Don't worry about coming back early from Alex's – I'll let them in.' She was practically dancing on the spot. 'It'll be amazing and won't cost you a penny.'

'Why?' Polly asked cautiously. 'What's in it for them?'

'Viewing figures,' Erica said, her earlier anger replaced with excitement. 'People can't get enough of these home renovation programmes. This is such an unusual house and living arrangement, the producer's really excited about it.' She spoke quickly. 'They'll want to interview us. Probably think we've got some sort of lesbian commune going on.' She laughed. 'That'll be a hit with the ratings.'

Polly's throat tightened, as she grasped the concept Erica was proposing. 'Filming in my house?'

Erica nodded. 'Exciting, isn't it?'

Louise ran her fingers through her new haircut. 'Will we all be interviewed?'

'Expect so. They'll want to have before, during and after chats with us about what our vision is, how we're coping with the upheaval, then the big reveal where we show how thrilled and delighted we are.'

Polly put a hand to her pendant. 'Showing where I live?'

'Only the house,' Erica said. 'They won't reveal the street name.'

Polly shook her head. 'No.'

'Don't worry about the upheaval,' Erica said. 'You'll have to move out while they're doing the big jobs – knocking down walls and things, but the studio should pay to put you up in a hotel. I will, if they don't.'

'No,' Polly said again.

Erica smiled. 'It's the least I can do to say thank you for looking after Jasmine.' She chose not to point out that Polly had looked after Jasmine so well she'd practically pushed Erica out. She needed to keep Polly sweet – there was nothing worse for a film crew than a difficult interviewee.

'No.' Polly twisted her necklace. 'No. No. No.'

'To which part?'

'All of it.' Polly's silver chain cut into her neck and she struggled for air. 'No recce. No cameras. No programme.'

'But someone's coming tomorrow to view it.' Erica's voice wobbled. 'It's all arranged.'

Louise frowned. 'It's free. Why are you turning it down?'

'Doesn't matter why. It's my house and I've said no.' Polly squeezed her eyes shut. She would not have a panic attack. She was stronger than that.

'Please, Polly.' Erica fought back tears of frustration and disappointment. Polly had to let Rob come. This was her one and only opportunity to make things right. 'Let them do the recce. You don't have to go through with it after that, but please let him come tomorrow.' She took Polly's hands. 'I know it's a big thing; you're bound to be nervous, but I'll deal with it all. All you have to do is—'

'No.' Polly met Erica's desperate gaze head on.

Erica saw the anger in her eyes and hesitated briefly before carrying on. 'I'll meet the production director while you're at Alex's, then—'

The knot in Polly's stomach exploded. She was nothing more than white noise to Erica. Despite having said no repeatedly, she still wasn't listening.

'I said no!' Polly screamed. Yanking her hands away, she hurtled up the remaining stairs, her feet slipping on the worn carpet. Erica ran after her.

'Leave her,' Louise called. 'Give her some space.' The fire door shut behind Erica. Sighing, Louise hauled herself up the stairs.

'Polly, please.' Erica burst into her bedroom. 'You don't know what this means to me.'

Polly stood by her bed, her eyes wide, her hands balled into fists. The doors to her wardrobe were open and an assortment of objects were strewn across the floor – odd shoes, a straw sunhat and a large cardboard box.

'I don't care what it means to you,' Polly hissed. 'It's nothing compared to what it means to me.'

'I don't understand—' Erica began.

'Just get out,' Polly shouted.

'But I—'

'Poll?' Louise edged inside the room and stood beside Erica.

Polly picked up one of Summer's teddy bears and hurled it at them. 'Get out, both of you,' she shouted as loudly as she could. 'Get out, get out, get out.' She clasped her hands to her head. Why wouldn't they go?

Erica looked on helplessly. She'd fucked up big time. Yes, there'd been an ulterior motive to the renovation programme, but she'd genuinely thought Polly would jump at the chance to have her house done up for free. Instead, it had triggered some kind of breakdown. Perhaps if she told Polly the truth, told her about Rob, she'd calm down.

She took a step towards Polly. 'Let me explain.' The floorboard beneath her foot came loose and she fell forward, her arms flailing. Her trainer caught on a cardboard box in the centre of the room and dislodged the lid, sending it spinning across the floor.

Polly felt the colour drain from her face. Her past was in that box. If Erica and Louise found out what was inside, it wouldn't be a case of her wanting them to leave her alone – they wouldn't want to come anywhere near her. They wouldn't be able to help but tell people they knew. She'd have to move and start all over again. She snatched the crumpled cardboard lid from the floor and wedged it back onto the box with trembling hands.

Erica picked herself up. She opened her mouth to point out that the loose floorboard was further proof that the house was in dire need of renovation but stopped when she saw Polly kneeling over the cardboard box, her arms wrapped around it.

'Just go.' Polly was visibly shaking. 'Go and leave me alone.'

Louise and Erica looked at each other. They couldn't leave her in this state.

Louise bent down and placed an arm around Polly. 'Come on, Poll,' she said firmly, helping her up from the floor. 'Have a lie down.'

Polly pushed her away, but Louise didn't give up. Eventually, too exhausted to fight any longer, Polly relented and allowed Louise to lead her to the bed and lie her down.

'Got to get back to Alex's,' she managed to say. 'The kids.'

'In a minute.' Louise placed a pillow behind her head.

Erica stood by the wardrobe, watching her anxiously. Polly's eyes fluttered open and shut. She was so tired. The panic attack at Alex's, followed by this hideous row and the paralysing fear of being plastered over the TV and her secret being discovered had sucked every speck of energy out of her and now she was powerless to do anything but lie there. Erica and Louise would go soon. If she lay very still and quiet, they'd get bored and go.

'Here, give me that,' Louise said.

Polly didn't know what she was talking about until Louise eased something out of her hands. Her blood went cold. It was the lid to the cardboard box. And if she had the lid, the contents of the box were on display. A shot of adrenalin charged through her and she pushed herself up to standing in time to see Louise bending over the box to replace the lid.

'You shouldn't keep old newspapers in here,' Louise said. 'They're a fire hazard.' She reached down and took one from the box.

'Stop,' Polly yelled. 'Don't read that.'

It was too late. Louise frowned as she absorbed the front-page story. Erica leaned forward to see the text more clearly. Polly's legs gave way and she sank back onto the bed.

'What is this?' Louise held the paper up. *Fireman Killed by Jealous Neighbour* was plastered across the front cover. Two photos dominated the page, with diagonal straplines running across them. *Lover* read one. *Husband* read the other. The photo of the husband looked eerily like an older version of Oliver, but without the softness Polly's genes had provided. His small brown eyes were cold. The other man was smiling in his photo. Laughter lines gathered around his bright, blue eyes.

Erica took another newspaper out of the box. 'There's a photo of you,' she said. 'But it says your name's Pauline.'

Polly held her breath.

'Is this story about you?' Louise asked. 'Are you Pauline?'

Polly nodded miserably. Yes, she was Pauline. Yes, the story was about her.

Chapter Forty-Six

Polly

It was his eyes she noticed first. They were a startling vivid blue. They crinkled as he smiled at her over the garden fence when she was hanging out the washing and he was mowing the lawn.

'Jammy git, next door,' Ian had said one evening, lying on the sofa, gripping the remote control to his chest. 'He's a fireman. Gets full-time wages for part-time work.' His feet tapped together in time to the *Top Gear* theme tune. 'They're coming round with their kids on Sunday for a barbecue. Get one of them trifles.'

Barbecues with Adam and Cheryl became a regular fixture. As did Adam and Polly's chats over the fence while the children were at school and Ian and Cheryl were at work. When autumn came, the chats moved into the house. For the first time, a man was asking Polly to talk about herself, valuing her opinion, inviting her to think. Neither her dad or her husband ever had. It wasn't her dad's fault. Consumed with grief over his wife's death and a fear of leaving Polly without anything, he'd thrown himself into work and encouraged her to do the same. 'Hairdressing's what you should do,' he'd said when she told him about her dream of being a singer. 'Forget this singing lark. Folk will always be in need of a haircut.' So Polly had got an apprenticeship at a local salon.

At the same time, Ian progressed from apprentice to peer in her dad's plastering business, having joined straight from school. Her dad started bringing him home every Thursday for tea, nudging him in Polly's direction. When he left them in the kitchen to go and watch the news, Ian would sidle up to Polly. She let him kiss her. She didn't know what else to do. Ian and her dad agreed to become partners in both the business and the family. They transitioned from kissing to married without any real input from her.

'You need someone to look after you when I'm gone,' her dad said when he was diagnosed with cancer. 'Ian can have the business. He'll look after you.'

Polly started cutting herself more often. Small slivers of pain along her arms that provided brief escapes from the pain in her head.

The kissing went from once a week to once a month, to a couple of times a year. Polly didn't seek to increase this. It was enough effort behaving exactly the way Ian expected during the day – quiet, grateful, in awe – without having to maintain it into the night too. Despite the lack of intimacy, Oliver eventually arrived. He gave Polly a joy she'd never known. He was so tiny, so precious, so dependent on her. For the first time since her mum had died, she had a purpose. Oliver loved her completely for who she was. She didn't need to worry about saying the wrong thing with him, or laughing at something that wasn't intended to be a joke or not laughing when it was, or not contributing enough to the household now she was freelancing, rather than working at the salon. She stopped self-harming. She didn't need to, now that she had Oliver.

Ian didn't like the attention she gave Oliver. 'Let him cry,' he'd say. 'It'll toughen him up.'

Polly ignored him and that's when the hitting started. Not often, but enough to make her fear him, to cower when he raised his hand, to flinch if he took a step towards Oliver with anger in his eyes. The day he took his belt to Oliver she tried to leave. He'd laughed in her face. 'Go and you'll never see your son again,' he'd said, pulling up her sleeve to reveal the row of angry scars. 'They'd lock you up in the nearest loony bin if they knew what you do to yourself. Can't take care of yourself, let alone a kid. Stay with me and you get to stay with Oliver.' Polly knew he was right. Knew he'd twist her words, her situation. No one would believe her. She was powerless. Except for one thing.

She made an appointment at the doctor's and got the contraceptive injection. Much as she wanted more children, she couldn't risk it. It was hard enough protecting Oliver, making sure she was always with him. She wouldn't be able to do that if there was more than one child.

Somehow Adam sensed what was going on. If Ian got angry because Oliver was making too much noise playing, or if his dinner wasn't on the table bang on six o'clock, Adam's head would appear over the fence or through the back door and he'd engage Ian in conversation and keep talking until Ian visibly cooled. It was only when Ian turned away that Adam's smile would turn into a grimace.

'I know he's bullying you,' Adam said one day. 'He shouldn't talk to you like that. Cheryl and I are only together for the kids – I've been in the spare room for months – but we're still civil to each other.'

Polly stared into her mug of tea, hoping he couldn't see the tears of shame that were threatening to spill over.

'It's not my place to say this,' Adam said, wrapping his fingers around hers, 'but you don't deserve to be treated this way. It's not right.'

Polly looked up and saw not only care and concern shining out of his bright, blue eyes, but something more.

'How can I help you?' he whispered.

The tea felt tepid compared with the heat that surged out of his hands. Even more so when those hands cupped her face, wound themselves in her red curls, ran across her body, made her come.

For six glorious months, Adam came to Polly's every afternoon he didn't have a shift. Her spirits soared when she heard the click of the side gate. She was high on happiness. Even Ian's brusqueness couldn't get her down. As long as she cleaned and ironed and cooked his tea and made his packed lunch the way he liked it, he had no reason to complain. In the mornings she cut hair for some of the mums from Oliver's school, so was bringing a little money in. And in the afternoon, when Adam wasn't working, they had two blissful hours together before she collected Oliver from school.

'Why don't you audition for *Sing to Win*?' Adam suggested at one of their Sunday barbecues. 'Fulfill your lifelong dream of becoming a singer?'

'Her? Sing?' Ian looked over from where he was turning the sausages with a pair of tongs. 'A strangled cat'd have more of a chance.'

'Do you like singing then?' Cheryl asked, showing Polly some rare interest.

Polly didn't know how to respond. She'd told Adam about her love of singing when they'd been in bed one afternoon. She hadn't expected him to bring it up in front of Ian. She could feel Ian's eyes on her as he swigged from his can of lager.

Adam tapped the heel of his hand against his forehead. 'Ignore me,' he said. 'It was a mate at work's wife who told me she wanted to be a singer.' He raised his drink. 'The beer's going to my head.'

'Chat up a lot of your mates' wives, do you?' Ian said. His tone was light, but his eyes were watchful.

'Sorry,' Adam whispered to Polly later on in the kitchen, as they cleared up. 'I wasn't thinking.' Adam leaned his shoulder against Polly's and she returned the pressure. A loud belch behind made them jump.

'Scuse me.' Ian patted his belly as he walked past on his way from the garden to the toilet and they leapt apart.

'We've got to be more careful,' Polly whispered to Adam the next day. They were on the landing outside Oliver's bedroom. 'If Ian finds out…' She didn't dare finish the sentence.

Adam ran a hand down her cheek. 'It's getting harder. I don't know how much longer I can keep up the pretence.'

Polly fought back tears. She didn't know how she'd cope if he finished it. Her hours with him had become as precious as the ones she spent with Oliver. Reliving the moments they shared was what got her through the monotonous evenings with Ian. On the rare occasions he wanted sex, imagining he was Adam was the only thing that stopped her recoiling with disgust. She couldn't bear to think of it ending. It would be the end of her.

'Do you want to stop seeing me?' Her voice quivered.

Adam stared at her in surprise. 'No. The opposite. I want us to be together properly. I want to marry you, Pauline.'

'Don't say that.' She stepped away and reached for Oliver's door handle.

'Let him sleep,' Adam said. 'Best medicine when you're ill.'

He took her hand and ran his fingers up her arm along the scars. 'I mean it. I don't want you to be with the man who drove you to this. Cheryl and I aren't happy. Why put ourselves through this when we could be together?' He pressed her hand to his lips. 'I love you.'

A lump formed in her throat. This hurt more than if he'd ended it – offering her everything she wanted when there was no way she could accept it. 'I love you too,' she whispered. 'But Ian'd never let me go.' She shook her head. 'You can't leave your kids, either.'

'I'd still be their dad. I'd see them all the time. They might even want to live with us. The three of us.' He nodded his head towards Oliver's door and smiled. 'Ian wouldn't have a choice. He'd have to accept it.'

'You make it sound easy, but it's not.'

Adam took her hand. 'It is. I'll look after you. All you have to do is pack some clothes for you and Oliver and walk out the door.'

Polly swallowed hard. Could she do it? Could she summon up the courage to leave? Could she have a fulfilling, happy life with a man she loved rather than a half-hearted existence with a man she'd come to despise?

A car door slammed outside and she and Adam jumped. They lived in a quiet cul-de-sac. Not many people came by unannounced. A mobile phone rang in the street and Polly's throat tightened at the familiar ringtone.

'It's Ian.' Panic coursed through her. 'Why shall we say you're here?'

'Tell him the truth. I came round to see if Oliver's better.'

Polly shook her head. 'He'll want to know why you're so interested.'

'Say I've come round for a trim, then.' Adam opened the bathroom door. 'I'll wet my hair.'

Polly ran downstairs and opened the front door. 'This is a nice surprise.' Her smile had never been so forced. 'I'm about to cut Adam's hair.'

'Alright, mate?' Adam came down the stairs, water dripping from his hair onto his shoulders. 'Early finish today?'

Ian ignored him. 'Why aren't you answering your phone?' he asked Polly.

'I put it on silent so it wouldn't disturb Oliver,' Polly said. 'Everything ok?'

Ian rubbed his thinning hair and a halo of plaster puffed out around his head. 'Can't find my rawl plugs. Must have left them somewhere.'

He pushed past Polly and ran up the stairs two at a time, flakes of dry plaster falling from his jogging bottoms onto the beige, flecked carpet. The ceiling above creaked, as Ian moved around their small bedroom. Polly and Adam exchanged nervous glances. If Oliver hadn't been off school sick, they'd probably have been in bed.

'Better get this haircut over with,' Adam said with forced joviality. 'Then you can get on with your day.'

They went into the galley kitchen and Adam perched on the bar stool. With trembling hands, Polly shook out her black barber's gown and secured it around his neck. Adam reached over his shoulder and squeezed her hand.

'It's ok,' he said softly. 'Just play along for now. You'll be out of here soon.'

He released his grip and she began to cut. Usually she loved running her fingers through his thick, dark hair and massaging his scalp. Today, his hair slipped away as she tried to grasp it. After a few minutes she placed the scissors on the work surface and wiped her hands on a tea towel.

'There you go,' she said. 'I'd best check on Oliver.'

'He's asleep.' Ian appeared in the doorway and a cold spasm shot through her. He stepped into the kitchen and walked his fingertips along the mottled work surface until they reached the fruit bowl. Adam and Polly watched him lift out an apple and take a large bite. He gestured to Adam's hair. 'What do you call that? Give the man his money's worth.'

'It's fine.' Adam began to stand.

Ian stepped forward and placed a hand on Adam's shoulder, pushing him back onto the stool. 'Do it properly, Pauline.'

Polly picked up the scissors. She was shaking so much she could barely prise the blades open.

'What's up?' A small chunk of apple flew out of Ian's mouth. 'Forgot how your fingers work?'

Polly ran a hand over her forehead. 'I don't feel great. Think I might be coming down with Oliver's cold.'

'Let's leave it.' Adam stood and tugged at the fastening of the gown.

'Sit down and let her finish what she bloody well started.' Ian formed his hand into a fist and tapped it against the doorframe.

Adam hesitated but sat down. His fingers gripped his knees through his jeans. Polly blinked back tears and tried to steady her hands. She could sense Adam's thought process as she combed the same section of hair over and over again. What did Ian suspect? What frame of mind was he in? What was he going to do?

Ian watched them from the doorway. 'Pauline ever told you how we got together?'

'Not sure she has,' Adam said evenly.

'Her dad employed me. Wanted me to take care of his only daughter. Make sure she had security. She's had some half-arsed ideas in the past. Wanted to be a singer when she was growing up.' Ian chuckled. 'I did laugh about that one. You – a singer.'

The scissors nicked Polly's finger instead of Adam's hair and she winced.

'Wanted to go to university at one point too.' He sucked at the juice in his apple. 'As if she could get in. Failed most of her GCSEs.'

'Only because I didn't have time to study,' Polly said. 'I had to do all the cooking and cleaning after school 'cos Dad wasn't here, and work at the salon every Saturday and in the holidays.' She'd regret saying that later.

'Bit touchy about that, are you?' Ian grinned. 'Don't like admitting you're not as bright as you think?'

Adam's knuckles whitened as he gripped his knees.

'I promised I'd look after Pauline, the same way he had.' Ian picked a shard of apple from his back tooth. 'I've kept my word, haven't I, Pauline? Put food on the table. Clothes on your back. Given you a kid. I'm good to you, I am. A good husband.' He motioned to Adam with his apple. 'And a good neighbour. How many times have we had you round for a barbecue? Hundreds, I reckon.' He paused. 'Yesterday's was fun, wasn't it?'

Adam gave a small nod. 'It was great, thanks.'

Ian nodded. 'Interesting, too.'

Neither Polly nor Adam responded. Where was this going?

'Interesting you knew about Pauline wanting to be a singer.' He flicked the shard he'd picked out of his teeth onto the floor. 'That's what did it. I've had my suspicions for a while. Couldn't bring myself to believe it though. I kept thinking, not my Pauline.' Blood pumped in Polly's ears. Ian swallowed loudly.

'But yesterday's barbecue. That's when I knew.' He hurled his half-eaten apple into the sink. It smashed against the stainless steel, denting the metal. Slowly, he turned to face them. His features were contorted with rage. 'That's when I knew,' he snarled, 'that you're fucking my wife.'

Polly felt the blood drain from her body. 'Don't be daft.' Her voice sounded as though it came from another room.

Purple veins stood out from Ian's neck. 'Daft, am I?'

Polly tried to step back, but she was wedged between the bar stool and the work surface.

'You must think I'm daft. Must think I'm a fucking idiot.' He thumped the doorframe and a cry came from upstairs.

Polly put the scissors down. 'Oliver's awake.' She squeezed out from behind the stool. 'I'll see how he is.'

Ian blocked her path. 'We're not finished yet, you slag.'

'Don't talk to her like that.' Adam stepped protectively in front of Polly.

'I'll talk to her however I want,' Ian growled. 'I'm her husband. You're nothing but the bastard who's fucking her.'

'He's not.' Polly fought back tears. 'You've got it all wrong.'

Oliver's cry quietened upstairs. Polly pictured him clasping his favourite toy and drifting back to sleep.

'No.' Adam shook his head. 'You haven't got it wrong. I'm sorry you found out this way and I'm sorry if we've hurt you, but Pauline and I...' he glanced sideways at Polly and then back at Ian. 'We want to be together.'

'Eh?' Ian frowned.

Adam nodded. 'I love Pauline. I want to take care of her and support her. Those things you mentioned – singing and a degree. She could still do them. There's nothing wrong with hairdressing, but she wants more. She wants to be happy. Together, we'll be happy.' Adam put an arm around Polly and pulled her close to him. 'I'm sorry – we're sorry – but that's the way it is. You deserve the truth.' Polly stood motionless at his side, not daring to move or speak or breathe.

'In love, are you?' Ian raised the back of his hand to his brow. 'How romantic.' He lowered his hand and smiled at Polly, a cruel smile which showed his barred teeth. 'You're not falling for this, are you? He just wants you to do his cooking and cleaning 'cos Cheryl's never home. Can't say I blame her.'

Polly clung onto Adam. She had to do this. She'd never get another chance. 'I'm sorry,' she whispered. 'I want to be with Adam.' She stared at the floor, too frightened to look Ian in the eye. 'I'll take Oliver and go and stay in a hotel. We'll be gone by the time you get back from work.' Adrenalin coursed through her body. This was happening. This was really happening. She was going to be free of Ian; free to live with the man she loved. Instead of tiptoeing through life, she could skip through it, her arms wide open, her face turned to the sun. What a life she and Oliver would have with Adam. A real life.

Ian laughed. 'Leave me? After everything I've done for you?' His eyes swivelled between Adam and Polly, eventually resting on Adam. Ian motioned to the open back door with his head. 'Piss off back to your house and don't come near any of us ever again.'

Adam held his hand out to Polly. 'Come with me.'

His fingers were poised mid-air. They offered freedom, happiness, escape. She looked at them longingly.

'You going then, Pauline? Going to run off and leave your son asleep upstairs?' Ian linked his fingers together and flexed them so they clicked. ''Cos you're not taking him with you.'

Polly looked helplessly at Adam. 'I can't leave Oliver.'

Adam took her hand and grasped it firmly. 'We'll get him together.'

He tried to walk past Ian, but Ian pushed him away, using the full force of his body to knock Adam backwards. His hand slipped out of Polly's.

'Get out of my house.' Ian held his fists up.

Adam steadied himself on the edge of the work surface and stepped towards Ian again. 'Let Pauline get Oliver. You can't stop her.'

311

'I'll kill you sooner than let you take him.' Ian launched a fist at Adam, and he ducked to the side.

'Stop.' Polly flinched as Ian threw another punch. She looked around and her eyes fell on her hairdressing scissors. Wrapping her fingers around the handles, she waved the scissors close to Ian's face. 'I said stop.'

Adam held his hands up. 'Steady, Pauline.'

She jabbed the scissors towards Ian again. She had no idea what she was doing. She just knew she had to get Oliver.

Ian laughed. 'Going to stab me, are you?' He pushed her hand away. 'You're even dafter than I thought.' He turned back to Adam. 'Some man you are. Can't even stand up for yourself.'

Tears scorched Polly's eyes. She dropped the scissors back onto the work surface. Ian was right. It was a stupid, empty threat.

'That's enough,' Adam said. 'You can't tell us what to do. Pauline's leaving, with Oliver, so stop being an arsehole and let her get him.'

'How fucking dare you?' Spit gathered in the corners of Ian's mouth. 'I'll kill you, you bastard,' he shouted. 'I'll kill you.' He lunged forward, ramming his shoulders into Adam's chest and hurtling him backwards.

Polly darted towards the empty doorway. An almighty crack, like a plank of wood splitting in two, stopped her. Behind her she heard panting, shuffling feet, something sliding, then a thud. She turned around slowly.

The first thing she saw was blood on the base of the corner cupboard. Her eyes travelled downwards, past the dark red spots on the work surface, past the smear of blood down the lower cupboard. Adam lay on his back on the floor, his body twitching. His head was on its side, his blue eyes staring vacantly. A pool of blood seeped over the lino. Ian was crouched over him, checking his pulse.

Polly's knees buckled and she dropped to the floor. 'You've killed him,' she whispered.

Ian turned to Polly, fear in his eyes. 'He should have listened. Should have left when I told him to.'

'You've killed him,' Polly said again.

'No, Pauline. It was an accident.'

'You said you'd kill him and you did.'

Ian grabbed her arms. 'I didn't mean it, you know that. But the police...' He tightened his grip. 'They mustn't know I was here when it happened. We'll say he fell and cracked his head and you rang me in a panic. I came home and tried to revive him before calling an ambulance. They'll believe you.' He shook her hard. 'Got that?' His fingers dug into her flesh. 'Tell the police he slipped. Tell them I was at work.'

Polly stared coolly at him. 'No.' She held her head high. 'I'm not doing what you tell me to do anymore. I'm telling the police the truth. That you killed him.'

Ian shook his head. 'You're in shock, Pauline. Getting in a muddle. Adam slipped and fell.'

'You pushed him.'

'I never knew the stupid bugger would fall against the cupboard. I just wanted him out the house.'

Hatred surged through Polly. How dare Ian call Adam a stupid bugger, as if his death was his own fault?

'If it wasn't for you, he'd be alive. That makes you a murderer.'

Ian stood up. His heavily creased eyes darted around the room. Polly turned her head to look at Adam. His beautiful, bright blue eyes were still open. She put out a hand to touch him. As she extended her arm, Ian reached down and grabbed it.

'You've broken my trust once today.' Ian's voice was low. 'Don't do it again.'

Something sharp pressed against Polly's wrist. Ian held the blade of her hairdressing scissors to her wrist. She tried to pull away, but the blade cut in more deeply as she struggled.

'Trauma's a terrible thing,' he said. 'Makes people do all sorts of silly things.' He pressed the blade down with his thumb. 'Do as you're told, Pauline.' Ian's voice was calm. It scared her when he shouted, but this petrified her. 'I'll kill you if you don't. No one would question it. It'd just be one more cut to go with all the others.' He grasped her chin with his free hand and forced her to look at him. He brought his face closer and closer to hers until his eyes merged together to form one eye. One enormous eye, full of hate. 'Imagine not being around to see Oliver grow up.' His eye glowered at her. 'Adam fell. He called round for a haircut, slipped and hit his head on the cupboard. I was never here.' He brushed a hand along her cheek and she flinched. 'Best not mention your disgusting affair. Don't want everyone knowing you're a whore.'

He pushed himself up to standing. 'I'm having a shower. Get your story straight before I phone an ambulance.' He paused at the kitchen door. 'Do as you're told, Pauline, or you'll never see Oliver again.'

He left the room and Polly heard his feet padding up the stairs. As soon as the bathroom door creaked open, she crawled over to where Adam lay motionless, his head turned awkwardly to one side.

'Adam?' She placed a hand on his chest. 'Adam?' He couldn't really be dead. This must be a trick to make Ian leave the room so she could get Oliver and they could leave together. 'Adam?' She lowered her ear to his mouth, not caring that her hair dipped into the pool of blood around his head, and willed him to respond. But he didn't move. He didn't breathe. His heart didn't beat beneath her hand. He was dead. A low moan resonated from deep within her. He was dead. And Ian had killed him.

As though sensing her distress, Oliver began to cry again upstairs. Polly clutched Adam's t-shirt, bunching it in her fingers, desperate to keep hold of him. His lips were soft against her ear. The same lips that not half an hour ago had told her he loved her, wanted to look after her, wanted to marry her.

Oliver's cry intensified. 'Mamma. Mamma.'

Polly uncurled her fingers from his shirt. Adam couldn't look after her now. She was on her own. A pain shot through her wrist as she sat up. There was an angry red mark where Ian had threatened to cut her. If he'd pushed the blade in any deeper, he'd have slashed an artery. Next to her hand was a lock of Adam's hair that she'd snipped off earlier. She picked it up and tucked it inside the pendant she'd inherited from her mother and always wore around her neck.

'Mamma. Mamma.' Oliver's voice was panic-stricken.

'Coming, Oliver,' she managed to call out. Her phone was on the side in the kitchen and she slid it into her pocket. 'I love you,' she whispered to Adam before leaving the room and closing the door.

Her legs shook as she climbed the narrow staircase to the small, rectangular hall. The bathroom door was ajar. Through it she could see Ian's silhouette behind the quivering shower curtain. His wet feet squelched against the bath when he turned to massage the shampoo out of his thinning hair with his chunky, coarse hands. Hands that would always have blood on them, no matter how often he washed them. Hands that would hold a blade to her wrist for the rest of her life. Hands that she would have to allow to touch her whenever he wanted. Maybe even tonight – to claim back what was his.

'Mamma. Mamma.'

Oliver was sitting up in bed, his cheeks creased from the pillow, his eyes red and heavy. She bent down and hugged him tightly to her. His little hands gripped the back of her neck, relaxed now that he was with her. How could she keep him safe if she was constantly afraid? How could she give him emotional security if she was living on a knife-edge? How could she teach him to stand up for what he believed in if she was too much of a coward to do the same? Tears ran silently down her cheeks into Oliver's blond hair.

The shower stopped running and the metal curtain rings screeched. There was a thud as Ian's foot landed on the bath mat. In a few minutes he'd be dry and dressed. He'd be phoning for an ambulance and silencing her with his eyes. Maybe he'd insist on holding Oliver. A display of dutiful family man to the police. A reminder to her of what she'd lose if she didn't confirm his story.

Oliver sniffed into her hair and she kissed his forehead. This wasn't just about her. It was about Oliver. She had to do the right thing for him.

'Come with me,' she whispered. 'Don't make a sound.'

The bathroom door was pushed shut and Ian urinated noisily into the toilet bowl. Polly hurried down the stairs, her bare feet moving silently on the worn carpet, Oliver following behind. She eased the front door open and pulled it shut at the exact moment Ian flushed the toilet.

'Where are we going?' Oliver asked.

'We're playing hide and seek,' she whispered. 'Let's be really quiet.'

If she could get to the end of the cul-de-sac and round the corner, she'd be out of sight from the house and on a busier road. A road where witnesses would see a man grabbing a woman and child. She ran along the payment, oblivious to the stones and cracked tarmac beneath her feet. Oliver cried out and she picked him up.

'Pauline?' The windows were open and she could hear Ian calling for her. Her breath came out in short bursts as she ran, Oliver heavy in her arms, the soles of her feet burning. Just another minute and she'd be on the main road.

'Pauline?' Ian's call turned into a shout. She could picture him running up and down the stairs, poking his head into each room, checking the garden, his frown deepening into a grimace, his cheeks growing red with anger. She was almost at the top of the cul-de-sac.

'Pauline.' His bellow was clearer.

Whimpering, she looked over her shoulder, petrified he was right behind her and would grab her and drag her back to the house.

He was leaning out of Oliver's bedroom window, his face contorted with rage. 'Get back here,' he yelled.

'Why's Daddy cross?' Oliver asked.

Polly reached the corner.

'Come back or I'll—' Ian started.

Polly turned the corner and leant up against the wall, exhausted. Her legs gave way and she slid down to the ground.

Oliver started to cry. 'Don't feel well,' he sobbed. 'Want to go home.'

Polly's throat tightened. Could she do this? Was she capable of standing up to Ian? More than standing up to him, was she capable of going up against him?

'You alright, love?' A man asked from his van.

Polly nodded automatically. He drove on and she stared numbly at her feet. They were smeared with blood. An image of Adam's body on the kitchen floor flashed in front of her. It wasn't a case of wondering *if* she could she do this; she *had* to. For Oliver, for Adam, for herself. Clinging onto Oliver with one hand, she took her phone from her pocket. Her call was answered immediately.

'Emergency. Which service do you require?'

'Police.' Her throat burned and she struggled for breath. 'Police,' she repeated. 'I need to report a murder.'

Chapter Forty-Seven

Erica, Louise and Polly

'Fuck,' Erica said, her eyes wide.

'I didn't do as I was told,' Polly said. 'I couldn't live the rest of my life knowing what Ian had done and being scared of what he might do to me or, worse, to Oliver.' She looked at the newspaper on her lap. She'd been so afraid to tell the story, afraid that reliving that afternoon would trigger another panic attack or that Erica and Louise would hate her. But it was a relief to be able to speak about it at last.

'Ian said he wasn't there when it happened, but some neighbours heard him shouting that he was going to kill Adam. The jury found him guilty.' Polly winced at the memory of Ian's twisted face when the verdict was called. 'Ian's sentence is fifteen years and he'll probably only spend half of that in prison. He'll be on licence in the community for the other half. I'll get plenty of warning when he's released, but it's still petrifying to know that one day he'll be out. That's why I moved here. To get away from him. He wasn't interested enough in my past to ask about my mum or grandparents, so didn't know about this place.' Polly looked directly at Erica. 'I can't be on TV. Ian could easily find out where we live if he knew what I'm called now. He thinks I'm Pauline Todd, not Polly Tomlin.'

Erica nodded numbly. 'Course.'

'That's why I'm always watching the children,' Polly added. 'I feel much better if I can see them. Stupid to be so paranoid, but I can't help it.'

Louise blinked slowly. 'A murderer,' she said faintly. 'Can't believe it.'

'Neither can I. It still doesn't seem real.' Polly eased her pendant open. 'When I talk about the man I love being dead, I don't mean Ian.' A tiny photo of Adam was in one of the frames. A lock of dark hair was nestled inside the other half. 'I thought this was all I had left of him, but it's not.' She snapped the pendant shut. 'I got his eyes.'

Louise made a gulping noise and shifted her weight away from the cardboard box next to her.

'Not his actual eyes.' Polly took a photo from her bedside table of Oliver and Summer. Placing it on top of the newspaper article, she pointed first to Adam's piercing blue eyes, then to Summer's.

The expressions on Erica and Louise's faces changed as they grasped what Polly was telling them. Louise looked astounded. Erica looked impressed.

'I didn't know I was pregnant for ages. I'd had the contraceptive implant, but it must have run out.' The realisation she was having Adam's child had been bitter sweet. As well as mourning Adam, she also mourned the loss of the dad her baby would never know. But it also meant she hadn't lost him completely; part of him would always be with her. 'Adam loved the summer. Seemed the best name for her.'

'Does Ian know?' Erica asked.

'He does now, but he didn't for a long time. I'd had her by the time the case went to court. When he found out, Ian's solicitor said it was new evidence and they could use it to request an appeal against the case.' She gripped her pendant tightly. 'The court rejected the appeal, but for a while I was really scared he'd get out.'

Erica reached over and hugged Polly. Polly tensed, then allowed herself to relax. It felt good to be hugged.

'I'm so sorry you've been through all this,' Erica said.

Louise patted Polly's shoulder. 'What about Oliver?' she asked. 'Does he remember his dad?'

Polly nodded grimly. 'He remembers the beating Ian gave him. He might decide he wants to see him when he's older, but I doubt it.'

'Fuck,' Erica said again. She wasn't displaying a great command of the English language, but these were unusual circumstances. 'No wonder you have therapy. Think I need some too, now.' She let Polly go. 'Can't believe you've dealt with all this on your own. You should have told us. How do you carry on day to day?'

Polly shrugged. 'Not sure I do always. Louise saw the state I was in a couple of years ago. She saved me.'

'All I did was encourage you go to the doctor's and tell you that time was a great healer. Had no idea all this other stuff was going on.' Louise felt embarrassed as she recalled encouraging Polly to make contact with her Zodiac Angel, after reading an article that claimed they could be called on in times of need. Even she had appreciated that this was stretching astrological probabilities, but thought it might bring Polly some comfort. That was when she'd thought Polly was a grieving widow. Instead, Polly's husband had abused her, killed the one person who could save her from that life and continued to torment her by appealing his prison sentence. It was going to take more than chanting to a candle to gain inner peace.

'If I hadn't been diagnosed with depression and given medication, I might have lost the kids. They could have ended up in care.' Polly's voice wavered. 'Oliver's brilliant, but there's only so much he can do.'

Louise shook her head. 'Dread to think how the twins would have coped if they'd had to look after me. I'd have had a breakdown for sure. George breaks everything.'

'I almost did. I'm still paranoid something will happen if they're out of my sight.' Polly sighed. 'I've got to stop being so protective.'

Erica remembered judging Polly for her paranoia when they'd been on holiday. She'd been so insensitive. The woman had watched her husband murder someone, for fuck's sake. And what about all the terrible things she'd just accused Polly and Louise of? She was such a bitch. Just a few weeks ago, they'd sat around the dining room table, toasting each other with wine and celebrating the success of their house share. Now they couldn't even be civil to one another. It was horrible. It wasn't them.

'I'm sorry for all those things I said downstairs. I didn't mean them.'

'Yes, you did. We all did.' Louise leaned back against the bed. 'If you ask me, we deserved them.' She frowned. 'Not that you did ask me. Got to stop saying that.'

'No, don't.' Erica nudged Louise with her trainer. 'It's part of you. I was being a cow.' Her behaviour since they'd moved in had been appalling. 'I'm sorry I took you both for granted and used you as my personal nanny. I've treated Jasmine terribly too. Don't know about you, but I didn't exactly run the house share past Jasmine for approval.' No, she'd just selfishly assumed it would be ok, in the same way she'd selfishly assumed it would be ok to carry on with the rest of her life. It had never occurred to her to check if Polly and Louise minded that she was rarely there. And then she'd had the gall to sulk when Jasmine turned to Polly. Erica was disgusted with herself.

Louise held out her hands. 'I should have owned up when I found out about the nightie and Tess stealing. I didn't want you to think badly of her.'

'I shouldn't have put them in the same room,' Polly said. 'They're too different. Bound to clash.'

'We could go back and forth all day, pulling apart what we said or who let who down.' Louise gestured to the newspaper in her lap. 'Never mind whose turn it is to unload the dishwasher – this kind of puts things into perspective, doesn't it?'

They sat in silence for a few minutes. Without the screeches and thuds and footsteps from the children, the house felt empty. Erica's own house was going to feel emptier too without

Dan. Jasmine would be devastated initially when they told her. Although the news that the creepy theatre masks would be leaving with him might soften the blow.

She cleared her throat. 'I know this is nothing in comparison, but Dan and I have separated.'

'Oh, no.' Polly sighed. Poor Jasmine.

'I'm sure it would have happened eventually, but the house share speeded up the process. Dan thinks it was an excuse to instigate change.' She pulled her knees into her chest. 'Sorry I pressured you into it. It was a selfish idea. Wasn't fair on you or the children or him. Instead of coming up with a quick fix solution, I should have looked at what was going on with Dan and worked on that.'

'You still could,' Polly suggested.

Erica shook her head. 'We've gone in different directions. He doesn't want to be bogged down with house admin and school stuff. Neither do I particularly, but I want to be more involved with Jasmine's life and that's all part of it.'

'And Dan doesn't?'

'Not sure he could. He's programmed to prove himself and further his career. It's great that he's so determined and driven, but we're not right for each other anymore.'

Louise patted her arm. 'Are you ok?'

Erica nodded. 'I just hope Jasmine is. She won't see Dan much. He's got a promotion and is moving to Dubai.'

'Dubai?' Louise squawked. 'Don't you want to go?'

'No,' Erica said firmly. 'I don't think it's right for Jasmine, either. Even if we hadn't split up he'd go, so there's really no point being together. The company will pay his rent out there and his bonus will pay off the loan, so at least money won't be an issue. Don't know how most people cope financially.' She looked across at Polly. 'How do you manage? You said the life insurance payment covers everything, but if Ian's not…' she trailed off.

'It's my dad's life insurance policy,' Polly said. 'Ian controlled it before he went to prison and I divorced him. It's my money now.'

Louise pressed her lips together. She'd like to get her hands on this Ian bloke. How awful that the man Polly loved was the one who'd died, while the horrible one got just fifteen years for his death. A thought suddenly occurred to her.

'Why was he charged with murder, not manslaughter, when it was an accident?'

Polly's green eyes flitted between Erica and Louise. Could she trust them with the truth? Would they understand? Would they want anything to do with her? She gripped her pendant. It was a big risk. They might be horrified or disgusted, possibly even wary of her. If they were, she'd have to move away and start again. It would be too hard seeing them at the school gates every day, pretending not to notice when they ignored her, knowing they were appalled by her actions. She couldn't bear that. When she'd been angry earlier, she'd convinced herself she didn't want them in her life, but the reality was, she needed them. Was she prepared to risk losing their friendship or should she take a chance and hope their relationship was strong enough to handle it?

'Polly?' Louise said softly.

Polly took a deep breath. 'If I tell you something, you have to promise you'll never say a word.'

Erica and Louise exchanged glances and nodded.

'I told the police that Ian bashed Adam's head against the cupboard deliberately.' Polly didn't dare look at them.

Louise inhaled sharply. 'You lied in court? That's perjury. You could go to prison.'

'You don't know what he was like. He was...' Polly hesitated. How could she describe living with someone who made her fearful of saying or doing the wrong thing? Who mocked every comment she made and scratched away at any confidence she'd once had until there was nothing left but the husk of what she might have been. Who might one day turn on Oliver. He was a vile man who'd made her life a misery. Her hands trembled in her lap. But did that justify what she'd done? Did he deserve to be locked up for the way he'd treated her or should she have pulled herself together and left? Her throat tightened. He'd never have let her leave. She'd done the only thing she could to give them a normal, decent life.

'The police had evidence and witnesses,' Erica said. 'The jury would have found him guilty. He *was* guilty. Why take such a massive risk?'

Polly ran a finger along the scar on her wrist. 'You get longer for murder than manslaughter. The longer he's in prison, the more time I have to start a new life. I don't blame you for thinking badly of me, but I did it for Oliver. I had to make him safe and this was the only way I could. Ian would have done something if he'd got off, I know it. He's not the sort of man to let go.' Polly wrapped her arms around herself. Despite the heat of the day, she was suddenly freezing cold. 'I might have exaggerated the fight, but it didn't change what happened. Adam died because of Ian.'

'But to lie in court?' Louise shook her head. 'That's breaking the law.'

'Yes, it is,' Erica said. 'But I don't think badly of you. If Adam hadn't fallen, who's to say Ian wouldn't have killed him anyway?' She placed a hand over Polly's. 'You did what you felt you had to do. No one knows how they'll react in certain situations. We've all behaved in ways we didn't expect to recently. Me especially.' She shook her head. 'I'm sorry for not being a better friend.'

'You don't have to apologise. You're an amazing friend.' Polly squeezed Erica's hand gratefully. Accepting and understanding her actions made Erica the best friend she could ever wish for. 'Even when we weren't getting on, it was better than being on my own, especially with all the kids here.' Polly paused, remembering Erica's accusation that she treated Jasmine as if she were hers. Erica was right. It had made her euphoric to know that the children preferred her to their actual mums. She'd wanted them to love her more. She'd encouraged it. She could see now that that was wrong. So, why had she done it? Had it been out of genuine love for the kids or had she, subconsciously, been punishing Louise and Erica for undermining her?

'I'm sorry if it seemed like I was trying to take your place,' she said quietly. 'The kids made me so happy. They were like some sort of life support system, giving me energy to get through the days and showing me that I could look forward to things.'

Erica shook her head. 'It's my fault, not yours. I neglected Jasmine. It's no wonder she wanted to be with you more than me. Sorry too for blaming you for Jasmine's accident. Louise is right. If I hadn't been with Rob—'

'Who?'

'A man I met through work. He was coming tomorrow to do the recce for the renovation show. That's why I arranged it, so I could see him.' Erica's cheeks grew warm. 'I was being selfish. Again.'

Polly ran her pendant back and forth along its chain. She didn't want Erica to miss out but couldn't have her home being filmed. 'Can you meet him somewhere else?'

'He wouldn't come. Besides, I'm thirty-six years old. It's about time I accepted the consequences of my actions.'

Louise looked at her sideways. 'You're forty-two.'

Erica pretended not to hear.

'I've got news,' Louise said. 'Nick and I are back together.' She tried to sound casual, but it burst out in an excited squeal.

'That's brilliant.' Polly clapped her hands together with delight.

Erica winked. 'Told you your new look would work.'

Louise's neck went pink. 'Actually, I was only wearing a towel when it happened. But he seemed to like that. Not that it stayed on for very long.' Giggling like a schoolgirl, she remembered their lovemaking, which had been so enthusiastic her giant teddy bear had looked in need of therapy by the end of it.

Erica's phone beeped and she slid it from her case. 'Dan's mum,' she said, reading the message.

'Everything ok with Jasmine?' Polly asked.

Erica nodded. 'She's asking for me.' She jumped up. 'I've got to go.'

'I'm so sorry about Jasmine's accident,' Polly said, standing up.

Erica shook her head. 'It was exactly that – an accident. And it should have been me here anyway, not you. Sorry you missed your date. Glad you and Alex are doing ok.'

Polly blushed and changed the subject. 'I shouldn't have told the kids the facts of life,' she said. 'Or got so involved.'

'Don't you dare apologise.' Erica gripped her hands. 'I'm the one who's sorry for not being there and for not giving you the respect you deserve. I didn't mean to trivialise what you were doing.'

Polly absorbed what Erica had said. 'So why did you? Is it because I'm just a mum? Because I haven't got a career? Is being a full-time mum a bad thing?'

Erica was ashamed to admit that Polly's assumption was correct. 'I used to think if a woman wasn't out there, making her mark, she was wasting her life. I was determined not to be a housewife like my mother. I wanted to have a career and be successful and pay someone else to do the dirty work.' Embarrassed, she looked at Polly. 'But I let you do the dirty work instead. Having looked after the children, I know it's harder than going to work.'

She squeezed Polly's hand. 'I admire you so much. I know I couldn't do it.'

'Why do you think I let Nick do the bulk of it? I couldn't have achieved half of what I have without him.' Louise twisted her wedding band. 'Now it's my turn to be supportive of him. Make sure he finishes his novel. There's no reason why I can't do more and give him some free time at the weekends.'

'You've changed,' Erica laughed. 'I thought weekends were prime time TV viewing for you.'

'Not anymore. Having a family means making some sacrifices. And if skipping the odd episode of *Midsomer Murders* isn't a sacrifice, I don't know what is.' Louise smirked. 'Notice I only said the odd episode.'

Erica was thoughtful. Someone else had spoken recently of the importance of making sacrifices for family. Someone whose positive outlook and harsh circumstances she couldn't forget.

'What went wrong with us after it started off so well?' Polly asked.

'Whoever you live with is going to grate now and again,' Louise said. 'Even when their star signs are compatible.'

'Grating's one thing; we practically turned on each other.' Erica shuddered. 'That argument just now, that wasn't us. We're supposed to be supporting each other. That was the whole point of moving in together.'

'If you ask me, we should forget that argument downstairs ever happened,' Louise said. 'Let's take what we've learned from it and move forward.'

'Sounds good to me.'

'And me,' Polly said. 'But what's going to happen now?'

Louise patted Polly's arm. 'Thank you for letting us stay, but we're ready to go home now.' She blushed. 'About Spain—'

'You go with Nick.'

'Sure?'

'Our passports won't have arrived anyway. I only sent the forms off on Tuesday.'

'Typical Pisces,' Louise said fondly. 'You can move into mine while the building work's going on, if you like?'

'Thank you.' Polly looked at Erica. 'When the roof's done, you're welcome to come back, but I reckon I'll be ok on my own, if you want to stay at home.'

'I don't know what I'm going to do yet,' Erica said. 'There's someone I need to speak to, then I'll have a better idea.' She kissed both women warmly on the cheek. 'I've got to get back to Jasmine.'

Polly nodded. 'I'd best go and find out how Alex is getting on with four children and seven dogs.'

Louise pushed herself up to standing. 'We'll have to meet him some time.'

'He's a nice man.' Polly reached behind her neck and unclasped her pendant. He was a very nice man. Although it was early days, she had a good feeling about their future together. Adam would have wanted her to be happy and know that someone was looking after her and the children. But if she and Alex stood a chance, she had to be honest with him. Oliver didn't want anything to do with his dad at the moment, but he might one day. And she was going to have to tell Summer the truth about her dad at some point. It wouldn't be an easy conversation, and it certainly wasn't one she could have if Alex didn't know. She dropped the pendant into the cardboard box with the newspapers. She loved Adam and she always would, but she was ready to move on.

'I'm going to tell Alex everything. I don't want any secrets.'

'Good for you,' Erica said. 'Speaking from experience, keeping secrets only leads to disaster.'

They stood and looked at each other. Was this really it? After two intense months of living, laughing, drinking, talking, fighting, was it going to end with a casual 'See you soon'? They smiled at one another, almost nervously.

The realisation that she was going to miss them came as a surprise to Erica. Living together might have had its ups and downs – she'd never fully recover from walking in on Louise washing her privates at the bathroom sink – but it had shown her that Louise and Polly weren't just mum friends, people she felt obliged to talk to at school events or that she occasionally deigned with her presence to secure babysitting favours. They knew her as well as her real friends in London did. Possibly better, at this phase of her life. Polly and Louise had been there when she needed support and now she couldn't imagine not having them in her life. They were as real as friends got.

'Group hug,' Erica said in an American accent. She winked at Louise, who looked horrified at the thought of physical contact. 'Come on,' Erica said. 'Or I'll force-feed you grapefruit.'

'Anything but that.' Louise linked arms with Erica and Polly and laughed as they pulled her in for a proper hug. The three friends wrapped their arms around each other and leant their heads together. They stood quietly, each reflecting on their time in the house and what the future held. They knew what they wanted, but none of them knew for sure if they'd get it or how the time they'd spent living together would affect what happened next.

Polly hoped Alex would understand when she told him the truth, but it was a lot to ask. A relationship with the ex-wife of a convicted murderer was unlikely to be what he'd expected when he first invited her to dinner. Erica knew she had to accept that she'd never see Rob again. Sad though that was, she would focus on Jasmine and how she was going to mould her career to fit around her.

Louise, in complete contrast to how she'd felt when they'd first moved in, was happy. Back then she'd been on an enforced break, her marriage to Nick dangling by a thread. Now they were more together than they'd ever been and she was never going to take him for granted again. She hoped he was still in bed when she got home so she could not take him for granted again. She smiled at the memory of how she'd left him – propped up against the pillows, a wide grin on his face, his hair sticking out at right angles.

The thought of Nick's hair made her aware of how close her head was to Polly and Erica's. She pulled away slightly and frowned. 'Please tell me you both got rid of your nits.'

Epilogue

Six months later

'Hi, I'm home.' Erica shut the front door and slipped off her Louboutins. She crossed the black and white tiled hall, admiring the framed photo of Jasmine that now hung on the wall where Dan's masks used to be. Not only was her picture much more aesthetically pleasing to look at, it didn't scare people.

The smell of soy sauce, ginger and chicken warmed her face as she pushed the kitchen door open and her stomach rumbled appreciatively. Erica walked over to the dining table and gave Jasmine a big hug before ruffling the long, dark hair of the little girl sitting next to her.

'Kumusta, Lillibeth.'

Imee clicked her tongue against the roof of her mouth. 'No Filipino. Only English.' She put a plate of adobo in front of Erica and indicated a bowl of rice.

'Sorry.' Erica winked at Lillibeth, who placed a hand in front of her mouth to hide her laughter. 'Thank you, Imee. You don't have to make me dinner, but I'm glad you do.'

'Is important for family to eat together.'

'You're right. I—' The trill of a mobile phone interrupted Erica. She looked across at her bag and then at Jasmine, who was watching, her brown eyes wide, her large front teeth nibbling at her lip. That face was more important than any phone call. Besides, if it was urgent, they'd leave a message. Her phone beeped, indicating a message had been left. Applying all the willpower of an addict coming off crack, or Louise resisting a

Curly Wurly, Erica forced herself to ignore her phone, sat down at the table and picked up her fork. 'So, girls, what did you do at school today?'

—

'Bye, boys.' Oliver and Max were so engrossed in their game of table tennis they barely acknowledged Polly. She smiled and closed the door of the den with its new, asbestos-free roof. Louise had personally overseen the final inspection to ensure it met safety requirements. The safety inspector had looked slightly bemused when Louise had turned up with her clipboard, but he'd gamely gone with it.

Polly stepped forward and a shin-high bundle of black fur ricocheted into her.

'Hi, Button.' Polly knelt down to stroke the small dog and he instantly wrapped his gums around her wrist, a habit she thought he'd stop after choking on Erica's Tiffany charm bracelet. Funnily enough, Erica hadn't wanted her eighteen-carat gold 'E' charm back after it had worked its way through Button's digestive system.

'Drop,' Polly said. The dog released its grip and sat back on his haunches.

'Why won't he do that for me?' Alex asked, coming out of the kitchen.

'You're not firm enough. Need to let him know who's boss.'

'Speaking of the boss,' Alex said, as Summer peeked out of the kitchen door. Maisie's head appeared next. She wore an apron over her school uniform and had a smear of flour across her forehead. 'Don't come in,' she said.

Polly smiled. 'What are you two up to?'

Maisie opened her eyes wide. 'Nothing.'

'Ok, I won't ask.' Polly planted a kiss on top of Maisie's head, then Summer's. They grinned and disappeared into the kitchen.

Polly walked to the newly erected row of hooks by the front door and took her coat down. 'What do you reckon they're doing?'

Alex took the coat from her and held it out so she could slip it on. 'I may have mentioned that it's our three-month anniversary of living together tomorrow.' He ran his hands along the back of her neck and scooped her red curls out from inside the coat so they flowed down her back. Her neck tingled at his touch. 'I may also have mentioned that you love chocolate cake.'

'I do love chocolate cake.' She turned to face him. 'And I love you.'

Alex slipped his arms around her waist and kissed her. 'Does that mean I can have your piece?'

'I don't love you that much.'

'Worth a try.' He opened the door for her. 'Love you too. Have fun.'

Pulling her coat tightly around her, she walked to the car. When she'd told Alex about Ian and Adam, he'd been shocked, understandably, and asked for some time to absorb the revelation. But a week later he'd turned up on her doorstep, Button in his arms with a blue bow around his neck, and promised her that for as long as she wanted, he'd be there for her. And the way she felt right now, she'd want him there for a very long time.

—

The tyre scraped against the curb. Louise pretended she hadn't noticed.

'I'll get out here,' she said. 'The drive's a pain to reverse out of in the dark.'

Nick relaxed his grip on the steering wheel.

'Hope you get lots of writing done.'

Nick smiled grimly. 'It's my turn to read tomorrow. Would you mind looking at it before the class?'

Louise nodded. 'I'll read it over breakfast.'

'Thanks. Nina said I was telling, rather than showing, so I want to get that right this time.'

Louise's neck grew hot. 'Who's Nina?'

'One of the other students. You'll meet her at the end of term dinner.' He placed a hand on her thigh. 'She's married, and not a patch on you.'

'Flatterer.' Louise bent her head to hide her smile. She took a bottle of wine and large bag of crisps from the footwell. It was bliss to have a healthy relationship with food again. She'd put a few of the pounds back on that she'd lost, but was relaxed about eating now, concentrating on having a balanced diet without depriving herself completely or gorging whenever she was alone. Best of all, she didn't have to eat grapefruits. Unlike her sister, who was living on them to lose her baby weight.

Instantly, she felt a pang of guilt. Her relationship with her sister had improved massively since she and Nick had got back together. Louise had admitted to still feeling resentful of her taunting when they were growing up. Rachel, in turn, confessed to being jealous when Louise did better than her at school. Unable to compete academically, she'd put Louise down at every opportunity, almost starving herself in the belief that being skinny would make her superior. It also made her infertile and it had taken several rounds of IVF before she fell pregnant. For the first time in her life, Louise felt that maybe she wasn't the dumpy, dud sister. Maybe she didn't need to be pissed off anymore. And maybe, in time, they could become close. Although she wasn't sure she'd ever forgive Rachel for stringing her oversize gym knickers up on the school gate.

Her top had gaped open as she leant down and she noticed Nick looking appreciatively at her cleavage.

'I won't be too late back,' she whispered.

His eyes lit up behind his glasses.

'Bye, kids,' she said over her shoulder to the twins in the back seat.

'Do you have to go out?' asked Tess.

'Yes. Thursday night is girls' night, but I'm yours all weekend.' She smiled at them. 'Want me to bring my whistle to the match on Saturday?'

'No!' George said, crossing his arms. A moment later he shrugged. 'Suppose you can if you want.'

'Have fun.' Nick kissed her goodbye.

George feigned a retching sound.

'It's ok,' Tess said to him. 'Mummy says she doesn't want another baby as she already has the perfect family, so they won't be doing "it" again.'

Nick's cheeks flooded with colour.

Louise smirked, pushed the door shut and walked across Erica's drive. She'd alleviate any concerns Nick might have about her not wanting to do "it" when she got home.

–

Erica closed Jasmine's bedroom door and made her way downstairs. The carpet was springy beneath her feet and there was no risk of splinters when she ran her hand along the bannister. She sighed contentedly. She loved her house.

Imee had managed to settle Lillibeth, tidy the kitchen and load the dishwasher in the time it had taken Erica to bath Jasmine and put her to bed. Jasmine drew it out for as long as she could, asking for 'just one more' story about twenty times. Erica was happy to indulge her, although she'd had enough of stories that ended with the handsome prince rescuing the damsel in distress. Where were the books featuring a strong, independent woman who rescued the prince? It had worked for Harry and Meghan.

She smiled at Imee. 'Everything ok?'

'I've dumped a load,' Imee said.

Erica blanched.

Imee pointed to the utility room. 'Is on timer. I hang out in morning.'

'Ah.' Erica breathed a sigh of relief. 'Better to phrase it as "putting a load in the washing machine".' Imee's previous employers had clearly had fun with her vocabulary. Hearing her ask the girls to put on their fucktards for gymnastics had been a particular eye-opener.

Language aside, phoning Imee six months previously and offering a salary and a home to her and Lillibeth in exchange for twenty hours a week childcare, had been an inspired decision, if she did say so herself. Their presence created a family atmosphere, which had been missing with their previous nanny, Phoebe, who'd disappeared into her room as soon as she heard Erica's key in the door. Now when Erica got home, she heard talking and laughing rather than the thud of feet up the stairs and Phoebe's door slamming.

Erica was able to get home much earlier now that she'd become an agent, specialising in fashion styling and sharing her experience, knowledge and contacts with eager young stylists entering the industry. She chose her own hours, ensuring she was home in time to put Jasmine to bed the majority of the time and could even pick her up from school sometimes. Occasionally she missed being in the midst of the action. Then she remembered hand-stitching sequins onto a wannabe's gusset so she sparkled with each high kick and the wistfulness stopped abruptly.

'Ok for me to go now?' Imee swept her long, black hair to one side and shrugged her small frame into a thick coat. 'Lillibeth is almost asleep.'

'Course,' Erica said. 'How's college going?'

'Very good. Teacher thinks I can move to next level after Easter.'

Erica smiled. 'You'll be a fully qualified nurse before we know it.'

Imee hoisted a bag of books onto her shoulder and walked out to the hall. 'Hope so. Then can get proper job and house and my mother can move to UK.' She opened the front door.

Louise stood outside, one hand raised to the doorbell. 'Hi Imee. Still ok to babysit tomorrow night?'

Imee glanced at Erica, who nodded.

'Smashing. See you at eight.' Louise and Imee swapped places and Imee headed out of the drive to walk to the local college.

Louise thrust her wine and crisps at Erica and unbuttoned her coat. 'Not too cheeky, is it? Getting you to babysit Lillibeth so Imee can babysit for me?'

'Course not. I'm here anyway. Nice for you and Nick to have a date night and it gives me a chance to catch up with *EastEnders*.' She rolled her eyes at Louise. 'Thanks for that addiction.'

Louise smoothed down her pencil skirt and followed Erica into the kitchen. 'Did you watch *Home Zone* last night?'

Erica shook her head. 'Just knowing he was behind the scenes would have made me feel crap.'

'Surprised your letter didn't work. It always does in the movies.'

'It probably stank of desperation.'

Louise shook her head. 'He wouldn't have been able to smell anything over all that Chanel No 5.'

Erica laughed. 'I didn't squirt it with perfume. It wasn't that kind of letter.'

'Don't suppose people send love letters anymore,' Louise said sadly. 'Just Snapchat photos of themselves topless.'

'Oh, I did that too.'

Louise's mouth dropped open and Erica winked to show she was joking. Three weeks earlier she'd come up with the idea of writing to Rob via the studio, saying again how sorry she was for hurting and misleading him, explaining that her feelings had been genuine and wishing him all the best for the future. She hadn't heard from him. Not that she expected to, but she hoped her words had made him feel better. Although a topless photo might have done that too.

Polly arrived and Erica hugged her and hung her coat next to Louise's. There was plenty of space on the coat stand now that Dan's various weather apparel was gone. Jasmine had been distraught when they'd first told her they were separating. Imee and Lillibeth moving in had helped distract her, and Dan had flown back to see her at Christmas – with a twenty-three-year-old girlfriend in tow. Erica wasn't jealous. Dan wasn't doing it to get at her; he needed someone by his side for security. And if that someone happened to be a show pony whose skintight, leopard-print dress emphasised her cleavage and pert arse, Erica wouldn't let it intimidate her. She had her own security – a great relationship with her daughter and a successful business. And the secure knowledge that she would never, ever wear velour.

She poured the wine, but Polly placed a hand over her glass. 'I'm driving.'

Louise spluttered into her glass. 'Bloody hell. You're not—'

'No! Four children and two dogs are enough for now,' Polly said. 'Got a rehearsal in the morning. Only two weeks 'til the gig at the piano bar, so I need a clear head.'

Erica took a bottle of sparkling water from the fridge. The change in Polly was unbelievable. A year ago she'd been quiet, insecure and wouldn't say boo to a goose. Although, in fairness, even someone with the confidence of a Kardashian was unlikely to actually say boo to a goose. Now Polly was a vibrant, fun, quietly confident woman who'd had the courage to respond to an ad in the local paper looking for a singer for their jazz band. She didn't know if it was Alex's influence or the relief of sharing her past, but she hadn't seen such a transformation since Nicole Kidman discovered hair straighteners.

'Are you looking forward to it?' Erica asked. 'I can see you stretched out on a piano, your red hair pooling beneath you, singing "Big Spender".'

'I'm more likely to be hiding under the piano than lying on it.' Polly sighed. 'I feel sick just thinking about it.'

'The first time will always be the hardest. The *Sing to Win* contestants were bricking themselves at the start of the series and we couldn't get them off the stage by the end,' Erica said. 'Can't wait to see you.'

'Me neither,' Louise said. 'But don't use it as an excuse to skive off Family Fitness in the morning.'

Erica rolled her eyes. She loved exercise, but her runs were therapeutic – a chance to cleanse her mind as well as her body. Doing jumping jacks and squats alongside a pack of middle-aged dads trying to outdo each other without inducing a heart attack was the opposite of therapeutic.

'Why did you have to take over the class?' she grumbled. 'I wouldn't feel guilty about not going if I wasn't letting you down.'

'Seemed like a good way of combining family time with keeping fit.' Louise smirked. 'And I love the power of the whistle.'

'You could always babysit Summer,' Polly said to Erica. 'Then I could go in your place.'

Suddenly the Family Fitness sessions didn't seem so bad.

Erica noticed Polly reaching for where her pendant used to be.

'Still seeing Becky?' she asked.

Polly nodded. 'We're down to once a month. They're checking-in sessions now, but I don't mind them anymore.'

Erica often thought about what Polly had been through; how petrified she must have been the whole time she was living with Ian, then living with the memories of what had happened, and the sadness that she hadn't been able to talk about Adam. Wondering what she'd have done in that situation was one of the things that often occupied Erica's mind when running. That and whether her Lycra leggings gave her camel toe.

Polly tried not to think about it at all. She'd done enough of that in the past. Alex, Max and Maisie had slotted perfectly into their lives. Her newly extended family was where her priorities lay.

Erica broke the silence. 'I've been talking to St Martins about teaching a class on styling.'

Louise refilled their glasses. 'Sounds fancy.'

Erica nodded. 'It'd only be an afternoon a week. I'm waiting to hear from them.' It had been strange going back to the college twenty years after she'd left. The course coordinator was probably still eating pureed foods when Erica was graduating. She remembered the call she'd missed earlier and got her phone out of her bag. 'Someone left a message earlier. It might be them.' She looked at the caller ID. It wasn't her contact at St Martins. It was someone else entirely. Her stomach folded in on itself.

Louise peered at the screen. 'She's got a voicemail from Rob,' she said excitedly.

Polly gasped.

'Looks like your letter worked after all.' Louise nudged Erica. 'Go on, play it.'

Erica cleared her throat. 'I'll do it in the hall.'

Louise looked disappointed, but nodded. 'Good luck.'

Erica shut the kitchen door behind her and sat at the bottom of the stairs. Her hands were shaking so much her touch ID didn't work. With trembling fingers, she keyed her passcode into the phone and held it to her ear.

'I got your letter.' Her heart pounded. 'I appreciate you taking the time to write it.' She closed her eyes and pictured his lips forming the words. 'It doesn't excuse anything, but I understand the situation a bit better now.' He hesitated. 'Sorry to hear about you and Dan.' There was another pause. 'That's bollocks. I'm not sorry at all.'

Erica let out a surprised laugh.

'If you still want to meet up,' Rob continued. 'Just for a coffee, let me know. It'd be nice to see you. Bye, Erica.'

Erica lowered the phone, stared at in disbelief, then replayed the message in case she'd misheard. He was giving her a second chance. This was more than she'd expected or hoped for or deserved. She glanced up the stairs towards Jasmine's closed door. She couldn't dive straight into a relationship though. Having seen the disdain on Jasmine's face when Dan introduced her to his girlfriend at Christmas – although that could have been directed at the velour dress – she didn't want to subject her to another 'new friend'. Jasmine deserved better than that.

Louise and Polly looked at her expectantly when she walked back into the kitchen.

'He wants to meet for a coffee.' She tried to sound casual, but her heart was pounding so hard it made her voice quiver.

Polly clapped her hands together. 'That's great.'

Louise raised her glass. 'I'd blow my whistle if I had it with me.'

Erica shook her head. 'I can't see him. It's too soon after Dan.'

'But you love him.' Louise looked as though she might cry. She was so head over heels with Nick that she wanted everyone else to feel the same way.

Erica could easily have put her head on the breakfast bar and had a good old cry too, but instead took a deep breath. 'Yes, I do,' she said, as steadily as she could. 'But I love Jasmine more. Don't think it'd do her any good to see me with someone else.'

'You can love them both,' Polly said softly. 'I was worried Oliver might not want Alex around, but he's thriving being part of a big family.'

'Weren't you worried about Summer?' Louise asked.

'Hardly. She'd ditch me for Alex in a heartbeat.'

Erica didn't join in with their laughter. Her stomach was churning with a mix of emotions – excitement and relief that Rob had forgiven her enough to call, but sadness and regret that she couldn't see him.

Noticing she wasn't joining in, Polly put a hand over Erica's. 'Meet him for a coffee. It only needs to be a quick, lunchtime drink, so you're not late back for Jasmine.'

Erica fiddled with her hoop earring. 'I don't know.'

'You've nothing to lose,' Polly said. 'You might realise your feelings aren't as strong as you thought they were. Or, if they are, you can take it slow. If he cares about you, he'll respect that.'

Louise nodded eagerly. 'When's his birthday? Let's hope he's a Taurus. They're the most patient.'

Erica politely ignored Louise's input, which tested her own, less virtuous, Aries patience, but she took Polly's words on board. Maybe it wouldn't hurt to meet for a coffee. They didn't need to rush into anything. Especially not a disabled cubicle. They needed to stay well away from those.

'I might do,' she said.

'Call him from the hall, we won't be able to hear,' Louise said, eyeing up the glasses to see which would be best to listen through the door with.

'I said I *might*.' Erica put her hand up. 'Enough about Rob. Thursday is girls' night. Girl power, sisters doing it for themselves, All that jazz.' She warbled the last bit and waggled her hands.

Louise snorted. 'Glad it's Polly singing on stage, not you.'

Polly's stomach lurched at the thought of it. 'Remind me again why I'm subjecting myself to this public humiliation.'

'You will not be humiliated,' Erica said firmly. 'You'll be adored by all.' She raised her glass. 'Here's to the start of your singing career. And to the Family Fitness franchise.' She winked at Louise. 'Move the class to eleven o'clock and the rest of the bottle's yours.'

'It's my bottle!'

Polly held up her sparkling water. 'Don't forget your agency. That deserves a toast too.'

Erica nodded her head in appreciation. 'Here's to all of us.'

They clinked their glasses together.

'Can't believe how much has changed in less than a year,' Polly said.

'One thing hasn't changed.'

'Your inability to frown?' Louise said.

Erica couldn't argue the point. She'd tried to go without Botox for a while, but why have aging lines and creases when there was a teensy little injection that could erase them? Yes, it was vain, but feeling good about herself was important. She wasn't trying to look twenty-three again; she wanted to look good for thirty-six. Or even forty-two.

'This hasn't changed.' Erica motioned to the three of them. 'Our friendship. Apart from those last couple of horrendous weeks in the house, but we got through them and learned from it. Hopefully we're better people because of it. I know I'll never take anyone for granted again.'

Louise looked down at her wedding ring. 'Me neither.'

Polly wound a red curl around her finger. 'Don't know what would have happened if you hadn't moved in. I was just surviving before. You two saved me from that. You were my life support system.' She smiled. 'Or "wife support system", as Alex calls it.'

Louise patted Polly's hand. 'We always will be.' She nodded at Erica. 'For all of us.'

The same surge of adrenalin that Erica had felt when she'd seen Rob's name on her phone coursed through her now. 'No matter what else is going on,' she said. 'We'll always be here for each other.'

'I think we need another toast.' Louise tilted her glass forward and Erica and Polly did the same.

'To wife support,' Louise said.

The three women smiled at one another. They'd been through so much together – good and bad – and come out the other side. There were no secrets now. No resentment or frustration or suppressed anger. No comparing or judging or complaining. All bad feeling had been vented that afternoon at Polly's and what remained was a united desire to help and encourage one another in their work, their aspirations, their family life and, last but definitely not least, in their friendship.

Erica, Polly and Louise clinked their glasses and smiled at each other. 'To wife support.'

A Letter From Kathleen

Thank you so much for reading my debut novel *Wife Support System*. I really appreciate it.

The inspiration for the book came on a typically frantic day. I was trying to test spellings, get to an after-school club, cook dinner, book a plumber and meet a work deadline. Oh, and complete the simple task of making a gas mask for a school project that was due in the next day. Many of my friends are struggling in the same way and it occurred to me that if we lived together, we could help each other out and life would be much easier. Providing I didn't ask for help with the gas mask.

I'm not as brave as the three women in my book to do this (although I am often as desperate – especially during lockdown!), but it was great fun imagining what issues would occur, both with each other and their partners.

I really hope you've enjoyed reading *Wife Support System*. If you did, it'd be great to hear your thoughts via a review. I know they take time to write, which is often hard to find, so if you are able to, I'd be very grateful. Providing it's a good review obviously.

Please also feel free to get in touch via Facebook, Twitter or Instagram if you'd like to talk about the book, or anything else. I'd love to hear from you.

Until then, take care and stay safe.

Warm regards,

Kathleen

Acknowledgments

I had the idea for *Wife Support System* years ago, but every time I tried to sit down to write, I got sidetracked by work, children, house 'stuff' and *Mad Men* box sets.

It was my nine-year-old daughter's words – 'Stop talking about writing a book and write one' – that gave me the motivation to get on with it. So, my first acknowledgment goes to Eve (who's now fourteen – I clearly watched far too much *Mad Men*). Thank you Eve for giving me the kick up the arse I needed (but don't use the word arse please #badmummy) and for your brilliant plot suggestions. I love our brainstorming walks. Elena, who's eleven, deserves just as much credit for keeping me company during lockdown when I was on a tight editing deadline. It was lovely to see your smiling face every few minutes. In the book, Polly says that nothing prepared her for how blown away with love she'd be when she had children. You two inspired that line. I'm blown away with love for you every day.

Thank you to my handsome husband, James, for making me coffee in the days and cosmopolitans in the evenings, for proofreading some of the chapters (the ones with the sex scenes obviously), and for letting me follow my dream. (The one where I get published, not the one I've been having about Han Solo since I was 15.) Oh, and for buying me some amazing shoes as a congratulatory present. Even though you don't know about them yet.

This book wouldn't have been written if it wasn't for my mum. She's supported me throughout, both financially (thank you for my mentoring with the brilliant author Jill Dawson through Gold Dust – and thank you, Jill, for your invaluable advice) and by believing in me. She's the best cheerleader ever. Although, thankfully, she doesn't wear the outfit. Sadly my dad isn't here to see my name in print, but he would have been so proud he'd have probably cried. He was a very warm man and not afraid to show his emotions – when I got married, when he met his grandchildren, when he fell down the stairs (fortunately he didn't break anything, but it clearly smarted a bit). I miss you, Dad. Enough said about that or I'll be the one crying.

I have to mention my brother, Adam, because I admire, respect and love him so much. I hope that by naming one of the characters after him, it'll make up for the time I locked him in the cellar.

Thank you to my in-laws. They're all amazing. I really lucked out there. Deryn, Linda, Jed, Laura and Andy and my gorgeous nieces and nephews (in age order), Brady, Isla, Charlie and Holly – I love you!

Thank you to my extended family and all my amazing friends for your encouragement and belief in me. A special thank you to those who read the book. I'm sorry I can't list everyone, but you know who you are. If you don't, that explains why I haven't had a Christmas card from you for years.

Those I do need to mention are my school buddies Becky, Marie and Tonya. Thank you for being loyal, loving, laugh out loud (LOL some say, but I can't see that phrase catching on), lifelong friends for more years than I'm prepared to admit to. Brigid, thank you for being the most amazing friend ever. I don't know what I'd do without your love, laughter, and willingness to go to work with a hangover. Thank you Strictly gals – Anna, Brigid (again – always around when cava's involved), Kate, Sarah, Sinéad, Vicky and Zoë – for championing me every step of the way, for being totally fab-u-lous, and for not talking through the *Strictly* final. You all get a Ten from me.

Thank you Girls Night Out gang Alex, Emma, Jane, Lea, Lisa, Lizzie, Sarah, Susan, Vicky and Wendy for 25 years of fun.

And for looking after me the night I fell from the top of a human pyramid.

Thank you to: Sarah T for making me laugh and for your nutritional advice, which ensured I didn't eat chocolate the *entire* time I was working; Sarah J for drinking cava even though you prefer prosecco and for keeping Eve and Elena entertained with dance lessons (when do mine start?); Clara for supplying me with one-liners that are much funnier than mine; Cinema Dean for watching period dramas with me (I do *not* thank you for making me watch Gerard Butler films in return); Sinéad for the brilliant dirty laundry strapline; Julie for printing out the many different versions of this book (approximately three million) so that I could proofread it on paper; Pauline and Geoff for hosting the best holidays ever; Emma D for our Drink, Shop, Do catch ups; Mark for taking my author photo in exchange for a meagre chicken wrap; Andy B for updating my website because I'm too incompetent; Magali, Rhianon and Vicky for our leisurely lunches; Transmission for being the best covers band ever and for having the best WAGs; Faye Sawyer for sharing details of her fun and exciting (but blooming hard work) life as a stylist with me. It was invaluable when describing Erica's career. I must stress that all other aspects of Erica's life came from my imagination – she's not based on Faye in any way – and that Faye never talked about her clients in any derogatory way or labelled them 'wannabes'. She was genuinely fond of them, but Erica's not always as nice as Faye is!

Thanks to Joady and Paul for your advice on police matters. If anything in this book isn't accurate, then that's down to my poor recall, not you giving me false information!

A special shout out to Zoë Folbigg and Catherine Bennetto, two incredibly talented authors, who have encouraged and supported me from the start. You must read their brilliant books. (After you've bought and gifted copies of mine to everyone you've ever met.)

Thank you to Bekah and the team at my local library. You must be sick of the sight of me, as I spent many, *many* hours

347

there writing *Wife Support System*, trying not to get distracted by all the wonderful books around me. Please support your local library. We're incredibly lucky to have this invaluable resource and if we don't use them, we'll lose them.

Thank you to everyone at the Romantic Novelists' Association. It's a brilliant organisation offering advice, information, events and networking opportunities and is full of the loveliest people you could meet. Loveliest of all are Alison, Annette, Christina, Giulia, Julia, Lynne, Maryam, Paula, Sophie and Tara. Thank you for being so much more than writing friends.

A HUGE thank you to my publisher Keshini Naidoo at Hera Books. Thank you for being so warm, witty, hard-working and enthusiastic, and for loving the book as much as I do. I'm so happy we met at the RNA winter party. Even if it was in the toilets.

And finally, thank YOU for reading this book. I really appreciate you investing the time and sincerely hope you enjoyed it.

Take care and stay safe. xxx